STATE TECTONICS

ALSO BY MALKA OLDER

Infomocracy
Null States

STATE TECTONICS

THE CENTENAL CYCLE, BOOK 3

MALKA OLDER

A TOM DOHERTY ASSOCIATES BOOK
NEW YORK

STATE TECTONICS

Copyright © 2018 by Malka Older

Edited by Carl Engle-Laird

A Tor.com Book
Published by Tom Doherty Associates
175 Fifth Avenue
New York, NY 10010

www.tor.com

Tor® is a registered trademark of Macmillan Publishing Group, LLC.

The Library of Congress Cataloging-in-Publication Data
is available upon request.

ISBN 978-0-7653-9947-2 (hardcover)
ISBN 978-0-7653-9946-5 (ebook)

Our books may be purchased in bulk for promotional, educational, or business use. Please contact your local bookseller or the Macmillan Corporate and Premium Sales department at 1-800-221-7945, extension 5442, or by email at MacmillanSpecialMarkets@macmillan.com.

First Edition: September 2018

Printed in the United States of America

0 9 8 7 6 5 4 3 2 1

FOR LOU, CALYX, PAZ

ACKNOWLEDGMENTS

Thank you, as always, to my family: Lou, Calyx, Paz, and Dora, Marc, Daniel. It is astonishing to be able to have a (figurative, which is all the more impressive) room of one's own within a house full of family, and I am so grateful for that.

Thank you to the Tor.com Publishing crew, especially Carl Engle-Laird, whose thoughtful editing made this book so much better, and Katharine Duckett and Mordicai Knode, who have worked so hard to get these books to as many readers as possible. I am in awe and gratitude of Wilhelm Staehle's covers. Thank you also to Irene Gallo and everyone else there who made these books a physical reality.

As always, thank you to all of those who have helped introduce me to new worlds and different futures.

In Dhaka, Harun Rashid and the Save the Children team and S.H.M. Fakhruddin.

En Cuba, gracias a Grisel Vázquez Arestuche y Zenaida Fernández Cabrera, Celia Gonzalez y Edilio, Nancy García Lamadrid y Eduardo Alfonso Prada.

My hopeful reimagining of the Presidio Modelo is in honor of Ricardo Vázquez and his compañeros, espero que no lo encuentren demasiado frívolo.

In Kathmandu, Sanjay Karki and the Mercy Corps team, Carolyn McKnight and the entire ELP group, and Arjun Basnet.

In Oaxaca (and in Queretaro and in Nice!), Tomás Luna. Also María Dolores Serrano for facilitating a trip to Chiapas that provided additional useful experiences. Nazuki Konishi, who accompanied me on my one trip to Estonia. In Nairobi, Elana Aquino, Abdi Mohamud, Mohammed "Mali" Ali.

Thank you to Lynette Coates for peace of mind at a critical juncture.

For language assistance, thank you to Thomas J. Connors and Hjalmar P. Petersen. All mistakes remain my own.

Part of my project with these books has been to connect this imagined future to our present. Thank you to Blair Glencorse and the Accountability Lab for the amazing work they've done and their partnership with me on *Infomocracy,* and to Amal de Chickera, Laura van Waas, and the Institute on Statelessness and Inclusion for their incredible work and their partnership on *Null States.* If you are interested in the issues in these books, take a look at what those organizations are doing in the world today.

Thank you to Marc Weidenbaum and the Disquiet Junto for making gronkytonk a reality; you can hear their stylings at https://llllllll.co/t/disquiet-junto-project-0302-gronkytonk/9621.

The Lumper is named after Lora Lumpe, who works on global small arms proliferation and other security issues. Thank you for your efforts and also for your graciousness when I emailed out of nowhere to tell you I had already named a fictional disarmament device after you.

Time capsule therapy is based on the work of Ellen Langer. If I have misrepresented it in any way, I take as my excuse the dilution of practice that would be likely to occur over the next sixty years, but if you are interested in the concept you should go to the source.

Finally, thank you to all the readers who made this series possible! It has been fun and fascinating to write; I hope you enjoy it as much as I did.

STATE TECTONICS

CHAPTER 1

The Dhaka street swarms with people, objects, and all of the existing data about all of these people and objects. Maryam, who of all people should be accustomed to words and numbers floating in front of her eyes, finds herself brushing at her face, as if to wipe away all that accumulated knowledge. It's too much. She turns on first one filter, removing any data uploaded before the last global election, then another that she rigged especially for this trip, muting personal data that is not directly related to her mission. But Maryam is a believer in fate and coincidence and a childhood reader of *Dirk Gently's Holistic Detective Agency*, and she can't escape the concern that her algorithm might exclude something vitally important. Miserably, she turns the second filter back off again.

A few months ago, a ban on high-emissions vehicles, already the norm in most of the world, was finally enacted for all of micro-democracy. Dhaka included a concentration of particularly recalcitrant centenal governments, and the moment the law took force, the streets emptied out and transportation (particularly of goods) became scarce. The foule responded immediately, taking over the pavement with no regard for the likelihood that cleaner motor vehicles would pick up the slack. Sidewalks, suddenly unnecessary for pedestrians, became valuable real estate, and capsule apartments were built in front of existing buildings, barely leaving access to the entrances. Hovels sprang up in front of the capsule apartments, sometimes sloping off the ill-repaired sidewalks into the street proper. The garbage collection system had been largely diesel-based, and although a team of rickshaw collectors now supplements the ragpickers who never stopped searching for anything worth selling, they are making little headway against the mountains of garbage that lean against walls and spill into the street.

A massive vehicle, retrofitted to scrape past the new standards, is forcing its way through the human-clogged artery that remains between all these obstacles, and its slow progress is pushing Maryam and, it seems, the entire population of the flooded delta of Bangladesh into the walls and the garbage and the shacks and each other.

This is not a context in which Maryam feels particularly comfortable. She grew up in Beirut and Paris and pre-earthquake Lima, and in decidedly comfortable segments of each, and until recently lived in sparsely populated Doha. She itches to deploy her crowdcutter, a translucent shell shaped like a shark fin that would not only give her a literal edge in moving forward but also isolate her from the press of bodies. But she left herself plenty of time to get to the sanatorium, and she doesn't want to attract any more attention than necessary. Anyone could be watching her, following her from feed to feed broadcast by microscopic cameras. But there are a lot of feeds in the world, a lot of people to watch. If no one is paying attention to Maryam, she doesn't want to give them a reason to start. And maybe this crowd is thick enough to get lost in. Cheering somewhat at the thought, she pulls her scarf lower over her forehead and presses on.

. . .

Maryam locates the sanatorium a few streets over. The neighborhood has taken a disorientingly quick shift for the better. It isn't one of the new wealth enclaves, with wide streets and gatehouses for armed guards, but the venerable residences are at least cared for enough to fend off the outgrowth of slums on the sidewalks. Maryam passes through a gate with the code she was given when she made her appointment, and then through a courtyard, hazy in the heat, to find the entrance proper. A plaque—an actual plaque, not projected or painted but engraved—explains the concept of time-capsule therapy and gives a brief history of its development, lists the names of major benefactors (including Information, Maryam notes with surprise; some of her bosses must be worried about aging too), and mentions the date of establishment: 2053. Maryam shivers at the thought of two decades crawling by while those within live frozen in the noughts. She pushes open the heavy door and walks in.

She finds herself in a large turquoise room with multiple closed doors leading off of it: a well-appointed reception center. Maryam had braced herself for the shock of stepping into a period drama, but everything seems normal: the receptionist is blinking through some data at eyeball level, an infotainment projection plays soundlessly in one corner, and the light fixtures in the ceiling are fluoron. Maryam gives her name to the receptionist, a skinny young man with luxuriant hair, and a few minutes later a small woman in her forties wearing a rose-and-green sari comes out to meet her.

"Welcome to the growling noughts," she greets her. "Saleha Rashid. We just have a few procedures we need to go through before you can go on to your appointment."

"Yes," Maryam agrees. "I have some projections that I believe I need transferred?"

"To compatible technology. We can help you there." Saleha leads her to a small office with an old-fashioned computer on a desk next to the workspace. "In fact, it was Taskeen who built the translation protocol, early in her stay here."

Maryam smiles. That bodes well. "Intent on keeping up with events, was she?"

"We don't forbid that, you know. Our clients are not institutionalized, and they are free to communicate with the outside world in any way they wish," Saleha explains as she works with the projection files Maryam tossed her. "We maintain temporal continuity in all the public spaces of the premises, however, which is why we need to check all of your modern devices here."

Maryam divests herself of her personal projector and handheld.

"You can keep your auto-interpreter, since it's not visible, but Taskeen won't be wearing one. Will you need an interpreter? We have several on staff."

"We'll be fine," Maryam says, hoping that's true. Her English is not great and she has no Bengali, but she can't take the risk of an interpreter and prefers not to advertise that her discussion with Taskeen Khan, creator of the Information data pathways and a personal hero, is going to be highly classified.

Saleha hands Maryam a flat device about the size of her thumb with a metal connector at one end. "Your projections are on this, or an approximation of them. You can use it with Taskeen's computer." She studies Maryam. "But before we go I'm afraid you'll have to do something about your clothes as well."

Maryam looks down at herself. She is wearing much what

she always wears: a black salwar kameez in pseudo-silk. The kameez is knee-length, with a simple micro-cutout pattern around the collar and cuffs, matching the dupatta she wears over her head.

"You can look like a foreigner, but you must be a foreigner from the turn of the century," Saleha clucks. "The pseudo-silk, the heat reflectors, the micro-cutouts. It's subtle, but believe me, someone from the past would notice. We have alternate clothing available." She opens a large cabinet to display a rack of colors and fabrics. "I'll be right outside. You can, of course, keep anything of your own that isn't visible," she adds as she closes the door behind her.

Maryam flips through the hangers, looking for something muted in the array of flowery fabrics and bright colors. Maybe this is an opportunity to cosplay a bit, even if it is a work meeting. She picks a style she recognizes from old movies, a full-skirted kameez and tight trousers in a bold geometric pattern. She looks around for a feed camera, remembers where she is, and grabs her handheld off Saleha's desk to take a picture of herself and send it to Núria.

There's a knock on the door. "All set?"

Maryam quickly puts her handheld back and opens the door to Saleha's pleasant smile. "Shall we go meet her?"

Saleha leads her through the door behind the receptionist, which opens onto a city street. Maryam blinks in surprise, and then blinks again. Information's detailed annotations and input don't appear, and the world looks strange. The vehicles parked on the sides of the street are all from the turn of the century, resting on pitted asphalt. Thick bundles of black wires sway above her head, suspended on posts, with subsidiary lines branching off toward each of the buildings. Posters—two-dimensional and unmoving—for ancient movies and long-discontinued products, like chewing gum, and disposable razors, are plastered to the walls.

"A bit disconcerting, isn't it?" Saleha asks.

"You must be used to it," Maryam says, not wanting to admit how strange it feels to walk into the past.

"Indeed. I've come to quite enjoy the shift."

"Are all these houses . . . real?" Maryam asks, gesturing at the three- and four-story buildings on each side of the road.

"Yes, we were able to purchase a block that hadn't been substantially upgraded since the early part of the century, although we did have to retrofit some of the accoutrements, like the electricity lines." Saleha nods at the sagging wires overhead. "And we made some alterations to close off our campus. There are no entrances other than our official ones, although it's not something you'd notice. We have simulacra of televisions that show contemporary programming on a set annual schedule, and—oh, you'll appreciate this," she says with the confidence of someone who believes everyone who works in tech is interested in all aspects of technology. "We have a purpose-built model of the 2010 Internet, with custom blockers that can set it to any year until 2005, completely self-contained!"

Maryam does appreciate that. "Very impressive!"

"Yes. Of course, Taskeen helped us with that, too."

It is strange to hear Dr. Khan, the visionary, academic, and technical genius, referred to so casually as someone who "helped" with a nursing home intranet. "And the shops?" Maryam asks. The building they are passing has a small grocery store on the ground floor, doors open for business, and in the one next to it she sees a jewelry shop. "Do you bring people in to staff them?"

"The businesses are all run by residents," Saleha says, with a tilt of pride in her voice.

"They work?" It must cost a fortune to live in this facility, and the octo- and nonagenarians still have to hold down jobs?

"Only the ones who want to. And of course, they keep what they earn. We find that many of our residents crave occupation, and having a local economy is beneficial for the neighborhood. Of course, it's a lot of work to manage it."

"You mean subsidies?"

"There's a great deal of arbitrage involved in getting the goods into this system and making them available for prices that make sense in the currency of the time. We offer some subsidies, especially for old products that we've had to commission, but there are also many administrative issues. But it's certainly worth it. Those who want jobs can have them, and everyone can shop within our campus, rather than simply receiving goods from us."

"You sound sold on this place," Maryam says. "Does it really work?"

Saleha smiles. "I've already invested in my spot in the sliding forties. You'll see," she adds, as they turn into the entrance of a small building to the right. They climb three flights of stairs—seems like a lot for an elderly woman to have to do every day—and Saleha knocks on the door.

"Taskeen!" she calls. "I've brought you a visitor!"

The door opens wide. The woman standing inside is small but upright. Her hair is black, but she probably modifies it— or dyes it; that's what people did at the turn of the century. She's wearing thick glasses and a warm smile that could be described as grandmotherly. Her skin looks soft and is slathered with artificial coloring—blush, lipstick—but without knowing her age, Maryam probably would have guessed her to be in her fifties or even forties.

"Come in, come in," Taskeen Khan says, stepping back so they can enter a narrow hallway bathed in warm colors from the cloth hangings on the walls. She gives Saleha a hug and takes Maryam's hand in both of hers. "I was just about to make tea."

Maryam sends Saleha a look that she hopes is not too rude. She needs Taskeen to herself, and her time is limited.

"Thank you," Saleha clucks, "but I have to be getting back to the office. I'll leave you to it and stop by sometime tomorrow."

After the door closes, Taskeen appraises Maryam with sharp eyes. "So. You're the hot new techie."

"I don't know," Maryam says, surprised. "There are always hotter and newer ones coming along."

Taskeen laughs, holds up her hands. "Sadly, I don't speak Arabic, although I always wanted to learn," she says. "English, perhaps?" she adds in that language, turning to lead Maryam down a short hall.

"My English is not so good," Maryam says, cringing at her own awful accent. "Français?"

"No," Taskeen says. "I'll make you some chai, yes?" Her volume has gone up a notch, even though she knows Maryam can understand her perfectly. "Don't worry, we have options. I've made some modifications to the era-appropriate translation software." She throws a wink at Maryam as she fills the kettle. "It's still a bit clunky, but we can use that."

"¿No entiendes Español, acaso?" Maryam asks.

"Oh!" Taskeen turns, kettle still in her hand. "Do you know, I believe I still do! I'd be hard pressed to speak it, but . . ." She turns back and fiddles with the gas stove, humming to herself. "Yes, let's try it. I speak whatever I want, and you speak Spanish, and if we get into trouble, we'll use the translator. Although we'll have to go into the other room for that." Nodding happily, she guides Maryam through an entranceway into a small study. A curtained window looks out on the street, but most of the wall is taken up by banks of humming electronics, and a large old-fashioned computer monitor sits between them, a keyboard on the desk below it.

"Wow," says Maryam, and then, remembering, repeats herself in Spanish. "Vaya."

"Yes, she's impressive, isn't she?" Taskeen pats the computer monitor fondly. "And most people don't understand how impressed they should be. I've souped her up quite a bit. She can do a lot of what your personal handhelds can do, although of course a lot slower."

Maryam, who had steeled herself to scrupulously avoid all mention of modern technology that was extraneous to her mission, coughs. "You, ah, keep up with the latest innovations?"

"I'm not in anachronism prison, you know," Taskeen says. "The therapy of being here is wonderful. I feel very young, and I'm grateful for it. But keeping my mind active is just as important. I can't keep relearning the things I learned when I was ten."

"Claro que no," Maryam says, automatically.

Taskeen seats herself in a wheeled chair by the computer and gestures Maryam toward a small sofa that probably already looked old in 2010. "So," she says, tapping at the keyboard. "What did you want to talk to me about? Something related to the Information substructure, I imagine. Oh, don't mind this," she adds when Maryam hesitates. "I'm bringing up the translation program in case we need it. Now go ahead." She rotates in her chair to face Maryam and folds her hands on her lap, smiling.

Maryam orders her thoughts. Fortunately she's been using Spanish a lot lately. "I don't know if you're aware of this," she begins, "but there have been some recent incidents attacking Information infrastructure."

"What kind of attacks? Blackouts? Denial-of-service?" Taskeen is leaning forward, already gripped. Information is the enormous global bureaucracy that collects, sorts, stores, and administers all of the world's knowledge, underpinning every modern activity; functionality outages can be devastating. The blackout during the election nearly five years ago brought global commerce and transportation screeching to a halt and almost caused several wars. But that's not the problem that has brought Maryam thousands of miles and decades into the past.

"No," she says, "it's not that; it's—" A whistle blasts through the apartment, and Maryam jumps, wondering if it's an earthquake or monsoon alert, or a fire alarm somewhere in this building without Information uplinks.

"That's the kettle," Taskeen says, patting Maryam's knee as she whisks by to the kitchen. "Nothing to worry about! I'll be right back with the tea."

Maryam has time to calm her heartbeat before Taskeen returns with two chipped ceramic mugs filled with milky tea. "Here you go, dear. Now, what were you telling me?"

After the respite, Maryam has to psych herself up all over again to divulge the tightly kept secret to this stranger.

"So far, the service interruptions have been minimal," she starts carefully. "In fact, that's what's confusing us. There have been a number of attacks on data transfer stations, and we can't figure out what the endgame is."

Taskeen purses her lips and swivels her chair back and forth. "Explain."

"In each case—there have been five so far—masked assailants break in, incapacitate the staff, disable the station, and leave, all before InfoSec can arrive. The longest they spent on-site was twenty-eight minutes, and that was in a remote area. No equipment has been taken, and the effect on the system . . ."

"Would be minimal," Taskeen says. "Unless something has gone very wrong since I left, rerouting around a single station outage should be a matter of seconds."

Maryam blushes, remembering that Taskeen wrote the protocol that has formed the basis for every product in her professional life. "At most, there were some stutters in access in areas local to the attack, and even that never lasted more than a few minutes. Getting the affected stations back online is a matter of hours."

"So, why are they doing it?" Taskeen mused, her fingers playing idly on the keyboard in front of her. She picks up her cup, blows on it, and takes a sip. "Tell me more."

Maryam looks up. "I can share the reports with you, but there's very little there beyond what we've discussed . . ."

"No, I mean the rest of it." When Maryam stares, the older woman puffs in frustration. "You're here. If you thought this was random violence, you'd be talking to a security expert, not an outdated programmer."

Maryam takes a careful breath. "Two years ago, there was an . . . issue, which raised our suspicions." A global pattern of assassinations of centenal and government leaders unwilling to go along with the misappropriation of Information infrastructure.

"*Two years ago?*" Taskeen puts down her cup in surprise. "You've known about this for two years and you haven't rooted them out yet?"

Maryam's brief had been to reveal only what was necessary, but she should have known that *necessary* would be more than she wanted to discuss when dealing with a retired and presumably bored genius. "We apprehended one suspect, who named two midlevel Information staff as their superiors. But the apprehension of that suspect was quite public"—as part of a failed assassination attempt—"so they had warning, and they absconded before we could arrest them. The thing is—"

"Absconded?" Taskeen wrinkles her nose. "Where to?"

"Null states," Maryam answers; outside of Information jurisdiction. "Probably Russia. The thing is, almost two hundred other staff disappeared at the same time."

Maryam can hear the quiet hum from the computer. "That does suggest a larger plot," Taskeen says finally. "My, my. What has upper management been doing?" Her tone sounds as though she tried to lighten the statement halfway through, and Maryam decides to ignore the criticism of her bosses.

"Most of them were Hub-based centenal support staff who, we've found since then, were implicated in attempts to reduce Information coverage. The details are complicated, but . . ."

"You think these attacks are continuing the same project." Taskeen taps at her keys some more. "Presumably as former employees, they understand the limited impact of shutting down individual transfer stations, so they may be using them as practice for a concerted larger-scale assault."

Maryam waits.

"Or they're trying to use the attacks to learn something about the system."

"That's where you come in," Maryam says.

Taskeen does not immediately leap into the problem the way Maryam would like her to. "So maybe not trying to reduce Information coverage so much as . . . take over?" She is leaning forward again. "You think they're trying to break your monopoly?"

"It's not a monopoly," Maryam says, the coldness of her tone diluted by the fact that she has to search for the word *monopoly* in Spanish.

"There are justifications for a monopoly on a public good, you know," Taskeen says mildly. She takes a swallow of tea. "Piggybacking on your infrastructure, that certainly makes sense, at least to start. Rebuilding all of it would be an enormous start-up cost."

"Exactly." Maryam tries to sound encouraging, but Taskeen isn't done with background yet.

"Two years is a long time."

Maryam offers a rueful chuckle. "Yes," she says. "I'm afraid it . . . it took us some time to make it a priority."

"Because you hoped you had nipped the plot in the bud."

"Yes." And because there were so many other things going on: internal battles over election rules and Supermajority terms and massive potentially planet-destroying infrastructure projects. And because nobody wanted to believe they'd been betrayed, and those who did believe it wanted to make sure no one else found out about it. "We still don't know for sure that the same group is responsible for the transfer-station attacks, but we've seen a recent upswing in data activity in various null states, most notably in Crimea and along the Baltic coast, which is where we think the majority of the former staff fled." She pauses, but Taskeen seems surprised by all of this, and it's easy to think of her as a colleague. "Exformation, as some of us are calling them."

"And I suppose the general public is taking this all calmly? The mass exodus, the attacks, the potential rival to Information's power?"

Maryam's smile disappears. "It's all public," she says stiffly.

This time, Taskeen's laugh doesn't sound surprised at all. "Public but invisible." She shakes her head. "Information needs to live by its principles. People are already too inclined to think the worst of it."

"It's all there," Maryam says, her face heating. "You can read about it. If you can get on Information, I mean."

"Mmm." Taskeen turns back to her computer and starts tapping again. Maryam wonders if it's possible that light touch is having some effect, triggering a recording mechanism. It seems unlikely, but she doesn't know enough about the outdated hardware, and her skin starts to crawl with suspicion. There could be recorders in the room, or some early twenty-first-century analog. She can't stop her fingers from feeling along the edge of her chair.

Maryam folds her hands back into her lap as Taskeen turns to her. "You've found nothing to indicate who carried out these attacks? Surely, you have cameras, data . . ." She gestures: *What good is your surveillance state if you can't use it to catch anarchist terrorists?*

"They put some planning into avoiding feeds," Maryam explains. Despite the near-ubiquity of cameras, the universal access to the feeds from those cameras makes it possible to avoid them if you work at it: you look at the image and work your way around its borders. "And they wear masks and robes over some kind of frame that hides body type and stride." She represses a twitch; she saw the footage for the first time while preparing for this visit, and even knowing what to expect, the blank and silent countenances were terrifying. "We've been putting more and more resources toward looking for them, but they seem to know the system extremely well."

"As if they had once worked within it," Taskeen notes grimly. She claps her hands twice, and Maryam expects a projection to leap out between them, ideally one with answers about unsolved data sabotage, but the older woman rises to her feet instead. "I forgot to bring the sweets."

While Taskeen is in the kitchen, plates clinking, Maryam quickly kneels to check under the chairs and the computer table. She straightens again, feeling like an idiot—*as if the recorders would be visible!*—and studies the framed pictures on the walls: Taskeen shaking hands with various dignitaries of the past half-century. She recognizes two presidents of Bangladesh, a prime minister of Nepal, the current queen of Bhutan when she was much younger, and Maryam's former boss Nejime when she was much, much younger. Maryam turns her attention from the better-known faces to those of Taskeen Khan at various ages, looking for clues in her standardized smile. Maryam wasn't sure about the gambit of coming here when Nejime suggested it. She's still not sure that this kind, spry old lady who has long been her hero isn't her enemy.

"So," Taskeen says, coming back with a bowl of amriti and the teapot. "You brought something for me to look at?"

"Updated diagrams of the current system. Since you retired, more structures have been layered on top, and it's not always easy to understand what's going on at the most fundamental level. We thought you might be able to see something we're missing that suggests what they could possibly gain from these attacks."

It sounds ridiculous now that Maryam says it out loud, but Taskeen settles into her seat and holds out a hand. Maryam starts the motion to throw her a file via Information, remembers where she is, and searches in her bag for the small device Saleha gave her. Taskeen takes it and plugs it into the computer.

"So, what are you going to do about this when you find the culprits?" Taskeen asks as she types and clicks away at her computer.

"*I'm* not going to do anything about it," Maryam says. She's watching closely, trying to figure out how the antiquated technology works. "I'm not a policy person. I don't make decisions, I just implement them—and only technical decisions, at that."

Taskeen chuckles softly. "Keep telling yourself that, if it comforts you." She hits one last key triumphantly, and the first diagram comes up. "All right, walk me through this one," she says, her voice shifting into management mode.

Maryam avoids hotel restaurants on the principle that captive audiences lead to decreased quality and value, but after pushing through the crowd that afternoon she has neither the energy nor the desire to go back out on the street. She finds a seat at the bar—a design feature, not a place for selling alcohol, as this centenal teetotals—and peruses the menu, annotated by Information with reviews and ingredient source data.

She has finished her kebab—middling—and is working her way through a salty lassi that's a little too salty when a man slides himself into the seat next to her. He is skinny and has a wide eager grin as he sits sideways on his chair to face her.

"Hello, miss," he says. "Where are you from?"

Maryam frowns at her lassi. Her public Information is projected beside her face for all to see. Working for Information is usually enough to discourage unwanted attention, but due to the clandestine nature of this assignment, she has muted that fact. The letters of her name shimmer with a subtle iridescence, but she wouldn't expect a straight man who tries to pick up women in hotel restaurants to catch that marker of queerness. She's surprised he didn't pick up on the font, which is a standard signal of being in a relationship. Maybe that's more geographically limited than she thought. Either way, she doesn't feel like dealing with him. She takes a last sip of her lassi and taps across the bits to pay for it.

"Miss, so sorry, I don't want to bother you." Against her better judgment, she glances at him: still smiling, but now modulated with apology. "So sorry, but you look like you're not from around here, and maybe this can help." He snaps, and an image appears. It looks like a travel guide, a lovely glossy photograph of a packed street in Dhaka, with tons of lines and arrows annotating it. Text flies up above it, briefly in Bengali before rearranging into Arabic under the influence of Maryam's visual translator and accompanied by a sonorous male voice: "Feeling out of place? Need to know more about the context around you? We can help!"

How odd. Maryam taps her fingertips against her thigh under the counter, composing some quick lines of code. "Why would I buy your travel guide," she asks, "when I can have as many as I want for free?" She snaps her fingers, imitating him, and four images jump into the air between them, the portals for Dhaka travel guides from four different Information compilers.

The guy laughs in admiration. "Ha! That's very good!" But Maryam is frowning at the image he called up, still hanging in the air between them. It looks uncomfortably like the street she was stuck in earlier that morning. She searches for herself in the crowd, but it is too dense to be certain before he flips it off. "You don't have to buy. This is a free sample, as a gesture of goodwill for a stranger in Dhaka. If you find it useful, maybe you will buy in another place. And you will find it useful. This guide is special. Ask your guides for the best chotpoti in the area, or what gangs roam the streets these days, or what this means in a Tejgaon neighborhood." He raises his left arm and clasps four fingers from his right arm on the opposite elbow.

Maryam stands up, annoyed. She's not going to run the searches and give him an opportunity to look triumphant when they're blank, or press his hard sell, or whatever his game is. She doesn't look back until she's left the restaurant, and then only to make sure he didn't follow her to the stairwell.

This hotel is so old that her room includes a Mecca-pointing arrow on the ceiling; Maryam notes it is a fraction of a degree off from the prayer-orienter she uses, projected in her vision.

Changed and in bed, she calls Núria, but there is no answer. The location monitor puts her somewhere over the Atlantic: deployed again. And heading farther away. Maryam curls into her pillows, turning the temperature up a notch on the climate-controlled sheets for comfort despite the warmth of the night.

To keep herself from checking where Núria is going, wondering if it's dangerous, speculating how long she'll be, Maryam projects up some content. She dithers at first between a ringle concert in Tallinn and an episode of *Petrarch*, a historical novela she's following with occasional winces. Then she notices a new episode of *Centenal Searchers* and immediately pulls it up. It's a great show. The insanely attractive hosts—two women and two men who have flirted with each other in all possible configurations—travel to remote single-centenal governments to explore their idiosyncratic laws and customs. It's a sweet show, laughing gently at the oddities of the world's isolated communities but admiring them at the same time, and Maryam relaxes as she watches handsome, goofy Samir interview an elderly man in a one-centenal government in Louisville about their annual horse-racing festival.

When she turns off the projector unease slips back, and before she falls asleep, she wonders if that weird travel-guide presentation was a random sales pitch, or if she's being targeted.

Maryam wakes to the sound of calamitous construction behind the hotel. She stretches in bed and realizes with surprise she's looking forward to going back to the sanatorium, almost giddy with it, in fact. Maybe it's the fun of dressing up in someone else's clothes. Or maybe slipping out of your accustomed era even for an afternoon has its benefits.

She takes a longer route to avoid pedestrian congestion, and because that photo from the travel guide is still creeping her out, and arrives at the sanatorium with her good mood intact. Saleha looks up from her workspace when Maryam comes in. "Welcome back! You can go to Taskeen's on your own if you remember the way. Here, I'll get out of your way for a few minutes so you can change."

Taskeen greets her warmly at the door. This time the tea is ready, the pot and the mugs waiting in the computer room. "There wasn't nearly enough intel in those reports," she chides as Maryam sits down. "The observations by the witnesses are sadly lacking in detail."

"I think they were a little distracted by the explosives and plastic guns."

"Hmph. My point is, there is not enough data to draw a solid conclusion about what they are hoping to achieve or how to stop them. However, I do have some suggestions." Taskeen sits at the computer and busies herself pulling up some diagrams. "So why did you move to La Habana?"

Maryam glances at her sharply. "You accessed Information!"

Taskeen winks. "I told you I keep my mind active. Why did you move? I know La Habana is gaining influence under Batún, but the Doha Hub is still far more powerful."

"Why did I leave?" *Because my boss, whom I like and respect, and my ex-girlfriend, who dumped me, are circling each other in a struggle for world domination. There is no way that works out well for me.* "It was a personal decision," she says, reminding herself that this elderly, once-powerful woman wants to show she's still linked in to the inner politics of

Information. No reason to imagine an alternative motive for the gossip.

"I see," Taskeen says, suddenly absorbed with her computer screen. "Here, take a look at this." She looks over her shoulder. "You'll have to come over here; it doesn't project up, remember?"

Maryam stands and leans closer. The glowing screen is filled with lines of code. Maryam has to stare for a few seconds before she can parse them through the antiquated two-dimensional representation of data and the dorky fonts. "Wow, you went right to the bricks of it."

"We built it brick by brick. That's the part I can help you with. It's the fancy casings and bells and whistles you people shellacked over it that I don't understand." Taskeen scrolls through the endless pages of code, pausing occasionally to dive deeper into subprograms. "I've found a couple of weaknesses, I'm sorry to say. But you know, it was a different time: these would have been difficult to exploit with the technology we had then."

"Oh?"

"Crash, yes. That wasn't so hard, so we had a lot of redundancies and hardware protections. But meaningfully exploiting the system, piggybacking on it in the way you're talking about?" Taskeen shakes her head. "That requires a more current level of computing and algorithmic power. Of course, I don't know that they're doing it at this level. If they're dealing with the superstructure, I can't do much for you." She scrolls some more.

Protesting too much? Maryam wonders. "By the way," she says. "What does this mean?" When Taskeen looks up at her she repeats the gesture the man made to her in the bar last night.

Taskeen blinks at her, accessing memory. "Stingy," she says, and turns back to the computer screen.

Maryam wonders if the gesture was a snide comment on her unwillingness to buy the product, or if the vendor uses the same examples on everyone. The latter seems more likely; he would have to know beforehand that the localism isn't covered on Information. Maryam checks quickly, and there is no reference for it, although apparently a similar gesture has recently evolved to mean something moderately rude along certain trade routes of West Africa.

"Okay," Taskeen says, finally finding the section she was looking for. "Now, I can't say for sure that this is what they're trying to do, not based on what you've given me, but this is what I would be after if it were me."

And what, Maryam thinks as she leans forward, *if it* was *you?*

CHAPTER 2

Maryam's flight back to Doha is delayed for four hours by dense fog, a once-seasonal irritation made unpredictable by climate volatility. Wandering the dispiriting airport, which hasn't been updated since (Information tells her) the fifties, she wishes for an office crow. Her errand is important enough to justify one, but the hope is that by flying commercially, she can stay under the radar. Yes, anyone who takes the trouble to look for it can find her travel itinerary, but it will appear less important, possibly personal.

After the rough landing (through a dust storm, because it's just that kind of a travel day) Maryam takes public transportation to the Information building and goes straight to the office of Nejime, director of the Doha Hub. Though she is no longer Maryam's direct boss, she's leading the investigation into the attacks.

"And?" Nejime asks without preamble when Maryam has been ushered in and the door closed behind her. The director's expansive office is spare, mostly devoted to seating arrangements, in various configurations, for meetings; Nejime's large workspace is configured to auto-hide all open projects whenever she moves away from it.

"She's willing to help and certainly competent enough to at least try." Maryam describes the sanatorium and her impressions of Khan.

Nejime laughs, unexpectedly. "I'd heard of temporal therapy, but I must admit I never took it seriously. Perhaps I should look into it."

"You're far too young to think of such things," Maryam offers in her politest voice, tacking on a *ma'am* for extra points, and Nejime laughs again.

"Flattery noted. So, explain her technical conclusions to me as best as you can."

"She thinks it's more likely they are trying to take control of the system than planning to knock it out by torpedoing a lot of data transfer stations at once—I'll spare you her technical rationale, but I also think she's focusing on the more challenging problem."

"The greater threat to us, as well," Nejime commented. "We've been shut down before. You reboot, you apologize, you move on. But someone else taking over our, so to speak, airwaves would sow doubt about the legitimacy of everything we provide."

Maryam waits a beat to acknowledge the truth of the statement and the unusual tension in Nejime's voice. "Taking that goal as the premise, she had a few suggestions for how they might go about it. I'll warn you, none of them has an easy fix." Maryam developed a metaphorical infographic on the flight, working at eyeball level so it was invisible to other passengers. She projects it out now, superimposed over a slowly rotating globe: a network of lines and symbols representing the entire patchwork of conduits, cables, broadcasters, storage sites, and other infrastructure constructed in asymmetrical waves over the past quarter-century.

"Is that all of our hardware?" Nejime asks, eyeing the globe with interest.

"An approximation," Maryam corrects quickly. "A single flight, no matter how boring, isn't nearly enough time to map our entire infrastructure. Also, remember that we don't keep tabs on all of it in real time, because governments bear responsibility for maintenance within their territories."

Nejime grumbles an acknowledgement and Maryam goes on. "Taskeen believes that their plan will require a hardware as well as a software hack—otherwise, it's unlikely they would take the risk of attacking the transfer stations, although it's possible they are using that experience to pinpoint a software weakness. Assuming hardware is involved, the most obvious loophole would be a power cut. You'll notice that was an element of every attack so far."

"We don't have backup power?"

"Some, but not enough, especially if multiple stations are attacked simultaneously. And, of course, we don't maintain or secure power grids, which are a matter for governments."

"I knew we should have put electricity under our mandate," Nejime mutters.

Maryam isn't sure whether she's joking, so she ignores it and walks her through simplified versions of Taskeen's other scenarios.

"Takeover would be difficult, but it's a legitimate possibility," she finishes, "and we don't have enough data to prepare for it."

"I want you to continue to work on this. It takes priority over election prep—I'll talk to Batún for you." Nejime pauses. "Do you think Khan would be an asset, if we could figure out a way for you to work with her?"

Maryam's first thought is *I can't move to Dhaka.* Her second is more professionally palatable, so she voices that instead. "Are you sure we can trust her?"

Nejime frowns. "No. Did she do something suspicious?"

"Nothing in particular, just . . . hard to figure."

"She always was," Nejime says, and dismisses the issue with a hand wave. "We'll leave her out of it for now."

The meeting could be over at this point, but Maryam doesn't leave. "What do we know about the people who left?"

It is unusual, within Information culture, to ask a researchable question, particularly of someone higher in the hierarchy. If you're not canny enough to find what you need in the all-encompassing data trough, you probably aren't qualified to know. "You seem to be taking the threat very seriously," Maryam amended.

But Nejime looks at her with surprise and what might be approval.

"We know at least two of them are disposed to violence," Nejime answers.

"Did you know them?" Maryam asks.

"No. Pemberton was based in Brasilia and Moushian in Dushanbe. Three people deserted from Doha . . ."

"Jensen, Ahmad Gibrail, and Alescio," Maryam says automatically. It was an enormous scandal at the time, the most shocking thing to happen since . . . probably since Maryam's own love life had intruded on her professional world. But when nothing happened—no arrest, no explanation, no sudden collapse—the fascination dissipated.

"Did you know them?" Nejime asks sharply.

"Only Gibrail, and him only to nod at in the canteen." Jensen and Alescio had been translators, six and a half hours a day smoothing and correcting machine translation. Maryam had always expected that if there were a revolution, it would come from the translator bay, although she'd been expecting a work stoppage, not a violent coup. Gibrail had been an analyst, not much higher up the hierarchy than a translator but more likely to come in contact with techies as he refined search algorithms.

"The sheer number of them," Nejime says, "the simultaneity of their departure—they must have communicated somehow beyond word of mouth, and now these attacks—"

"What happened after they left?" The usual answer, *They went to the null states,* is used like *They lived happily ever after* or *Exit, pursued by a bear,* as if the null states are unknowable wastelands where nothing further could occur, but that can't be true. People live their whole lives in the null states, even if their lives aren't minutely documented the way micro-democratic lives are. And now Exformation is returning, having presumably outwitted the bear, to attack data transfer stations and wreak havoc.

"As far as we know, Pemberton ended up in Vladivostok and Moushian in Crimea. We believe other groups found their ways to Chongqing, the Baltics, and perhaps Saudi. Up until now, our intel from these places has been extremely scant."

"Up until now?"

"We have a new source which suggests that they remain scattered and dangerous, and are receiving some support from Russia. Also, there's the timing."

"You think they'll make an attempt on the election?"

"It's the joint in our armor, the weakest point in our high and impenetrable wall," Nejime says. "As the last election made abundantly clear." Two different kinds of sabotage, a recount, and a revote triggered confusion and distrust that took years to clean up. "We have to assume they've learned from that: from the tactics used against us and from our response."

"You think they'll try to start a war?" Maryam feels a

remembered chill as she says it. Five years ago, Maryam was young and mired in her own romantic melodrama; when she found out how close they had come to war, it had been as shocking as if she were told that the bubonic plague was sweeping the world again. She has heard enough real-world conflict stories from her friend Roz's SVAT work since then to feel jaded, but the word *war* still resonates with danger.

Nejime strides over to the sun-shielded windows. "I would like to believe that war is an expensive anachronism and that we should be worried about a subtler means of taking and holding power. But if there is a war, Maryam, remember: the militias will not necessarily be on our side.

"They're coming for us, though, that I am sure of." She turns back into the room. "One way or another, these petty, violent fools are going to try to take down the system we've spent decades trying to balance and counterbalance with careful featherweights of policy increments and procedural nuances. Despite all this hope and effort and intelligence we've expended to improve the conditions of democracy, all Exformation have to do is get people to trust us a little less, make them hate us a little more. And they will try it, Maryam, on Election Day or before." Nejime takes a deep breath, and Maryam can see her banking her fires, submerging into the calm aloofness that has been her trademark as a director. "It almost makes me glad that the term was shortened to five years. Peaceful transfers of power, that's the game. If we can just get through the election . . . if this new structure adds legitimacy, gives dissenters an additional outlet . . . we might survive."

"If they're trying to take over," Maryam says, trying to make her tone steady and comforting, "they need to use our infrastructure, at least to start." That's what Taskeen said. "They can't build an infrastructure at that scale without us noticing."

"In that case," Nejime says, "let's make sure we're paying attention."

While she's in Doha, Maryam finalizes the sale of her old apartment. She could have done it remotely, but this seemed like a good opportunity to wipe out any trace of regret. When Maryam moved to La Habana six months ago, she kept her Doha apartment out of hesitation to cut her moorings. Now, with the benefit of distance, she is happy enough to let it go. It's good to be back for a visit, but the flavor of Doha has gained the complicated, bitter taste of misguided love affairs.

With her apartment finally gone, she stays with her friend Roz. Roz's husband, Suleyman, greets her warmly at the door and then tactfully retreats, leaving them to catch up. They spend the evening out on the terrace, Roz's ankles propped up on the railing.

"So, you'll be living in Kas?" Maryam asks.

"It seems so," Roz says. "At least for the first few years. But only after the birth; I'm not ready to rely on the medical facilities out there." She picks out another oyster from the cold box, pops it open, and switches the shucking knife for a handheld microbiome scanner to check for contaminants and bacteria. Convinced, she slurps it.

"You're okay with that?" Maryam sips her fizzy kumquat juice.

Roz shrugs, rubbing her belly. "I've gotten fond of the place. And I had trouble thinking of anywhere I'd rather raise a young child, to be honest. Suleyman has promised we can move someplace more cosmopolitan when I get the itch to."

"It sounds like a good solution," Maryam says blandly, wondering when she'll see her friend again. It's not easy to find an excuse to visit a small town on the eastern edge of the Sahara. She promises herself again that she'll be better about calling Roz, set up a regular time maybe.

"And how's La Habana? Looks like you're loving it there."

"I am, more than I expected. I needed a fresh start, and it's a good place for that. But that doesn't mean it's perfect." Roz raises her eyebrows, and Maryam offers an extravagant shrug in response. "It's good, you know, it's just that Núria travels so much—okay, we both do."

The pause draws out. Roz takes another oyster, checks it, hands it to Maryam. "This one's fine if you're not pregnant."

Maryam looks at it skeptically, then shrugs and slurps. She's definitely not pregnant. Besides, she'll be back in La Habana tomorrow, with its excellent hospitals. "Do you remember back when you first got together with Suleyman, and you were worried that the two of you were too different?"

Roz nods. "You're feeling something similar?"

"Well, not as extreme," Maryam says, although she wonders. "Obviously she's not as isolated as Suleyman was. But she's a *soldier*, Roz! What am I doing with a soldier?"

"You like her."

"It would be one thing if she were InfoSec, or something like that." Maryam goes on as if she hadn't heard, the spring inside her uncoiling. "But she's a government soldier! Your-Army, no less."

"She's good at her job," Roz says, around a mouthful of mollusk. She speaks from personal experience; she was working with Núria in the Caucuses when Maryam met her now-girlfriend.

"Yeah." It does seem like Núria's career is on the upswing, with all the travel they have her doing. "But it's—we're so different. And there are so many things we can't talk about!"

"That part is tough," Roz agrees, rubbing circles on her belly. "Although at least it's both of you, so you both understand the situation."

"But she acts like—like everything's fine! Like the relationship is already settled, like it's decided that we're together and there's nothing more to worry about, like she's not worried about us at all!"

Roz is silent for a long moment; Maryam imagines her piecing together a response that doesn't point, heavy-handed, at Maryam's recent bad experiences. "You know," she says finally. "Suleyman proposed way, way before I was ready. And so I made him wait."

"I don't think a proposal's in the cards," Maryam says, although her nerves curl at the thought. *Would that be enough? Would that prove to me that she really likes me? Or would I find new ways to doubt?*

Roz is waiting for more, and Maryam wishes she were more contained, less stressed and emotional about these quirks of private life. Tonight, she decides, she will be. No more whining. "What did you decide to do about work?" she asks instead.

"We're paring down my responsibilities now. As of next week, I'll be down to two projects."

"The Wall?" Maryam guesses, taking an oyster.

"Of course," Roz says, not hiding her pride. The Wall is a compiler she set up to collect visual and animated interpretations of the news drawn by youth from around the micro-democratic world. Recently she added a training and data-art education component, "a tiny step toward making SVAT work unnecessary," as she calls it, and while usage is still low by Information standards, it has been growing steadily. "But I've been delegating more and more, so that if I do decide to take a lot of time off, the other staff can manage it without me."

"And the other thing?" It's both a relief and a disappointment to be talking about something other than her relationship, but Maryam leans into the feeling of withdrawal.

"The mantle tunnel mess." Roz shifts in her seat. "Do you think maybe we could use something to go with the oysters? Toast with chutney or something? The date chutney they make here is really good."

Maryam grins and pulls up the menu page from the building kitchen to put in the order. How many nights have they spent here over the years, ordering late-night snacks and talking? Or, in her case, whining about her love life. "And how is that going?" she asks.

"Ugh, it's a mess," Roz says. "Horrible legal issues that are totally new and have to be thought through for the first time, horrible environmental issues that no one can fully predict, angry people on all sides." Permission to start excavating the first mid-haul travel tunnel through the mantle was granted almost two years ago, but the project was halted almost immediately by a series of challenges from the governments it would pass under, and the battles have been ongoing ever since. "I'm going out to Berlin next week—you know 888 already broke ground there for the tunnel connecting to Istanbul?"

"Even with the PhilipMorris tunnel stuck in red tape?"

"Yup. Nothing to stop them excavating their own territory on spec. It's only when they cross under the border that the problems start. I guess they are hoping for momentum."

"Hell of an investment," Maryam says, sipping. "And that's a lot of travel for you, isn't it?"

Roz shrugs, hands curled around her belly. "They let me use a crow, so it's pretty manageable. And it's just Rome, Cairo, Berlin, and Istanbul, nothing very far."

"Still, it doesn't exactly sound relaxing."

"Well, I'm just doing high-level analysis," Roz says. The real reason she's stayed on the project, as they both know, is her fierce distrust of highly technical, insufficiently understood infrastructure projects. This still surprises Maryam: because that anger is rooted in Roz's personal history, she had long avoided mixing it with her professional life. Maryam suspects that Suleyman convinced her to get involved.

There's a silence, but it's as swollen with unseen meaning as Roz is.

"Have you been following the Williams trial?"

Maryam, who thought they were not-talking about Roz's environmental conflicts of interest, looks up in surprise. "Of course," she says. "The headlines, anyway."

Roz is fiddling with the microbiome scanner, beeping it across the balustrade, the armrest of her chair. "What do you think?"

Maryam has to take her time with that. Especially over the last few days, focused on her mission, she's been skimping on the detailed reporting, but everyone in Information, plus most of the rest of the world, is riveted to the case. Nakia Williams, a midlevel Information analyst based in the New York City hub, has been accused of tinting the presented interpretation of data in accordance with her own political beliefs.

"It's a tricky one," Maryam says finally. "I don't feel like I have enough of the data to make a judgment. It's not like Blanton or Yadav." Both Information officers who, in the past, have been convicted for using their influence to amass personal wealth. "It makes me grateful that I'm on the tech side and not dealing directly with live data." She shifts in her seat. "What about you?"

"It's . . . worrying," Roz says slowly. "Of course, if people do something like that, you don't want to let them get away with it. But it's also a problem if analysts self-censor."

A bell dings, and Maryam goes to get the food from the dumbwaiter in the corner, ignoring Roz's halfhearted offers to get up and get it herself.

"I met her once," Roz adds, after she's spread some chutney and taken a bite.

"Williams?" Maryam asks.

Roz nods around another bite. "Did some SVAT work in the Hudson Valley after the last election. She was our liaison to the local hub." Before the semi-sabbatical of approaching maternity leave, Roz frequently worked on Specialized Voter Action Tactics teams, which use direct in-person approaches to extend Information's data outreach to the most recalcitrant—and conflict-prone—voters. The last election, almost five years ago, spawned a plethora of missions for them.

"What was she like?"

Roz shrugs. "She's cool. Helpful, competent. She's a friend of Mishima's."

That brings it closer to home. "Do you think she did it?"

"I don't know," Roz says, putting down her half-eaten toast in dismay. "It's— We can't be completely neutral, obviously. No one can. So I guess they're asking whether she skewed the data on purpose and— That's not a clear line, you know; she could have sort of known it was coming out on the side of what she wanted but thought that was just the way the data pointed . . ."

Maryam waits, surprised to see Roz so worked up. When Roz doesn't go on, or go back to her toast, she ventures a guess. "You're worried you can't trust yourself?"

"I'm worried I can't trust this organization!" Roz bursts out. "Especially . . ." Her voice drops again. "Especially on the mantle tunnel. Everyone knows how I feel about it. Maybe I should request a transfer." Another pause. "I guess I am worried about trusting myself, a little. Both."

"I don't understand," Maryam says. "Information analysts have *always* had to walk this careful line, right? You have processes?"

Roz nods, mouth full again: the crisis has passed.

"So, what happened? Why are they suddenly cracking down on this one person?"

"Maybe because there have been accusations against Information's neutrality . . ." Roz trails off, because there have always been accusations. "There's a SVAT team out there now, trying to calm the situation down."

They munch quietly. The light breeze brings the sound of music from somewhere in town.

"Have you heard anything about the—all those people who left?"

Roz turns to look at her. "No, nothing official. Although I think about them every time we go to Kas and I see how the new Information infrastructure is coming along."

"Has it changed much?"

"Immensely. It's almost like normal now." When Maryam was there, Kas had been notably lacking in cameras, feeds, and handhelds. "But I always think about all the other projects they had planned with the feed money. Power generation, irrigation."

"Doesn't quite make up for assassinations, though, does it?" Maryam says.

"Of course not." Roz shifts her weight. "Wait, are you asking because they're back? I thought that was over."

"Erm." Maryam hedges. "Some people suspect they're behind these transfer-station attacks."

Roz shudders. "I saw an alert about that and avoided it. There's only so much awful news I can take at a time."

"And with the election coming up, there's sure to be a surplus."

The next morning, Maryam boards a commercial crow for La Habana. It's usually a good bet, since there are only a few possible stops between Doha and La Habana, but they get stuck with a stop in Praia, another in Montserrat, and three in eastern Cuba, and the journey is two hours longer than usual.

Even once they arrive there's a long line for municipal public transport crows, so Maryam takes a taxi. It lurches annoyingly through the heavy evening traffic, windows all rolled down and no breeze.

At least she knows from her locator that Núria is home. As she drags her suitcase down the hall, though, she is assaulted by what is first a premonition, then a suspicion, then a certainty. The apartment is in an old building, and while the plumbing and floors have been renovated to modern standards, the walls still efficiently transmit the sound of eager chatter.

There's nothing to be upset about. Núria didn't know exactly when she would get back. Yes, she could have checked, but crow ETAs are unreliable, changing as additional passengers board at drop-off points and the algorithms are updated. What was she supposed to do, send her camaradas home in the middle of a tertulia?

Maryam pushes open the door to the apartment, and light and laughter flood out into the dim hall. "Oh, hi," Maryam says, pulling her bag into the living room after her. Her first impression is of a crowd, but it's only four extra women, eighty percent of Núria's band of revolutionary friends. Magdalena stands by the window, tumbler in hand; LaForet is on the barstool, long bare legs twirled together; Zipporah and Carme are on the sofa; and Núria is curled beside them, her feet tucked up under her and almost touching Carme's thigh.

"Darling!" Núria jumps up and dots a kiss on Maryam's travel-chapped lips. "Welcome home! You must be exhausted." She tugs at Maryam's bag, her soft curls briefly obscuring Maryam's view of the other women and their chorus of hellos.

"I got it," Maryam says, wishing she'd been quick enough to properly return the kiss instead of just receiving it. "It's— It's fine, I've got it."

"What do you want to drink?" That's LaForet, slipping off her stool to slide to the liquor cabinet. The camaradas never remember that Maryam doesn't take alcohol.

"I'm feeling pretty grimy; I think I'll get a bath first," Maryam says, and drags her suitcase out of sight of their smiling, relaxed gazes. Safely in the bathroom, she runs the water long and hot, then slides in. Baths are another great advantage La Habana has over Doha. Even here, though, it doesn't do to waste water, and she and Núria usually soak together. She lingers in the tub, hoping the ladies will take the hint and go home, or that Núria will leave them to their chatter, but the door to the bedroom doesn't open, and occasionally the laughter from the sala is exuberant enough to be heard over the lapping of the water.

Maryam drags herself out when the water is already a shade too cold and she has lost the glow of its initial warmth. Hopefully not a metaphor, she thinks, wrapping herself in a robe. She sits on the bed for a while, debating whether to get dressed again and go pretend to enjoy the soiree, but she is exhausted from the flight and the disappointment. She pulls on her pajamas—black, of course, and pseudo-silk—and, after dithering, slips out the door and through the sala to the kitchen to get a glass of water. She pauses in the archway to the kitchen, unwilling to cut through their talk again, unwilling to be the loser who goes to bed, but unable to join in.

"Information is still ignoring marginalized perspectives, though," LaForet is saying. "I heard they did *another* algorithm-scrubbing last year, and yet . . ." With a gesture of the hand not holding the wine glass, she throws up two rapidly overlapping piles of vidlets and articles, one set committing the failure—racism, misogyny, assorted phobia—the other set identifying and excoriating it.

"And that poor woman in New York," Zipporah puts in, hand over her heart. "Can you imagine what she has already gone through in her career to get to where she is, and *this*?"

The sad relaxation of the bath falls away as Maryam's shoulders tense up. She does not want to defend Information on the Williams case, and she doesn't understand it well enough to add nuance. To avoid drawing their attention, she turns back to the kitchen and adds some more water she didn't want into her glass.

"They're going to fire her for—what? Doing her job?"

"Firing her would be the least of it; she could be thrown in jail!"

Maryam turns back to the doorway in time to see a projection Carme has put up showing diversity stats in the grunt and middle-management ranks of Information compared to those at the top. "But you have to unpack this," she adds, pointing at the numbers in the executive rank. "Okay, yes, there is some multiculturality up here, but if you look at these people's status in their own cultural-national paradigms, they are usually near the top in wealth, social capital, and whatever the relevant ethno-racist categories are." Maryam feels her face go hot and has to turn back to the kitchen again. She shouldn't take this personally: she is hardly executive-level at Information, and based on the fashions the camaradas regularly wear, they are far richer than Maryam has ever been, absolutely or relatively. And yet it stings. At least Carme was incensed enough to sit up, incidentally increasing the sofa space between her and Núria.

"The question," Magdalena says—she has moved to the divan, and Maryam can hear the coldfactor clink in her glass as she gestures, "is how do we hold Information accountable when they are the only game in town?"

"They could be a lot worse," Núria says. Maryam glances toward the sala in time to see her not looking at anyone.

"Of course they could be, but 'could be worse' is not enough of a standard, don't you think?" LaForet works for a news compiler and so is arguably part of the system, but it is a somewhat fringe organization that (according to their mission statement, plastered beside LaForet's head in her public Information) *aims to draw attention to underserved populations and stories.*

"It's well past time for a revolution," says Carme.

"After twenty-five years?" Zipporah asks. "That's not a bit quick? The United States got two and a half centuries, the People's Republic of China got nearly a century, the French Fifth Republic seven decades."

"History is speeding up," Carme answers with a wink.

Tertulias about Information's faults are Maryam's least favorite kind of tertulia. *How long are they going to stay?* She blinks up the time, but it's only 10:32, barely early evening by La Habana standards. Her eyes are tipping shut because of the long flight and the jet lag, but she feels like a pathetic girlfriend instead of an international jetsetter.

"Well, I'm off to bed," she says as she walks through the sala, and immediately wishes she hadn't. They all stop their conversation and trill out versions of "Good night!" LaForet even gives her a little wave. Then Maryam shuts the door, the cool dimness of the bedroom so soothing to her gritty eyes that she crawls right into bed, sure she won't be able to stay awake any longer.

She's wrong, and spends most of the next two hours listening to the dim sound of laughter through the door, the large bed empty around her, until she finally dissolves into unconsciousness.

CHAPTER 3

Jetlag wakes Maryam up early. She is relieved to find Núria's arm around her, quiet snores against her cheek, and wishes she wasn't. *Enjoy it*, she tells herself, but after a few moments of immobility she eases herself out of bed, quietly pulls on the first clothes she finds, and goes out to get breakfast.

There is food in the kitchen, but Maryam likes taking advantage of that first effortless early morning of jet lag to soak in some Habana life. True, a majority of the inhabitants are still sleeping off the pleasures of the night before, but early hours after dawn offer another side of the city. Delivery bots trundle by with their loads. The clack of dominos calls from the glassless window of a café. Joggers and speedbladers cruise along the sidewalks around her, heading in the direction of the Malecón, the recreational course along the high parapet that has been erected against the encroaching seas. Maryam considers following them, but it's a moderately long walk and she still has that lightheaded jet-lag feeling of consciousness slightly detached from her body.

In the park, a group of people slow-motion their way through a tai chi routine, a bright government logo projected into the air above them: this is an 888 centenal, and the government has been trying to brighten its corporate branding with a number of soft-power social programs. Next to her favorite bakery she finds more evidence of prosperity: a new construction site, several orders of magnitude quieter than the one in Dhaka. An early-twentieth-century building is being renovated and reinforced, and the dense coverage of microbots cleaning its façade winks in the sunlight.

There's a line in the bakery even at that hour, although most people go straight to the pickup side for orders they placed ahead on Information. Maryam prefers to look at the options in person, so she waits her turn and orders two pasteles de queso, two de guayaba y queso, and, after checking the chain of origin on Information to reassure herself that they are 100 percent beef, two de carne. She adds two café cubanos; the espresso never seems to come out the same from the cafetera at home, and she likes the tiny recyclable ceramic thermoses they serve takeaway orders in. On her way home, she detours to find the sugarcane vendor, a pushcart with a hand-crank machine that cores the caña, pulps the inside, and pours it back into the hollow stalk, which is then sealed for easy transport. She orders one straight and one with a squeeze of lime for Núria.

The apartment is still quiet when she gets back. Maryam begins setting out plates without being too subtle about it, and before she's done Núria wanders out of the bedroom, dark curls adorably rumpled. "Ooh, breakfast!" she says, and kisses Maryam briefly on the lips before settling onto the high stool by the counter. "Thanks, amor."

Maryam feels her nerves flutter under her skin. She caught the undercurrent of morning breath when Núria kissed her and it didn't even dilute her desire, a chemical phenomenon she will never understand. "No problem. I miss this stuff when I'm away."

"Me too!" Núria says fervently. "You know I just got back myself."

"Where from?"

Núria glances up through her eyelashes: Maryam could have found out if she wanted to. "West Africa." It's a staggeringly vague answer, and Núria amends apologetically: "A tour, five centenals in three days."

"Wow," Maryam says, wondering what a soldier can accomplish in such a short time.

"I was advising on security plans, that sort of thing," Núria says, as if reading her mind.

"After all that, I'm amazed you had the energy to hold a salon." Maryam takes a sip of sugarcane juice, hoping she didn't sound too jealous.

"Oh, you know, we had already planned it before the trip came up. And it's not really a tertulia; they just come over! Besides, I slept on the flight back—I doubt I would have been able to go to bed early."

Núria is good at that. Maryam can never seem to sleep on flights.

"I have to leave again Saturday," Núria says.

"Saturday?" It's a sinking feeling. "Where to?"

"Oaxaca."

"Oaxaca?" Maryam searches her memory for any ongoing conflict there, then searches Information. "More advising?"

Núria rolls her eyes. "Ugh, it's nothing. You remember how that centenal there opted out of micro-democracy last election? They call themselves the Independentistas? Well, of *course* the neighboring Liberty centenal is *convinced* that this means the Independentistas are their enemies and likely to attack at any time to expand their territory, so they requested security assistance."

"¿En *serio*? And you have to go?"

"You're the ones who pay for it." Núria raises her eyebrows at Maryam, who sighs.

"Government sovereignty."

Núria shrugs. "You know, we in the security forces are like an ambulance. If they call us, we have to go. Even if they're hypochondriacs. Anyway, we do it on short rotations so no one gets too bored. I'll only be away for ten days. And it's not that bad an assignment. The food is great!"

"I bet," Maryam says, as enthusiastically as she can manage. She doesn't want to be the needy lover, and they knew going into this that they'd both be traveling a lot.

"What about you?"

"Me?" She's still distracted by trying to hide her disappointment.

"How was your trip?"

"Oh." Maryam remembers why she's not supposed to be annoyed about Núria's obfuscations: she has to do the same thing. "It was fine. Dhaka and Doha." She tries to think of something she can say about it. "I finished selling my apartment!"

"Congratulations," Núria says. "Did you see Roz?"

"Yes, she looks great," Maryam enthuses, and then recalls the more troubling parts of their conversation. "She's doing really well." A pause. "She and Suleyman are going to move back to Kas after the baby is born."

"Wow," Núria says. "That's a commitment."

"Yeah."

"Any more travel coming up?"

"Nope," Maryam says. "Not that I know of." She's ready to say something about having a deep-research project that should occupy her for the next few weeks, but that might lead to questions she can't answer. She bites into a pastelito instead.

Drawing on years of training in controlled motion, Mishima eases her trapped arm free. In ultra-stealth mode, she rolls smoothly to her feet, then creeps through the dim room toward the door. She slips out into the corridor and draws the door silently closed behind her.

Only then does she allow herself a deep breath. The baby is down for a nap.

Not so much a baby anymore; Sayaka is nearly two, toddling and stringing together disjointed words and gestures into stories that Mishima follows anxiously.

Mishima twitches her fingers, turning on the audio baby monitor and tuning it to a specific frequency that she isolates to her left ear. Mishima's fame and life experience have made her too paranoid to use vid for anything she doesn't want to share with the world, although she does enable a small window of baby-sleep status indicators—breath rhythm, temperature, heart rate, REM—in the bottom left of her vision. Then she turns up the ongoing conference call in her right ear and switches her input stream from typed to spoken.

They are still trudging through some of the murkier details about the proposed advisory council for the upcoming tweak of micro-democracy, and Mishima wanders around the apartment, picking up toddler detritus as she listens. Normally, she doesn't have to multitask quite so dramatically. Mishima's so-called job, which became official three months ago when an Information-wide primary chose five candidates to go into the global election, has only rare schedule

requirements, and Ken's work is even more flexible, allowing them to juggle childcare between their responsibilities
most weeks. Today, however, Ken is in Surabaya; although
the official campaign season for the upcoming global election won't open until next week, scoping out opportunities
and strategy development are well under way, and Ken is at
a regional centenal governors' conference for western Java.
Until a few months ago, Ken was working as director of citizen engagement for Free2B, their current government, but
in preparation for the election he's been promoted to their
government-wide campaign strategy director. Mishima is
increasingly aware that their current work-life balance isn't
going to stand up to the pace of the election, but the campaign
period is only four weeks. They'll manage. Afterward . . .
depends on whether Mishima wins.

A part of her is looking forward to a more hectic schedule
as much as the other part of her dreads it. She misses urgency.

And these conference calls don't provide it. At the moment, Valérie Nougaz is making a last-ditch reprise of her
argument that there should be more Information representatives on the advisory council, or whatever it is they eventually
name it. Mishima wants to jump in and point out that tipping the council in Information's favor will only make
people more suspicious of them, but she holds back. She and
Nougaz are the top two candidates for the currently single
Information seat, so the two of them arguing over the number of seats is not a good look.

Nejime, who has been hovering over the awkward incep-
tion of this council with more concern than any emperor
penguin ever showed, advised her not to get involved in the
preliminary structural arguments. It makes sense but it
hasn't been easy. Mishima is usually the smartest person in

any room, and while she can freely admit that in this particular group—the upper echelon of Information's strategic thinkers—others could claim that title, it's debatable enough for her ideas to merit attention. In fact, if you count intelligence *plus* recent real-world experience, she's undoubtedly the person best positioned to redesign this stupid system.

However, as Ken reminded her at one point when she was ready to chew the walls with frustration, this is not about the best idea. It's about politics.

Case in point: she got into an early argument with Nejime and al-Derbi about why the Information representative should be globally elected.

"It doesn't make sense. This person represents *Information*; it should be Information staff who chose whom they want in that position."

"That's not the point." Al-Derbi spoke softly, as usual. "Information already has influence."

Mishima was so focused on system design that she hadn't seen the larger picture. Of course, Information would continue to influence the world the way it always has: through the subtle, often unintentional control and weighing and presentation of data. The point of the Information representative wasn't to advocate for this already-powerful entity but to garner the reflexive legitimacy that people would assign someone who was globally elected. To make people feel like they were involved. Illusory democracy.

After the slightly embarrassing pause of working through it, Mishima turned on Nejime. "I thought you told me this was going to be a real job," she snapped, perhaps more sharply than she should have, because she was annoyed with herself for missing it, annoyed with them for playing these games.

"It is a real job," Nejime answered. She raised her voice

as rarely as al-Derbi, but soft was not the adjective that leapt to mind when she spoke. "There will be decisions made in this assembly, and the skills and quick thinking of the representative are of utmost importance. But it also needs legitimacy, and we need greater engagement in the process as a whole. With any luck, this restructuring will salvage, little by little, the system we have worked the past quarter-century to build. But perhaps you expected you would be ruling the world?"

Mishima almost walked away right there. She would have done it with a smile, but it would have been absolutely irrevocable, and she still had doubts, mostly in the form of a gauzy image of her sitting in some august chamber, making sophisticated arguments and voting on difficult measures with Sayaka cuddled to her chest or sitting on her lap. "I expected not to be bored," she said instead. She should have stopped there, but she was still mad. "I expected not to be a celebrity spokesperson. I expected not to be a veneer on the endless mechanics of bureaucracy."

"Do you think Valérie Nougaz would be running for an unimportant, boring position?" al-Derbi asked pensively.

That's the best proof anyone has offered so far, but Mishima was still feeling ornery. "She's old. Maybe she's looking for semi-retirement."

Nejime and al-Derbi, both of the same era as Nougaz, ignored this, although Mishima has a feeling it's going to come back and bite her in the ass some day.

She shifts her attention back to the ongoing discussion long enough to register that they're talking about the name of the council now.

"Supreme Board of Advisors?" Gilchrest asks. Mishima

thinks he's being sarcastic, but his tone always sounds dry and deadpan, so it's hard to say.

Nougaz shakes her head, too annoyed to laugh. "We've had enough problems with this stupid Supermajority moniker. How many conflicts have been caused in the past quarter-century because people overestimated its importance?"

Nougaz is right, as she so often is, but the name of the entity is a problem Mishima cares very little about, and that little is mostly annoyance: it should have been decided long before now. It's more than a pet peeve about the inefficiency of bureaucracy (as she's explained to Ken more than once); it's a foreshadowing of how problematic the building of consensus is going to be for this council.

Not wanting to get too irritated, Mishima uses the time to catch up with the latest news in Nakia's case. It's an odd feeling, scrolling through accumulated stories instead of popping news alerts as they appear in the moment, but between the kid and the prep for the new role, she has fallen behind. There is a faint overlay of guilt, as well: she hasn't contacted Nakia since the allegations came out. She hadn't contacted her in months, maybe years, before then, either. Their friendship was one of food and chatting when they happened to be in the same place, not so much reaching out in between, and in the wake of the accusations, Mishima hasn't figured out how to change that. It's impossible to forget that writing to her would look bad from a political standpoint, but Mishima hopes that's not a factor in her decision.

The case itself is fascinating and frightening enough to attract her attention even if she didn't know the principal. Pre-campaign polls in an 888 centenal in commuting distance of Manhattan have been showing for several months that AmericaTheGreat, a nationalist government that barely hides its white-supremacist platform, is a strong challenger.

As one of the political directors of the New York Hub, Nakia was involved in framing and presenting the situation and oversaw the annotating advids or content from the contending governments. She also lived in the centenal in question and, given that she is not white, would have to move if AmericaTheGreat won. The easy retrospective consensus at cocktail parties and in plazas is that she should have recused herself, but Mishima knows the situation is well within both policy guidelines and customary practice. It's impossible for directors to recuse themselves from every issue that affects them, and Nakia was part of a team working on the coverage; any given item would have gone through at least three and up to eight different levels of overview.

Nonetheless, AmericaTheGreat saw an opportunity and attempted to paint her as a partisan abusing her power, leading to a flurry of annotations, retractions, blockages, and, finally, a challenge to an algorithmic analysis. The requisite algorithmic tribunal determined an 86 percent probability of bias, and the case was automatically referred to human judgment, with a charge of *influencing or attempting to influence the outcome of an election* with the exacerbating factors *from a position of power* and *before the start of official campaign period.*

The scandal should have ended there. There was already a fair amount of attention from news compilers and activists because of the continuing controversy over what beliefs made a government too awful to be allowed to win an election. Failing the algorithmic tribunal was not rare—37 percent of all cases that went to algorithm failed, as Mishima was reminded by Information annotation every time she read about the case—but it always adds to the notoriety. Still, at that point a quick yes or no human verdict, complete with transparency analysis, would have ended the case, with at worst a thirty-month jail sentence if Nakia had been found guilty.

Even jail might be a better outcome for Nakia than this continuing morass of suspicion and indeterminate suspension from her job. A resolution would be better for Information, too, especially going into the election. Mishima can't understand why the board hasn't come to a decision. There must be something unusual in the data, but while normally all Information data, including authorship and editing markers, are publicly available, the posts that triggered the case have been sequestered because of the ongoing investigation.

A message comes up against Mishima's vision: her assistant, Amran, has pinged her to let her know that the attendees are putting anonymous suggestions for the name of the council on a board. Mishima rolls her eyes but invents one (Multiperspective Government Interaction Committee) and throws it up. This seems likely to be one of those situations in which anonymity is touted but participation still counts.

AmericaTheGreat has twenty-seven centenals; it seems like a large number in the context of horrendous and irrational prejudice, but in the grand scheme of micro-democracy it's tiny. More importantly, of the eight centenals it won in the second election, six voted themselves out again in the third. Mishima doesn't have to configure this data herself: there is a sub-group at Information dedicated to tracking and analyzing what they call "quasi-democratic governments" within micro-democracy, so she's confident in the assertion that between the outmigration of out-group inhabitants and poor economic competitiveness, their electoral victories rarely last long.

That's the primary justification within Information for allowing them to continue to exist. The official position of the organization is that the Basic Law on Human Rights marks the lower boundary for acceptable action within the microdemocratic system, but when someone argues that the law should be expanded to prohibit coerced migration or segregationist intent, the response is usually *They're going to fail anyway. Let them work it out of their system*, people say. *Let their voters experience for themselves how poorly these ideologies work in practice.* But that's a dubious argument when faced with evidence of how such groups affect people's lives during the time they are in power. Mishima suspects the rationale for winking at them has to do with the more powerful groups that, if less fascist in their ideology, still bend toward segregationist or colonialist tendencies: 1China, for example, or the AlThani government in Doha, the unusually generous host of its regional Information hub. Or even PhilipMorris, with the harsh distinctions between their producer and consumer centenals. And while AmericaTheGreat and their ilk tend to fail, the overall centenal share of identity-based governance is growing.

Amran pings her again, and Mishima realigns her feeds to prioritize the meeting. They've decided to call it the Secretariat, which fulfills the blandness criterion at least. One thing has been accomplished on the call, which already puts it well above the average. Mishima feels comfortable zoning it out completely.

From her Saigon centenal where Free2B is polling at 82 percent, she can shrug off AmericaTheGreat's rising poll numbers as a tiny and probably temporary threat to the New York centenal where Nakia lives, and as all but irrelevant to the system as a whole. Her narrative disorder, however, al-most immediately produces a perspective that might be Na-kia's: a beloved neighborhood and community, under attack by people who hate her for no reason; a majority that will expel her from the place she's lived for the past eight years; a decisive, popularly sanctioned rejection of her humanity. Just imagining it makes Mishima bite her lip with anger. Is it possible, then, that Nakia consciously or unconsciously let some of that anger or the disdain over the utter illogic of it slip into her intel decisions?

It seems almost impossible that it *not* affect her work. But that isn't surprising: despite the patina of neutrality, every-one within Information knows that personal preconceptions and preferences are always going to slip in somehow. That's why the regulations have, over years of wrangling, become so extensively detailed. So why is this taking them so long to decide? Her guess is that they are working out a new detail in the rules. Or maybe they're throwing a bone to the government-sovereignty faction in the face of ever-increasing complaints about Information's power, but this seems like a particularly poor example from which to argue for stronger governments.

It gives Mishima the shivers, even though she's never been in the position of picking and choosing what data to present and how. Although if she wins this data-forsaken election, she'll be in exactly that position, and with a powerful spot-light focused right on her.

Ken is fifteen minutes early, but when he walks into the hotel restaurant, his former boss is already seated, the tiny flickers of updates and messages playing against his corneas. Suzuki's hairline has crept up a few inches, and Ken wonders why he hasn't had it reseeded. He must like the éminence grise look.

"How are you?" Suzuki asks warmly as Ken slides into the booth across from him. "It's been a long time."

It has been years since they've seen each other: since they both left Policy1st, Suzuki because of a scandal, and Ken because of burnout and disillusionment. They have been in irregular but not infrequent contact since then, usually through Suzuki throwing some of his speaking engagements Ken's way, but they've never had a reason to meet in person, or even via projection.

"Fine," Ken says. "Doing great. You're looking well."

Suzuki brushes that off with a pleased smile. "And how's your baby?"

Ken always feels a twitch of annoyance when people he hasn't seen in a long time ask him about Sayaka. He didn't tell Suzuki about having a baby; he didn't have to. Mishima rocketed into unsought superstardom due to an almost-but-not-quite-perfect spy mission, and her pregnancy was impossible to keep private. "She's terrific," he says, forcing a smile and convincing himself that he would want Suzuki to know anyway. "So, what's going on?" When Suzuki contacted him two days ago he claimed he was just taking advantage of a coincidental overlap in Surabaya, but Ken has lived with Mishima far too long to buy that.

Suzuki flexes his fingers and dives in. "This election is crucial; I don't have to tell you that. More crucial than the last one, even. If we lose now—if Heritage wins, or even one of the other big corporates—they will say policy-based governments can't cut it. That we talk big ideas but we can't run things. It will be an excuse for anyone who is ever tempted by the easy promises of corporates when their better instincts tell them to vote based on policy. We need to win this one."

All true, but why is he saying "we"? The scandal that enveloped Suzuki was indelible and defining, complete with amusing vid clips. There's no way they'd give him a leadership role, especially during an election, and Ken doesn't see Suzuki accepting anything less.

"I've set up a consulting firm to support Policy1st's campaign, and I'd like you to join me."

Ah. The popular "not staff but still important" consultancy. "I appreciate the offer, but I'm running Free2B's campaign." Ken says it with mingled pride and regret: yes, he's in charge, but Policy1st is the defending global Supermajority and Free2B is miniscule. They are only contesting five new centenals, and two of those only because Ken is ambitious.

"Come on, Ken!" Suzuki says. "I appreciate your loyalty, but we need you! You were always my right-hand man."

"Thanks but no thanks," Ken says, more decisively. Being Suzuki's right-hand man was rocket fuel for his early career, but it's not where he wants to end up. He still feels guilty, though. "Maybe we can set up some joint events or something."

"No, you're right; you should concentrate on your own priorities." Suzuki couples it with a paternal pat on the shoulder as he rises, but Ken's not sure if his former mentor is refusing out of spite or because joint campaigning is likely to be more valuable for Free2B than for the Supermajority. "But stay in touch, and please let me know if you change your mind. Remember"—he locks Ken's eyes—"how high the stakes are." And then he's gone.

CHAPTER 4

The Berlin site management headquarters for the 888 mantle tunnel construction project is a temporary building so luxurious it makes Roz itch, although she tries to comfort herself with the idea that most of the gold plating is nano-layer ormolu. The domed room is spanned by a 1:1000 scale projection of the proposed tunnel. Enlarged sections at either end show the planned areas around the entrances at each terminus—a climate-controlled pleasure garden in Berlin, a covered shopping area in Istanbul—complete with animated, multicultural customers, a constant flow of them stepping into the model capsules that depart along the tunnel every half hour. A separate, smaller display along one wall linked to geophysical sensors for real-time updates shows the current status: a shovelful of dirt missing on each end, along with a filament that has been threaded along the proposed route for data collection and micro-mapping purposes.

Even that tiny alteration to the Earth's mantle makes Roz nervous. Sure, it's not a tunnel, just an underground cable like so many before it. But it's very deep, and she can't stop remembering the horrifying vids of the Kanto earthquake five years ago, which might have been caused by early-stage mantle tunnel excavation. She doesn't broach her concerns, because that's not why she's here, but she's relieved when someone else raises the question of whether the scanning filament could cause problems. She's less relieved by the environmental engineer's airy response: "It's a tiny, tiny cable. Believe me, that is the least of our worries."

Roz is supposed to be monitoring the institutional structures around the groundbreaking of the tunnel, but 1) it's five degrees below freezing out there, so 1.1) most of the institutional partners are inside the temporary building; 2) as far as Roz is concerned, a hole in the ground is a hole in the ground; 3) this is a highly premature and symbolic groundbreaking, with at least twenty-six pending legal challenges to settle before they can dig more than ten meters. Also, though she hates to put it on the official list, being six months pregnant is more exhausting than she expected, and a comfortable seat in this cozy warmth is hard to pass up.

Thanks to 1.1, she is able to do her work inside. She's currently watching the project's chief environmental engineer, one Ana Djukic, run through an infographic-illustrated projection on major concerns and how they are addressing them. To her right are several representatives from centenals above the projected route; on her left sits Veena Rasmussen. The former co-head of state of the Policy1st Supermajority government left her post a year ago to concentrate full-time on stopping the mantle tunnel projects. Quixotic, yes, but probably less so than Policy1st's global rule. In any case, she's an utter nightmare for Djukic.

"Your cost-benefit analysis fails to take in externalities," Rasmussen interrupts early on, then: "That methodology for testing seismic interference is highly debatable; it's only been examined in a handful of studies," and finally: "What about all the risks you haven't thought of?"

Roz keeps quiet, in part because she's not here as an environmental crusader, even if she would like to be, and in part because she's already surprised at how openly critical Djukic's presentation is. If Veena would let her finish, she might learn something useful to one of the dozen lawsuits she's supporting. Roz is not completely convinced, of course: it's probably a subtle form of greenwashing. *See how honest we are about all the environmental dangers? Surely if we're responsible enough to tell you about the concerns, you can trust our judgment that we should go through with our risky and poorly understood plan to conquer the world.*

Djukic, who started with the "questions at the end, please" tactic and quickly realized that wasn't going to cut it, has moved on to smiling agreement and deflection. "Thanks for that question; I was just getting to it," and "Excellent point." By the time she finishes, her smiles are more grimaces, but she got through the presentation, which Roz grudgingly admits is a win, for her and for the tunnel. The audience sighs and disperses, some to poke at the controls of the large projection model, others choosing another of the ongoing presentations to join. Veena has moved forward to take on the environmental engineer one-on-one; Roz hasn't yet convinced herself to stand up.

"Can I interest any of you in a snack?" A young man from the project PR staff slides by, gesturing at the trays of charcuterie being brought in from the cold and deposited on a table against one wall.

"Um." Roz wishes she hadn't left her microbiome scanner in the crow. "Um." She's too embarrassed to go get it, but this hurts: she doesn't get pork very often. "Thanks, I'm fine."

Rasmussen says nothing, but the word *vegetarian* doubles in size and starts flashing in her public Information. It's not the politest way to get her point across, but Roz sympathizes: she must be in this situation constantly.

"Oh—uh, there are some crackers over there."

Veena waves her hand: she's fine. Roz, on the other hand, levers herself out of her chair and drifts toward the table with the crackers on it.

"Amazing thing, isn't it?"

Roz looks up, mouth full of her fourth and fifth crackers.

The centenal rep—his public Information shows he's from a EuropeanUnion centenal not far from Budapest—nods at the model. "This kind of transportation speed and efficiency—and practically energy-neutral!"

Roz swallows the crackers. "The construction process is not energy-neutral." She's surprised by this guy's enthusiasm; it's not like the tunnel will have a stop near Budapest so he can get on.

He waves his hands. "That will be quickly offset in the energy savings as people forgo other types of transportation."

"Energy use isn't the only measure of environmental damage," Roz adds, searching the cracker selection for something more exciting. They have some pâtés and vegetable spreads, but she doesn't dare touch any of them without her scanner.

"You heard the woman—their tests have found no indication of substantial environmental degradation."

Roz wished she didn't care enough to educate this guy, but out of both personal inclination and professional training, she can't let that half-truth slide. "The environmental engineer said 'so far.' The testing up to this point is extremely limited compared to the impact of the full tunnel."

It doesn't even scratch the surface of his gusto. "There are always risks, but the benefits will be incredible," he says cheerfully, taking a cracker himself and smearing it liberally with pâté. "Trade, cultural exchange, tourism, all at a previously unimaginable scale. The intangible values are important too."

Suspicious, Roz pulls up recent EuropeanUnion proposals at eye level and searches by *tunnel*. It's the first entry: a route from Budapest to Belgium. "Even if one is harmless, which seems unlikely," she hears herself say before she can self-censor, "what do you think will happen to Europe when its substratum looks like Swiss cheese?"

Before the guy can respond, Roz hears a voice at her shoulder.

"Excuse me, Ms. Kabwe?" Djukic has finally extricated herself from Veena's coils and is hovering. "Could I have a moment of your time?"

"Sure," Roz says, wondering what this is going to be.

The environmental engineer waits until they've stepped away from Mr. Mantletunnel and lowers her voice. "There's something I'd like to show you, if you wouldn't mind joining me at my workstation?" She nods toward the door.

Roz grabs her jacket and follows Djukic out of the insulated trailer. The project site is as yet untouched by any noticeable digging, but it's been cleared and the wind is sharp through the desolation. Roz's heated jacket doesn't close around her belly anymore. She pulls it as tight as she can and hurries to the environmental section's pop-up shelter. If this is an attempt to lobby her for Information support on some greenwashing scheme, it is not going well. Or maybe Djukic wants her help promoting an environmental agenda? More appealing but still impossible, given her position.

"What can I do for you?" she asks once they're sealed into the warmth of the shelter. It's a small space, divided into three workspaces and littered with models and instruments.

Djukic walks over to what must be her workspace and fires it up. "We found something on the scan of the route."

That polite deference disappeared fast. "Is it serious?" Roz asks. She's not sure why they're coming to her all hush-hush; there are procedures for this.

"It looks serious, but it's not environmental." The engineer pulls up a three-dimensional projection of the tunnel route and points at a line that crosses the trajectory several dozen meters closer to the surface.

"What is that? A fault?" On these trips Roz is constantly jumping at every vibration and loud noise, expecting the next mantle tunnel–caused earthquake.

Djukic shakes her head. "It's straight, so that means it's human-made."

"Some kind of infrastructure?" Roz asks, knowing it's a stupid question even as she does.

"Nothing goes remotely that deep. And if there was, we would have found out about it during the permits-and-research phase."

"So what—" Roz stops. A deep, clandestine, artificial tunnel. She says something she never expected to say in her career. "Can I ask you to keep this quiet? For now," she adds, hoping that mitigates her hypocrisy.

Djukic doesn't seem to care. "Why do you think I called you in here by yourself? I want no part of this."

"You're going to be a part of it," Roz says. "We're going to need your help to figure out what this is."

"It's another tunnel," Djukic says, standing up and jabbing her finger at it. "Obviously!"

Roz looks her over sharply. "What's your position title again?"

"Chief environmental engineer. But I'm an independent contractor; I don't work directly for 888 or for Ground Works"—the contractor building the tunnel.

"Okay," Roz rubs her forehead. "So, you're telling me they don't know about this yet."

"That's right," Djukic says, annoyed. "If they did, you'd be hearing this from them."

"A tunnel," Roz says.

"Or a pipe, maybe," Djukic points out. "A line of some kind."

"What does it link?"

"If we assume that it's built on the principles we're using, which prohibit curves sharper than five degrees, that gives us an approximate trajectory. But from this fragment, we can't tell how far it goes."

"So, even though it's shallower than this tunnel, that doesn't mean it's shorter?"

"Not necessarily."

"Okay, show me the trajectory. There can't be that many major cities along it."

There aren't.

"Oh, no," Roz says.

Djukic nods with the slow pleasure of watching someone else put the last ominous puzzle piece into place. "That was my conclusion as well."

"Tell no one about this!" Roz no longer feels conflicted. "Above all, no Information communications even hinting at it. You understand?"

"I'm not telling a damn individual," Djukic says. "Don't make me regret I told you!"

This woman has clearly seen the films: she knows what happens to scientists who, through innocent rigor in their research, discover something of geopolitical inconvenience. "Okay," Roz says, starting to pace the tiny confines of the pop-up tent, smaller than the hut she lived in when she first went to DarFur. Djukic pointedly moves out of the way of her belly. "Here's what we're going to do. I need you to manufacture some kind of environmental concern."

Djukic snorts. "No need to manufacture one. I've got plenty."

"Unexpected and serious?"

"Since no one's been listening to me, I guess it'll be unexpected."

Roz has been listening, or at least reading her reports. "Seismic activity or groundwater contamination?" She manages to make herself sound bored, as though she doesn't lie awake every night, waiting for tremors.

The engineer flashes a toothy grin. "All right, then, something new." She collapses the scan projection, much to Roz's relief, and pulls up another one. "Here's something I've been working on."

The topography in the projection collapses inward, slowly at first and then with gathering speed.

"City-size sinkholes," Djukic says, with grim satisfaction.

"There's a nightmare I did not need."

"Highly speculative," Djukic says, "but not impossible. 888 is going to be pissed if you stop construction for this, though, especially with PhilipMorris moving forward."

"The PhilipMorris tunnel isn't moving anytime soon," Roz says. She was in Cairo a week ago and didn't even get near the site, because all the action is in the courtrooms now.

"And we're not going to stop construction. We're going to do some additional testing."

"Ah, better. And this is perfect for that, because it will require extensive assessment of the mantle and crust *above* the planned tunnel."

"Okay," says Roz, going back to pacing. "This is what happened. You brought that problem up to me, and I scoffed at it, or at least told you we need more data. I go home tomorrow as planned, and I talk to my supervisors. In a couple of days, I send you a message asking you to come to Doha to present your data."

"*Doha?*"

"Don't worry; between us, we'll figure out a good reason why it's urgent you come in person. In the meantime, not a *word* about this to anyone, especially"—Roz groans—"Veena Rasmussen." The last thing they need is the embattled Supermajority getting wind of this. "Not a *breath* of it on Information, got it?"

"I got it before you did," Djukic says. "But . . . you want me to do the further testing, right?"

"Whatever testing you would do for sinkholes. Don't make a big deal out of it, but keep an eye out for any further details you can find about this—" Roz waves her hands, too angry to name the combined environmental and political disaster. "Tell us about them in person, in Doha."

The engineer still looks worried.

"I'll have a quiet word with the head of security," Roz says. "Tell them you've gotten threats from environmental groups and that they should keep a close eye on you."

"Make it *business interests.*" Djukic glares at Roz as she opens the door. "And make it good."

. . .

The first official polls do not look good for Policy1st, and Vera Kubugli has put out a brave (and irritable) vid statement hammering on the unfairness of the shortened term and minimizing the role of the Supermajority. *We are here to focus on the good of each and every Policy1st centenal, and we hope that people vote for us for the improvements we can make for them locally. While we are proud to carry out our responsibilities as Supermajority, we welcome the new structure that we hope will provide an equitable and balanced approach.*

Heritage, the previous Supermajority, has been shaken twice in the past five years by massive scandals. Their last head of state, Cynthia Halliday, is currently avoiding prosecution in Guantánamo's criminal haven after an attempted secession from micro-democracy (the more serious charges against her, that she attempted to poison Valérie Nougaz at a fancy-dress gala, have gone largely unreported, the evidence all but invisible on the feeds of the event). For reasons no one seems to understand, Heritage voters elected her abandoned husband, Tobias Agambire, as their new head of state. Not only is he tainted by questions of his criminal involvement, he lacks his estranged wife's charisma, and so far has been an indifferent candidate. Heritage has fallen to somewhere between fifth and ninth place in government rankings.

For the moment, 888 and PhilipMorris are the top contenders in the Supermajority race. Policy1st is holding on to third, with the other big corporates, 1China and, surprisingly, SavePlanet all clustered in the next eight. There is still time for a lot to happen before the election, though, and with the uncertainty about how the Secretariat will affect government power, opinion pieces on how to vote strategically are hugely popular in plazas and on compiler sites.

When she's done everything she can with the polls, comparing across sites and running analyses and breakdowns, Mishima checks up on some of the more unsavory elements that tend to gather during campaigning in attempts to disrupt governments, elections, or the entire system. She does it obliquely, and with a pang of guilt. This is no longer her job, but it was so integral to her experience during the last election that it is easy to fall back into. She has to worm around for a while on various shady plazas and sites, but most of these people want to be found, and she remembers the mindset they're looking for. Anarchy has been relatively quiet during the interim, seemingly focused on building their following. Mishima swears under her breath when she finds indications that they attempted to influence the shortening of the Supermajority term. They must have calculated that the change would tend toward destabilizing the system. She's not sure they're wrong.

Recently, there has been an uptick of both spending and plaza activity by Anarchy's predominant members—despite all evidence, they refuse to call themselves leaders. Before she can stop herself, Mishima sends a message to Nejime suggesting a closer watch on the group.

She approaches her next target with greater circumspection and greater guilt. It takes a correspondingly longer time for her to pick up the trail, but eventually Mishima finds a trace. What puzzles her is where she finds it.

Before she can follow up further, she gets a call. It's from Nejime, and Mishima winces: she was in the mindset of lonely late-night working, but it's still a reasonable hour in Doha.

"Since you're not so terribly busy with your job," Nejime

begins, and Mishima feels an immediate spike of adrenaline, like joy, "there's something I'd like you to look into."

"Go on."

"We've noticed some odd incidents." *Incidents* is not promising, but Mishima reserves judgment. "Campaigning that doesn't make sense."

"Doesn't make sense how?" Mishima asks. She blinks up the volume on the audio channel to Sayaka's monitor long enough to hear her slow breathing, then closes it again.

"We've found campaign advids for localized governments running in places we wouldn't expect those governments to contest." Nejime sends Mishima a file.

Mishima chooses the globed visual representation first, to get a sense for the scatter—sparse instances, but distant leaps—then switches to tabular. Only three cases: advids for a two-centenal Tamil government playing in what was once Wales; the single-centenal government of the Faroe Islands touted in pop-ups in Jakarta; and an Andean-centered government advertising in Dakar. Governments can campaign wherever they like, but all these governments are strictly focused on local issues and have never attempted to gain centenals outside their geographic heartland before.

"Could it be a mistake, a glitchy targeting blast or typos in the address?" Mishima asks, checking to see if the advids were produced by the same company and then setting up a quick program to eliminate transpositions or easy substitutions in the numerical references for the centenals in question. Both return negative.

"It's possible. But note that the centenals in which these incongruous advids are playing are closely contested. A few votes for an uncompetitive party could affect the outcome in any of them."

"And yet," Mishima says, as she rapidly calls up poll numbers, "they're not being contested by the same governments." The western British centenal is hovering between a local Welsh government and one of the new policy-based governments, also quite local in reach for the moment; the Jakarta centenal is in a tight three-way race between Philip-Morris, 888, and SavePlanet; and in Dakar, the corporate Liberty is battling it out with a West Africa–focused corporate called NousSommes and, somewhat further behind, 1China. "It's unclear who benefits."

"Other than those who oppose the whole system. I thought you'd like this," Nejime says.

"How did you find it?" Mishima asks, intrigued. This is exactly the sort of oblique, small-sample-size data that would be dismissed as a coincidence by pattern-recognition programs and missed by human analysts.

"An Information grunt in Jakarta saw one of the ads from FríuFøroyar and got curious. You're not our only employee with intuition and initiative, you know."

"I hope you promoted them," Mishima says.

"We're certainly keeping an eye on him. But I'd like someone a little more experienced to follow up. And since you seem to be interested in nihilist anti-election movements . . ."

"On it," Mishima answers.

"Just don't get too caught up in it. Don't forget about winning the election," Nejime says, and signs off before she hears Mishima's snort.

Maryam manages to forget entirely about the first official day of campaigning, until she steps out of her apartment building and smack into a haze of pop-ups smoothly extolling the possibilities of this or that government. She blinks them away in annoyance and some surprise: she wouldn't have thought this centenal would be so hotly contested. As she walks down the street, she counts ads from six different governments, each with a response from the current incumbent, 888, that is a masterpiece of visual storytelling demonstrating deep knowledge of the centenal through a panorama of anecdotes set in and around beloved neighborhood institutions. She has to grudgingly admire the artistry of it, but every ad she sees reminds her time is running out to figure out and foil the attack Nejime predicts: Election Day is in four weeks. She is relieved to reach the ad-blocked shelter of her workspace.

Maryam has been working in a café down the street from her apartment. It's a change for her, but searching for exploitable weaknesses in the bones of Information infrastructure in search of clues to a massive conspiracy from her desk in the office makes her nervous. The café, ironically called El Chismoso, has wraparound bank seating in individual, dual, and small-group configurations, all with scan blockers and conversation-muting sound architecture: a reaction, Maryam assumes, to the country's repressive history and its tradition of neighborly spying. She is not overly worried about the latter; what she's doing wouldn't make much sense to anyone without a firm grasp of Information's underlying technology. Still, she is careful: doing her work at eye level even within the cocoon of the solitary booth, examining micro-modules of the problem to keep the larger issue unidentifiable, muting her public Information so no one can infer what kind of infrastructure she's considering. Occasionally, she gives in and opens, in the corner of her vision, a small live feed from one spot or another along the Liberty/Independentistas border in Oaxaca. Even though they talk every night, she finds it soothing having that tiny link to Núria, and the intense concentration of her work is punctuated by momentary distractions whenever she sees a YourArmy uniform saunter through her view.

Maryam was initially trying to match the vulnerabilities Taskeen suggested with what data they have gleaned about the transfer station attacks, but she didn't find anything conclusive. She has moved on to looking for other evidence that a weakness has been exploited: scouring communications to and from null states; searching for underlying code modifications in the areas Taskeen pointed out. It's painstaking, and even if she's right about the modalities it's unlikely that she'll hit upon the exact places they are using them. Also, irrational as it is, she can't avoid a faint unease, as though those eerie white masks are searching for her as well. She has been taking increasingly long breaks to work on the normal election-related maintenance instead.

Frustrated, she stands and stretches. The café has gotten crowded, so she puts in a deposit to hold her booth for fifteen minutes and edges her way along the aisles to the door. After the muted environment of the café, the street is loud with pregoneros and passers-by and bright with sunshine and campaign ads. She lets her eyes drift along the pedestrians and up the façades, stretching her arms and shoulders. An ice cream vendor passes on a bicycle, her projected menu shimmering above the cooler, and three men walk by laughing.

"¿Señora? ¿Señora? ¿Ey, señora?"

Maryam doesn't realize at first that the low urgent voice is accosting her. This is partly because she's usually addressed as *señorita*, and so she's already a little annoyed when she turns her head. The speaker is young, maybe that's why: slight-built, androgynous, baggy light blue guayabera, public Information muted, which is much more common in Cuba than in Doha.

"Señora, you look like you're not from around here. Maybe this can help?" They project up an image of the old cathedral at night framed by bright text about hotels and restaurants, and cut it off again, quick as the flash of a trench coat opening.

"I live here," Maryam says, offended again.

The person gives her a long look over: her loose head scarf, her black pseudo-silks, her perforated leather slippers. "Sí, claro, señora," they say, and walk on.

Maryam remembers that she's been speaking Spanish, her clunky accent obvious, and resists the temptation to switch to Arabic. Like that would make her seem more like a local. Belatedly, something clicks in Maryam's memory; she pulls up nearby feeds, hoping she can find an image of that photo. Did that text bubble really read *Everything Information doesn't tell you*?

"Wait!" she yells, starting after the vendor as she continues to blink through the feeds. "Wait, I'll take one."

The vendor glances back over their shoulder, and Maryam tries an encouraging smile. *Look lost*, she tells herself. "I'll take one. Please?"

This time, the vendor's gaze is warier, probing Maryam's eyes instead of her fashion choices. "Paper only for you, señora," the vendor says, pulling a crumbly folio from their shirt pocket. "Six bits."

"I'll take three," Maryam says, gesturing urgently with her payment toggle.

The vendor takes off.

"Wait!" Maryam yells again, senselessly, and then runs after them. The vendor is quick and lithe, dodging through a gap between two of the chatting men and skidding around the crowd of schoolchildren clustered around the ice cream vendor. Maryam loses sight of them around a corner. She speeds up, wishing she was wearing better shoes for running, which is especially embarrassing since the vendor is wearing the local favorite, self-adhesive shower sandals, hardly the most ergodynamic footwear.

Turning the corner at least puts her in the shade, and she catches a glimpse of the scurrying figure ahead. Maryam pounds after them. An old woman sitting on a stoop, knees wide apart under her long skirt, cackles something at her that even her translator doesn't catch. She hears snatches of three piropos of varying levels of rudeness and admiration, but she keeps running until she sees the vendor worm their way into the rows of vendor carts clogging the entrance to the Parque Coppelia and disappear in the lunch-hour crowds.

Slowing to a jog, Maryam diverts toward the Malecón and then turns back south, aiming for the other side of the park. She opens a bunch of feeds along Calle 25, on the assumption that the vendor was heading east rather than trying to lose themselves in the crowd and double back: crossing Calle 25 would take them to the university and, beyond that, away from the open-grid pattern of the Vedado into the tighter, named streets of first Chinatown and then La Habana Vieja. Flipping through six sets of three feeds each while avoiding pedestrians turns out to be impossible, so she posts up in a doorway on the angle of Calle 25 and sweeps both directions while more slowly reviewing the feeds from the last three minutes.

"¡Ey! ¿Qué haces allí?" A shutter flaps open, slamming

against the wall, and a wiry old woman leans out the window and waves Maryam out of her doorway, rapid-fire invective following her as she walks up the street while still flipping through feeds. The vendor could be anywhere by now. She should go back to the office and conduct the search in a more professional manner, but instead she follows a hunch toward the university. If she can't find the vendor, maybe she can find some evidence of their product.

CHAPTER 5

Maryam finally gets back to the office, hot, tired, and slightly annoyed at losing her deposit on the table at El Chismoso, but in possession of four wrinkled pages she picked up from a table outside the bursar's office at the university. The first page of the pamphlet announces itself as an atlas of local microculture. She's not positive yet whether it's of the same provenance as the clandestine guide she was offered—the cover image is different, and there is no direct comparison to Information—but her instinct, or pattern recognition, tells her they're related. She leaves it at her workstation and goes to find Batún, the Habana Hub Director.

"Have you heard anything about non-Information tourist guides?" Maryam asks him, once he's gotten off the top-level meeting about campaign monitoring.

"About . . . what?" Batún is clearly still stuck in the discussion about borderline fact misrepresentation and enforcement of polling standards.

Maryam has been in La Habana long enough to know him, and so she waits while he rubs his large hands over his lined forehead and follows him when he trundles down the hall to the cafeterón.

"¿Quieres uno?"

Maryam starts to shake her head and then changes her mind and accepts, and Batún puts in the order for a colada.

He takes the coffee and the stack of miniature cups and they head back to his office, where he pours. He takes a sip, rubs his hands over his forehead again, takes another sip.

"Now," he says. "What are you asking me about?"

"Anything, any rumors or hints or anything at all about someone distributing local data that's either not available on Information or available through a different source. Maybe paid, maybe not?"

Batún leans back in his chair to think it over. "Nothing comes to mind," he says at last. "You said *tourist guide* before?"

"That's how it was presented to me, at least." Maryam tells him the story of the vendor. When she gets to the part about the text that may have said *Everything Information doesn't tell you* he leans forward.

"But you're not sure that's what it said?"

"It was something to do with Information; I'm not sure of the exact phrasing."

"No feeds?"

"I've been checking, but so far I haven't found an angle that would show that projection. It looks like they put it up two-dimensionally, and they might have known where the feeds were."

Maryam hadn't planned to go into the full, embarrassing story of the chase, but he's interested enough that she finds herself telling it anyway, and then going back to her workstation to get the pamphlet. As she hands it to him, a corner of the front page crumbles off.

"Cheap material?" Batún asks, handling it carefully.

"I suspect it's designed to self-destruct." Maryam remembers the vendor's face when they refused to give her a digital copy. "A safety mechanism that allows them to disseminate widely without committing to unvetted buyers." She hesitates. "I had another encounter that may have been with these people, but the modus operandi was so different that I'm not sure it's connected." She tells him about the odd incident in Dhaka.

"So, you have a copy of that one?"

"No, I turned it down."

"Why?" Batún asks, carefully flipping through the pamphlet on his desk. "It was free, right?"

"It was creepy," Maryam says, annoyed. "Clearly you've never been a woman traveling alone."

Batún laughs his deep laugh and then reins it in with a grimace when Maryam doesn't smile. "Fair point," he says. "Sorry. You want to follow up on this?"

"I—I don't really know what to make of it." Maryam had been hoping to hand it off. "It's not exactly my area."

"Well, it might be," Batún says thoughtfully, handing the pamphlet back to her. "I'll admit I never thought of tour guides as the way they'd take us down, but if the Exformation crew are starting a separate datastream outside of Information, I would say it's very much your area. You better scan that, first thing," he adds, as another bit of intel crumbles into dust against her fingertips.

Ken is happy that Free2B is doing so well, particularly in its incumbency centenals. It is, as he's said at least a dozen times this week, the best indicator of governmental success. However, he has to admit that it makes this campaign cycle lack a certain urgency that he remembers fondly from the last one. Five years ago he felt like the future depended on Policy1st winning as many centenals as possible, and he and others scoured the globe to find places where their efforts could make a difference.

Now he has to argue for days with the Free2B leadership over any expansion to their campaign. If it were up to him, they'd be competing in every centenal that adjoins one of their incumbencies, and looking for other opportunities as well. They have a great platform of policies and principles, very appealing to a lot of people: not too strict, not too lax, a laid-back aesthetic with a social compact at its heart. (Or at least that's what the campaign copywriters have put together.) But that laid-back aesthetic also translates into a lack of ambition, at least on the part of the government leadership, and so far they've refused to contest more than four additional centenals, two of them fairly safe bets. "Bigger isn't always better, you know," the head of state told Ken gently on the last projected conference. "Expanding too quickly could hurt our model. Maybe when we have better immigration numbers, or a little more name recognition."

Ken is trying to sharpen his ingenuity and political acuity on the nine centenals they are campaigning in, but it's hard to get excited about his job, and as much as he appreciates being home for Sayaka, it's weird to leave the office at 6 P.M. during an election. He has just left the Free2B campaign office in Saigon to wend his way home when he gets a call. He jumps when he sees the ID: Vera Kubugli, the remaining Mighty V and head of state for Policy1st.

"Ken!" she says as soon as he picks up. "Good to speak with you again. It's been so long."

"Hi!" Ken says, uncertain how to address her. He met

Vera a few times when he was working for Policy1st, but only briefly. He wouldn't have thought she knew his name. "What can I do for you?"

"Ken," Vera says, her chumminess morphing into gravity. "As you know, this election is of vital importance to our government, and to the world. We are being monstrously outspent by corporate governments, and we need all hands on deck." A pause for that to sink in. "I know what great work you did for us during the last election, and I wanted to ask if you'd consider coming back to give us a hand."

"Oh." Ken suddenly feels like jelly. "I would lo—I'd be honored to help, but" (as Vera must know) "I have a job with Free2B. I've been working with them for years now, and I'd hate to leave them this close to the election."

"Of course," Vera purrs. "Commendable, indeed. But you have to consider where your efforts will have the greatest impact. Eking out another centenal for Free2B will affect at most 100,000 people. If Policy1st loses the Supermajority—in this election, after half our term was stolen—that will be a disaster for millions."

A disaster might be overstating it, but Ken *is* still mad about the five-year thing. He reminds himself that he's campaign director for Free2B. "What exactly is it that you think I could help you with?"

Vera knows what he's asking. "We were thinking Executive Strategy Developer," she says. "Leading our centenal mapping and prioritizing, working closely with the communications people in charge of messaging, finding innovative ways to present ourselves to skeptical voters in centenals we haven't previously contested."

Ken is breathing fast. She knows exactly what he wants, what buzzwords to drop and buttons to push. He tells himself that it's probably too good to be true. "Can I get back to you?"

Mishima asks her assistant, Amran, to do some preliminary searches on the unexplained ads. It's not so much a necessary delegation as a mentoring exercise. Well, not so much a mentoring exercise as an experiment. She was given budget for an assistant three months ago, and picked Amran over several people with more relevant experience because Roz had vouched for her, but also because she had heard that Amran had been diagnosed with a level-four narrative disorder. As part of her lifelong informal and self-directed research project on her condition, Mishima finds it useful to observe the narrative expectations of someone with an entirely different cultural and family background, and this assignment is the perfect test case.

Amran starts by giving her a decent, if uninspired, rundown of the facts that Mishima already knows, with a few additional instances she's managed to dig up: a Burmese nationalist centenal apparently advertising in Luanda, and a small policy-oriented government with no current centenals promoting itself on the northern bank of the Rio Grande. "It's not certain yet whether that last one fits the pattern," Amran clarifies. "Since they don't hold any centenals and don't have a specific local or nationalist focus. But they are based in and primarily campaigning in and around Dushanbe. Every indicator—demographic, ideologic, or other—says that centenal is unlikely to be a strong target for them."

"What about the money?"

"The advertising seems to have been paid for out of the campaign funds allocated to those governments. I say 'seems to' because I've spoken to representatives from all of the governments, and none of them will admit to authorizing the ads; they haven't found any missing funds, either. It looks like the perpetrators found a way to announce for an additional centenal and then used the additional money for the ads."

"It's amazing that rule doesn't get abused more often," Mishima mutters. Governments receive campaign funding for each centenal they officially contest, with the money, other than an overhead percentage, constrained to be used in that centenal alone.

"People don't like to lose," Amran notes, and it's true: governments care about their win-to-contested ratio.

"And they didn't notice they're contesting more centenals than they planned to?"

"These governments are campaigning only in a few places, most of which they are almost certain of winning. It's not as hard to keep track of three centenals as a global election; they probably don't spend too much time thinking about it."

Mishima forgets that not everyone is as obsessed with the election as she is. "The account signature was hacked." That should narrow the suspect list.

"Or . . ." Amran hesitates, continues when Mishima nods at her through the projection. "Possibly someone within each government authorized the ads."

"Possible but unlikely, unless there's a single person working for all of these tiny far-flung governments. Or a consulting firm?" Mishima has to repress a shudder: ever since being ambushed by consultant assassins with incredible hacking skills, she's found consulting firms highly sinister.

"I've checked, and there's no overlap in their consulting profile either," Amran says.

"So hacking seems more likely. Anything else? Motive?"

"I haven't found any pattern in terms of who benefits," Amran says. "It feels more like pointless chaos."

"You investigated the home centenals of these small governments too, right? If someone is stealing their campaign funds . . ."

"None of them is in a particularly close race." Amran hesitates again.

In the three months since she hired her, Mishima has tried to get used to Amran's insecurity. It's not something she's ever had a problem with, and yet she can imagine, if circumstances had been slightly different, if she had ever confused the uncertainty of distinguishing narrative from real with uncertainty about her own intelligence and ability . . . For the first time in her life she is, while not exactly grateful, aware of the advantages of an early diagnosis. "Was there something else?" she asks, hoping she sounds encouraging.

"Looking at the ads longitudinally across the five cases," Amran says, "they are escalating."

Mishima frowns.

"It's a small sample size," Amran says hurriedly, "so it's hard to be sure." She flicks an infographic into their shared projection: the extrapolated line is shallow, but it is indeed trending upward. "It's odd because . . ." Another hesitation. "The other data seems to suggest general disruption, but escalation points away from that."

Mishima nods, pleased to hear her own intuition echoed. "It could be a small planned increase after an initial trial."

"Or maybe a viral pattern?" Amran suggests. "Something self-replicating?"

"Hard to do with this kind of activity," Mishima points out. "The ads have to be tailor-made for each jurisdiction. Keep an eye on this, okay? I'm going to snoop among likely suspects." She knows just where to start.

Maryam was not convinced when Batún suggested that the tourist guides might be related to the ex-Information group she's been stalking. Part of it is that she wants nothing to do with tourism, or obnoxious vendors who pick her out of a crowd to accost, or strange outdated technologies. Part of it is that it seems too small and ridiculous: she is looking for people who are trying to take over the world, not touts.

Then she scans the pamphlet. As the sensors touch the surface, it disintegrates. Maryam jumps away. This outdated technology has some very up-to-date technology built into it. It creeps her out even more now, but she's also galvanized: this may turn out to be important, and it's a neat challenge to boot. Within minutes, she's set up a program to comb every feed she passed through this afternoon to get pictures of the pamphlet and search for the vendor. While it runs, she starts designing a more complicated search for references to obscure travel guides, but she's distracted by a news alert: another transfer-station attack, this one outside Luanda. Maryam gets swept in, obsessively following along with the commentary on the Information intranet. Coverage outside of Information is muted, which reminds Maryam of Taskeen's uncomfortable point about public but invisible data. She flips through the feeds in the surrounding area, dreading the occasional oblique shots of those featureless masks but unable to resist dwelling on them when they appear.

She emerges an hour and a half later with no clues but one new idea.

"A data transfer station?" Batún asks, when she finds him in the canteen and corrals him back to his office.

"I want to take a look at one and see if I can figure out what these people are after when they attack them. They can't just want to inconvenience us."

"There are a couple of small transfer hubs in the city, but they're mostly automated," he says thoughtfully. "Your best bet is probably the one on Isla de Pinos, at the Presidio Modelo."

Maryam blinks up the details and has to repress a shudder: it's not a cute etymology lost in the dust of time. The data transfer station is housed in the remains of a refitted panopticon prison from the late twentieth century.

"I know some people there," Batún says. "If you're sure this is a good idea?"

"It's the only idea I have right now, and we're running out of time."

CHAPTER 6

Getting to Isla de Pinos used to mean taking a ferry from Puerto de Batabanó, but Maryam sees no reason to be circumspect about this trip, and Batún offers her one of the office crows. She flies almost directly south from La Habana, follows a straight road inland from the coast that leads her past a residential zone and a baseball field and straight to the former prison.

Isla de Pinos has a population just short of the normal 100,000 benchmark but, like many other islands, it was granted its own centenal anyway. Information has carved out a small section around the data transfer facility under their own jurisdiction. As usual, Information has gone out of its way to concretize their principles in the landscape, as an optional projection when she enters the site shows in detail, contrasting historical footage side by side with what she sees in front of her. They've reforested the once-stripped grounds, and the cylindrical buildings, which old vids show as tattered hulks with holes in the roofs, have been sheathed in heat-reflectors and solar cells, and painted or projected with swirls of brilliant color.

"We're trying to make something good out of the site," explains Veronica de la Campana, the site supervisor, who welcomes Maryam at the gate, thanks to Batún's introduction. "Of course, the data transfer facility is useful—and pleasantly ironic for a former panopticon—but we also wanted to build a beautiful, multifunctional space for the community, something inspirational, that they would look to for hope and maybe use as a park, for picnics, games . . ." The sentence ends in expansive gestures. De la Campana speaks at Cuban velocity and with a slight rural accent, and Maryam turns on her translator set to subtitles in case she misses something.

"Has it worked?" Maryam asks.

De la Campana shakes her head slightly. "Not yet, not so much. They remember the bad times. It will take more work, more outreach. Maybe a tourism program, the local businesses would appreciate that, but it's so hard to do properly." She nods at three people inside a small hut that Maryam's Information tells her is a recent addition.

"New security protocols?" she asks.

"For what it's worth," de la Campana says. "It's obviously much easier to get in here now than when it was a prison."

They are approaching two cylindrical buildings, with another, larger one visible between them. "Over there is our on-site power generation," de la Campana says, pointing to the rightmost building, which is done in brilliant sunburst colors. "But there's not much to see. Let's start here." She guides Maryam toward the building on the left, adorned in a resplendent interpretation of *Starry Night Over the Rhône*.

The interior is less colorful and looks nothing like the photos of the former prison. The panopticon design mandated a central plinth from which the guards could see into every cell lining the circumference. They've kept the pillar, which in a nice inversion of design has been turned into an automat food dispenser, the little doors mimicking the grid of cells that once girded the walls around them, but the rest of the building is entirely different, a spiral of office floors punctuated by stairs at different points on different levels. From where she is, Maryam can't see into any individual offices—even on the ground floor, all the doors are turned away from her—but by peering up the wavering column of stairwell openings, she can see all the way up to the roof, giving her a sense for the overall layout of the building.

"Wow."

"Isn't it something?" De la Campana leans in slightly. "Designed by Afolabi. Such an amazing dialog with the original structure." She gives Maryam another few moments to gaze around and recover, then leads her to the first staircase, a graceful curve of broad, shallow stairs with no handrail. "Have you ever been in a data transfer station before?"

"Only hubs," Maryam says, slightly embarrassed. Until now, she had assumed that they were basically the same thing, minus the senior leadership and administrative functions hubs provide. "Can you tell me how they're different?"

"There is some overlap, of course," de la Campana says, comfortingly unsurprised by the question. "For example, we have a bloc of translators in the southwest cylinder that manages overflow from La Habana and Mérida Hubs. As the system has grown, hubs and data transfer sites have both multiplied, and grown, and grown more similar, as we have needed more and more of the functions that are provided by both."

"Like translation."

"And analysis, sorting, distribution management." The first floor is done in cool aquamarines and blues. As the corridor they are following spirals close to the outer wall, Maryam sees that the casing is translucent, and the light glows through it in deep blues, with startling gold around the stars and reflected lights. "Hubs tend to have more analysts. Data stations, on the other hand, include storage." She gestures through the slightly rippled transparent wall toward where the largest of the cylindrical buildings looms. "And, obviously, we have a strong focus on distribution management. Initially, these were minimally staffed sites composed mainly of storage and transfer hardware."

"Do you still have that old infrastructure?" Maryam asks.

De la Campana smiles with a touch of smugness and opens the door to her right to reveal a closet clogged with cable. "We do."

Maryam wonders if the attackers could be planning some kind of hardware hack, and gazes at the cables in hope of inspiration, but she doesn't know enough about anachronistic electrical engineering. They continue the tour, going up to the next floor.

"So what do you think they're after, attacking these sites?" Maryam asks as they walk past a series of collaboration rooms.

"I don't know," de la Campana says. "They seem like stunts to me." (The word she uses is *comemierdería,* which Maryam's auto-interpreter never knows what to do with, but Maryam has heard it often enough since moving to La Habana to get the gist.) "This type of attack could take us offline for a few days"—the station in Mandalay was down for a week, Maryam remembers—"which is annoying for us, but in the grander scheme it doesn't matter. Data gets rerouted around an inoperative station. Maybe a few of the nearby stations are overloaded for a little while, but nobody outside of our staff would even notice."

"How many would they have to knock out at the same time to make a difference?" Maryam asks.

"I don't know; dozens? Hundreds? Surely someone has done the calculations."

Trying to envision it from an attacker's perspective, Maryam pulls up the feed for the entrance road. The camera angle includes the guardroom and much of the road; she can see a small group that has just passed the guards moving toward them. It wouldn't be hard to go around the feed, she thinks; the trees would make it difficult with a vehicle, but on foot—

One of the figures on the road looks up at the camera, and the face is bone-white and featureless.

Primordial horror grips her: an icy clench of wrongness passing over her body in a wave. As reason slowly clunks back online, Maryam registers a more specific terror. "They're here," she whispers.

"¿Perdón?" De la Campana turns to her. Maryam opens her mouth to try to force words out, and the image disappears as Information blinks off. There's a muffled *boom*.

"The attackers," Maryam manages, though her tongue doesn't want to move. "They're here."

De la Campana's face goes ashen. One hand reaches out for the wall, and she flutters the fingers of her other.

"Information is out," Maryam gasps, but de la Campana has already figured that out, and is lurching toward a nearby office.

"¡Directora!" The young man inside steps away from the workstation he was frowning at in frustration. "I'm sorry, Information doesn't seem to be working . . ."

Ignoring him, de la Campana finds a button on the wall and jams at it with her palm. "¿Seguridad? ¿Seguridad?"

Standing in the doorway, Maryam begins to pull out of her daze. "They don't hurt anyone," she says, and then she manages to say it a little louder. "They leave everyone unharmed." The analyst at the workstation looks over at her, and she sees his face change as he interprets her words and realizes what they must mean. Fear spurts over his face, transmitted like a virus. "They don't hurt anyone!" Maryam snaps at him, and he nods, pulling back from panic.

There's another *boom,* this one closer and louder. The door, Maryam thinks. De la Campana's emergency button must have sealed it.

De la Campana turns to Maryam. "Hide!" she says, urgently. "¡Escóndete!"

"They don't hurt anyone," Maryam repeats. An unfrozen part of her mind twitches in annoyance at the lack of a new response.

"Maybe not, but anyone could have known of your visit here, and I'm not taking any chances." With surprising strength, the small woman takes Maryam's bicep and speedwalks her back down the hall.

"Not the cable room," Maryam quails, her brain jerking back into action. "That might be what they're after!"

"Claro que no." De la Campana opens a different door and stumbles to her knees, hands scrabbling on the wall. There's another explosion from below and a sudden uptick in the background noise in the building. "Here." De la Campana stands and pushes Maryam through the doorway. "You can stay here. If you hear them coming, there's a panel to let you behind the wall there. It's not comfortable, but it's hard to find."

"Temperature scans!"

"There's a climatization unit in there that will hide your heat."

"But you—"

"Everyone knows who I am and that I'm here. It will seem odd if I am missing. But you—even if they know you came, you could have gone for a walk in the woods." De la Campana stands, and tugs her tailored T-shirt down at the hips. "Besides. They don't hurt anyone." She flashes Maryam a grimace that was probably meant as a smile and then turns and walks away, only a little unsteady. "¡Cierra la puta puerta, coño!" she adds over her shoulder, and Maryam scrambles into the closet.

A s Roz expected, when Nejime sees that projection of the scan, she wants to bring in the environmental engineer immediately. Roz talks her down to a day and a half, and sends the official request to Djukic. She shows up thirty-six hours later. "It's good you gave me a little time," she tells Roz as she leads her through the corridors of Doha Hub to Nejime's office. "I was able to run preliminary scans—not enough, mind you, to be sure we won't be facing large-scale sinkholes, but I have better projections of the other tunnel."

She opens them as soon as Nejime's door closes behind them. The line Roz saw in Berlin has grown slightly longer before petering into the unscanned and unknown, and the projection swings in for a close-up showing an ovoid curve cross-section.

"How big is this?" Nejime asks, tracing the line of the mysterious tunnel.

"Nowhere near as big as the tunnel 888 is trying to build," Djukic answers. "We can't be completely sure, because so far we can only see it from the bottom, but the bottom half is quite narrow. It could be high and narrow, but not too disproportionately."

"How narrow?"

Djukic holds out her hands about the width of a door-frame.

"So, it could conceivably be used to transport people?"

"Yes, but not many at a time. Nothing like the superhigh-ways 888 and PhilipMorris have planned."

"They couldn't keep something that big a secret," Nejime muses, turning back to the projection.

"They wouldn't have wanted that, anyway," Roz puts in. "Russia and Switzerland may trade and share intel occasionally, but they're not on the best of terms. They wouldn't open a channel that would allow one of them to invade the other."

"Could it be for sharing intel?" Nejime asks, turning on Djukic. "Some kind of analog system, a cable perhaps?"

"Sure," Djukic shrugs. "Why not?"

"No way to know without opening it up?"

"How would there be?"

"Scans, listening devices, echolocation? You're the engineer."

"*Environmental* engineer." Djukic frowns. "I am not an intel techie." She doesn't need to glance around the office to make her point: *This is the mothership of intel techies; why are they asking her?* "As far as I am aware, there is no way to find out what's inside without opening it."

Nejime turns her full attention to Roz. "Let's get in there, anywhere along the line, without them knowing about it." She pauses, blinking. "A data transfer center in the Caribbean just went offline. Presumably another attack."

Roz takes her cue. "We'll work on this."

"Find a way in," Nejime says, her attention already elsewhere. "There's too much we don't know right now."

· · ·

Maryam spends the first nine minutes after de la Campana leaves her in the dark, crouched, listening as hard as she can. She doesn't hear much. There are three more explosions, all of them farther away—probably at the other buildings. A faint pattern of voices, occasionally rising, from the ground floor. Doors slamming as people on this floor leave their offices and either try to run to the roof or make their way downstairs. A few yells, and the sound of footsteps pounding quickly down the hall. Maryam cowers and reaches for the wall panel, but the pounding rushes by the closet door, and there are no shots, and no one screams. At some point, she becomes aware that she's whispering, *They don't hurt anyone,* over and over to herself, and she stops.

How long has she been crouched in here? She blinks up the time: 11:06. What time did they attack? None of the attacks have lasted longer than . . . what was it? Twenty minutes? Twenty-five minutes? Her fingers twitch, but Information isn't there to answer. No longer than half an hour. That's all she has to do, sit out half an hour. And how long has it been now? Maybe fifteen minutes? Surely not twenty already. Maryam shifts, rolls her shoulders. Or maybe this is the attack they've been planning for. Maybe they aren't waiting for Election Day. Maybe data stations are going down all over the world. Maryam fights the cold tremor of panic. She reaches automatically for her de-stress set—a calibrated puzzle game with a cycle of Nusrat Fateh Ali Khan qawwali at background volume—but that's not there either. She makes a mental note to pull a copy onto her handheld when she gets back on Information, and somehow that reminds her that her handheld tracks motion. She checks: it has been nine minutes since her position changed.

Maryam lets out a long breath and feels it tremble. It feels like it's been much longer than nine minutes. But at least now she knows. She can hold out twenty more minutes, and if it lasts longer than that, then she'll know the pattern has changed.

She wonders what's going on below her. In the previous attacks, the brigands tied up the staff and left them in meeting rooms or lobbies before disappearing into the buildings, away from any feeds. Have they already rounded up the staff? She can't hear anything, or at least nothing identifiable: maybe some whispers of ambient noise that could be faraway voices or the normal functioning of the building. Maryam eases her aching legs into a sitting position. Around a thousand people work in this complex, but without Information, she's not sure how many are in this building. Or maybe what they're after isn't in this building at all: Maryam remembers the looming shape of the storage building, the sunburst colors on the energy building.

At that moment, the dim light that filtered around the door edges from the hallway extinguishes, and the background hum of the building cuts off, replaced briefly by a rush of voices and cries from below. A moment later, the hum starts up again, louder, along with a fainter, blue-tinged light: backup power.

Maryam wonders if de la Campana is all right, if she's tied up, or if she stood up to them foolishly or heroically and has been hurt or . . . She remembers the director saying, *Anyone could have known of your visit here,* and all the calm she had regained dissolves in a cold flood of nausea. Could it really be chance that they attacked this site, out of the 7,924 data transfer stations worldwide, less than an hour after Maryam arrived? She huddles down into herself on the floor, trying not to make a sound, imagining over and over what will happen when the door is ripped open and she is staring once again into that terrifying mask.

This panic is deeper, but Maryam surfaces faster. 11:10. Twenty-five minutes to go. Information Security is on the alert for anomalies out of data transfer stations; they'll know this one is offline almost immediately. If the attackers aren't close already—Maryam presses her senses against the quiet of the building and hears nothing—it's unlikely they'll find her before help arrives.

What could they get done in such a short time? Curiosity (or boredom) gets the better of fear, and Maryam tests her access to the internal systems. The processors are active and running a diagnostic, although she can see a steep drop in processing activity ninety-two seconds ago when the power went off. They must have tied processor and memory backup into the emergency power, because it doesn't look like there was much of an interruption . . .

Maryam gasps, and immediately covers her mouth with her hand as if she could smother the sound after it escaped her. This isn't an auto-diagnostic. The attackers must have launched it.

She doesn't remember that from any of the reports on previous attacks.

She should disconnect immediately, before they notice someone else in the system. But if they're running a diagnostic, that confirms the attacks are trial runs. They're probing the system for weaknesses.

Or maybe a specific weakness.

Maryam squeezes her eyes shut for a second. The attackers aren't outside the closet door. They aren't about to leap out of the darkness and grab her. Logging into the system won't change that.

She plunges in.

Her first step is to call up the initial diagnostic command, hoping that the parameters will offer hints to what they're looking for. But the command is already gone, and so, when she looks, are the beginnings of the output: they're erasing as they go. They must be dumping data directly into portable memory and wiping; that's why this wasn't in the reports.

A new routine starts up. She sees it running through every connection point, and it jangles through her nerves like a slap, like the moment she saw that mask looking into the feed: they're coming for her.

They're trying to triangulate her location, and it's not even going to be hard, because in her rush to get on before she could get too scared, she didn't try to mask her access point. Muttering imprecations through lips numb with fear, Maryam cuts her connection. She huddles for a moment, cursing helplessly—she doesn't even know if they found her before she cut off—and then builds a quick-and-dirty bounce program to fold into the connection command. It won't hold long, but she throws a ridiculous coefficient on it, so maybe, maybe, it will hide her until InfoSec arrives.

It almost doesn't matter. Exposing herself is better than cowering in the dark with no intel beyond the uncertain interpretations of her eardrums.

Maryam hits the connection, wastes a few milliseconds confirming that the bounce subroutine is working. Her fingers are trembling so hard, she has trouble with her controls and almost goes to verbal, but decides that would take too long. Deep breath. She orders a copy of the outputting diagnostic results into her handheld memory. And then, a more daring thought—she wonders if she can divert the attackers' output so that they don't get what they need. It serves them right, she thinks, pawing through the code they haven't bothered to protect. While they're diverting Information's intel, she can yank theirs. Along the bottom of her vision she can see their search routine barreling through the bounces she set up. Maybe if she—and there it is! She changes the address for the output dump and, for a few seconds before they figure out how to reroute it, their data is hers.

What chance that those few seconds will make a difference?

At least she doesn't have to do anything until they reroute the diagnostic or find her hiding place. Maryam watches the search across the bottom of her vision, the diagnostic output down the right sidebar, and dabs at her cheek with the back of her hand. She is damp with sweat: the climatization and air circulation functions aren't supported on emergency power. The search program is creeping closer, but there are still two false nodes left and she's poised ready to re-scramble when the entire system cuts off.

Maryam blinks in the darkness, afterimages of her interfaces glowing faintly in her vision. They killed it. Her stomach lurches again into the familiar crease of terror: did they locate her? They could have been running a hidden program while she was distracted by the obvious one. She pushes her palms against her eyes and listens. But instead of pounding or yells she hears a growing buzz. Information blinks back on: a portable aerial broadcast, located twenty meters up and ten meters to the northwest of her position. There is a banner across the top of her vision, its message reiterated into her earplugs: *This is a message from Information Security. You are now connected. We are securing this site. Remain in your current location and await further instructions.*

Maryam slumps back against the closet wall. She will wait, happily. She has no desire to move.

CHAPTER 7

It's a clear night after a streak of heavy rain, and Mishima and Ken are out on the balcony, enjoying the warm air and a bottle of sake.

"You're ahead!" Ken is looking at Mishima's polling so she doesn't have to.

"And that's good, right?"

"Three points," Ken says, ignoring her. "Which is a point more than the margin of error."

"So, basically tied." Mishima hadn't been able to decide what she expected the polls to look like, but regardless of their configuration her reaction feels inevitable: jaded, sardonic, pessimistic.

Fortunately, this is Ken: he knows it's a front. "There's a decisive age split, but that was to be expected. Hmm."

"Hmm?" *See? She does care.*

"Nougaz has the edge on 'strong, decision-maker.'"

"Well, she is a strong decision-maker," Mishima says. She means it: she's seen the downside of that strong decision-making a few too many times. Her tone comes out strange: admiration crossed with the irony-sarcasm-sardonic axis. She was hoping for flat and unbothered.

Ken is trying to figure out how anyone could be a stronger decision-maker than Mishima, but he supposes most poll respondents have never been stabbed in the leg by her. "It's not like that's the primary quality for an Information representative on the Secretariat," he tells Mishima instead. "What people should want for that role is someone low-key and restrained. Rational. Geeky."

"Mm." Mishima doesn't feel like parading her cynicism again, but she has no faith that people will vote for the kind of person they should want, if *should* even means anything in elections. In her experience personality outweighs logic, self-interest, and the requirements of the position every time.

Ken shifts Sayaka's weight on his chest and turns his focus to government-level polling data, projecting it up so they can read it together.

"Free2B is looking solid," Mishima comments.

"In all five centenals," Ken grumps.

"And you've got a good shot here and here." She traces the map facet with her forefinger.

"Hmm," Ken says, and brings up the data for Policy1st.

Mishima tries to look on the bright side. "They've improved over the last three days."

Ken shakes his head but says nothing. Mishima doesn't push it: it's going to be hard for Policy1st to close this kind of gap. True, nobody expected them to win the last election, but they were swept in by a perfect storm of two separate corruption scandals. It seems unlikely to happen again.

"What would you do differently if you were working for them?" Mishima asks, a gentler way of saying *Do you really think you would single-handedly save the world this time?*

Ken sighs and stretches, careful not to disturb the sleeping toddler. "I know, you're right. But I still feel bad for not helping when . . ."

"It's a shitty move, this five-year shift," Mishima says. "But Policy1st losing won't be the end of the world."

"No, not the end of the world, but I think . . . not a good

outcome. Not just because of what Policy1st does or doesn't do when in power, but because it unfairly misrepresents the potential of policy-based governments in general." Ken knows it's the Policy1st line, but he agrees with it.

"Unfairly," Mishima repeats, trying to keep her voice as gentle as it was before.

Ken shrugs, annoyed, and Sayaka murmurs and turns her head without waking. He rubs her back as he answers. "It's unfair because five years isn't enough time to get a grip on governing, not enough time to work their way out of the complications Heritage left for them."

"Politics isn't fair."

"No, but we should want our systems to be. As fair as we can make them, anyway."

Mishima leaves a long pause, because this conversation isn't going anywhere. "In any case, I still think you are doing more good with Free2B."

He perks up slightly, which is a good sign: if he wanted to hear that, he must be leaning away from the Policy1st job. "Really?"

"Really. But you know if you want to switch, I'm with you."

Ken shakes his head. "They made the job sound great, but . . . I feel bad about it, but I just don't trust them anymore. I think I would get there and it wouldn't be anywhere near what they are implying."

Mishima reaches out to rub his arm. "You're so much wiser than I am."

Ken takes his cue. "You know everything is going to change once the election is over and you're a member of the Secretariat. *That's* the job you want. The campaigning is just what you have to go through to get there."

"Maybe," Mishima answers, looking back up at the sky. "I'm more and more doubtful that the job will be worth it."

"Then you'll quit," Ken says, with perfect faith.

Mishima sighs. The past five years have given her some opportunities to dismantle her loyalty to Information, but she's not sure it's completely dead yet. Besides: "And disrupt this whole carefully planned scaffolding of new governance?"

"They have a plan for filling vacated seats, right?" Ken shrugs. "Chaos is part of democracy too."

He gets a weak chuckle out of her for that.

The debrief is tedious: two and a half hours of questions about twenty minutes sitting in a dark closet. The repetition of "I don't know" becomes so physically irritating to Maryam that she begins to suspect she is overreacting, that her annoyance is at least partly trauma-fueled. At least they agree to let her continue the discussion back in La Habana. She insists on seeing de la Campana before she leaves. The small woman is trembling but composed, and manages a smile when she sees Maryam. "They don't hurt anyone," she says to her. "You were right. Everyone is accounted for."

Maryam wants to ask her what it was like; whether the crowd control tactics were exactly like the previous attacks; if she learned anything; whether it was as terrifying as she imagines; but when de la Campana leans forward to pat Maryam's shoulder, she catches a hint of vomit on the older woman's breath. She can learn all of that from the reports later, except for the degree of terror, and that she doesn't really need to know.

The InfoSec officers give Maryam some sugary energy chews on the crow, which don't exactly steady her but do make her feel better. She spends most of the hour-long flight eyeing the shower facilities but decides she'd rather wait for her own apartment. When they get to La Habana, the Info-Sec named Martín escorts her to one of the secure meeting rooms. Maryam expects Batún, but it's Nejime, projecting in, who interviews her.

"We want to keep this as tight as possible," Nejime says, though Maryam hasn't asked. "You say they were aware of your actions?"

"They were absolutely aware someone was interacting with them, although they may not know who. There was no way of avoiding attention." Nejime sighs. "Sorry."

"Don't apologize; you've just brought us the biggest break we've had since the attacks started. I'm just frustrated with my own lack of understanding on the techie front. So. What did we learn?"

Exhaustion clobbers Maryam, and even shrugging feels difficult. "I haven't been able to look through the output I saved yet. I passed it on to InfoSec, but what they were after may not be apparent . . ."

"It's fine. Go get some rest; we'll talk about it later. And, Maryam?" Nejime's eyes are down, as though in her Doha office she's already looking at something else. "You know whom to talk to if you are feeling effects from the trauma?"

"Yes, of course," Maryam says automatically, trying to re-member. There's some kind of employee support service, although she's never used it before. She supposes she can find it if something convinces her she needs it.

It is not until she is back to her own workstation that she remembers she wanted to tell Nejime about the disintegrating guidebook. The guides seem drastically less important since the morning, but also more appealing to work on than on the data she collected in those terrifying minutes on the Isla de Pinos. Maryam knows she should go home and try to sleep, or whatever it is people normally do at four in the afternoon after hiding from masked assailants in a broom closet, but it is easier to sit down and go back to work.

Maryam starts composing a program to sift through recent intel from La Habana and Dhaka looking for tourism reviews mentioning unusual guidebooks. It is relatively mindless and settles her so much that she is reluctant to stop, even after five. Maryam hasn't forgotten that Núria arrives home from Oaxaca tonight, but she's achieving a torturous sense of virtuosity by not checking on her current location. The longer she can stay at work, the more likely it is that Núria will be home alone waiting for her instead of the other way around.

She's trying to figure out how to better mask the intent of her search when she gets a ping from Núria: *Home! I know you're busy but I can't wait to see you!*

Maryam is out the door before she knows what she's doing, and has to do a remote check to make sure she closed all her files. It's already dark out, and La Habana is coming to life, public transport crows raucous and crowded, the streets twisty with couples and groups on their way to shows or drinks. Maryam skips the crush and splurges on the first cab that passes.

Getting into the unknown tunnel—the null-states tunnel, or nunnel, as Roz has started calling it mentally—proves to be a nontrivial problem, as Djukic explains.

"Look, it's shallower than 888's planned mantle tunnel, but it's still very, very deep. Digging down that far requires big equipment, and you would need a place to put the dirt. Not easy to hide."

"So, how did they do it?" Roz wonders.

Djukic shrugs. "They dug it in the null states, without feeds watching their every move?"

Roz cocks an eye, wondering if that's anti-Information feeling she hears or a statement of the obvious. "Yeah, but we have satellite imagery."

"Well, take a look. Maybe you'll find something. Still not sure how that helps us dig into the tunnel without them noticing."

"Could we mask it with the work on the mantle tunnel?"

"Not easily. Remember, the tunnels only cross at one point, and it's near the middle of 888's trajectory. There's no reason to dig above the middle; in fact, we really don't want to do that."

"Part of a test, maybe, for your sinkhole theory?"

Djukic scoffs. "Picking, out of the entire length of our tunnel, the one place where they cross? Besides, we wouldn't have to go that deep to take samples."

The baby kicks, or elbows, and Roz rubs her stomach absently. "Okay, so let's say we do it closer to the supposed terminal. Switzerland is not large; if we look for some place close to the border, the tunnel should be shallower as it arches toward the surface, right?"

"Definitely," agrees Djukic.

"Let's say we just want to get something really small in there. A tiny feed camera."

"That would be better. We don't want to disrupt the structural integrity of the tunnel."

Another problem to worry about. "And supposing it's being used to transmit data. How are we going to hack into that?"

The environmental engineer gives her an *are you crazy* look. "Definitely not my department."

Information has never been great at internal data dissemination. It's a fact that is brought up again and again at meetings, usually with *what can you do* grins or head-waggles and some reference to irony, but Rajiv has never found it surprising or funny. Rather, it's emblematic of everything that he hates about the organization: the hypocrisy; the bread-and-circuses approach to avoiding the strictures of their trademark transparency; their disregard for their own staff; their patchy, politically motivated competence. Information never bothered to create a strong organizational structure, preferring a pretense of egalitarianism that lets the worst personalities accrue power; of course intel-sharing is haphazard, along with human resources, opportunity, and funding.

But if Rajiv despises Information, he is also used to it. Like a hated apartment he's lived in far too long, he knows every creaking board and leaky faucet and quirk of the composter. Rajiv knows how to navigate Information. (Long ago, before he gave up on them, he used to joke with his colleagues that in order to spy *for* Information, they had to be able to spy *in* Information.) He has elaborate alerts webbed through his interface and catches everything anyone writes or whispers about the transfer-station attacks, so he knows almost immediately that the latest one went wrong.

Rajiv reads everything he can about it on the intranet and

from public compilers, then goes for a walk. He follows his normal route to the chess café he frequents several times a week, but deviates into a narrow, feedless alley and dodges into a tiny shop front festooned with flags: Russia, China, Switzerland, Saudi, Western Sahara. The proprietor, blinking through some content or other, ignores Rajiv as he steps into one of the booths and closes the cheap soundproofing behind him.

Rajiv enjoys all the awkwardness of the call center—the prepaid cards he buys, the grimy booth—because it reminds him how hard these communications are to trace. Not impossible. There are not so many people living in Kathmandu who have reason to pay the staggeringly high fees to speak with someone in the null states, and almost all of those want to call China. But there are enough people calling relatives or, less often, business associates in Russia to muddy Rajiv's pattern, and he makes sure it's difficult to pinpoint his visits to the call center. He's already won three centenal chess championships, thanks to all the practice he gets while he's covering his tracks, and he doesn't even like chess.

Rajiv taps in the long-memorized phone number and murmurs the password calculated from the previous day's average temperature on the Baltic Sea.

"Hello?"

"What happened?" Rajiv hisses. There is something liberating about this antiquated form of communication. Invisible and with his voice distorted by ancient lines, it's easier to loose his frustration. "I told you increasing the frequency of the incursions was going to be risky."

Moushian, used to Rajiv's irascibility, laughs. "We knew it was inevitable. Someone was going to get a look at the diagnostics eventually. I doubt they figured out what they were looking at."

Rajiv snorts. "If anyone can figure it out, it's her."

"What? Who found it?"

Rajiv gives a brief synopsis of Maryam's career.

"Dangerous," Moushian says thoughtfully. "But also possibly disgruntled?"

"You think she might join us?" The possibility hadn't occurred to Rajiv, but he's gotten used to assuming that he's locked in irreconcilable enmity with everyone around him.

"Can you create an opportunity to find out?"

Rajiv sighs. "I'll see what I can do."

"Carefully, though—we need you for the live run. Don't compromise yourself."

"Everything else going well?" Rajiv can't keep himself from asking. It's safer for him to know nothing about the other fronts, but now, so close to the decisive point, he feels the absence of that knowledge like a blindfold. He has kept his heart rate down during countless mental-emotional scans and stealth operations, but this slow-motion toppling of the world order is nerve-wracking.

"Progressing as planned; don't worry."

It is very late that night when Núria realizes Maryam can't sleep.

"What's wrong?" She props herself up on her elbow and tweaks the bedside lamp to emit a modicum of light.

"I—" Maryam stops to consider whether she's being indiscreet. The attacks on the data transfer sites are public knowledge, if so downplayed as to have gone unremarked.

Her travel plan was obvious, as de la Campana pointed out. Núria might not put the two together, especially given their tacit agreement not to peer too closely into each other's work travels, but it's there for her to see if she looks.

Maryam decides that's license enough. "I was at a data transfer site today when it was attacked."

"What?" Núria sits up. "Are you all right? What were you . . . What happened?" Even in the dim light, Maryam can see her eyes moving as she blinks up the intel.

Maryam intends to sketch the outline of it, avoiding the details of her virtual exploits, but once she starts talking she can't seem to stop. When she describes the mask staring up at her through the feed Núria grabs her hand, and when she gets to the part where InfoSec shows up, Núria grabs all of her in a tight hug.

"Querida," she whispers. "I'm so sorry you had to go through all that. How terrifying!"

Maryam's voice comes out steady and calm. "I'm fine. It's all fine." She is glad Núria can't see her face. "Nothing bad happened. I was never really in danger. Not like . . ." *Not like you are, every time you go out there.*

Núria pulls back and shakes her head at her, the modified strands in her hair glinting copper in the light. "You were very brave. And what you did with the"—she motions with her hands, indicating complexity—"the, what? Can we call that *hacking*? You were amazing."

"I only took obvious countermeasures," Maryam answers, bemused.

"*I* wouldn't know how to do any of that."

"It's just what I do," Maryam says. "You must do much more impressive things all the time." Núria's shoulder is smooth and curved above the bedsheet. Maryam wants to touch it. She reminds herself that they are together, she is allowed, and reaches out to run her hand along the soft skin, wishing she didn't feel so awkward.

"Oh, my work is not so heroic these days. I consult on security measures or patrol silly borders." Núria leans back against her pillow, relaxing into Maryam's touch. "It is a little . . . frightening, though."

"Your work?"

"No, I mean . . . with the election coming up, all the talk I'm hearing, the insistence on having that border guarded, it's like something is building up . . . like these attacks. I didn't know how many there were until now. It feels like we're on the brink of something, like it might all fall apart."

Maryam feels terror return to her belly, thinking of what that might mean. Especially from a soldier. "You've been spending too much time with the camaradas." She tries to make it sound teasing, but Núria doesn't laugh.

"At least they think about these problems, try to face them."

Her tone isn't accusatory, but Maryam feels stung anyway. "They complain about what's wrong," she says, realizing she sounds petty and defensive. "They don't seem to have many ideas for what to do."

Núria doesn't seem bothered, shrugging her delectable shoulder as she snuggles into her pillow. "Well, they try. But hopefully, since Information has your super hacking capabilities, we won't need to worry about it."

Maryam, staring at the ceiling, is unconvinced. "I didn't *do* anything. I didn't find out anything."

"Not yet," Núria murmurs, and rolls over to curl into Maryam's arms. That, at least, feels perfectly natural, and Maryam starts to relax. "But you will."

CHAPTER 8

The next day Maryam feels twitchy. Maybe it's a reaction to the trauma, or delayed uncertainty about telling Núria so much. There must be a reason that Information hasn't asked YourArmy to help secure the data transfer stations: they want to keep these attacks as small as possible in the public consciousness. And, she keeps reminding herself, no one got hurt. If anything was lost, it was only data.

Work helps calm her: she spends the day focused on election-related techie stuff, which is challenging intellectually but not ethically. Maryam does feel guilty about not analyzing the data she culled from the attack, but every time she thinks about it she gets a wave of nausea. Other people are working on it, so she gives herself a pass. She's braced for awkwardness at home, but that night, she and Núria cook together with almática music in the background. Their sex is less urgent than the night before but more comforting, and afterward they curl up together in bed and watch *Centenal Searchers* together: pretty much the perfect evening, and suggestive of stability and commitment.

The next night, Núria has plans to go to Magdalena's place for another camaradas tertulia.

"You should come!" she tells Maryam. "It'll be fun."

"I'd love to," Maryam lies. She *would* love to go if it were fun, but she has never been able to find her rhythm with those women, all united by culture, ideology, and attitude. "But I need to catch up on work. You know, after the past couple of nights."

Núria rolls her eyes at her weak attempt at flattery but doesn't push it, which plunges Maryam into doubt again. She wishes she had gone, instead of sitting alone worried about what might be happening there without her.

Work, then. Maryam is still reluctant to look at the transfer station data—she feels as though it might infect her, might give her away to those masked fiends—and instead she combs through the results of a program she set up to trawl for references to guidebooks. The initial hits all seemed to be about legitimate, Information-based tourist intel combined in various forms by compilers. Maryam adds the terms *scoop, unbelievable, intellicious, secret,* and *pro-tip,* with a secondary filter for responses containing *couldn't find it* or *not where you pointed,* and reconfigures her search to look for items that are either designed for virality or tightly restricted by audience. She still nets a lot of standard travel guide promotion, but 314 results in she finds:

> Super-weird secret tips! I was in Delhi last weekend and found an amazing travel guide *on paper* that told me every little detail about the neighborhood. Very useful! Unfortunately it was poor quality paper and has already deteriorated, so I can't share.

Maryam opens a globe and places pins in Havana, Dhaka, and Delhi, then goes back to her search results.

> Some sketchy guy in Alexandria tried to offer me a secret "tourist guide"—has anyone else come across this scam?

Does Information know everything? These intellicious travel guides say no—but they're almost impossible to find.

Almost impossible to find, indeed. But now she knows they're out there, and on at least three continents.

She can feel her concentration slipping as the evening continues. Her thoughts keep straying to the salon that she decided to skip. Who showed up? Is it one of their raucous evenings or a quiet one? Does Núria miss her?

Anything is better than jealousy. Maryam resolutely opens the cache of attack data and dips into it. A system diagnostic is not the most fascinating reading, but she does feel virtuous, justified in missing the stupid salon.

She could, of course, speed through the feed closest to Magdalena's door, figure out who went to the tertulia and whether they are all still there, or whether most of them have left already . . . Maryam catches herself and slams shut the tiny projection she had just opened. This is ridiculous. She has just made up her mind to go to the tertulia, pride and laziness forsooth, when she gets a secure comms call from Nejime.

"Good evening," Nejime says, and Maryam remembers that it's very late—or, rather, very early—in Doha. "How are you feeling?"

"Fine. Really." Or she will be. "I'm glad you called; I was just looking at the data from the attack." She gives Nejime the chance to cut her off with results from some of the other experts who have been working on it, but the older woman is silent. "They were testing transmission paths, running contingency after contingency—if such and such a node was out, how would the data get from A to B, and millions of permutations thereof."

"What does that mean?"

"Probably that you're right: They're investigating how to disable and co-opt our infrastructure." She hesitates again, this time because of the weight of what she's about to suggest. "Have you considered leaving the transfer stations that have been attacked offline?"

"They've all been checked for malware . . ."

"I know, but if those are their most up-to-date data points in the network, they may become the entry points."

"I'll look into it," Nejime says. The network will function without those nodes, but taking the transfer stations offline means reassigning or putting on leave thousands of workers, a logistical nightmare that will only be exacerbated by the campaign season.

"I'm sorry I didn't learn anything more useful."

"Don't worry about that," Nejime says. "I appreciate your insight, but we've also got a whole InfoSec team looking into it. What I need from you is intel from the ground. How up are you on the Independentistas?"

Maryam has a panicked moment wondering whether Nejime saw how often she opened feeds off the Independentista border last week. "I . . . am familiar with the basics." She wonders if Nejime has put together *why* she was watching that border.

"We're seeing some unusual data along their frontiers; that is to say, data not sourced from Information."

Maryam's pulse quickens. "Don't they have their own intel-gathering mechanism?"

"Yes, but this seems unusually sophisticated. It's unclear whether they are deliberately broadcasting it into microdemocratic territory, or whether it seeped across the physical border unintentionally, but I'd like someone to take a look.

And just in case it is related to the ex-staffers, I'd like it to be you."

"You think they might be based there?"

"We've been focusing on the null states, but the Independentistas, for all their connections with micro-democracy, don't have an extradition treaty with us. Knowingly or not, they may have become a staging base for attacks on our system."

"That sounds . . ." *Dangerous. Active. Non-techie.* "Serious."

"For now, we just want to get a sense for their data infrastructure. Hassan thinks that even if the ex-staffers aren't there, looking at a completely different system might be helpful in thinking about our problem."

"To get ideas about how Exformation—sorry, the ex-staffers—could be piggybacking on our connections," Maryam says, intrigued.

"You will have to go there," Nejime adds. "We don't have access to their intel processes."

"And they will grant me on-site access?" Maryam asks, uncertain.

"No," Nejime says, annoyance putting some bite into it. "You will hack in once you're there."

There's an awkward pause while Maryam tries to figure out what to say to that, whether to base her concerns on technical or ethical grounds.

"You can go as a tourist. There are very high tourism rates from La Habana. Take three or four days, hack in to get a sense for the infrastructure, look around for any evidence of organized opposition to Information. If you have any concerns about your safety, leave immediately and we'll send someone else in to deal with it, but I don't expect that. Think of it as a research trip."

"If you really think . . ."

Nejime sighs emphatically. "You are close by, you are working on this issue, and you are best qualified to deal with the technical issues. We need to know and we need to know soon." After a pause during which Maryam wrestles with herself, Nejime adds, "The sooner you get back out there, the better."

Twenty-two days until the election, and the data from the transfer station attack didn't tell them much. Maryam would prefer to stay in her safe Hub office for the duration, but at least nobody has attacked the Independentistas. And if anything does happen, at least she knows there's a YourArmy deployment along one of the borders. "I suppose it's better than going to Russia."

Nejime laughs in surprise. "Yes," she says. "Yes, I'm confident that it is. I'm sending you contact links to the local staff around Independentista territory. We do not have any permanent staff within their jurisdiction, although that's something we're working for in exchange for a foreign rep seat for them on the Secretariat. However, all of their borders except the one with Liberty are completely open. Stay in the urban area, and if you sense any threat, which I don't anticipate, get into micro-democratic territory as quickly as possible. Good?"

Maryam nods and Nejime cuts the connection before she has time to change her mind.

Maryam spends forty-nine minutes researching the Independentistas and their tiny nation, and downloading additional intel to store on her handheld for later. Then she grabs her bag and leaves the office. If she's about to travel again, she's going to spend every moment she can with Núria before she does. Even if it means an evening with the camaradas.

R oz sifts through endless satellite imagery of the areas they suspect as likely termini of the nunnel, one in Moscow and the other in a rural area of the null state of Switzerland, but she finds nothing suspicious, even after cross-referencing with the pictures of the initial illegal mantle tunnel Heritage started in Tokyo five years ago and the two currently in legal stasis. The images of Moscow trigger a fascination with the unknown and forbidden: that strange, overdeveloped city that she has almost no data about and has never seen except from 200 miles directly overhead. The blocks of massive buildings give her an idea: surely, there's enough space inside some of those to hide a dig site.

"Certainly possible," Djukic answers her carefully worded query over projection. "It's what I would do."

From that, she manages to communicate that Djukic should identify a location in Zurich that will allow them to dig into the nunnel from inside a building. A few days later, she gets a message from Djukic informing her that she and a small team she considers reliable will be setting up shop in Zurich to carry out "those tests we talked about," in an environment with similar geology far enough away from the planned mantle tunnel so as not to cause problems with the eventual construction. Roz approves with some unease, nervous about agreeing to something discussed in ad hoc code and simultaneously worried that the code is too transparent.

Roz doesn't plan to fly out until the enhanced electronic surveillance tool she assumes they're using makes contact with the shell of the mystery tunnel. It's not just that she's seven months pregnant; she also has better things to do than wait for a flexible cable to bore twenty-five kilometers into the ground. She has to keep up with the Wall, for one thing. Also, none of this secret drama has affected the processes on the sanctioned mantle tunnels in the least (with the exception of Djukic's temporary removal from the 888 team), and she needs to keep up to date on all the legal and engineering challenges. Besides, her presence would risk drawing attention to the operation.

The first attempt turns up blank.

"What do you mean, you didn't find it?" Roz asks, distracted from a ticklish discussion about a particularly sensitive Wall panel proposition when Djukic appears in her office. "And what are you doing here?"

"I didn't want to explain over Information," Djukic says, as if it were obvious. Roz whispers a quick excuse to the Wall team and closes all her projections.

"So," she says, trying to focus. "How is that possible?"

Djukic has thrown up a sketched projection of their project. Apparently, they are digging in the basement of the massive leisure, entertainment, and sports complex that was once the Zurich Hauptbahnhof. "We always knew we were guessing about the termini." Djukic is phlegmatic about the whole thing; Roz wonders how often her engineering calculations go totally wrong in practice. "We are probably correct in assuming that there are no sharp turns, but even slight bends will have a significant effect over a distance. We're going to retract the cable slowly, running spherical geolocation scans in a fifteen-meter radius every ten meters. Hopefully we find it. If not, we'll have to reassess the hypothetical trajectory. And find another large building willing to let us play under their roof." Djukic turns to leave, then turns back. "By the way, we should figure out a secure communications channel."

"Oh, right," Roz says. "I'll—" She is about to say *I'll ask Maryam* when she remembers that now also requires secured communications. "I'll look into it, but for the moment, if you need me to come out there, send me a message about new environmental problems that you think I'd want to see, or something like that."

"In Zurich?" Djukic smirks. "All right, I'll think of some excuse."

"If they've been looking for this sort of thing, they've probably found us by now," Roz says, wondering who the most likely *they* are in this scenario. "But yes, let's try not to raise any more flags than we have to."

Maryam usually feels like she and Núria are doing reasonably well, with their two government incomes and the manageable cost of living in 888 in La Habana. She saves a little every month, doesn't feel bad about the occasional indulgence, and can afford to buy environmentally neutral products. Maryam's father is always offering to send her money if she ever needs it, but she's been independent for years.

Magdalena works for YouPengYou, one of the world's largest social-capital investment firms and a member of the 888 consortium. Maryam knew this, in some highly judgey corner of her mind where she reluctantly stores basic facts about the camaradas, but she had assumed it was some kind of middle-management job or below. Seeing Magdalena's place makes her reevaluate. She lives in a mansion, and not a small one; when the public transport crow drops her off by the half-circle driveway, Information tells her it used to be an embassy. Maryam looks Magdalena up, and there it is: VP of Scalability. That would do it.

The elaborate ironwork gate glides open before Maryam reaches it—onto a courtyard with a three-level fountain and an extraordinary mural depicting obreros, global data flows, and the crossed flags of Cuba and Catalunya. As Maryam passes close to the mural on her way to the open door to the interior, she sees that it is actually a micro-mosaic. Magdalena's not just rich; she's ridiculously rich. And she still has the nerve to put socialist and accessist motifs in her mural.

Maryam lets her semi-hypocritical outrage carry her into the daunting situation: a party; that has already started; in a mansion screaming chic yet socially conscious wealth; featuring the five radical Catalá glintelligentsia nemeses who fascinate her girlfriend.

Magdalena greets her at the door, hair in a classic wave-back reminiscent of the 2050s, body encased in a silvery robe that molds to her figure in constant piling waves. "Maryam! I'm so glad you could make it." She leans in for a cheek kiss. Maryam reciprocates but pulls back after the first, Cuban-style, making it awkward when she has to go back in for the second peton. "We don't see you often enough," Magdalena goes on, leading Maryam back into the house once they've cleared the kerfuffle.

"So glad you could get away." Núria is waiting for them at the door of what must be the sala (or one of them). She's wearing her fluttery red sleeveless jumpsuit, one of Maryam's favorites, and Maryam hopes her glow is because she's shown up and not for somebody else here. With her, there's just the one kiss on the mouth, and Núria links her arm through Maryam's to walk in together. Maryam wonders if Núria has realized how nervous these women make her.

"A drink?" Magdalena sways toward the full bar.

"Juice?" Maryam asks.

"Oh, of course. Maracuyá? Or a batido, maybe? Mamey, guayaba, anon?"

"Maracuyá would be great." Maryam takes her drink and turns back to the room. Alba, Maryam's favorite of the group because she's relatively low-key, nods at her from across the room, and LaForet offers a little wave from beside her. There's music, some kind of pared-down neo-trova; after a few minutes, the tambor and voice pairing ends, and applause and the rumble of conversations are audible before the next song starts. Maryam checks the source—the music is being piped in live from a popular downtown bar.

Magdalena sways away from them, and Núria smiles at Maryam. "I'm glad you could make it," she says again, pulling her a little closer.

Maryam smiles back, but apologetically. "Something came up," she explains. "I have to leave tomorrow. Just for a week or so," she adds, feeling both pleased and guilty about Núria's disappointed expression. "Routine work became much less important than spending a little more time with you." Even if she would much rather they were alone.

"Do you want to go home?" Núria asks, and even though she does want to, the unexpected offer gives Maryam the fortitude to shake her head.

"We're here now; we might as well stay for a little bit." She opens her mouth to tell her that she is going to be on the opposite side of the border Núria patrolled last week, maybe to ask for some local suggestions, and closes it again. "I don't mind, really," she says instead, kissing her on the cheek. "Enjoy yourself, and we'll go back when you're ready."

Fortunately, the tertulia is not as painful as Maryam expected. She is quiet for the first stretch, trying to catch the rhythm, the levels of facetiousness and daring. There are plenty of bons mots, but what intimidates her the most is how relaxed these women are with each other, as though every one of them were at home in her pajamas instead of dressed for a red carpet in a bejeweled mansion. Maryam doesn't usually think of herself as socially awkward. A mild introvert, perhaps, but she's always been able to sparkle in small talk. But these women are terrifying.

The conversation has turned to borders: apparently, one of the tiny nationalist states in Europe—not Catalonian in this case, but Tyrolese—has put a referendum on their citizens' election ballot about the construction of a border wall around their centenal. Other nationalist governments, including at least one Catalonian (*Could it be Núria's?* Maryam wonders), have started debating the idea. The camaradas treat it as a joke. Micro-democracy allows every government to decide its own immigration and border policies, but most governments prefer to encourage both immigration, which tends to benefit the incumbent in elections, and casual visits, which tend to boost the economy. The exception are those nationalist governments that care more about "purity" or "cultural protectionism" than growth or power. As Carme puts it, "If they want to shoot themselves in the collons, let them!"

"It's an ugly precedent, though," Zipporah says. "And only perpetuates segregation and misunderstanding."

"It will preserve small and unusual cultures as well," Magdalena says, and shrugs when they all look at her. "I think it's worth trying to see both sides."

"A physical border, though! It's not like walls keep culture out, not in this world! And so expensive and environmentally harmful."

"And *economically* harmful," Carme adds. "Can you imagine going through a, a—what, a border control?—every time you need to buy something not available in your centenal?"

Núria's eyes meet Maryam's from the bar across the room, and it occurs to her that they—the Information techie and the soldier—have far more experience with physical borders than any of these women. For the first time, Maryam wonders whether Núria ever feels out of place among the camaradas too.

"When I was a teenager in Beirut, there was a physical border between two centenals." Maryam is almost surprised to hear her own voice: it sounds loud in the room, as though she is forcing herself into the conversation, although she is fairly sure she spoke into a neat pause.

"Just between two?" LaForet asks. "Not around the whole centenal?"

"Just between the two," Maryam confirms. "It wasn't intended as isolationism or even to prevent all contact between citizens of those two centenals, because they could easily go around. The idea was to prevent impulsive contact between the two—basically to force people to take a breath before they aimed flamethrowers at each other."

"How long was this thing up?"

"I don't know—five years, maybe? It's gone now." Maryam shrugs, feeling that her story has fizzled. "The funny thing," she starts again, "is that there was a border crossing, a gate in this wall. I mean, people could just go around, right? But to save them the . . . I don't know, half an hour that might take, they had opened a big, fortified, staffed border crossing."

"I'm picturing a moat with a portcullis," Carme says, and they all laugh.

"Not far off," Maryam admits, when they've quieted. "No moat, of course, but it was a heavy metal gate with spikes on top, not one of those easy-up easy-down barriers." She grins at the camaradas. "Naturally, my friends and I used to find any excuse to go through that gate."

"And what? They would ask you questions or something?" Magdalena asks.

"There were guards," Maryam says, "but they got to know us pretty quickly." She stops, remembering: one of the guards was killed a few years later in a traffic accident. "They would ask strangers to show their public Information, ask them their business, that sort of thing. Again, it wasn't so much that they were supposed to stop people as make them pause for a few minutes before they rushed into a fight."

"And did it work?" asks Alba.

"Mostly," Maryam says, and falls silent, remembering the time it didn't.

"Did it cause longer-term problems?"

"Hmm?" Maryam rouses herself back to the present. "It did, in fact. Even though contact was still possible between those two centenals, it was marginally more difficult. Interaction rates went down, and suspicion and hostility went up."

"See?" Zipporah says, and the conversation spins back to the hypothetical future. Maryam falls back into isolation, wondering what that border looks like now.

If Ken hadn't been pushing for Free2B to campaign in additional centenals, he wouldn't have noticed when they did, but in between checking the polls obsessively he occasionally glances at the official election registrar. When he sees an additional target centenal, he has to count three times to be sure he's not imagining it. *Why didn't they tell me?* he wonders as he looks up the centenal number. He's asked them to expand enough times. Maybe it was an impulsive decision and they haven't decided if they really want to contest that centenal yet. Or maybe they have some problem with him as Campaign Director? Then the centenal data loads, and he's even more baffled.

"I don't understand," Ken says when he finally gets through to Geoff Forth, the Head of State of Free2B. "Look, I'm thrilled that you added another centenal to the campaign, but I've sent you several breakdowns of the most accessible targets, and this . . ." He trails off, gesturing at his projection of the demographic breakdown for centenal 3829471. Trending middle-aged and up; currently a Liberty government; top-ranked issue areas are agriculture and law and order. "This is not an easy win for us."

"What are you talking about?" Geoff asks without meeting Ken's eyes. The automatic read is dishonesty, but Ken knows it's more likely that he hasn't stopped doing whatever he was doing when Ken called. "I thought you added the new centenal. Was a little annoyed you didn't clear it with me first, actually."

Ken has never been particularly fond of Geoff, which is uncomfortable, given how much he appreciates the government he founded and runs, but at least he doesn't have to interact directly with him too often. "Of course I wouldn't do that," Ken says, trying to keep his tone bro-friendly. "That's why I kept asking you to approve new campaign areas." He wants to make sure that's clear before moving on; Geoff is capable of associating this faint disapproval with him for weeks without remembering what it's about or that he didn't do it. "You're sure you didn't add this to the list?"

"I haven't touched it, haven't even looked at it in weeks," Geoff says. He's still focused on something else; Ken's betting an interactive or one of those competitive crossword puzzles he's so into. Much as he hates the founding-genius narrative Geoff cultivates, he has to admit it was brilliant to design a government that required almost no work on his part. "Must have been Phuong; she's also been harassing us to expand."

Ken doubts that, but he thanks Geoff quickly to forestall the coming rant about the overly optimistic Saigon office and goes to Phuong to confirm.

"Nope, haven't touched it." The Free2B Saigon centenal governor has been Ken's boss for years. "What do you think, should we cancel or go for it anyway, since Geoff hasn't let us add any of the ones we actually want?"

"Maybe we can switch it out," Ken suggests. "But let me look into it first—maybe there's a reason whoever it was picked this centenal."

Ken tries not to take work home, because (unlike Mishima) he believes in dividing work time and family time. But he wants to decide quickly on that extra centenal—the excitement of planning a new campaign, even or especially an underdog effort, battling with his better sense—and so he ends up scanning the data after Sayaka goes to bed. When Mishima asks, he tells her what he's working on.

"Wait!" Mishima says, when he gets to the fact that no one has admitted to targeting the centenal. She puts her hand on his arm, and Ken feels the familiar frisson: he's never been sure if it's driven by his attraction to her or the energy she exudes when she's on the hunt. "You're telling me no one knows who added the centenal?"

"It's probably someone from the council," Ken says. "Probably too embarrassed to admit it now that it's becoming an issue. You know how Free2B is." Lax with permissions and security.

"It's just . . ." Mishima hesitates, but all the data she's working with is public, even if the pattern has not yet been picked up anywhere. She throws him her file on the mystery ads. "It doesn't exactly fit the pattern, or rather, it fits as a significant escalation. Free2B is both larger and more geographically widespread than these other governments, but . . ."

"You think we're being trolled?" Ken asks gleefully. "Ha! I can't wait till Geoff finds out!" Mishima glares at him. "What? You know he thinks he's too cool to be made fun of."

"Maybe it is just a joke."

"What else could it be?" Ken's pulse has accelerated in a way that this election has not provided so far.

"Either it's a very sophisticated attempt to sway the results in certain centenals, which would be bad, or active discrediting of the entire election process, which would be worse."

"You want me to go out there?" Ken asks, meaning the new target centenal. "No ads have run yet; we must have caught it in process."

"No," Mishima answers, squeezing his arm lightly. "It's better if they think you haven't noticed. Ask around quietly to see if you can confirm that it wasn't an official source who placed the campaign registration, but only in person. I'll take care of the rest. Don't worry," she adds at Ken's expression. "If there's any way to involve you in the fun, I'll let you know."

They are both sleepy when they tumble out of the party, and Núria is mildly drunk, so they decide to take a taxi home instead of the public transportation. Maryam gets in first and leans her head against the window, tired but relieved that she not only survived, but possibly even enjoyed an evening with the camaradas. Núria gets in and leans against Maryam.

"Mmm," Maryam says, and puts her arm around her girlfriend. *Girlfriend.* Why is it so hard to believe that is real, when they've been living together for a year now?

Because we travel all the time and barely see each other.

Because I love her more than she loves me.

Because I always manage to fuck these things up.

Maryam shakes her head, trying to dispel the sudden gloom.

Maybe everything will be all right. Maybe this time I can—

"By the way," Núria mumbles.

"Mmm?"

"Something happened in Oaxaca that I thought I should tell you about."

Maryam's stomach and her sense of comfort both experience a sudden drop, and she's unhappily wide awake: is Núria about to tell her she cheated on her during the deployment? But Núria is still talking and her tone sounds puzzled, a little hesitant, but neither guilty nor grief-stricken. And she would feel something if she were ending the relationship, wouldn't she? She isn't Valérie.

"I was approached by someone who . . ." Maryam holds her breath. "A child, giving out cards, you know, about a sort of datastream—"

Maryam thought she was awake before, but now she's sitting up, accidentally dislodging Núria as she does so. Her only thought is how to stop Núria from talking without being too obvious. "Hey, look, we're almost home," she says desperately. Everyone knows the auto-taxi feeds are constantly mined for content and reposted as candid serials. Núria must be drunker than she thought to talk about *anything* in one, even if she doesn't know how sensitive it is.

"Oh, yeah," Núria says, and finds a new position against her shoulder, either sleepiness or OpSec training reasserting itself. Fortunately, they *are* almost home, and a few minutes later, Maryam is helping Núria out of the cab and they are swaying together toward the door of their apartment building.

"Sorry, sorry," Núria murmurs into Maryam's ear as they wobble down the hall. "I shouldn't have said that; I just, I kept forgetting to tell you . . ."

"It's fine," Maryam says. Núria's hair is in her face, and it smells fantastic. She puts her fingertip to the door lock, struggles them into the sala, and drops Núria on the sofa. "Tell me now." She goes into the kitchen to pour a glass of water and grab an anti-inebriation pill. "Something about a datastream?"

"That's right," Núria says. "There were these cards, telling you how to access it; kids would give them out on street corners."

"And?" Maryam hands her the water and the pill and watches as she drinks gratefully.

"Bé, I thought you should know because their big selling

point was that it was not Information." Núria frowns. "Whatever that means." She eyes Maryam over the rim of her glass. "Did you know about this? You don't seem terribly surprised."

"Sort of," Maryam says, too wired for the moment to wonder about what she should tell and what she should keep to herself. "Did you take it? Did you look at the intel?"

"No way," Núria says. "It was too weird, and accepting strange programs or documents is totally against operational security protocols. But . . ."

Maryam pounces. "But someone else did!"

Núria nods. "Some of the other officers were talking about it."

"And the intel really wasn't on Information?" Maryam plops down next to her.

"It was a matter of some debate whether the data were just repackaged or really new." Núria shrugs. "I didn't think too much of it, because even if the data were new, if it was all about the Independentista territory, that wouldn't be exactly strange, since they're not covered by Information. But even a repackaged news compiler that's not on Information is strange for us, so people were making a big deal about it."

"*Was* it all about Independentista territory?"

"I don't know, I never looked, I just assumed . . . No," Núria says slowly, and it sounds like she's sobering up now too. "No, I think I remember some people talking about what it said about the election . . . unless there's an election in Independentista territory now too?"

"Do you think I can see the channel? Do you have the card?" Maryam asks. She slips her arm around Núria, inhales the scent of her hair again.

"I never took it," Núria stretches against her, sleepy. "But also . . . I think there was more than one channel," Núria starts. "I'm not sure; that was another thing that we wondered about, if they were really different or just different names for the same thing. I mean," she adds with a yawn, "how much content that's not on Information can there really be?"

"Did you see more than one? Do you know how they were accessed?" Maryam finds a thread of metallic garnet in Núria's dark curls, the modification she put in for hair that would otherwise turn gray.

"No," Núria says. "But I did wonder . . ."

"What?"

"Whether they were approaching us because . . . you know, because we're YourArmy. Because we're not known to be big fans of Information."

If there is a war, Maryam remembers, *the militaries will not necessarily be on our side.*

"I mean stereotypically, you understand," Núria adds into the sudden silence. "In general."

"Stereotypically." Maryam smirks. "In this case . . ."

"In this case"—Núria pulls her down to horizontal—"The biggest fan."

CHAPTER 9

Mishima has to admit (although not to anyone other than herself) that she is just as inappropriately eager as Ken to go haring off after these mystery advertisers. She goes so far as to look at flights that will get her to centenal 3829471 before giving in to the fact that, as a candidate to the Secretariat, she is at least as visible as Ken and even less likely to take a random trip in the middle of the election.

"I could go," Amran says unexpectedly when Mishima is briefing her.

"I don't know if it would be helpful to be there in person," Mishima says, repeating the arguments she's used to talk herself out of going. "We have no evidence of in-person campaigning, and they could be creating and placing the ads from anywhere. We should prioritize remote vigilance."

And, it seems, Amran does. Two days later, she comes back with an update. Even through the projection, Mishima can feel her nervous energy.

"I found someone in 3829471 who is looking into the false ads," she says.

"Oh?" Mishima flicks her fingers out of her assistant's line of sight to bring up Amran's search activity over the last few days. "A curious citizen?"

"I don't think so. The ads haven't appeared yet."

Mishima laughs. "That seems conclusive." She likes Amran's approach to the investigation, an oblique search that broadened the enquiry enough to catch others searching along the same lines, but she does note that it has been seven hours and twenty-two minutes since Amran saw these results. Even given the time for reading and processing, her assistant is ambivalent about something. "You want to go check it out?"

Amran takes a deep breath. "Yes, I do."

"We could send someone else . . ." Mishima is running through the Information spy corps in her mind: Irepani, Rajiv, Yulya, Simone . . .

"I know the case," Amran insists. "Besides . . ." She hesitates. Mishima waits. "The target is Somali diaspora."

"It doesn't mean you have to go if you don't want to," Mishima points out. "There are plenty of other ways we can build a connection. Or we could just spy on him from a distance."

"I'm already running cross-references on his contact history immediately before and after his research, and facial recognition on any public in-person meetings, so I'll see what comes up. I've also looked at his previous searches, and he does seem to have an extreme interest in local quirks and history." She sends Mishima another file. "Otherwise, a short-term casual acquaintance to see what comes up, with a strict time constraint."

"A traveler or a tourist?" Mishima has to admit Amran is making a good case for herself. Clearly some of the intervening time has been spent in prep. But she suspects there's also a degree of anxiety. Best to bring that out before deployment. "It might be dangerous. I'm just speculating"—it's pleasant to say that phrase to another person with narrative disorder, who might calibrate properly instead of giving it undue importance—"but one of the groups I'm looking at for this is Anarchy."

It takes Amran a moment to place the name—they haven't been very active inter-elections—but then her eyes widen. "The ones who tried to bomb the debate in the last election?"

"It fits their disruptive approach, and they have the technical savvy to pull it off."

Amran is looking down at her hands. "Still . . . there's been no suggestion of violence related to this effort so far, has there?"

"No. But we don't know what they're planning yet." Mishima relents, aware that some of her reluctance is because she wishes she could go herself. "I'm just worried about you going without being trained for this sort of thing."

"I'll be careful," Amran says, her eyes still down. "Just observation."

"No, I think you can go beyond observation. A casual acquaintance with a built-in time limit is not a bad idea." Amran brightens. "You'll need a cover identity." Mishima is talking to herself more than to her assistant now. "I'll speak to Nejime about it. And I'd like you to get some training, but you will need to get on the plane as soon as possible. I'll send you some manuals and we'll backfill later. In the meantime—" Mishima pauses, searching for a practical piece of advice. "Do you have a knife?"

Djukic's message comes a few days later, vague and urgent. Roz walks into the landscaped caverns of the former Zurich rail station with no idea what they've found. She works her way around the wave pool—particularly popular now as winter encroaches outside—and down the stairs to the basement. Djukic and her team have done a nice job: setting up pop-up shelters even within the building to screen their activities, and putting up large UNDER CONSTRUCTION signs to make it seem like some kind of work is being done on the building itself. Roz opens a few doors to empty temporary offices before she finds them: Djukic and two others, huddled around a projected map and brainstorming board.

"Hi!" Roz says. "What did you find?"

Djukic turns to her with a puzzled grin. "I think you'll have to explain it to us—geopolitics is not my area. We found the tunnel, almost on top of the path we predicted, but considerably shallower."

"Shallower?"

Djukic nods, drawing Roz over to the three-dimensional map and pointing out the line passing through empty space well below everything recognizable. "We went right by it on our way down, only off by a couple of meters. It's only three meters deep here, already sloping up out of the mantle into the crust."

"So . . ." Roz feels slow.

"So the terminus is closer than we imagined. I don't think this tunnel could reach the nation-state of Switzerland."

Roz gapes. "It's not a nunnel after all." *Or, at most, only half nunnel.* "Where does it end?"

"There's still some wiggle room in the calculations, because the slope can be slightly adjusted depending on various factors. But we're fairly confident it terminates in this centenal's territory." Djukic spins the map to show the surface and highlights a modestly sized semi-rural centenal just outside the Zurich coalition.

Roz staggers back until she finds a chair and sits. "Heritage."

Maryam isn't sure what to expect from Independentista territory. She recognizes plenty of preconceptions about the Independentistas themselves—in her head, they are a more proactive, less privileged version of the camaradas—but it's harder to fit their Territorio de la Justicia, as they call it, into her stereotypes. It is not exactly a null state. For one thing, the Independentistas have a trade agreement with Information. They import updates from selected news compilers and handpicked educational material and programs. In return, they export certain intel about themselves as well, so before she arrives Maryam is able to research their population, politics, and economy, and follow the back-and-forth the Ministerio de la Educación/Guendariziidi has been carrying out with Information over the colonial biases inherent in their educational programs. The Independentistas have gone so far as to make their own modifications and export them back into the micro-democratic world via Information, although the low production values have kept them from winning more than a loyal but narrow following.

Why, if they're already exporting their locally compiled data through Information, would they be broadcasting a non-Information channel?

Maryam scans through their modified programs and is surprised to find herself itching to fix the technical issues to help them transfer ideas more effectively. She shakes her head at herself: either the camaradas are getting to her more than she thought, or she's emotionally susceptible for some reason. Why would she, an Information employee, help a revolutionary anti-Information government? But they do make some good points. And it's not like they're an enemy of micro-democracy. Maybe she could volunteer her expertise to the Independentista government as a way to ingratiate herself with them.

There's no airport in the Territorio de la Justicia—too much environmental damage—so Maryam flies into Oaxaca-LibreYSoberana, a micro-democratic centenal with close ties to the Independentistas, and takes an augmented bicycle taxi from there. It is not a long journey—the Independentista territory includes several neighborhoods within the city of Oaxaca, extending from there out into rural areas—but it's a novel sensation to be driven by a person, triggering both a pleasant old-timey feeling and an uncomfortable layer of guilt. The driver is chatty, especially after the stored energy capacity kicks in. Coasting along, he points out major landmarks, talks about the work that's been done to improve the road without long-term environmental harm, and offers a full buildup to crossing the invisible border between micro-democratic territory and the fragment of Information-free government that is their destination.

Unmarked and unguarded though the border might be, the change is immediately obvious. Election ads and other pop-ups are cut off from one block to the next, and all of the casual data Maryam sees overlaid on her vision—intel about the age of the houses, the nearest pharmacy, the weather forecast—disappears. When she blinks to bring up Information, she sees instead a different, clunkier interface offering her the choice of an education portal, a general knowledge portal, and a current events portal. After a few false starts, she selects *current events*, which takes a ridiculously long time to open, and is given sample slices of four well-known global news compilers, two more that are specific to anti-colonialist and liberation theology traditions, and a regional one, along with what looks like a locally produced news show with production values out of the '50s. There's also a local plaza, apparently all text. She can't imagine any of this stuff appealing to people with access to real Information. She flicks it off.

The taxista is still talking, waving his hands at buildings and pointing in the direction of the zócalo. Maryam is supposed to be a tourist, so she might as well take advantage of the driver's loquaciousness. "So there are no cameras here at all?" she asks, looking around in affected wonder and taking in the stone-paved streets and packed dirt alleys, the large covered market surrounded by street vendors selling flowers and wooden toys.

"None!" the taxista says, with a flourish of his hand. "And let me tell you, as someone who has lived in three different centenals"—he counts on his fingers—"Libertad, Oaxaca-LibreYSoberana, y NuevoPRI, I don't miss them at all!"

Sure, Maryam thinks. *Nobody misses cameras until they need one.* "I heard there were tensions between the Independentistas and Liberty," she says, trying to sound timid.

"Pff! Just the elites panicking. If you want, later I can take you to the border they put up, give you a tour, even take you through the control point." He leans back to line-of-sight her his contacts. Maryam accepts, then points him quickly back toward the road, her timidity now unfeigned: a cat is darting through traffic, causing the solar bus in front of them to jerk to a stop. The bicycle swerves on its own and the driver laughs. "Don't worry, señorita! We still use crash-prevention technology. It is just the power that comes from the people."

This sort of enthusiasm for the Independentista project

could get old fast, Maryam thinks as they pull up in front of her hotel, a two-story building near the central urban area of the Territorio de la Justicia. The lobby is cool and humid after the brilliant heat outside, a small fountain playing against tile in one corner. Again, she finds a person where she least expects one, an elderly woman who checks her in with gentle slowness. Maryam wonders if these are all make-work jobs to keep the economy running, or a natural consequence of the absence of Information.

Her room is small and has the same damp air as the lobby, but when Maryam opens the two windows onto the courtyard it quickly fills with the smell of pine: a cultivated microclimate. She inhales deeply, then sets up a modified workspace. It's a bit like those very few times when she briefly locked herself out of any but the most urgent updates in order to concentrate on a project: the isolation only becomes unnerving if she remembers that she can't turn Information back on whenever she wants. The taxista's contact details give her the first fingertip-hold in the Independentista system, and she worries away at that until she has more.

A mran wishes she had been able to get the training—*In what? Spycraft? Self-defense? Weapons?*—before she left. She was able to talk herself onto the plane without too much difficulty, but it's a long flight. She can only stave off the fear for a few hours before it takes over. Images of the debate attack five years ago play through her mind: shattering glass, chaos, terrified people. She restrained herself from looking up Anarchy before she left, which was probably poor spycraft, now that she thinks of it, and she wonders what else they have done. She wonders how vicious they are when they

aren't making a political statement; when, say, they are dealing with an Information spy.

At least she has a lead. Her subject, Dalmar Dualeh, met
yesterday with a woman named Radha Langer who is not
from the area. Langer is checked in to a hotel in the centenal adjoining 3829471, and the cross-reference found a recent visit to Porthmadog in Wales, where ads for a small
Tamil government are playing. It could be a coincidence, but
all the mystery narratives Amran has ingested have told her
there's no such thing. Besides, Information hasn't helped her
find any connection between Langer and either of those
places. In fact, as Amran reviews the profile again, Information is a little thin on Langer all told. Her intuition—her
narrative disorder, Mishima would say—twitches, and her
fingers twitch in response, but she holds back: the linkups
on planes are notoriously easy to hack and regularly trawled
for sensitive data revealed by bored passengers. She can take
another look when she lands, and decide whether to fabricate an acquaintance with Dualeh or go straight for Langer.

In the meantime, Amran has to try not to be terrified.
And (Mishima's suggestion for the flight, as if she *knew* the
idleness would make Amran fidgety and scared) get used to
her cover identity so that she doesn't stutter over her new
name when introducing herself to someone. She reviews the
public Information that will be displayed next to her face
again, hunched over even though she's projecting at eye level
and there's no way the person sitting next to her will see
anything but flickers.

She is Idil Farah, content designer for Puntland Studios,
a small content developer in Nairobi. Mishima guessed correctly that Amran would have a thorough knowledge of their
catalog. "And you fit the profile of someone who would work

there. We've settled it with them so that they will claim you if anyone asks." Amran's hypothetical position had to be fairly low-level so no one will expect to see her name in the credits, but that, Mishima told her, will make sense because she's so young. (Amran doesn't feel *so* young, although she guesses in comparison to Mishima's vast experience she seems that way.) She's traveling for work to research a new project, a diaspora-based love story they are developing.

It is a bit exciting, imagining this different life for herself. Amran has never before pictured herself as a content designer. She was always sure she wanted to go into either government or Information, but Mishima is right: now that the idea has been planted, it makes complete sense. The neat details devised by whoever manufactures these false identities (she thrills again to the idea of something false coming out of Information) make it astonishingly easy for her to build a whole fantasy world out of it. *Yes,* she imagines saying, *I worked on* Mysteries of the Night; *I only had a small job, but I was able to meet Leylo Daud, and she was very pleasant to work with. Yes, content design can be hard work, but my colleagues are wonderful and we have fun even when we work late. I hope to move up in the company soon. I would really like to be generating new concepts . . .*

This is pleasantly distracting enough to take her mind off the fear, and eventually Amran/Idil manages to fall asleep.

CHAPTER 10

S o," Djukic says, leaning close over the tiny round table. "Are we breaking into the tunnel or not?" They have decamped to one of the cafés on the upper level of the Hauptbahnhof; Roz asked Djukic to brief her away from the team.

"I think . . . not yet." It has not escaped Roz that the projected terminus of the tunnel is the Heritage centenal where William Pressman, former head of state for the former Supermajority, holed up to evade arrest until his successor, Cynthia Halliday, turned on him a couple of years ago. If this tunnel was his means of communicating with the world outside of Information surveillance, there's a possibility it's no longer in use, but Roz can't imagine Heritage would let so valuable an asset go to waste. In either case, it will be an enormous scandal. Roz wants to seek guidance before unleashing that level of chaos in the middle of election season. "I'm going to get an answer on that soon. Is there anything more you can tell me about the tunnel itself, now that we've found it?"

Djukic leans back. "It's more or less what we thought. Maybe big enough for a person-carrier, but not big enough for very many to travel at the same time."

"Still, the fact that it is at least that large . . . if it were just for comms, they would have made it smaller, right?"

Djukic offers one of her characteristic shrugs. "Perhaps. Maybe they wanted the option. Or they wanted access maintenance. Or perhaps they found the engineering challenging. That's the other thing we noticed: based on the technology, this tunnel is at least a few years old. There has been a lot of progress in mantle-boring technology in that time as more governments started researching the possibilities of sub-crustal travel."

A few years . . . That fits with the timeframe for William Pressman's house arrest. One would think Heritage would have given up on drilling through the mantle of the earth after their first attempt cost them the Supermajority, but some people never learn.

"Okay," Roz says. "Give me a minute to call in." She stands and walks through the main hall of the building and out into the chilly air. She finds a corner more or less out of the wind, where she can be sure no one has line of sight on her, checks public feeds to make sure her face is not visible on any of them, and calls.

Roz generated some single-use encryption codes before coming, seeding most of them with Nejime's assistant Zaid (and the remainder with Suleyman, just in case). When she calls Nejime using one of them, there's a slight delay before her face appears, lips pursed. "You don't think this is an excessive level of security?"

By the time Roz had explained the situation, Nejime is completely focused. "Very interesting." Roz can see her start to pace. "Not totally confirmed?"

"No, not yet," Roz says, "but the engineering data looks conclusive."

"Last time we talked, they thought it went to Switzerland," Nejime grumps, and then looks up. "I suppose this calls into question Moscow as the other terminus?"

"I suppose it does," Roz agrees. "It's still a possibility, but there are at least two other Heritage centenals within the tunnel's possible trajectory—as well as those of other governments, of course."

"Heritage's secret communications," Nejime muses. "We knew they had some sort of system set up during the secession crisis, but I always assumed it was code-based, not an entirely separate physical channel."

"It makes sense that Pressman would want sequestered communications, given the risk of prosecution." Nejime, still pacing, doesn't answer. "So, we hold off for the moment?" Roz asks, hopefully. It feels creepier to break into the systems of a micro-democratic government than those of a null state, even if those systems are illegal.

"No," Nejime says, snapping out of it. "We're assuming that this channel is defunct, but they could be using it right now to conduct clandestine communications—on unapproved infrastructure, no less!" Roz is surprised by the force of Nejime's fury. "Even communicating centenal to centenal within Heritage threatens the legitimacy of the election. And if this does go to a null state, they may be a part of the conspiracy to attack us openly!"

Conspiracy? Roz thinks, but she doesn't dare vocalize it.

"This is the problem with sovereignty, with the so-called Supermajority! You give these governments self-determination, they use it to eke out every shred of power and secrecy and economic advantage they can! And people still dare to argue that the system would work better without us, the governments left to self-regulate!" Nejime reins herself in, modulating her voice back to something like normal. "We need to know what's being transferred down there. The first debate is in four days and we're only a few weeks from election day. If they are still transmitting data, we need to take care of it now. Get them started on the prep. I'll send Hassan and Niamh tomorrow; if we find comms cables as we expect, they'll do the sniffing so it won't be noticed."

Probably.

Centenal 3829471, a segment of the city of Guelph, is not at all Free2B's target demographic. Not that Amran has ever been to Free2B, although she harbors hopes that Mishima will invite her to the Saigon centenal some day. But in the meantime, she has done a lot of research on them, and this is definitely not a centenal they are likely to win. Guelph has a university, but it's not in this centenal, and most of the students live on campus or nearby. This centenal is older, whiter, and staider, and seems unlikely to be swayed by policies like subsidized diverse food trucks and holistic herbal health care strategies.

Amran wonders what premise the false-flag ads could have here. None have appeared yet, both encouraging and a little worrying: what if this is all some misunderstanding? She spends some time wandering around town to orient herself, although only after she has set up tracking on Dualeh and a facial recognition program to run Langer's image against other identities. That will take a while, even though she told it to start with known Anarchy associates.

In the meantime, she explores the bare-branched residential blocks and occasional tacky shopping street. There's not a lot of colorful design or informal economic activity or other interesting things to look at, so while trying to understand the layout (in case she has to flee on foot), she lets herself concentrate on election ads. Liberty doesn't seem confident that they've got this centenal locked up, and the streets are blanketed with pop-ups in the brazenly cheery comic-book style they've adopted for this election cycle. Based on ads, the main contenders seem to be local or regional: O!Canada!, a retrograde government trading, like so many do, on nostalgia; and, less prominently, AgFutures, which targets farmers but also attracts agricultural scientists and people who believe themselves "culturally farmers".

Tired and not particularly enlightened, Amran stops for some coffee (bland) and donuts (overwhelmingly good). She is tempted to go stake out Langer's hotel, but that seems like the sort of thing she should be trained for first, so she decides to start with Dualeh.

W e go in tomorrow," Roz says. "They're sending a couple of people to help analyze the pipe."

She had thought Djukic would be pleased, but the engineer is frowning. "You discussed this over Information?"

"We're using one-time codes for encryption," Roz says. "Not perfect, but it should do. Look, the sooner we get this done, the sooner you can go back to your job."

Again, Djukic doesn't look as happy about that as Roz expected. Consulting as an environmental engineer for a mantle tunnel can't be that much fun. Still, she quickly organizes the two workers to start digging the person-sized access tunnel, promising to take a turn herself when she gets back from dinner. Fortunately, with the tunnel so much closer to the surface than they expected, it won't take long, and the excavation detritus will be manageable.

"We should reach the tunnel tomorrow, early afternoon if we take our time."

"Perfect. The techies should be here by then." Roz sops

up the last of the juice on her plate with sorghum bread. Djukic insisted on a moderately long walk to find a pub for dinner—"Nothing by this ridiculous fake-sports complex is going to be any good," she proclaimed with expressive handwaving—and Roz has to admit her rabbit stew was excellent.

Djukic shrugs. "Whatever you say, boss." She taps in an order for schnapps. "Want something to drink?

"Oh—thanks, but I'm not drinking." Roz pats her belly.

Djukic's eyes widen. "You don't have an alcohol neutralizer?"

"I do," Roz says. "But in that case, what's the point?" She doesn't trust those things to keep her baby safe, but she doesn't want to sound like the paranoid luddite she probably is.

"Suit yourself," Djukic says, taking a shot, and then asks belatedly, "It doesn't bother you if I do, does it?"

"Not at all," Roz says. In fact, she finds it entertaining to watch how matter-of-factly Djukic goes about getting herself drunk. Probably a requirement for surviving as an environmental engineer in this age of environmental destruction. Especially if you're willing to work on things like the mantle tunnel.

"Why *are* you working on the mantle tunnel?" Roz asks some time later. Even just drinking herbal tea, she's feeling more relaxed, and nothing should offend Djukic after the quantity of schnapps she's ingested.

Indeed, Djukic shrugs without ire. "If I don't do it, who are they going to hire?" It seems like a rhetorical question, but she pauses for a moment as though waiting for Roz to answer. Just as Roz is getting ready to say something, she goes on. "They'll hire someone who doesn't care as much as I do, that's who. Someone who'll set up some pretty, very pretty, very fragile straw people"—she shapes them in the air—"very pretty, very convenient environmental concerns that will be very easy to fix, and then they will tell them how to fix them, probably with a product they sell." Djukic is drifting now, gestures getting wider as she follows her tangent. "Yes, maybe they'll sell it like greenwashing, but often, they find a way to ask someone to pay them for using the extra land or material or whatever to make it supposedly safer, and then—"

She pauses for a sip, and Roz dives into the breach. "It must be frustrating, though. Do they listen to you?"

Djukic expels her breath in a well-marinated laugh. "They listen to me exactly as much as they have to," she says, tilting her glass and rolling it around on its edge until Roz taps in an order for another shot. "Actually"—Djukic perks up after the first sip—"that's the fun part."

"Oh?" Roz asks, taking a sip of her cooling tea in solidarity.

"Yeah, figuring out how to make it seem like they have to listen this time. You know"—leaning in conspiratorially—"finding the combination of legit danger, potential expense, and public relations damage that will make them shell out more cash." She cackles. "I know *you* get it, Roz!"

Roz feels the sudden warmth of unexpected inclusion along with the slight unease she always gets when she wonders whether someone has figured out where she's from and what that means. It's silly, because the data is not only public but obvious to anyone who looks at where she's from. The name Mwanza has ceased to be a place for most people and become a shorthand for environmental disaster. But she has obscured it by using the old village word for her now-underwater neighborhood, and so few people bother look it up that it feels like a close-kept secret. "I understand why you do it," she says at last. Her voice sounds formal and restrained compared to Djukic's loose warmth. "But how do you manage it without"—*without feeling incredibly sad? without triggering major depression?*—"without giving up?"

Djukic drinks. "I'm afraid of what will happen—to me, to my children, to their children if they choose to have any, to everyone—if I give up."

"That's . . . a lot," Roz says. She has just figured out why she is so interested: she is imagining an alternate career, a different mission for herself, if she had chosen the Earth instead of data, nature instead of government, engineering instead of analysis. "How can you live that way?"

"You're right. You're right, of course. It is very hard. All I can do is hope that somehow, by doing this, I make things a little less bad. Even if it's just a little. And"—she cheers suddenly—"I know my friends are doing the same! There are many of us." She claps Roz on the shoulder. "I'll introduce you!"

A mran's cover story about developing content for a diaspora love story is, as per best practices, based on truth. There is a sizable Somali-descent community in Guelph, although not in the Liberty centenal. Some come direct from the horn, primarily out of Baidoa, and there are also a substantial number of second-order immigrants who moved from Dearborn decades ago, when the United States collapsed. Dalmar Dualeh, who falls into the latter group, attends the largest mosque in the centenal, and Amran turns her steps there with hope and wariness. This is the superpower she gains for being part of a small, proud, and poorly understood community: an intel source she can tap that Mishima and the other super spies cannot. But being among Somalis makes her feel more nervous about her cover identity: surely, someone there will have an aunty or a friend or a former colleague who will be able to disprove it? She takes comfort in the fact that few of them are from Nairobi, as both she and her cover identity are, and eventually relaxes into the familiarity of the language heard without auto-interpretation, the ritual, and, after prayer, the food.

At the restaurant that many of the young people adjourn to after prayer, she manages to seat herself next to her target. She doesn't have to do much; he introduces himself, with charm, as Dalmar, and chats her up about the content factory ("Somallywood, huh?") and Nairobi before turning the conversation to him. As she already knew from Information, he's an algorithmic logistician for a new regional transport start-up. "So, if you decide you want to go to Niagara or Toronto during your visit, just let me know," he says with a wink, passing her his data via line-of-sight.

"Oh, thanks," Amran says. This seems too easy. Disoriented by his interest, she doesn't mean to sound unimpressed, but it must come across that way, because he goes on with a smile.

"That's just my day job, though." He leans forward, smile getting bigger. "Mostly, I'm a spy."

"A . . . spy?" Amran asks, wondering if this is some kind of trap.

Dalmar leans back, pleased with himself. "Not a government spy, of course. Just someone who collects intel and passes it along."

Amran is catching up with herself and is able to creditably play naïve. "To Information, you mean?"

He laughs, perfect white teeth gleaming before his mouth falls back into the default friendly smile. "Not exactly." He leans forward. "You can keep a secret, right?"

He *can't* be serious. "Sure," Amran says, offering a smile of her own. "Try me."

"There are other data channels besides Information. I work for one of them."

Amran laughs, because she doesn't know what else to do. "You mean a compiler?"

"No, no." Dalmar is whispering now. "There are these new channels. Most people don't know about them yet, but they're going to blow up soon. But they need intel that isn't already available on Information; that's why my spying is important."

Amran keeps playing disbelief. "What new channels? You're making this up!"

"No, they're real, like—like the tour guides; have you seen those?"

Amran shakes her head.

"I can show you," he says, voice still low. "But not here."

Wary, Amran laughs again as though she's still not taking it seriously. "If it's such a big secret, why did you tell me? You don't even know me."

Dalmar leans back, confident and suave. "Everyone will know soon enough. But I don't want these guys to get the same idea and start cutting into my profits. Getting in early is how you get the advantage! Which reminds me." He winks. "You're from Nairobi, right? I know they're looking for people all over the world. And if you join, I can get a bonus."

Ah.

"You could do the same," Dalmar adds quickly. "Once you're in, I mean."

Amran's still not convinced this is more than an elaborate pickup line, but knowing what's in it for him makes it more plausible. She decides Idil, a sophisticated content designer, would be skeptical too. "So . . . you're telling me you work an exciting, attractive, clandestine job, and you have no evidence of its existence?" She smiles indulgently.

Dalmar laughs self-consciously. "I can show you, but not here." Amran raises an eyebrow and he holds out upturned palms. "We can't let it show up on Information, right? Not until we're ready to launch."

Launch? "How does the intel get to anyone, then?"

"There are ways," Dalmar says, relaxing back into his seat. "For example, sometimes they use paper."

Amran is skeptical. "That can't possibly reach very many people. Or travel far. Is this a local operation?"

"It's *very* local," Dalmar says, proudly. "But globally connected as well. You know, like a government."

Amran doesn't know.

"You don't have to join with us," Dalmar says, worried again. "But you should be careful. I know content designers are going to be in high demand, and there are other groups that might try to recruit you . . ."

An alert makes Amran miss his next few sentences: one of her searches has returned a success. It's Langer's facial recognition, but not from the hotel, and not from Anarchy. Langer's face belongs to Gowri Misra, a former low-level Information analyst at the Delhi Hub who disappeared two and a half years ago.

Amran stares at the two images, too startled even to pretend she's staring at Dalmar instead, although hopefully that's what it looks like. There are differences between the faces, as one would imagine after more than two years of hard living in a null state, but it is the same woman, or her twin. Exformation! Energy shoots through Amran, and suddenly she has to move.

"Let's go for that walk after all," she tells Dalmar, pulling up a map at eye level to direct her toward Misra/Langer's hotel.

"Sure!" he says, and chatters on amiably as they go. He occasionally tries to suggest a different turn, but Amran's determined stride brooks no dissent. She catches shreds of his conversation (". . . see, it's all in how you look at things . . ." ". . . people don't *like* Information . . ." ". . . amazing opportunity . . .") but she's preoccupied. The mythic status of the rogue Information staff has grown every day that they have evaded capture. Public conversation might have been muted by the usual misdirection and downplaying, but in the corridors of the Information Hubs, people still whisper rumors about where they went, what they are planning, why they took such a desperate step. Amran is sure she's not the only staffer who has fantasized about finding one of the elusive criminals and bringing them to justice, or (better) single-handedly tricking valuable intel out of them. She thought she had correctly identified that as an impossible daydream and not something that might happen in real life.

The route to the hotel skirts the Liberty centenal, and almost as soon as they step across the border, one of the myriad pop-up ads littering her view jumps out at her, flower-child lettering in a glittery gold font: *Vote Free2B, and be yourself during your golden years!*

Amran stops cold, staring at it. Dalmar, who has taken another few steps, realizes she's fallen behind and turns back. "What is it?"

"This ad," Amran manages. "It's odd. Do you see it?"

Dalmar does a double-take. "Free2B," he says slowly, and then shakes his head. "Never heard of them." He adds brightly, "Do you know anything about them?"

"No, not about the government," Amran lies. "But look at the ad. It's targeting old people. We shouldn't even be seeing it."

Dalmar looks at her with admiration. "See? You're so observant. You'll be perfect for this job."

"I have a job," Amran says automatically.

"So do I," says Dalmar. "I spy in my free time. You interested? The pay is good."

There is only one answer that Amran, aspiring covert agent, can give. "That sounds amazing. If it's true," she adds, with what she hopes is a mildly flirtatious twinkle. "Can we talk about it more tomorrow? I've got a work call to get to."

After four hours of steady work, Maryam has a general understanding of the way the Independentista data and communications systems are set up. She doesn't see any obvious way for them to transmit outside of the trade-agreement pipeline, but then it wouldn't be obvious, would it? Going any further will mean crossing a line: she hasn't hacked into anything yet per se, and she decides to take a break before she does. She's supposed to be a tourist; she had better act like one for a while instead of sitting shut up in her room. If she can find one of these mysterious repositories of data, she should be able to trace it from that end. Knowing what she's looking for will make the hacking part easier. Besides, the room is starting to give her a queasy feeling that makes her want to scope out escape routes.

It's only five short, square blocks to the border with

OaxacaLibreYSoberana, which would be more comforting if Maryam could imagine outrunning anyone who came banging on her hotel room door. She dawdles on the border, scanning for illicit feeds, but finds nothing. No children handing out paper cards on the corner, either. She gives herself a few more minutes to tap into Information and make sure there have been no urgent messages or world-shaking events. Blinking away the interface, she realizes that she has been standing alone on a street corner, staring at nothing while people walk past. Anyone watching her would know she was logging on and be able to guess that she is getting her fix and therefore staying in Independentistas territory. Feeling exposed, she turns back into the Territorio de la Justicia. Surely, lots of tourists feel compelled to check in with Information even while they're on vacation from it? Indeed, as she strolls back, she notices a few cafés on that block with prominent SE CONECTA AQUÍ signs in their windows and increasingly impressive antennas on their roofs.

As she strolls through the city, casually aiming herself at the closest point of the NuevoPRI border, Maryam sees more evidence of the tourist economy. There are restaurants offering canela panqueques and mole lattes dusted with açaí, art galleries featuring impressionistic paintings of Oaxacan streets and market scenes. She finds a stall selling broadcloth headbands with a capilliphelic coating that makes it easy to capture hair under them. Remembering the bright outfits at the sanitorium in Dhaka, she buys one with rainbow stripes as an alternative to her usual black headscarves. Then Maryam sits down at one of the outdoor tables of a café and has a tamal con rajas y chapulines and a tejate while she wonders how she's going to find any ex-Information staffers that might be hanging around.

What would they be doing if they were here? Hiding out, she supposes. Studying the local intel infrastructure, like she is. Maybe making forays into Information infrastructure, which would mean hanging out along the border, maybe in some of those cafés she saw, or renting a room close enough and buying an antenna. Since she has no idea how to distinguish them from tourists and Information-hungry locals, she goes back to the hotel and gets to work.

After another few hours of excavation on the local processes, Maryam takes a quick evening stroll to find some dinner. Taking a recommendation from a tourist compilation she downloaded before she came, she finds a gorgeous flor de calabaza soup in a cute basement restaurant two blocks away. Lingering over her espresso after dinner, she worries about how predictable it is to go to the border and stare into Information every time she leaves the hotel. It would be even more suspicious to pretend she doesn't care about messages, social capital funds, plaza conversations, and news, though.

It's comforting how familiar the walk to the border feels already. In the warmth of early evening, Maryam can see individuals, couples, and small groups leaning against walls and standing under streetlights, their eyes flickering with content or updates. It's an eerie cross between streetwalking and drug addiction, and Maryam does a quick download and starts reading as she walks back to the hotel. There's a sweet but brief message from Núria, and something bland and unimportant from Nejime that Maryam interprets as a request to check in, so she doubles back to send an equally anodyne answer. By the time she gets back to her hotel, she feels exhausted, even though it's at least three hours before her usual bedtime.

The climate control on the bed is antiquated and there's a small sign on the wall asking guests to refrain from using it unless absolutely necessary because of limited electrical power. Maryam is tempted to sleep with the window open for the cool courtyard air but feels too nervous. Even after she's tucked in and sweltering, she finds herself glaring anxiously at the door, wondering if shadowy ex-Information workers have been tracking her searches and are coming for her in the night.

CHAPTER 11

Maryam wakes refreshed, if sweaty. In the light of morning, her fears seem silly. She gets a breakfast of chapulines rancheros in the hotel dining room and goes back into the work eagerly: it is fascinating to look at such a stripped-down system. She is building a model of the nodal connections as she goes; it looks something like a small airport, with a few crisscrossing runways and smaller tracks for baggage vehicles. She can imagine a similar model of even a tiny corner of Information—say, her centenal in La Habana—looking like a star map.

One difference that leaps out at her is the bottleneck where this system connects to the outside world: there is a single, though robust, channel to Information. It is not controlled by a censor, human or algorithmic: Information only sends across what the Independentistas pay for. And yet they still channel everything through the government before distributing it; people can see the Information data only through the government portal. Maryam spends some time in that channel checking to see if additional data is being sent clandestinely, and also observes the slimmer return channel, over which the Independentistas send back their local news program and demographic data as agreed. For kicks, Maryam takes a look at the local news program. She sometimes streams local compilers in La Habana to learn more about her new city and keep up with crime, weather, and restaurant openings; compared to those, the Independentista programming is painfully amateurish. She wonders how many people watch it, but no numbers are available, and she doesn't want to waste her hacking time on it. Instead, she starts looking for other gateways into the system.

All the thinking about crossing points has reminded her of the border that Núria spent ten days patrolling, and when she's ready for a break she decides to go check it out. Maybe she can find some hint of the clandestine channels there. Maryam considers calling the taxista to take her there, but after looking at a map—available through a projection port in her room—she decides it's close enough to walk.

Following the border along its length reminds her of the story she told the camaradas. The technology here is totally different: instead of poured concrete and metal, the wall involves a close grid of feeds, nanosensors, and simulated electric-shock transmitters. It could be almost transparent, but Liberty has papered it over with patriotic projections. That's probably a temporary solution until they can fit something more solid into the budget, but it makes the point: this isn't only about preventing people from crossing over easily, it's also about erasing the idea of an independent government from the experience of Liberty citizens. She shakes her head over the hysteria about a non-hostile foreign government and daydreams about Núria patrolling the other side of that border in uniform, which is why she doesn't notice the man loping alongside her until he says something.

"Heeyy." The man is dapper in a lavender guayabera open nearly to his navel, with a rangy swagger and hair in two-millimeter twists. "Look at you."

Maryam sends him a death glare, and he holds up his hands. "Not verbally assaulting you, I swear. I'm just saying, we don't see many Information staff around here."

The death glare gains laser focus, but he laughs. "Come on! You think you don't stand out?"

"I'm on vacation," Maryam spits, and immediately regrets engaging.

"Sure you are," he agrees amiably. "So am I. So refreshing to get out of Information territory for a time and still have access to almost all the amenities of home."

Maryam peers at him, not sure whether he's being serious or sarcastic. "So, you're not from around here?"

"Not in the least! But I keep it on my list for when I get kicked out of micro-democratic territory for good."

"And why would that happen?"

"I'm a bad influence. But I'm not sure yet whether I could stand to live here permanently. It's a bit provincial for my taste, and these Independejos take themselves so seriously."

"Seems easy enough to cross over into OLYS or Nuevo-PRI," Maryam offers, falling into the rhythm of his banter.

"For now," he says, darkly, and then offers his hand. "Domaine."

Maryam disdains it. "Why did you approach me?"

"I told you. You obviously work for Information, and we don't get many of those. Except for that famous one a while back."

The memory hits Maryam in the guts, and she can't believe she forgot about it: Valérie took a hyper-publicized holiday trip to Independentista territory right after her breakup with Vera Kubugli. The compilers were all over it: vid of her in a stringkini by the pool, walking down the picturesque streets, sipping coffee under a straw hat with augmented eye shading. Even the memory stings. Maryam, in the early stages of her relationship with Núria, was trying to ignore the breakup as much as possible, but the images were everywhere. To make matters worse, Nejime was silently furious that Nougaz was providing so much publicity to a non-micro-democratic vacation spot. It was part of the impetus that finally overcame her inertia and got her to move from Doha.

Maryam glances over at Domaine, but he doesn't seem to have noticed her discomfiture. "And because I'm such a bad influence," he's saying, "I can't exactly call Information to complain."

"Complain about what?"

"Hierarchy, monopoly, poverty, democracy as distraction, the cost of elections, the advantage of large governments, that appalling show trial in New York—should I go on?"

"You want me to listen to you complain about the things Information is actively working to improve and still does better than anyone else?" Maryam asks, letting her boredom into her voice. What *is* it with the weirdos picking her out of the crowd lately?

"Isn't it nice to hear from someone who doesn't hang out in the Information fandom?"

"Oh, right. We *never* hear from anti-Information people, since they're so restrained and nonconfrontational. Why do you think my public Information is muted?"

"Because nobody uses that shit here, and you're undercover anyway?"

Maryam forces a laugh. "Information staff can't take vacations?" A glint from a nearby wall catches her eye, and she turns her head to look.

"You like it?" Domaine asks. "My work. The design, that is; I'm not an artist."

It looks like sprayed-on, analog graffiti but sparkles like sequins under a disco ball. Maryam is almost sure it's a projection, if a beautifully crafted one.

"IntelliGeneration?" she reads, finally deciphering the script. "What is that, some kind of reproductive assistance service?"

Domaine laughs easily. "You'll find out; don't worry." And just like that he turns away and walks off.

Maryam stares after him, wondering if she offended him, and then shakes herself. She doesn't care if he's offended.

"Oh, by the way," Domaine says, turning back and tossing her a bit of line-of-sight data. "Here's a great place to get tlayudas. Not in the guidebooks, or at least not in the ones on Information. Local knowledge is still worth something." And he winks before turning again and disappearing into the crowd.

Uneasy, Maryam turns back to her hotel. She triggers a script she wrote years ago to detect people following her—developed for creepy male stalkers rather than political spies—before remembering that it won't work without feeds. She's disturbed enough to duck into a café and drink some chocolate with a view of the street. She doesn't see Domaine—can that be his real name?—again, and she decides it's safe to return to the hotel. She has work to do.

Maybe because now she's looking for it, she notices another two IntelliGeneration signs on her way back. She sets up a search on the neologism to run as soon as she has Information access again. And another on Domaine, in case that slightly odd name turns anything up.

. . .

Djukic's team of workers are chuting the dirt directly into a compressor, which packs it into more easily stored bricks, and stacking the bricks in the basement rooms. It's moving quickly, but not quickly enough for Roz. She is exhausted from the night before and a little annoyed that Djukic doesn't even have a hangover.

"Any guesses?" Roz doesn't really care about guesses, but she's not drinking coffee, and she needs some kind of conversation to stay awake.

"Guesses?"

"What we'll find."

"Not my department," Djukic says.

Roz turns away, suddenly annoyed by Djukic's go-to answer.

"But based on the engineering specs, as far as we know them . . ." Either sensing her annoyance or interested in the question, Djukic decides to speculate. "Comms are a safe bet, but you're right; from the size, it's something more. Yes, probably human transport, but I think not regular. It wouldn't be very comfortable. Maybe an escape hatch."

Not a bad guess. Roz tries to remember Pressman's arrest, and when she's still not sure, she replays the footage. Halliday was careful not to give Pressman any notice, so maybe he did have an escape route that he never got to use. It would be an interesting historical footnote, but as Nejime pointed out yesterday, and again in an irate message this morning, the real issue is whether the tunnel is still in use. Roz can feel herself getting twitchy again. She wishes the election were over already. She sits down, rubbing her belly. More bricks clunk out of the compressor.

"Where do you live?" Roz asks, again trying to stave off boredom and nerves. She had a pre-conception vision of herself as the serene and graceful pregnant woman, but instead she spends most of the time feeling sweaty and off-balance.

"EuropeanUnion," Djukic answers, kicking a clod of dirt. "One of the Belgrade centenals. And you?"

Roz shrugs. "I live in Doha. All the centenals there are AlThani, based on the local royalty."

"What's that like?" Djukic asks.

"It's okay," Roz says. "I live there for work, and they like having so many of us there bringing in business, so they make it convenient for the office and comfortable in terms of living. But . . ." She pauses, realizing she's getting personal, and then forges ahead. She was the one who asked first, after all. "After the baby comes, we're planning to move to my husband's centenal, part of the DarFur government, in a small city called Kas."

Roz can see the flashing against Djukic's eye as she looks it up. "Wow, it's in the middle of nowhere! What's *that* like?"

"It's . . ." Roz finds that she is smiling as she searches for a descriptive to convey the feeling of it. "You know, when I first went, I didn't like it at all, but I guess it's grown on me. It's quiet, people know each other, and yet there's this wildness too, because the desert is right there . . ." She shakes her head and changes the subject. "And EuropeanUnion? How is that?" She rarely asks people about their governments. She hates feeling like a pollster. Besides, she has so many data-driven opinions on all the major governments that it seems disingenuous to ask citizens what they think.

"Oh, you know," Djukic says. "It's okay. They have some odd old ideas, but they're pretty good about protecting the environment, people's rights . . . I would have liked

SavePlanet, but there was no chance of them winning a centenal in Belgrade, and EuropeanUnion is a decent compromise. Pretty good schools for the kids. Our head of state is a genderqueer sociologist, which says something about the electorate. And no smoking—there's a PhilipMorris centenal adjoining us and the fug is—" She scrunches her nose and waves her hand expressively.

"Is it looking pretty safe in the election?" Roz asks, pulling up the data as she does.

"Probably," Djukic says, but her tone is uncertain, and Roz sees what she means: EuropeanUnion has a lead but not what she would call a safe one. PhilipMorris is next, building off their neighboring constituency, and EasternPromise, a regional group somewhat smaller than EuropeanUnion, is in the mix.

Roz is about to ask whether Djukic plans to move if the smokers win when her belly stiffens to the ache point and she winces.

"You okay?"

"Sure," Roz says, rubbing and then standing up. "Just a practice contraction."

Djukic had sounded only mildly concerned, so Roz isn't surprised when she answers: "Oh, ugh, yes. I had lots of those with my second son."

"I get nervous about going into early labor." Roz glances at her wrist, where a bracelet over her vein is monitoring oxytocin levels: no spike.

"You are still a couple of months away, though, no?"

"Six weeks or so, but you never know. That's why they let me use the crow for these trips," Roz says. "I can start back immediately if I need to."

"Nice."

"I appreciate you not asking before," Roz says, trying to keep the rapport growing. "I got so sick of people asking when I was due that I thought about putting the date in my public Information in big pulsing letters."

Djukic guffaws. "Why didn't you?"

Roz shrugs. "It seemed unprofessional." She remembers Rasmussen using her public Information to emphasize her vegetarianism; maybe that's how you get to be a head of state, by not caring. "Also, that would make it even more public. The ideal is less to tell everyone than to have no one ask, because why do they need to know? Fortunately, my husband is . . . He tends to quell frivolous questions." Suleyman is neither large nor rude, but the command he exudes makes people think twice about idle chatter.

"Useful."

"It is. I wish he could teach me how he does it."

Djukic goes over to take a look at the progress on the dig, and wanders back.

"You don't have to answer if you don't want to, but are you going to use nanobots for the delivery?" Djukic asks.

Roz can't repress a wriggle of discomfort. "I . . . don't think so. I know everyone says they speed and smooth the process, but just the idea of them . . . down there . . . and then that they're on the baby when it's born . . ."

Djukic laughs. "Yes, I understand. I turned them down for my first one but used them for the second birth."

"Did it make a big difference?" Roz asks, not sure she wants to know.

"It did," Djukic answers. "But they say the second is easier anyway, so I'm not sure how much of it was the bots."

Roz knows that rates of nanobot usage in delivery, like other controversial pregnancy and birth technologies, correlate strongly with government of citizenship. The only stronger indicator is the government where the attending doctor or midwife did their training. She keeps her mouth shut; she doesn't want to suggest that Djukic's choices, already in the past, were influenced by politics or dodgy data.

Djukic, on the other hand, is happy to continue the conversation. "What about painkillers?"

Roz gets an update at eye level. "Hassan and Niamh just arrived," she reports, relieved not to have to answer. "And just in time, too." The hole is only a few feet short of the tunnel. "I'm going to go upstairs to meet them."

A mran doesn't find Langer, or Misra, at the hotel, though she spends the rest of the evening planted in the lobby coffee shop, with feeds from all around the entrance dotted across her vision. It's possible that Langer is in her room, huddled (Amran imagines) in front of a workstation filled with quickly written Free2B ad copy. Or maybe she's out late, scouting locations or gathering local knowledge, or maybe she found a way to sneak back in without being seen. Seeing the Free2B pop-up has unsettled Amran. It triggered something in her narrative disorder that has convinced her, despite all the efforts of her conscious mind, that Langer has already left the city. She spends quite a lot of time scanning through airport and train station feeds, even as the facial recognition programs run on them. Sometimes you need human eyes. But she finds nothing, neither in the automated scan nor in the tiny fraction she scrutinizes personally.

As she scans and lurks, Amran tinkers with a draft message to Mishima. She's sure she will be recalled from this assignment as soon as she alerts Mishima, either because it's dangerous (Exformation is at least as dangerous as Anarchy) or because they simply don't trust her, untrained as she is, with such a delicate assignment. Amran is tempted to wait longer, but she doesn't want to be the stupid expendable character in this story, getting killed or messing up the mission with her temerity. A little before midnight, she gives in and sends the coded message, then goes back to her hotel to get some rest.

The next morning Amran wakes up and checks the dropsite plaza to find, as expected, a message suggesting she take the first flight home. At least Mishima didn't think it was important enough to break protocol and buzz her. Taking courage from that, Amran replies to the effect that she has a few loose ends to tie up and will fly out late that night or the next day. She checks her feed notifications, but there is no sign Langer has been back to the hotel, and Amran concludes that she's gone. Then she goes to meet Dalmar for bagels.

Roz makes small talk with Niamh and Hassan, none of it involving birth, for twenty-two minutes before the compressor judders noticeably to a halt. "We're there?" Roz asks.

"Just about," Djukic says. "We have to slow down now; we don't want to hit the tunnel, in case they have motion sensors."

"They're going to feel something anyway when we break into it, right?"

"It depends how sensitive their security is," Niamh says. "We have ways to avoid detection."

"We were planning to use a nano-cutter on a low setting," Djukic says.

"That could work, but we have some modifications to help further," Hassan says, and throws up a projection, drawing Djukic into deep technical discussions. Roz wanders away to call Suleyman; this is going to take a while yet.

She's still talking—minute details of the ever-evolving pregnancy experience, the baby's movements, the food in Switzerland, what he's been doing in Doha—when a message from Djukic pops up: *We're at the casing.* Roz signs off and walks over to the hole.

They've set up a live projection from the bottom of the pit, where Hassan and one of Djukic's engineers—no, Roz decides, looking around, Djukic herself—are hovering in climbing harnesses. Hassan is documenting the smooth curve of the tunnel, and then Roz sees his hands as he sets up the nano-cutter. Djukic is holding the motion sensor, instructing Hassan on how to adjust the settings. Hassan cuts at an angle so the oval won't fall in once it's cut through. As he slides it off and Djukic cautiously swings her legs in, Roz has an uncharacteristic moment of wishing she was the one lowering herself into that dim hole, but comforts herself with the reality that at the moment she wouldn't fit through it.

"There's definitely room for a vehicle," Djukic says, her light playing on the narrow space. "Not much more than a two-seater, I'd guess, unless they . . . Hassan, you better get down here. That is a *lot* of comms cables."

Maryam debates whether to go to the tlayuda place Domaine suggested. She doesn't particularly want to meet him again, especially if he takes her presence as encouragement. But the vibe she got from him wasn't sexual, exactly, more cryptic and knowing. If she takes him at face value, he was clear that it was her job, not her appearance, that interested him. And his nod to tourist guides is intriguing. Still, she checks with the hotel staff before she leaves.

"Not . . . exactly a restaurant," the young man at the desk tells her. "It is very informal, you understand. Yes, they have food, but if you would prefer something with, perhaps, a roof, I can recommend an alternative."

Maryam lets him do so, mostly to create doubt about her location in case someone is trying to follow her, and then heads for the tlayuda place, which apparently doesn't even have a name. As she walks, it occurs to her that she's more worried about random gender-based violence than targeted violence based on her work. That's something she should probably reevaluate. The thought gives her chills but also an odd sort of satisfaction.

When she gets to the tlayuda—*alley,* she supposes is the right description—it is comfortingly normal: brightly lit by cheap fluoron curls hung across the entrance and along the adjoining walls, not to mention the flames from the fire pit; plenty of people sitting around the makeshift tables, and more in the short line that indicates where she should order; a tambora oaxaqueña version of "Hava Nagila" playing from someone's amplifier. Maryam has eaten some excellent meals since arriving in the Territorio de la Justicia, but the tlayudas, bubbly and blackened in patches and dripping with cheese and beans, are amazing. Maryam licks her fingers and almost orders a third, but the line has grown while she ate. Instead she sets out for the border to check in, comforting herself with the plan of a return for more tlayudas the following night.

Sated and satisfied, Maryam meditates on the way cheap

hole-in-the-wall food can reach a level of appeal that more polished preparations can't achieve as she meanders toward the closest border, the one with NuevoPRI. As she crosses, she is almost immediately bombarded with campaign pop-ups, reminding her of the advantages to being away from Information, at least during election season. This neighborhood is nothing like the cute touristy area she downloaded in yesterday: instead of little cafés with sunscreen umbrellas and pastel-and-tile two-story houses, there are blocky apartment buildings and no shops. As long as that means none of the junkie ambience of tourists sucking in their Information fix, Maryam is fine with it.

She walks down a long boulevard more or less parallel to the border while she blinks up Information. There is the now-expected meaningless message from Nejime, which she immediately answers with a single Yes so Nejime will know she's okay and available. Hopefully, she'll get back to her quickly if there's anything she wants to talk about. After that, Maryam dusts quickly through her work messages—not urgent, not urgent, annoying but not urgent—and is taking a quick look at headlines and polls when something in one of the pop-ups snags her attention. Maryam blinks away her interface. There, blinking faintly between a campaign ad for Liberty and a promo for the latest Hillbilly Hitman motion novel, shimmers the graceful script of the IntelliGeneration logo.

Maryam's fingers twitch toward it, but she hesitates midgesture. Was it a coincidence that Domaine approached her right before she saw the IntelliGeneration ad? He said he worked on it. She flips her view to check the metadata: the link leads to data situated in the Territorio de la Justicia, but not through the government channel—a completely separate system. Is this the non-Information stream Nejime was looking for? It's a diffuse network, making it difficult to track the exact physical location. Maryam leaves that for later.

She opens the link. The interface flows around her, tendrils of intricate design surrounding a range of infotainment options. Maryam's practiced eye assesses the graphics as substanceless, purely cosmetic, but beguiling nonetheless. She is reminded, uncomfortably, of her reaction to the Independentista portal: this is as far ahead of the Information standard as that interface was behind it. It's not *just* graphics, although it gives Maryam a disloyal feeling to admit it: there's a design element that makes the interface appealing to use. Still, anyone can manage something like that if they put enough effort into it. Not without a feeling of apprehension, she chooses a stream of content: series criticism.

She emerges with a sigh ten minutes later, looks around, and realizes she has walked three blocks while reading. The sctup was no more immersive than Information, but Maryam has always had a tendency to lose herself. Terrible security practice. She flashes quickly back through surrounding feeds to make sure no one followed her.

As for the content itself: not so different from Information, particularly some of the edgier news compilers and commentators. That's basically what it is, Maryam thinks, an audience-oriented news analysis compiler, except that the content isn't (she checks) mined from Information but bespoke. It's pretty good, too—there was an interpretation of *Crowbinders,* for example, that she thought was particularly astute—but it's clearly less professional than Information: a few glitches in the translation, minor editing errors. Maryam can't decide whether to feel contemptuous, threatened, or intrigued.

While reading Maryam was dimly aware of the pings and buzzes that indicate low-priority messages, search results, and updates. The IntelliGeneration search brought up a handful of hits on Information, but nothing that makes it clear what's going on: graffiti, unexplained pop-ups of the single neologism, its insertion in plaza discussions in a way that suggests a viral campaign not yet come to fruition. Their effort for name recognition is clear, but as far as she can tell no one has yet clarified what it is for. They are trying attract customers while evading Information scrutiny.

As of right now, they've failed. IntelliGeneration will have to be shut down. It might be tricky to control the source, since it's located in the Territorio de la Justicia. Maryam isn't sure what, if anything, their agreement with Information says about this situation. But there must be a way to cut off the transmission into micro-democratic territory.

Still thinking about that technical problem, Maryam opens a newly arrived message and stifles a jolt of dislocation: it's from Taskeen in Dhaka.

What is she doing, writing to me? Maryam had hoped that no one noticed their contact, that anyone who followed her movements closely enough would have lost her at the sanatorium, leaving her ultimate reason for visiting uncertain. At least the message is oblique.

Dear Maryam,

I hope all is well since our last correspondence. I wanted to let you know that I was able to find some data on your old teacher, even after all this time. Please get in touch so I can pass it on to you in person.

Yours in tech, Taskeen

What is Taskeen doing? Is this the early-twenty-first-century version of wink-wink-nudge-nudge? To Maryam it sounds like a screaming klaxon of clandestinidad. "Old teacher." She snorts and shakes her head, then frowns when she reaches the last line. "In person." Surely, she doesn't mean . . . Maryam rubs the nape of her neck. She opens a message to Nejime, closes it, opens it again, closes it again. If she flies to Dhaka, it will be as obvious as sending a message. She could try calling Taskeen on a secure channel—if she can even get one into the sanatorium—but the only clear thing in her message is that they have to meet in person.

Undecided, Maryam goes on to the last notification: the results of her search on Domaine. There is some ambiguity; apparently an M-rap star who goes by that moniker emerged a few years ago. But when Maryam reads the Information intranet results all the comfortable assurance of the last few hours melt away. He's a known agitator, suspected of violence, confirmed to have involvement with a range of militant anti-Information groups. How could she have been so naïve? That couldn't have been a chance meeting. *"You think you don't stand out?"* He must have known she was coming, followed her somehow. Which means he listened in on Nejime's calls.

Hands shaking, Maryam books a ticket on the next flight to Doha.

CHAPTER 12

Maryam has to wait nineteen minutes before she is ush-ered into Nejime's office. It's not surprising, since she made no appointment and is supposed to be on the other side of an ocean. Her only regret about it is that she doesn't get to observe Nejime's reaction when told she is here. Was it annoyance? Anger? Anticipation of some important develop-ment?

By the time she walks in, Nejime's mode is gently teasing. "Have you decided to come back to the Doha Hub, then?"

Maryam laughs along obediently, wondering if Nejime used the nineteen minutes to call Batún, or to update her-self on Maryam's movements. "I'm afraid not," she says, and projects Taskeen's message up between them.

Flutters of surprise and irritation cross Nejime's face as she reads: so, she wasn't scanning Maryam's recent comms. Maybe she *was* in a meeting. "What *is* this? Did you suggest she contact you in this way?"

"Of course not! It came out of nowhere."

"And so you got on a plane." Nejime no longer sounds angry, more resigned.

"A crow, actually," Maryam says, and then hopes it didn't sound flippant. Nejime doesn't seem to be paying attention, anyway.

"A little paranoid, no? We have no evidence they've been

able to break into protected communications. But perhaps it's warranted. It certainly seems to be going around—"

"It is. Warranted," Maryam puts in. "Either that, or someone got incredibly lucky." She tells Nejime about her encounter in the Territorio de la Justicia. When she mentions Domaine's name Nejime blinks up a file, courteously putting it at workspace rather than eye level. Maryam has seen most of it before, so she waits until Nejime has finished.

"Ah, yes, *that* one. I thought he sounded familiar. Made some trouble during the last election. Nothing too serious," she adds, eyeing Maryam, whose hands are shaking again.

"Still," Maryam says, a little defensive. "He knew who I was and that I would be there. He must have snooped our conversation."

"That or he saw your flight reservations and drew his own conclusions."

Maryam isn't sure that's less creepy. "He would still have to know who I am. Unless I really do look that much like an Information worker."

Nejime chuckles obligingly, then gets back to the point. "You could have drawn his attention any number of ways."

It's true; Maryam thinks of her searches about the tourist guides, and the shot about the tlayuda place not being on Information.

"I'm curious as to what he wanted," Nejime says, "but I don't think you were in any danger."

"There's more," Maryam says, trying not to sound defensive. IntelliGeneration doesn't have broadcasting capacity that will allow it to be accessed beyond the immediate vicinity of the Territorio de la Justicia, but she recorded her own brief dip in its data stream, and she projects it up for

Nejime. "You don't get the full experience this way," she explains, pointing out how the interface works, "but this gives you a taste of it. This is, I think, what you heard about?"

Nejime pages through the recording. Her face looks tighter and colder than usual.

"It's not so bad," Maryam says, and then wishes she hadn't: downplaying this doesn't do anyone any favors.

"It's the most daring example of data peddling I've seen. They put a lot of resources into this interface for an illegal activity that could be shut down at any point. Although we can't easily stop them while they're in Independentista territory." Nejime frowns. "Is the data stolen?"

"I don't think so," Maryam says. "It doesn't fit the parameters of any of data we've identified as missing. But it's hard to be sure. It's certainly not on Information anywhere."

"Hopefully we can block the transmissions, and quickly. They do seem to be coming at us from all sides." Before Maryam can ask what Nejime means, she brushes her hands together, moving on. "Well. We just have to get through the election. Go on to Dhaka. Find out what Khan wants. Oh, and while you're at it, keep an eye out for the person who tried to give you the guide, maybe even ask around discreetly."

"That message could be a trap." Maryam hopes she sounds cautious rather than shaken.

"Of course it could be," Nejime says dismissively. "But if they're already reading your communications and following your movements, why bother with such a ridiculous message? Why not simply approach you in La Habana? No, I suspect this one is all Khan interacting awkwardly with the modern world." She taps her fingers in quick annoyance, and Maryam wonders if she is reconsidering her interest in time-capsule therapy. "Taskeen was one of the great minds, probably still is. She may have something useful for you. And we owe her the benefit of the doubt, even if she is long retired. But—" Index finger raised, Nejime preempts any opportunity for Maryam to ask about why Taskeen is owed and whether she can be trusted. "I am going to arrange for some training—for *both* of you—on clandestine operations."

Maryam is both flustered and flattered. "Spycraft? That's not really my area."

"Isn't it?" Nejime asks with asperity. "You use tech to find things; don't tell me you've never thought about using it to hide them? And we're not going to make you a spy; it's election season, and much as we need additional observers right now, it is no time to be training new ones. You're going to learn some best practices so that you can cultivate this informant in a safe and professional way. And after all this is over, you need to think about taking on more of a leadership role; spycraft is pretty much a requirement for navigating at a higher level."

"Leadership role?" Maryam asks faintly.

"Of course," Nejime says, as though it should be obvious, as though they had talked about it before. "The reorganization—assuming we survive long enough to achieve it—is going to lead to all sorts of new opportunities, and you are in an excellent position to take advantage of them."

Maryam swallows *I don't want to take advantage of them* and *What would I do in a leadership role?* and nods along as Nejime continues. "You have the technical know-how, you understand the wider goals of Information, you have useful extra-Information contacts"—meaning Núria, Maryam supposes—"and whether you like it or not, you possess the bedrock of leadership skills."

"I don't even know what that means," Maryam answers.

"We can talk about it later," Nejime says. "For now, focus on figuring out what's going on with Taskeen Khan and learning all you can about these opportunistic datastreams."

Maryam was hoping to hang out with Roz while she was in Doha, but her friend is out of town—in Zurich, of all places—and cagey about what she's doing. Maryam hopes it's just the paranoia Nejime said was going around. Roz tells her she should get in touch with Suleyman and stay at their apartment anyway, but Maryam begs off, explaining that she needs a quiet night. She ends up in the one of the three hotels Information recommends to visiting staff. Built by a Japanese firm angling for business travelers in the middle of the century, it combines the compact, careful aesthetic of an Osakan business hotel with nods to the luxury expected in the Gulf states at the time. Maryam takes a stroll along Al Meena, noting which of the shops she knew have disappeared to be replaced by new ones, and eats a lonely meal at her favorite restaurant, Medeterranée, before returning to the hotel to snuggle into the climate-controlled futon and wish she were home. She tries her usual balm of watching some content, but everything has been taken over by the election, so she ends up examining the polls instead.

Maryam is not a big politics geek—she wouldn't go so far as to say all governments are the same, but they do fall into a narrow range between *horrible* and *less horrible*—but at this stage, the campaign is pleasantly distracting. She looks at the numbers on her centenal in La Habana first. So far, 888 is still in the lead, but HerenciaHatuey and, of all governments, Liberty are in close pursuit.

HerenciaHatuey might be interesting; she generally

expects nationalist governments' focus on ideals and/or unscientific notions of group boundaries distract them from governance, but she's also found that they're more idiosyncratic, often finding quirks or tweaks to the citizen experience that the larger governments rarely think of. As their name suggests, their ideology is somewhat militant, but they've never expressed any expansionist tendencies and instead focus on emphatic minority and environmental rights programs and proactive solidarity linkages with other small governments that have similar agendas.

Liberty, on the other hand, lost all her sympathy during the last election. Maryam still remembers Roz's friend Ken's face after he got beaten up in a Liberty centenal during the blackout. Maryam also spent the better part of six months unsnarling the changes that Liberty made to localized Information disbursement code allowing them to show one reality to their citizens while everyone else saw a different one. Their logo alone is enough to give her a sensory flashback to those months: gritty eyes, growing horror that eventually shifted to dull irritation, the frustration of picking through someone else's drastic, uncommented, inelegant hack, and the smell of myrrh in the scent profile of the colleague stationed next to her. She shudders. It is beyond her how anyone can vote for those people, and Maryam spends a few moments considering whether she would be willing to leave her comfortable apartment and pleasant neighborhood just so she wouldn't have to live in a Liberty centenal. She comes to the conclusion that yes, she would, but of course it depends on Núria, too. They've never talked about that hypothetical.

Maryam was not particularly excited about moving to an 888 centenal when they were looking for an apartment, but she has to admit she's liked it more than she expected. That reminds her to look at the Supermajority stats. She knows most of the people she works with are rooting for Policy1st on principle (or pretending to root for them out of peer pressure), but she's never understood the appeal. Evidence-based policy is great, but she's not convinced by Policy1st's analytics. There's something a little too planned-economy about their work. She also deducts points for smugness. So, she's not unhappy to see 888 polling ahead by a little over a thousand centenals, even if it's too early for it to mean anything. The first debate tomorrow should define the situation better.

You . . . agreed to what, now?"
Amran wasn't confident enough of her protocol to be sure when she should contact Mishima directly, especially since she now has a new spying gig that Mishima doesn't know about, so she waited until Mishima called her. As she should have expected, this does not improve Mishima's mood.

"I was offered a job? And I thought it could be useful, or at least . . . possibly I might learn something interesting . . . because after all, the offer came from the subject of the investigation." Amran pauses, but Mishima says nothing. Maybe she hasn't figured out what to say yet? Amran hurries on before the silence can lengthen. "So I'll be sort of . . . spying, I guess you could say—that's what they said to me, anyway—for them, but really I'll be spying for you."

"Start at the beginning." There's a resignation to Mishima's tone, but Amran is careful not to draw too much hope from that. She's back in her flat in Nairobi, which is definitely

not the living space of a cool, up-and-coming content designer, and other than identifying Gowri Misra—which
should, she thinks, count for something—the only thing she
has to show for her few days in Guelph is a place and a time
for a job interview, five days hence.

"Why was this guy so eager for you to get the job?"
Mishima asks. She sounds distracted.

"He gets a commission. Or something like that. For recruiting me." Dalmar coached Amran on how to act during her interview: play it cool; don't act like spying is a big
deal; don't try to know everything about the local neighborhood, because they'll ask at least one trick question about an
invented bit of trivia; be honest about how much time you
can work. "They're supposed to show me an example of
how they compile intel during the meeting."

"It's good work," Mishima says, her eyes coming back
into focus on Amran, who is already listening for the *but*. "I
just want to make sure you're safe." A pause. "We'll have to
extend your identity into Nairobi; they'll probably track you."

"Maybe not, if they're trying to avoid Information?"

"Let's assume they will," Mishima says, gathering brisk-
ness as she goes. "So, you'll need to go to your job."

"At Puntland Studios?" Amran asks, startled. "You can—I
can—I'll be going there?"

"Of course," Mishima snorts. "They were already on
board to back up your story; they'll be happy to take you on
for a couple of weeks. I hope you were paying attention
to diaspora culture, because they really are developing that
series."

"That's . . . They . . . It's really fine for me to pretend to
work there?"

"Are you kidding? Content studios love this sort of thing,

even when they can't tell anyone about it. Maybe especially when they can't tell anyone about it. It appeals to their sense of the dramatic."

"What's happening with the other thing?" Amran was trying to curb her curiosity, but she can't resist.

"What other thing?"

"That former Information staffer."

"Oh, Misra." Mishima sighs, and Amran wonders if she knew her, had worked with her. "We suspect she left in a private crow, the day you arrived."

Amran freezes. "Did she . . . Did they know?"

"Maybe, maybe not. It could be she finished her mission. You said an ad went up, right? There may have been no reason for her to stay longer."

"Where did she go?" Amran asks, starting to recover from the idea of being made before she even started her work.

"We lost the crow over northern Europe."

"Russia."

"Maybe," Mishima says, repressively, then sighs in admission. Of course it's Russia; they already know significant numbers of ex-Information staffers are exiled there. "In any case, this intel you brought us, that they're behind the false ads instead of Anarchy, puts a whole new spin on things." Mishima waits, but Amran is still elated that she brought them worthwhile intel and has no interpretation to offer. "Anarchy seeks disruption for disruption's sake. They have an anti-Information agenda but no plan for what to do instead. But these former Information staffers . . . they want something."

"Revenge?"

Mishima's mouth twists: Amran has worked for Information for only five years, and already she imagines vengeance as the first motive of her ex-colleagues. "I was thinking of a power grab, but you may be right."

In the interests of finding the man with the tourist guide, Maryam stays at the same hotel in Dhaka, but when she arrives in the restaurant for dinner, the tout isn't there. There are two couples sitting at tables, speaking Bengali and Sinhalese, according to her auto-interpreter, and a couple of men sitting separately at the bar, one apparently local and one who speaks to the waiter in Nepali. She hesitates at the corner to see if any of them offer her a tourist guide, but though the local glances at her while chewing, neither of them shows any sign of getting up. She decides to go out for dinner.

On her way down to the lobby, Maryam starts searching for restaurants. Her usual approach is to filter by distance and average review (and price, when she isn't traveling for work), but she remembers what that tout said to her about finding the best—what was it, chotpoti?—through his guide. It occurs to her that she could try compiled tourist guides instead. She's never really understood the point of those things: why take the time to read some fancy writing paired with artificially lit, unrealistically beautiful photos when all the relevant intel is so easily available? But if she's going to look for illicit tourist guides, she should try to understand the appeal.

Maryam sits down on one of the extruded chairs in the lobby to read up, opening feeds to the three most popular tourist guides for this neighborhood of Dhaka and browsing on a comparison pattern. Her first impression is that guides are as useless as she thought. There's a general agreement in tiering the local establishments that doesn't vary far from her average review list. When she tries to narrow it down, the guides either hedge or disagree.

> Some hits and misses, but great atmosphere.
> On our first visit the curries were excellent, but the second time they were lackluster and the rice was cold.
> Three of us loved the passion fruit lassis, but the rest of our team thought they were too sweet.

Then she reads a description of a macher jhol so mouth-watering that she immediately places her order and walks to the restaurant in question.

Maryam enjoys the food, and although she wouldn't have been as hyperbolic as the reviewer, she comes away feeling satisfied, not cheated. That helps her understand why people use tourist guides, but why one that doesn't use Information? What can this organization, so slapdash they have to hand-sell their wares in streets and hotel restaurants, provide that Information can't?

Once again, Maryam finds herself looking forward to her visit to the sanatorium. She even has an outfit in mind to try on, and she flips cheerfully through the clothes until she finds it. Once she's suitably retro, Saleha sends her on to Taskeen's apartment, and Maryam dawdles to suck in the feeling of anachronism, peering in the windows at the jewelry store to see if she can find something quaint and romantic for Núria. She's tempted to wander beyond Taskeen's building, although she doesn't think the site goes much farther, but she doesn't want to be late, and instead climbs the stairs quickly. Taskeen opens the door before Maryam can knock:

Saleha had called her (on a telephone!) to let her know Maryam was coming.

"Faster than I expected," the older woman says, letting her in. "I do appreciate you coming; I wasn't sure you would."

The strict and probably patronizing speech Maryam had planned dissipates. "I didn't realize you would need to contact me," she says instead. "We should set up a more secure channel."

Taskeen laughs as she turns on the kettle. "Was my message not coy enough? I'm afraid I'm a bit sheltered from all the miscreancy online. Part of why I like it here, to be honest."

Maryam gets annoyed again with Taskeen's cloistered-innocent act. "You had something to tell me?"

"Ah, yes," Taskeen says, leading Maryam back to the computer room. "I've been thinking about these attacks on the data transfer stations. They must be stopped. I know you said no one has been hurt, but it's only a matter of time . . ." She ignites the computer with a firm push of her thumb and turns around, stopping when she sees Maryam's face.

"I was caught in an attack," Maryam blurts.

"What?" Taskeen searches her face, then guides her over to the armchair and pulls her desk chair in front of it. "Tell me everything!"

Maryam stumbles through the story. The terror feels impossibly distant now, especially since she can't conjure up pictures of the masks and of the looming, painted towers of the former prison the way she would if she were telling it with Information available. Still, Taskeen seems affected.

"Poor dear," she says, patting Maryam's hand as she jumps up to get the tea. "I hope you've been taking it easy since your ordeal," she adds, edging back in with the tray.

"Oh, uh." It would have been easy to keep talking, spill straight into the uneasy tale of the Territorio de la Justicia and accept Taskeen's comfort, but something holds her back. "I took a short vacation." That segue seemed a little too care-less, Taskeen a little too solicitous. "Made even shorter when I got your message."

"Of course," Taskeen replies briskly, handing Maryam her cup. "We should get to work. I do hope coming out here is worth your time."

"The attacks have to be stopped," Maryam says, feeling bad about the sharpness.

"I couldn't agree more!" Taskeen has rolled her chair over to the computer. "In the interest of that goal—I don't sup-pose you can share the data from their diagnostic with me?"

"Oh—I have it, yes, but I didn't convert it."

Taskeen opens her mouth, and Maryam thinks she's about to say she has developed her own translation program, but instead she shakes her head. "Tomorrow, then? Don't forget to ask Saleha to convert it when you come in. It will be very useful. I was thinking that instead of trying to stop them with security measures, which is impractical given the number of sites and risks greater violence, we should re-move their reason for being there."

"We don't know their reason for being there," Maryam objects.

"We know they want to take control of Information infra-structure." Taskeen spins away from the computer and skew-ers Maryam with her gaze. "I am sure of it, Maryam; that's their game. They can't do anything without the hardware, or they wouldn't be taking such risks. That infrastructure is your capital. You—we—have invested in it over decades.

That, along with Information's more fragile and less trans-ferable legitimacy, is your advantage; it is the barrier to en-try that prevents you from being overrun by competitors."

"You almost make that sound like a bad thing," Maryam comments.

"Well." Taskeen holds her eyes for a moment longer, then whirls back to her computer screen. "Whether it's a good thing or a bad thing is, I suppose, a problem for the econo-mists or the sociologists, not us techies." Maryam can't tell whether she's being sarcastic. "But if you want to maintain control, you must protect that infrastructure at all costs!"

"But not with security?"

"Security is great," Taskeen says. "But it will take too long to raise your security levels at all the transfer stations. They're obviously targeting the election. If you can stave them off for—what is it now, a few weeks?"

"Twelve days," Maryam says, amused that Taskeen doesn't know.

"I'm sure they'll try something different after that, but if you can block the current attempt, it will take some time for them to think up something new. You can use that time to enhance physical security. So, what we want is to keep them from accomplishing what they're trying to do at the transfer stations. Some kind of quick software change that can be implemented across all the stations immediately."

"They've already hacked in once."

"Yes, but remember their time limits! They only have a brief time on site before security shows up, and only eigh-teen days before the election. A software change will prob-ably foil at least one attempt and possibly delay them enough to put off the whole plot." She spins back to Maryam, smiling now. "Come on! I'm sure you and I can put something fun together in a day or two!"

There's a knock on the door. Maryam jerks out of the reverie inspired by the thought of working together with Taskeen Khan. Taskeen looks just as startled as she is.

"I wonder who that could be," the older woman says, jumping to her feet. "I'm not expecting anyone." Maryam follows her to the door in time to see an apologetic Saleha and, behind her in the corridor, a neatly built man who looks to be in early middle age.

"So sorry to bother you while you have a guest," Saleha says, "but this gentleman wanted to see you. He said your mutual friend Nejime recommended he stop by? I was going to call, but . . ."

"Oh!" Maryam blurts, blushes, and then starts again, turning to the stranger. "Won't you join us for some tea? I know Nejime as well; I'm sure we'll have a lot to catch up on."

Saleha gives Taskeen a questioning glance before stepping out of the way, but the old woman nods with her eyes on Maryam. A moment later, Saleha has waggled her goodbyes and the three of them are moving into the kitchen. Maryam's face is still burning: she wonders if she just flunked her first spycraft test. She takes a moment to marvel at the unexpected directions her career has taken over the last few weeks.

The stranger speaks first. "Rajiv," he says, holding out a hand to Taskeen, then to Maryam. When Taskeen brings her hand away, it's folded around something, and she works the miniscule item out to the tips of her fingers. Rajiv taps his ear.

Taskeen looks amused. "You're not supposed to bring this in here," she says, but she fixes the auto-interpreter into her ear anyway.

"Nejime asked me to stop by and offer some suggestions

on secure communications." Rajiv looks comfortable and composed, a light smile on his face as if he hadn't just sauntered into a stranger's house. He's no taller than Maryam and built wide—a broad flat chest, a wide face—but it is not until Maryam registers that he's speaking Nepali that she remembers where she saw him before.

"You were in my hotel last night!"

Rajiv's smile grows as Taskeen looks back and forth between the two of them. "Yes, I was. Well spotted."

Maryam doesn't mention that she only noticed him because she was looking for a tourist-guide tout.

"So, secure communications, is it?" Taskeen shoots Maryam a look that says, as clearly as a private message, *This joker is going to come in and explain to us,* us, *how to manage coded intel?* "Do go on."

Rajiv can't have missed the look, but he doesn't lose his smile as he starts flipping projections into the air.

Fortunately for him, the training has nothing to do with coding. He's there to teach them how to navigate the world of Information without attracting the attention of those who might be looking for you, or looking for the same bit of data you are. They spend the morning talking about nonprogramming methods of infosecurity, and he defers to Taskeen whenever the subject even comes close. "I'm not going to tell you how to code your way into pretending you're someone you're not—you'd know much more about that than I would." He nods at the older woman. "But these are a few ways where you can shape your footprint on Information to reduce your exposure. They won't protect you as much as a manufactured identity, but they are less intensive and—the big advantage—will not give you away if they fail the way a new identity or other flash coding approaches will."

Taskeen sniffs at that—Maryam can almost hear her retorting, *My covers don't fail*—but listens as Rajiv explains about drop-sites in plazas, misdirection, overcrowding, and oblique searches. "Most of these are venerable techniques, adapted for the digital world."

"What about using the telephone?" Taskeen indicates hers, possibly facetiously.

"Too easily bugged," Rajiv answers, and moves on. In the safety of the sanatorium, where Information has no feeds or (publicly avowed) interfaces, they practice designing parameters for searches, communications, and travel. "Information claims to be transparent, but that is deceptive," he says. "Look at where the attention of the world is focused and use that glare to distract from what you're doing."

"For example, the election?" Taskeen suggests.

"Exactly."

Maryam stays quiet, wondering if the tension between them is something more than the jousting between experts in competing fields.

After three hours, Taskeen begs off, claiming a fatigue that Maryam can't quite believe, but Rajiv doesn't seem surprised or disappointed. "If it's acceptable to both of you," he says, a phrase that Maryam reads as a concession to politeness rather than a request for permission, "we'll meet here again tomorrow morning to continue, and then you and I"—nodding at Maryam—"will practice street security." He turns to Taskeen. "I take it that sort of training is not useful for you?"

"Of course it isn't," Taskeen says. "I almost never leave the compound, and only reluctantly for unmissable family events."

Rajiv and Maryam leave the sanatorium together, which seems to comfort Saleha—she waves them a cheerful goodbye—but it also allows Rajiv to lean in just before the outer door opens and ask, "Do you trust her?"

By the time Maryam has finished gaping in surprise, they are out on the street, back under the feeds, and she doesn't know how to answer. She shuts her mouth and watches the passersby—a series of six skinny men in dhotis carrying piles of bricks on their shoulders, a gaggle of college students in bright colors—until her overworked brain has finished porting over what he taught them about Information to the real world. Then she waits until a truck lumbers by, and covers her mouth with a corner of her headscarf, pretending to cough. "I'm not sure," she says, loudly enough for Rajiv to hear over the clatter of the vehicle, and then quickly blinks through the surrounding feeds to make sure neither her voice nor her lip movements appeared on any of them.

"Not bad," Rajiv says, face turned toward her as if in concern over her cough. "But check the feeds first, ideally not in such an obvious way, and then you can use angles instead of cloth. Subtler." He grins, then goes serious again with startling swiftness. "I'm interested to hear more of your experience with her. She's such a legend but . . ." Maryam raises her eyebrows. "I have concerns. We'll revisit the question tomorrow?"

"Okay," Maryam says, but she's distracted: she had forgotten that the first government debate of the campaign was happening while they were in the time capsule, and she can see just from the volume of traffic on the Information intranet that something newsworthy happened.

Mishima finds the election debates a lot less fun now that she's preparing for her own event. Her typical mix of intellectual fascination, gossipy obsession, and personal interest in the result is tempered by the awareness that she will soon be performing herself. Everything that happens at the government debate will be fair game for questions to Secretariat candidates, so there's also the feeling of cramming for a critical and wide-ranging exam. More than that, though, she is registering in a new way how professional spokespeople and heads of state deploy nuances of gesture, tone, and phrase, wondering what she can cull for her own use and what will seem artificial.

There are differences between the debates, of course. There will only be five Information candidates on her stage, and the first government debate has seventeen. It's a significant reduction from the number included in the previous election's first debate, which is partly because Information tightened up the criteria for inclusion, but—frowning over numbers during the opening statements—Mishima wonders if it's also indicative of a consolidation of power among large governments.

She surfaces from the data long enough to hear the Liberty spokesperson talking about fresh starts and becoming better through experience, and expands her datacubes again. At least number-crunching—never her strong point—will distract her from the smarm. Ken, next to her, is making incoherent angry noises and yanking at his hair.

When Mishima looks back up from her (inconclusive) data, she finds that whoever's in charge of the official Information debate projection is doing the same thing. Debates are audio-only, much to the chagrin of the better-looking heads of state, and while most of the projection is taken up with annotation of the ongoing speeches, someone has started putting up infographics ranking the participating governments along various metrics on a slide screen.

Mishima notices that while Heritage remains number one in inequality, followed closely by 888, Policy1st has crept up quite a few spots over the past few years. They naturally jumped when they won the Supermajority, with many centenals that had been in higher-Gini governments moving over to them, but the fact that they've continued in that direction suggests that some aspect of the Supermajority status may benefit the already-wealthy more than others. Mishima makes a note to throw that question to the economists. Odd, having access to a staff of experts in various subjects, instead of muddling through everything herself. And that's just the official candidate perks; actually winning would probably spoil her completely.

Vera Kubugli won the randomization and gets to make her closing statement last. Listening to her rich tones, Mishima remembers how in the last election Policy1st presented a different spokesperson at every debate, supposedly part of their focus on policy rather than personalities. She wonders if they're going to do that again this time; she can't think of anyone with a stature anywhere near Vera's. Have they noticeably centralized power since Veena left? Her brain, catching something her conscious mind missed, jerks her attention back to the content of Vera's speech.

". . . and because we believe in local policy determination, we'll be taking our own approach to this a step further. We are introducing mechanisms to allow centenals that vote for us to maintain their local government identity while benefiting from the experience, economies of scale, and umbrella policies that Policy1st can offer."

Mishima slams upright and opens the official Policy1st site in a separate projection. Even as her eyes take in the structural diagram posted in pride of place to describe this move, she opens the Information intranet because she knows people are going to be losing their shit over this.

"What?" Ken is yelling next to her. "How did they—" He jumps up and starts parading around the room, talking to himself in fragments that, Mishima notes, have a distinctly triumphant sound to them. She scans the diagram while intranet comments drift in front of her vision and the rest of Vera's speech washes over her.

There's a lot of shrieking going on at Information over whether this is legal; Mishima will wait for the lawyers, but it looks like a neatly borderline case to her. The diagram clarifies that centenals who take this plan will have no official status with the local government they would have otherwise chosen, but they will receive an explicit contract ceding specific policy areas to the second-choice government. The initiative seems designed to skirt the law requiring merging governments to completely align their platforms.

Mishima opens a call to Nejime, but there's no answer. She must be flooded with calls from freaked-out staffers. Mishima toys with the diagram while it rings, and then stops suddenly. She can see both sides of this, but she's not going to have that luxury for long. This is exactly the sort of thing the Secretariat would decide on, which means she's going to have to have a position.

She ends the call unanswered.

CHAPTER 13

Possibly taking a hint from the previous day, Rajiv is even more deferential with Taskeen on their second meeting. "How would you do this?" he asks. "Is there a coding solution that would let you communicate in this way?" "This would be more useful if we could hardcode the message path to avoid certain nodes; is that possible?"

Taskeen does seem mollified. She smiles at Rajiv once or twice, and when they break for tea, she brings out the sweets right away. Yesterday he got no food at all. But Maryam is pretty sure that Taskeen is holding back in her answers. Either that or she really is dotty. When Rajiv asked if she trusted Taskeen yesterday, Maryam honestly wasn't sure. Now she's positive that Rajiv shouldn't trust the elderly maven, but she feels much less inclined to warn him. The techie sisterhood, it seems, is thicker than Information loyalty.

"Now that we've covered some basics," Rajiv is saying, "let's get a little more specific about what we're doing. You're working together to find these ex-Information staffers, right? What do we know about them?" Drawing them out, he lists known and suspected activities, capabilities, and weaknesses. "We need to think like them. Put yourselves in their position. What do you think they're doing?"

"Acting desperate," Taskeen snaps. They both look at her

in surprise, and she tries again. "They're probing for weaknesses."

"That seems reasonable," Rajiv says. "So, what do we expect from here?"

Taskeen coughs around something that might have been "incompetence" or maybe "nonsense."

"More of the same, presuming they haven't found what they're looking for," Maryam suggests.

Taskeen rises to clear the tea. "Weren't you going to practice—what did you call it? Street security?—today?"

They take the hint.

"She is acting a little odd," Maryam says once they're safely away from the compound. She still has no intention of telling Rajiv about the techie stuff he (presumably) missed, but her curt dismissal was so obvious that to pretend not to have noticed would be strange.

"I wonder." Rajiv seems lost in thought. "In any case, hopefully we've gotten through to her enough to keep her from sending any more reckless messages."

We? thinks Maryam, her sense of techie sisterhood thickening further.

"By the way, is it true you were in the Isla de Pinos station when it was attacked? Can you tell me about it?" When she nods reluctantly, he looks around and guides her into an unassuming teashop on a corner. Maryam, who has just had two mugs of Taskeen's excellent blend, is not in the mood for a cup of swill, but she supposes there's an operational security reason. She sips the lukewarm brew sparingly in between describing the experience a second time. If Taskeen's warmth yesterday brought out the emotional side of it, Rajiv seems more interested in the narrative and technical details. "In a closet! Where was it located? How frightening! And they didn't look for you? What about heat sensors? How did you hide your identity when you logged into the station's systems?"

When she's finished, he leans back. "I haven't been following Exformation too closely—not my billet—but these station attacks are scary. Amazing they don't hurt anyone, though! Almost a Robin Hood aspect to it."

Maryam looks at him skeptically. "You think they're distributing the data among the poor?"

He laughs. "No, but I imagine it could garner them some sympathy. Daring attacks with no victims."

"Sympathy?"

"Oh, I think plenty of people would be on their side, don't you?" His eyes search her face, and Maryam focuses on the dregs in her teacup. "Especially, I hate to say it, but especially Information staff. I think everyone can relate to the feeling of workplace dissatisfaction."

"Is that what it's about?" Maryam asks, doubtful.

"Since they worked for Information before, I assume they have some grievances."

"Sure," Maryam nods, feeling that it's better to agree at this point. "Don't we all?"

"Maybe even deeper philosophical disagreements with the organization."

She gives him a questioning look.

"It's possible they are acting on some principles—say, questions of privacy, or responsible neutrality, or unelected hegemony—as well as a desire for power." There's an earnest glint in his eye, and Maryam forces a smile.

"Oh, no doubt," she says, swallowing an inclination to retort, *Or at least that's what they tell themselves.*

"I'm sure we've all had our disagreements with the bureaucracy." Rajiv chuckles. "I know I've had my share."

There is a *crack* and a moment later a rapidly accelerating *pock-pock*: a monsoon is drenching the pavement just outside.

"See, like that," Rajiv says, yelling to be heard over the sudden crushing noise of the rain. "Why didn't they warn us?"

Maryam can't tell if he's joking.

This is a *great* opportunity; it's a win-win." Ken realizes he is using buzzspeak and takes a breath. "We can get the best of both worlds." Not much better, but said slower, it *sounds* more thoughtful. Besides, this buzzspeak is probably the best way to communicate with Geoff Forth. "We can combine the power of the *sitting Supermajority* with the quirky local flavor and freedom of Free2B. I still know a lot of people at Policy1st, I'm sure I can work out advantageous terms, it could be—"

"We are all well aware of your continuing contacts at Policy1st," Geoff says, in the driest of takedown tones. "Ken, you've been of incredible value to us and you're doing a great job as campaign director, but after all these years, I'm not sure you've fully aligned your perspective with that of Free2B."

Ken, already thrown off by the attack (*Does Geoff know Policy1st was trying to poach me?*), leaps back into the breach, fueled with indignation. "I love Free2B! I came here because this was where I wanted to live. I have turned down every higher-profile, higher-salary offer, I—"

"And we *appreciate* that, Ken, but the bottom line is you still think bigger is better, that ambition is a virtue. That perspective informs all your work. But that's just not what Free2B is about."

"Was I just fired?" Ken asks Phuong after the meeting.

She frowns. "I'm not sure. Geoff hates coming out and saying uncomfortable stuff like that."

Ken is trying to figure out whether he wants to be fired or not. On the one hand, it would be a great excuse to take the Policy1st job. On the other, he loves his apartment, and his neighborhood, and really the whole government. Would he have to move, if only for pride's sake?

"You shouldn't be," Phuong is going on. "They'll never find another campaign director as good as you." Ken swells, ready to stay. "At least not for the price, and not this late in the game."

"I wish he'd tell me one way or the other," Ken grumps, deflated again.

"You could make some tiny adjustment in the strategy document and take it to him, see what happens," Phuong suggests. "I'm pretty sure he'd tell you one on one."

"That could tip him against me," Ken points out. "Geoff and I have never done well one on one."

"Then keep your head down," Phuong says. "Just do your job, okay? I, for one, want to keep my centenal."

Rajiv doesn't know Dhaka well, but he looked up call centers in the city before he arrived—using carefully oblique searches for *low-income businesses* and *obsolete tech still in use*. The one he selected is festooned with posters and pop-ups advertising short-term labor contracts in Saudi. He's concerned that a call to Russia will stand out, but at this point he's willing to take the risk.

"Maryam might be amenable in the future, but she's not ready," he says as soon as Moushian picks up. "I'm not willing to risk it."

"What about Khan?"

"Still dangerous," Rajiv says. "She might suspect me. I managed to take some imaging of her computer screen, which I'll send you as soon as I get back to Kathmandu. I think they're looking at data transfer software."

Moushian is silent.

"Are we ready for the event?" Rajiv asks, unable to help himself. "I don't know what Khan is planning, but Information is on alert."

"We're ready, but I think we need to go to our contingency plan. Get yourself to the site."

R ajiv doesn't show up for training on Maryam's last day in Dhaka. She waits for thirty-two minutes, then, wondering if she's breaking a key rule of dealing with spies, asks after him at the hotel desk. He checked out the night before, leaving no message. Odd, but maybe he was called to an emergency somewhere. Maryam is not too sorry to miss the training. Instead, she goes back to the sanatorium to visit Taskeen one more time. It feels almost like an obligation, as if Maryam's been neglecting an elderly relative: Taskeen was the one who called her here, and then they were interrupted by Rajiv, and she's barely spent any time with her.

When Taskeen opens the door, however, her brisk pleasure in seeing her is nothing like a lonely old woman who had been hoping for another visit. Maryam tries to pull herself back into professionalism while Taskeen puts on the kettle.

"Well?" the older woman says. "How was your time with the spy? Did you learn something?"

"Something, maybe." Maryam chuckles self-consciously. "I'm not sure it's the type of skill you can pick up in a few days."

"That's just what a spy would say," Taskeen says in what Maryam hopes is a teasing voice, tapping her on the back of the hand. "Tell me though: do you trust him?"

"Rajiv?" Maryam asks, not even surprised anymore. The conversation with Rajiv in the teashop was entirely weird, but she's gotten into the habit of not answering that question with the truth. "He seemed nice enough. But trust him? No, I don't trust him. But I trust Nejime."

"I don't!" Taskeen snaps. "I don't trust him, I don't trust Nejime, and I don't trust Information."

"I thought you and Nejime were friends," Maryam squeaks, her eyes straying to the photo of the two of them together on the wall.

"Friendship has nothing to do with it. If you think your boss or your organization has your best interests at heart, you're a fool." Taskeen gestures impatiently, as if trying to brush away the effects of her harsh tone. "It's fine to say you're just a techie, but at some point, you have to start thinking for yourself, you understand?"

The kettle whistles on cue and Maryam jumps, and Taskeen laughs, then pats her on the hand again as she goes to make the tea. Maryam stares at the room cluttered with the detritus of an influential life. When Taskeen gets back, she waits for her to either resume or explain her rant, but Taskeen sets out the cups in silence.

"What kind of changes were you considering?" Maryam asks finally. Taskeen looks up sharply, her face bright and poised. "For the data transfer software, I mean."

"Oh, that," Taskeen answers, but she still looks eager. "I think we can shift a few things around, maybe change some command definitions, and that ought to slow them down."

They dive deep into it, long enough for Maryam and Taskeen to be finishing each others' sentences as they work through the problems. It's been a while since Maryam's done such straight-up tech work, and even longer since she's done it together with someone who could hold their own. Every time she remembers that it's *Taskeen Khan* she's working with, she shivers.

They finish their work, but Taskeen puts the kettle on again and pours them more tea, and they chat about less consequential matters. Taskeen wants to hear about those former colleagues of hers who are still at Information. Some of them Maryam knows only by names; she has spent most of her career at the Paris, Doha, and now La Habana Hubs, and her circle is somewhat limited.

"And Nougaz?" Taskeen asks, after Maryam has updated her on the scant gossip that hovers around Nejime. "I understand she's still trying to run things?"

Maryam chokes a bit on her tea. "She's . . ." Oh, yes, there is a non-personal update she can offer. "She's running for the Information representative position on the Secretariat."

Taskeen wrinkles her nose. "I've seen this Secretariat thing mentioned in the news compilers, but what exactly is it?"

Maryam glances at her sharply when she mentions news compilers, but Taskeen has admitted to staying abreast of current events several times already. "It's a . . ." Again, Maryam stops; that's a harder question than it seems. Like everyone in her set, she has an awareness and a working knowledge of the new structure, but not an actual definition.

Maryam blinks to bring up the official Information line, but of course it doesn't come. "It's an attempt," she starts bravely, "to add structure and . . . oversight to the system. Since Information is supposed to be neutral"—she and Taskeen share a knowing grimace—"and the Supermajority doesn't, and shouldn't, have much oversight power, the Secretariat is meant to be a committee staffed with representatives of various interested parties that can deal with procedural disputes, set the kind of umbrella laws that Information is reluctant to touch . . ." She trails off with a shrug. No one really knows yet what the Secretariat is going to do, although she's heard there's a list of possible issues pending its decision once it exists.

"And . . ." Taskeen frowns. "I've heard that there will be null states involved?"

"Oh, yes," Maryam says. "It's supposed to include a range of stakeholders: quite a few government representatives, including several seats designated for small governments or coalitions of small governments; one from the Supermajority; and Information. The null states representatives will only have an observer status, but even so their inclusion offers sort of a side benefit, I think, as far as Nejime's concerned. Information is interested in improving relations outside of micro-democracy, and they saw the Secretariat as an opportunity to create open, consistent communication of some kind. That's why they're making such a big deal out of the non-debate tomorrow to introduce the null states representatives, even though no one here is voting on them."

Taskeen harrumphs. "Well. I suppose it is some kind of evolution. A bit tepid, though, no?"

"I don't know," Maryam says, a little defensive. "It's an experiment."

"Experimenting is good," Taskeen says. "The system was always supposed to evolve. But this might be too little and too late."

"Nejime is worried it might be," Maryam says before she can stop herself.

"Then she should have done more, sooner," Taskeen says, snappish again. Then she smiles. "Next time," she winks, "we need to build it in to the code: tectonic shifts in the structure every fifteen years or so. Enforced adaptation!"

They laugh together, and then Maryam starts the process of leaving.

"I suppose we'll be able to keep in touch better now, after Rajiv's helpful training," Taskeen says, standing to walk her to the entrance.

"Mm," says Maryam noncommittally. Taskeen's tone is odd, and Maryam isn't sure whether she was being sarcastic or not.

"Just in case," Taskeen says, and Maryam hesitates, looking back at her from the dimness of the entrance hall. "I noticed that all the tricks he taught us? They would make it easy for someone who knew those tricks to find our communications."

"I suppose . . . easier at least, if not easy . . ."

"Just in case," Taskeen repeats, "we should have another protocol. In case you ever have reason to doubt."

To doubt Rajiv? Or to doubt Information? "Like what?" Maryam asks cautiously.

"Well, we could always use agreed-upon plazas and code phrases, like he suggested, different ones that he doesn't know about. I'm pretty sure I can set up a simple interface allowing me access to those plazas with the tools I have here."

Maryam suspects that interface is already coded and running.

"Or we could set up an unmarked channel. It's something I've toyed with before. I'll show you." Taskeen sits down again and opens an interface to Information on her computer. Maryam hesitates, then drifts back into the sitting room, since she's obviously not leaving yet.

The channel they create is not impossible to find, but once they've stripped all the connection and location data from its nodes, making each accessible only from the other, it is well hidden. The connection won't appear on any search; it won't even be apparent to the programs that distribute data packets, so Information won't use it to send anything other than what they create. It would be possible for someone to stumble upon it by entering random locations, but the odds against that are astronomical.

"There," Taskeen says when they're done. "Doesn't that feel more secure?"

Only, Maryam thinks, *if it's Information you're trying to hide from.*

CHAPTER 14

On the flight back to Doha, Maryam reflects that she doesn't still feel confident with clandestine work. If anything, Rajiv's training made clear how limited her abilities are. She can think through the approaches Rajiv gave them, but it's the sort of thing that you need to be able to do without thinking for it to be effective. It has to become second nature, and the only way for that to happen is through lots and lots of practice, which Maryam hopes she will never have.

It did open her eyes to how easy it is for the people who do have that practice—Roz's friend Mishima springs to mind—to maneuver undetected. Maryam had always believed Information to be basically omniscient, at least in the public sphere. She never found this to be particularly disturbing, maybe because she was so young when Information was established, and surveillance was already near universal before that. With so much data out there, she generally assumes that nobody would be looking at the details of her life unless they had a good reason to; on the other hand, the intel was there, neatly stored and (with a few exceptions) equally accessible to all in case there turned out to be a reason to confirm any of it later.

Now she realizes that there have always been plenty of interstices for people to slip through if they want to. Rajiv

told her he could walk from one end to the other of Dhaka—
or pretty much any other city in the world—unseen, simply
by studying the feed placement and weaving from side to side
like a drunkard with sways timed to avoid them. It seemed
obvious once he said it, and yet it had never occurred to
Maryam that people, except the most desperate and gifted
of novela-style criminals, would go to those lengths.

She thinks again about Mishima. She's only met her a few
times, but she's heard enough about her from Roz to have
an idea of what she gets up to beyond the public persona—
or used to. Maryam knows that for most of her colleagues
and peers Mishima is the candidate of choice to represent
Information in the Secretariat. She's even heard the camaradas rave about her "radical physicality." But thinking of the
facility she must have evading surveillance makes Maryam
somewhat uncomfortable with the idea of her promoting
Information in the Secretariat. Not that she wants to vote
for Nougaz instead.

To avoid thinking about that, she follows thoughts of
Mishima, which lead her to the Nakia Williams. Remembering her last meeting with Roz, Maryam decides to use the
flight—plane instead of crow; she has no patience for extraneous stops on this return trip—to read up on the trial. It
is not going well. There is clarity that Information has
presented a negative view of AmericaTheGreat, and even
though all the negative statements made were true, accusations are being made about the overall tenor and the
lack of balance. From what Maryam reads, Williams hasn't
made much headway defending herself. It's a little scary,
because Maryam can imagine all too easily how difficult
that defense must be. She wonders if Williams has started

to question herself, doubt her own version of the events and her motivation in doing what she did.

Even scarier, though, are the comments.

Fortunately for everyone concerned, Mishima hasn't had to do much campaigning. While government spokes-people and heads of state regularly hold rallies and angle for favorable coverage from news compilers, the Secretariat po-sitions are untested and technocratic, and individual pos-turing has been limited. Still, Mishima is aware that the factions of Information behind her candidacy—Nejime's clique, primarily—aren't above political stratagems, and every once in a while they ask for her cooperation. Today she's supposed to do an interview with an influential com-piler, which means allowing the compiler's editor to follow her through her day.

"It's to give the voters a sense of you as a person," Nejime's assistant Zaid said while cajoling her into it. "That behind all the glamour, you have a normal life."

"What glamour?" Mishima grunted, but she agreed on the condition that Ken and Sayaka be kept out of it. This is like trying to use a cocktail umbrella in a typhoon, given how public Sayaka's life has been so far, but she figures not sanctioning her exposure is the least she can do for the kid. Still, as the compiler argued to Zaid—and Zaid, apologeti-cally, passed on to her—she could do something to reference family commitments without involving her family. Maybe she can go shopping and buy some toddler food or some-thing. "Also, they would love to follow you on a speedblading routine."

Mishima decides to go swimming that day instead,

subjecting them to a hundred repetitive laps. "I'm afraid the rest of my day is going to be pretty boring for you," she says with satisfaction. "I spend most of my time studying issues and concerns on Information." She's walking them toward a café where she works occasionally, since she doesn't want them in her house.

"Oh, that's fine," whispers the editor, who is intimidated by Mishima but not intimidated enough. "We'll montage what you're working on; it'll be great."

Anticipating this, Mishima has prepared a day of work that a) doesn't point at anything the wider public can't know; b) brings up issues she thinks the wider public should pay more attention to; and c) looks more or less productive. After an hour and a half of comparing oversight structures in the governmental and private sectors over the past three centuries, she's bored, resentful, and has run through her prescheduled tasks. She's never felt such a strong urge to look up Nakia's case, or check on Amran's progress with the shady spying gig. Instead, she calls up the latest polling: not for the Secretariat, which would look desperate or egomaniacal, but for the government election.

Policy1st is still trending upward relative to the leaders, although not nearly steeply enough to win them the Supermajority. 888 is starting to plateau, leaving an opening for PhilipMorris or one of the other top corporates. To her annoyance, Mishima notices that even Liberty is gaining ground. *How can people forget so quickly?* she wonders, and considers requesting a poll specific to that question—do they not *remember* the last election? Do they still believe Liberty's promises? Do they not care as long as they get their discounted Nestlé products?—before she remembers that anything she orders will be seen as politically motivated. Maybe she can get Roz or someone else to do it? Although in light of Nakia's trial, she doesn't want to expose anyone else to accusations of partisanship.

"Okay," Mishima says, standing up. "Time to stretch our legs."

The editor rises gracefully, her camera handler slightly less so. *Shopping,* thinks Mishima. *Family commitments.* She walks them from the café toward a wet market she's been to a few times before. She and Ken rarely shop for groceries, relying on takeaway, delivery, and regular cooker supply services, all cheap and simple in Free2B and in Saigon more generally. In point of fact, Mishima's familiarity with this market relies on the food-truck belt encircling it. Passing through that zone, she gets a wave from the woman from the Thai arepas truck; a few steps later, the pissaladière vendor calls a greeting, which Mishima answers through gritted teeth. Hopefully the editor won't notice the utter lack of such rapport with the produce sellers.

Not that they won't recognize her. Everybody recognizes her. Mishima is wearing a check scarf wrapped around the bottom of her face and large sunglasses of the so-called stealth variety, but that just means a delay of one to four seconds before oncoming pedestrians go through the standard expression spectrum: hesitation, recognition, awe. But only the people she's interacted with are likely to speak to her. Most people stare for another two to three seconds and then scramble to get out of her way.

As Mishima enters the market proper, she convinces herself that this outing is good for her, regardless of the newszombies following along. She could be more . . . *domestic* is not the right word, but, say, proactive about managing household tasks. It feels virtuous to be out here, squeezing mangos and smelling passion fruit—or is it supposed to be the other way around? She frowns, and considers a jackfruit; Sayaka loves them, but cutting them up at home is such a pain. Better to order the pre-peeled version.

Mishima is taking her time among several varieties of leafy greens, hoping that her deliberative moue makes it look like she's judging freshness by some traditional intuitive trick instead of looking up the names and usages on Information, when she becomes aware of a shift in the clutter of sound around her. Without conscious decision, Mishima refocuses, pulling up the news alerts. The first glance reminds her of what she had managed to forget: the null-state debate.

It is not actually a debate, although the rhyme and the parallelism have proved irresistible to most news compilers, and so far Information is letting it slide. All the null states have been offered observer status in the Secretariat. Their processes for choosing their representatives are their own, unpoliced and unremarked on by Information. However, given the micro-democratic population's lack of familiarity with null states and the newness of the Secretariat, the powers that be decided a public introduction would be useful, while the news compilers inexplicably felt they needed more drama during an election season.

It is a non-event event, not really part of the election, not really a debate, and Mishima had decided not to pay any attention to it. She is trying to concentrate on issues and pivot points, and not the noisy superficia of the election.

And of course, the one event she decides not to watch may have the most impact of all. When Mishima tunes in to the audio, she doesn't hear platitudes about civilization or peace or diplomacy but a recorded, repeating statement cloaked in the otherworldly eeriness of voice distortion: *Why don't you get to vote on those with the real power Why don't you get to vote on those with the real power Why*

"Anarchy," Mishima breathes, and then presses her mouth closed, hoping no one, in person or via camera had an angle on reading her lips, nabbing that stupid assumption as quickly as it slipped out of her. No time to check. She pulls up the Information intranet, scans through what is known about this crisis:

> broadcast interrupted from the null states debate
> reroute! if the algorithm isn't doing it do it manually, use
>   brute force if necessary to find a clear path
> HOW is this possible?
> negative, looks like they've cut the connection from the
>   conference center
> ohhh the Chinese are going to be pissed about this
> cut it how?
> status within the hall?
> data transfer station on Gozo not responding
> another attack?
> evacuating personnel from—

Mishima hears an echo to the monotonous repetition of the audio statement and whirls around. Someone in the market has thrown up a large projection of the feed from the debate. It's becoming a trend when there are disasters or big news events, and while Mishima understands the impulse—*we're all in this together*—she also finds it incredibly annoying. It does draw her attention to something: there's a weird undercurrent to the sound that she thought was the murmur of people around her reacting. Now that it's magnified, she recognizes a separate audio track repeating at a lower volume. She isolates it and listens: *Information. Omission. Spying. Lying. Information. Omission. Spying. Lying.*

It's eerie, almost subliminal, and precisely targeted to reinforce the most common villainous qualities assigned to Information. Mishima focuses back in on her feeds, her data, all the threads she knows how to pull. The current theory is an attack on a data distribution center was used to hijack the feed, which shouldn't be possible because of network redundancy. There's no intel yet from the conference center. For all they know, there could have been an attack there too, on people as well as data. If null-state representatives are killed or even hurt during an Information-hosted event . . . Mishima remembers the Anarchy attack during the last election, the ghostly persistence of the remote-controlled crow, the bomb . . . She should be there, like she was then. She should be at the null-state debate, or on call somewhere nearby. They would have sent her to the distribution center as soon as the attack was launched; she could have stopped it, reconnected the communications, maybe captured one of the attackers . . .

". . . some sort of problem with the null-state debate," Mishima hears. "We're here with Secretariat representative candidate Mishima as we learn more details about this devastating attack. What do you think is going on? What can be done to prevent these attacks in the future?"

It's the editor, of course, and from the sound of it, she's gone live—that's the only explanation for her slight delay in coming to harass Mishima. She hears the questions, but they are stupid questions, and she shouldn't be here, squeezing fruit in this market so that the fucking voters can get a fucking sense of her as a person. She should be *there*, helping. Fighting. She hears the silence stretch, hears it extend beyond the length of dead air that should be allowed in a broadcast, then twice that. If she were there, at the site of the crisis, Mishima would know what to do, and even if she didn't know, she would be doing it. Here, she can't even figure out what to say.

Whenever Roz has been home for them, she and Suleyman have watched the debates, and now this null-state non-debate, together. This event is taking place on a floating conference hall off the coast of Malta, in order to avoid having to decide on a government or null state to honor with the headache. It falls in the late morning, Doha time, but Roz has been working from home a lot as her pregnancy advances. Suleyman massages Roz's feet, which he swears is what has kept her ankles from swelling, and Roz talks at the projection and sometimes to him, although she makes sure all the questions are rhetorical. Roz knows Suleyman isn't as engaged with global politics as she is, and although she finds it slightly baffling, she tries not to hold it against him. Whenever he says something that reveals his ignorance of the intricacies of Supermajority-level intrigue, she reminds herself of every old saw she's heard about the importance of local government; Suleyman's grasp of the politics in his home town is deep, subtle, and canny.

In the case of the so-called null-state debate, Roz can't blame him for being uninterested. She had hoped that even without a debate, there would be some discussion of planet-wide issues, in particular the mantle tunnels and their environmental effects. Instead she gets overly crafted self-aggrandizements. They vary slightly according to the fashion of each null state (Russia restrained, the Saudis religious, the Swiss passive-aggressively neutral, the Independentistas proudly revolutionary, and so on) but the overall tenor is the same: *We are flourishing without micro-democracy, but we're willing to take part in your games if only to demonstrate how great we are.*

There is Information annotation of the statements, but it is exceedingly mild. Reading along, Roz can almost feel the hesitation of whatever poor sap is on duty for this.

"They're not calling them on anything!" she complains to Suleyman, but then has to add, "I suppose there isn't enough solid data coming out of the null states to prove or disprove much." At least Information agreed to allow video, so they can people-watch foreigners during the soporific content.

"And they probably don't want to admit how much they do know," Suleyman says, once again showing himself to be savvier than she gives him credit for.

Roz is about to make a joke to that effect, maybe with a kiss, when the Chinese diplomat's speech gets interesting. "Unlike Russia, which works to destabilize the delicate balance of world relations, the Pax Democratica you have so carefully built, we aim to preserve and work within this highly effective world order." The Russian representative is on her feet, complaining, and Roz is leaning into the rush she gets in those rare moments when something more or less momentous breaks through the cautious veneer of international politics. Then this goes from less to more. The projection disappears and the elegantly modulated voice of the Chinese representative is replaced with a jerking, artificially distorted drone: *Why don't you get to vote on those with the real power Why don't you get to vote on those with the real power Why don't you*

Suleyman leaps up and goes to the terrace, leaning out to look up and down the street. Roz hasn't moved, but she's doing the same thing in her own way: opening local news compilers and launching early-warning algorithms to look for any signs of disturbance here. She knows the non-debate is—was?—more than three thousand kilometers away, but the disappearance of the projection and the invasion of that voice make it feel like they're under attack, and Roz's heart is racing.

"Anything?" she asks as Suleyman comes back into the room.

He shakes his head. "Nothing visible."

"I don't see anything either. Local, that is." The quick glance was enough to alert her to the attack on the data distribution center. Someone is already stringing together a timeline of the previous attack and any other distribution center oddities.

The distorted mantra drones on. Roz becomes aware that there's a sort of counterpoint or chorus accompanying it at a lower volume, but she's more disturbed by how long it lasts. The voice and its message are both annoying, and Roz is tempted to mute it, but she wants to know when it ends. When Anarchy attacked the debate during the last election, they controlled the audio feed for thirty-five seconds. This disruption is already at 268 seconds and counting. Of course, last time the appropriation of the broadcast was only part of an attack that also included violence. She hopes that in this case, the focus is on data, and everyone at the event itself is safe. She can imagine the Chinese and Russian diplomats, oblivious to the incident, continuing their duel of honed insults for an imagined audience.

Roz levers herself up to standing: there's no reason to, but sitting suddenly feels too passive, and besides, she's supposed to be moving around as much as she can because exercise is good for the baby and for smooth labor, quick recovery, blablabla. She paces the room, hugs herself, and then moves over to her workstation in the corner. "Let me see what's going on."

Suleyman nods; ten minutes later, Roz discovers a cup of mint tea by her hand. "Shukran," she says, noting that the repetitive audio has ended (or been cut off by Suleyman), and dives back in.

U nusually for her, Maryam dozes through the last half of her flight, missing the subtle buzz as those who kept their news alerts on reacted to the reports of data hijacking, prompting anyone who's not immersed in content or asleep to check their own Information. Instead, she wakes up disoriented and then, as is her practice, focuses on dealing with the various airport processes as efficiently as possible. She dozes again on the public transportation crow heading for the Doha Hub, forgetting that her news alerts are still off.

And so, she's unprepared to walk into the Doha Hub and find a whirlwind of muted activity. "What's going on?" she asks Saeed at reception, her eyes tracking up the figures crisscrossing the seven stories of galleries lining the covered atrium.

Saeed gapes. "You haven't heard? There was an attack on the null-states event—"

"What?" Maryam blinks frantically to page through news sites. "No casualties," she reads aloud, liquid with relief. *They don't hurt anyone.*

Saeed leans forward. "They—we still don't know who it was—had full control of the audio feed for twelve minutes and eleven seconds."

"*Twelve minutes?* But . . . how?"

"That's more your department than mine."

Saeed's right; it is exactly Maryam's department, and her eyes stray upward again, this time searching out the techie-infested fourth floor. Yep, it looks like the volume and agitation of people in the corridors are notably higher there.

"Can you let Nejime know I'm here?" She gives him her suitcase to keep behind the desk. "I'm going to see Hassan on the way up. And Roz."

"Roz is working from home," Saeed calls as she turns away. "She might be in later."

"Ma'alesh," Maryam answers, already heading for the stairs. She'll stay at Roz's tonight anyway.

"*Twelve minutes?*" Maryam repeats when she gets to Hassan's office—formerly her office. "What happened?" There are three members of Maryam's old team clustered around Hassan's workspace, and three more entering or leaving the office as she says it, but Hassan answers her, even though he hasn't taken his eyes off of whatever he's got projected up at eye level.

"We don't know yet. There should have been plenty of redundancy, even at that floating venue."

Maryam pauses, taken aback for the second time. Hassan is more perturbed than she expected. "The attack on the data transfer station?"

Hassan throws up his hands, still not looking away from

his work. "Sure, that was the most default route for the data. But there were fifty, a hundred others for the routing algorithm to substitute. It's like it didn't see them," he adds, almost to himself.

Maryam is silent so long that Hassan eventually looks up from his projection. "Something to add?" he asks.

Maryam shakes herself, then shakes her head. "Sorry to interrupt," she says. "Let me know if you want extra help on this." She turns to go.

"Hey! Of course we want your help, if you have time."

"I have to see Nejime, but send me what you're working on and I'll take a look later."

Once out of the office and after a quick glance to make sure she was alone, Maryam posts up against the wall to leave a message for Taskeen in one of the plazas they agreed on. She's sure Taskeen would prefer she use their secret tunnel, but Maryam isn't in the mood to play with network failures.

She expects to have to wait to see Nejime, but Zaid ushers her in immediately. "She's been waiting for you," he whispers. The office is full—Leung and a group from his team clustered around a projection in one corner, Nejime conferring with al-Derbi in another—but as soon as Nejime sees Maryam, she asks everyone but her and al-Derbi to leave.

"What's going on?" Maryam asks, unnerved, as the door closes behind the foreign relations team.

"Maryam." Nejime reaches out as if to touch her hand. "I'm sorry. I feel terrible."

"What is it?" Irrationally, Maryam blinks up Núria's location, *Surely she wasn't there, surely she wasn't hurt . . .*

"We only have the first reports, so I can't say that this is completely confirmed yet, but it seems that Rajiv used his authority to slip the attackers past security. He was there, he got them in, and he fled along with them," Nejime clarifies, seeing how stunned Maryam is.

"Was he . . . a hostage? Was he under duress?" Maryam asks.

"As I said, we don't have all the intel yet, but witness reports suggest not." Nejime pauses. "Maryam, I made a mistake asking him to interact with you and Taskeen. Do you think he could have learned anything from you, anything that he could be taking to the rest of this group as we speak?"

"He did act a little strange . . ." Maryam tries to remember everything she said to him. "I was being careful, but it never occurred to me he might be a—" She chokes a little on the drama of it.

"A double agent," al-Derbi says gravely.

"But he said a few things that seemed odd, so I didn't offer much. And Taskeen—Taskeen lied to him a couple of times, or misled him, I guess."

"How do you know?" Nejime asks sharply. "You two discussed it?"

"No, she misrepresented technical details in a way that must have been intentional. She was rude to him, too. I thought she was just being crotchety, but maybe she suspected something." Between this and the apparent technical sophistication of the data attack, Maryam's mind is racing into conjecture. *Could Taskeen have been working with Rajiv instead of deflecting him?*

CHAPTER 15

A*tunnel?*" Maryam and Roz are sitting on the veranda again, and Maryam bites her lip: she said it too loudly.

Roz laughs softly. "It's fine. I turned on the airscaping before we came out; I don't think anyone can hear us. That was my reaction, too."

"And it was full of comms cables?"

"Packed with them," Roz says. "Well . . . lined with them—they left space in the middle for personal transport. An escape pod, maybe."

"But why so many cables, when the tunnel only goes between two fixed points?"

"It depends, in part, on where point B is," Roz says. Djukic is working on that. "But I think . . . I suspect Heritage was selling channels."

"Selling channels to whom?"

"To other governments. We've only worked our way through a few of the data streams so far, but it looks like they're all encrypted under different systems."

"You mean other micro-democratic governments?" Maryam asks, sitting up. "They were paying Heritage to transmit data behind our back?"

Roz sighs. Her reaction, two days ago when the idea was first floated, was much the same. Now she wonders how it could be surprising for anyone in their line of work. "People are constantly trying to get around Information. There's this addictive fetishization of privacy, even when it's not for any particular purpose."

"That may be," Maryam says, taking a bite of candied kumquat. "But if you're right, we're not talking about chisme or petty private scandals. These are governments digging a secret tunnel through the mantle of the Earth to keep people—not just Information, the constituents they supposedly work for—from knowing what they're doing."

Roz nods agreement. "We're considering the possibility that this may not be governments but the individual corporations within Heritage's coalition. Corporations have secrets too."

"Very true," Maryam agrees, taking a piece of papaya this time. "Election time makes it seem like everything's about governments, but that might make more sense than Heritage cooperating with other governments, even for money."

"Of course, if they were talking to a null state without our knowledge . . ."

"Scary," Maryam agrees. "So there's still the possibility this could be Exformation."

"Yes, but . . . I keep coming back to the question of why so many cables. You would think they would only need one."

"When I started researching these weird tourist guides," Maryam says, "I was baffled by the idea of data not available on Information. But now . . . there's so much out there, so much we miss."

There's a long-enough pause that Maryam thinks Roz isn't going to answer. When she does start to speak it's slowly, as if thinking it through as she talks. "I started to see that in Darfur. The edges, the gaps in coverage. And then there are the null states, and the places near them. And then there's everything people try to hide from us, successfully or not. And the things we don't see at all, because we don't think they're important or we don't know what to look for." Maryam realizes that Roz's measured tone is that of someone guiding a friend through an epiphanic doorway, invisible from one side, impossible to miss from the other, that she has already passed through long ago. "And sometimes it . . . it seeps further. It grows. People are used to hiding things, and they keep finding new ways to do it."

"Until they dig tunnels hundreds of kilometers under the surface."

"So it seems," Roz sighs. "My point is that while this tunnel is a dramatic and extreme example, people hide data all the time. In a way, it's part of the system, a natural outgrowth . . ."

They think about that in companionable silence. Roz's belly is noticeably bigger than the last time Maryam saw her, or maybe it is just the effect of the loose neck-to-ankle dress she is wearing. Maryam's mind flits back, as it has been periodically, to the last moments of her visit with Taskeen. She still hasn't received a reply to the message she left in the plaza, and she's not sure whether Taskeen simply hasn't checked the site—it is, after all, a bit more complicated for her than blinking, and she might not expect a ping so soon after Maryam left—or if she is trying to force Maryam to use the channel they built.

"Dealing with an actual tunnel would be so much easier . . ." she says dreamily.

"Easier?" Roz asks, remembering the piles of dirt slowly mounting under the old Zurich railway station.

"I just meant because then we would know the channel, we'd be able to see it."

"You know," Roz says after a pause. "Maybe we're over-reacting."

Maryam shoots her a skeptical glance without bothering to sit up from her slump.

"We're basing this on the theory that terrible people have been planning terrible things for years and no one has been able to find them or stop them! How realistic is that?"

"You think they're not actually doing it?"

"I'm just saying we see hypothetical tunnels and data oubliettes and who knows what everywhere! Just because Nejime is freaked out about getting through the election doesn't mean someone is trying to blow it up."

Maryam shakes her head. "You found an actual secret tunnel."

Roz waves her hands. "Those enemies, we knew about."

"You still don't know for sure who's on the other side," Maryam points out.

"You see my point, though."

"They attacked an election event! They hijacked our data stream for *twelve minutes*." Maryam can no longer say the word *twelve* without mental italics. It's not that twelve minutes is such a terribly long time, but it is very long, *very* long, in proportion to the amount of effort expended on the attack. Once Rajiv got them through the door, it only took six attackers ten minutes to take it down. Maryam hopes, vindictively, that the software assault took ages to code and involved lots of thorny debugging.

"And what did they do with those twelve minutes?" Roz asks. "Repeated the same three-second clip over and over. *They* probably didn't even expect it to last that long."

Maryam flinches; that almost sounds like criticism of the tech department. She's been reacting to that sentiment all day, and she's still not sure whether non-techies are actually thinking it or whether she's just being defensive.

"When that voice came on," Roz goes on, "Suleyman walked out and looked up and down the street. For rioters, or terrorists, here! I did the same thing virtually." She shakes her head. "Over nothing! This tiny disruption. It wasn't just that it startled us. We're all waiting for something big. Something global."

"A revolution," Maryam says, and then thinks of the camaradas revolucionarias and their theories about the life-cycle of political regimes.

"We overreacted," Roz points out. "It was just . . . those losers again, trying to get attention and knock things down without any plans to pick them back up again."

"We don't know what it was yet," Maryam says, with a little more force than necessary. Something's happening. She's never tested high on the narrative-disorder spectrum, but in this case, it feels inevitable to her. "Maybe we're right to expect something big, and it just hasn't happened yet."

Roz doesn't answer, but the words seems to coalesce in the air around them, like a threat.

"Or." Maryam isn't sure if she's talking because the last thing she said is making her nervous, or if this really needs saying. "What if it's the other way around, and we're under-reacting? What if the revolution is happening, right now, and we're not seeing it?"

"What do you mean?" Roz asks.

"What if they're making their move, spewing out modified intel, and we don't know because the people who see it don't know it's modified?"

"How would we even test for that?" Roz wonders.

"I don't know," Maryam says. "Remember in the last

election how Liberty changed Information for people within their centenals?"

Roz groans. "I can't deal with that right now!"

Maryam cedes, and they are silent for a while.

"What do you think their goal is?" Roz asks.

"Hmm?'

"If they change Information for some populations. Liberty had a reason. They wanted support, votes, immigration. Why would this . . . this nebulous, nameless group do it? How does it help them?"

"It undermines us," Maryam offers.

"People do hate us," Roz sighs.

There's another pause. Maryam debates it internally, then line-of-sights Roz some of the ugly commentary she found about the Williams trial. Roz is silent, presumably reading. Then she line-of-sights back the latest decision on the PhilipMorris mantle tunnel proceedings: government sovereignty doesn't extend as deep as the mantle, and the construction is authorized. It's not a final go-ahead, as there are other challenges pending, but it's indicative.

"The Secretariat might solve some of these problems," Roz says, but she sounds doubtful.

"Do you ever think about what it would be like if there were other sources of intel?" Maryam asks.

"There are, kind of," Roz argues. "Different compilers present different opinions and perspectives. They're just not allowed to lie."

"Lying is subjective."

"Sometimes! Not always."

"Okay, but you know what I mean. In those certain cases . . ."

"To have a more distinct viewpoint? Maybe." Roz is silent for a while, and then adds, "I think more about privacy."

"Privacy?"

"You know. Whether fewer feeds would really be such a bad thing."

Maryam has to think about that for a while, but she still finds it creepier that people are avoiding feeds than that there are feeds everywhere in the first place. "What about competition?"

"Competition?"

"You know. In data management and provision."

"Theoretically, competition would improve the quality of the information provided," Roz says, but she sounds skeptical.

"I guess what I'm asking is, are we sure that whatever these people are trying to do is really such a bad idea?"

Even in the darkness, Maryam can tell that Roz has turned to look at her. "You think they're trying to compete with us?"

"Would it be such a bad thing," Maryam says into the night. She says it very quietly, without even the inflection of a question to raise her tone.

"Sometimes I wonder," Roz answers, just as softly.

They don't speak for some time after that, tasting instead the changed flavor of the silence between them.

After she came back from Zurich, Roz considered her responsibility on the secret tunnel complete. She handed management of the problem over to the code-breakers and returned her focus to the Wall. She's less and less eager to travel as her due date approaches: even at the end of the twenty-first century, no one can tell her with any certainty what week her baby will be born, what the first signs of labor will be, or how long she will have to find competent medical care once labor begins.

Fortunately, the mantle tunnel work is at an ebb for the moment: PhilipMorris, encouraged by the ruling in their favor, is trying to push through the additional cases, and 888 is waiting in hopes of useful precedent. All Roz has to do is to keep up with what is going on in the courts, while waiting for any change on the ground.

One of the more frivolous lawsuits, filed by a far less reputable group than Veena Rasmussen's, claims that the contractors may have already caused irreparable damage through the insertion of the preliminary scanning cable along the proposed route. There's plenty of literature about how it is impossible to observe without affecting, but almost nothing covering concrete probabilities of environmental impacts. Roz considers calling Djukic to get her thoughts on it. She hasn't contacted Djukic since getting back; she thought about doing so once or twice, but it seemed weird to revive the friendship, or whatever it was, without the excuse of work. She initiates a call, hesitates, and then shuts it down.

Instead, she goes by Hassan's office. "Keif?" she asks, leaning in his door. Since her time in Darfur, and getting together with Suleyman, she's been taking every opportunity to practice Arabic, and they chat through the usual greetings and make small talk for a few minutes.

"Any update on the comms from the tunnel?" Roz asks, lowering her voice automatically.

"Not much," Hassan says, leaning back in his chair and

stretching his arms behind his head. "We haven't gotten data from all of them yet." He and Djukic put readers on all the cables, braided them into a single thick strand, and threaded them out through one small hole in the tunnel carapace and up into a newly rented and locked office in the basement of the old train station. "The messages we've skimmed are solidly encrypted. What with all the fluster around the attack on Malta, we haven't been able to put much effort toward breaking the codes."

"Are any of them the same or . . ."

"Different encryption on every single one. As far as we can tell, unrelated systems. We'll get through them, but it will take a while, and we'll need significantly more data from each one." He throws up a projection to give her a sense: a long row of silos, some completely empty, others showing different levels of data. As they watch, a few more strings of incomprehensible characters drop into one of them.

"Still in use, then," Roz comments.

"Most definitely. At least these twelve strands. Haven't seen anything on the others yet. No sign of vehicular movement in the tunnel."

Roz leans back against the wall, pondering. "Do you think, hypothetically, is it possible that the scanning cables for the two legitimate mantle tunnel projects could be transmitting comms?"

"No reason why not," Hassan says. "But wasn't there oversight when they were scanning?"

"There was," Roz agrees. "And a lot of press. But it was focused on the process, and the route, and possible environmental issues. I don't know if anyone outside the government studied the composition of the cables."

Hassan clucks, appalled at this oversight.

"How hard would it be to check on that now?"

"Not technically difficult," Hassan answers. "Kind of awkward politically."

"We couldn't do it without them noticing?"

"Well, the cables only surface at the excavation points, so it's either dig another hole or find an excuse for examining them at crowded, guarded, media-heavy construction sites."

"How long would it take?"

"To check the composition? Not long. If you want to put a reader on . . . but then, a reader attached at the surface at the busy excavation site is likely to be noticed."

"Hm." It occurs to Roz that if they find evidence of illicit communications, they don't necessarily have to keep it secret; they could bring charges against the government. They would lose whatever intel they could get from reading the comms, though. And she'd hate to drop a bombshell like that during the election, even if it's deserved.

"Could you ask your engineer friend to examine the 888 cable?" Hassan asks.

Roz makes a face. "I don't know if she's that good a friend." Djukic came to them with the secret tunnel but hasn't said anything about what she'd seen of the 888 tunnel. "And if she is, I don't want to involve her in this. We'll have to come up with something else."

Explain exactly what it is you want me to do?" Amran is trying to combine skepticism, curiosity, and professionalism in her tone, and is annoyed with herself when she hears the interrogative upward tone anyway. Hopefully it makes her sound suspicious rather than unsure. Mishima told her reluctance would be less suspicious than eagerness, with the added advantage of being able to ask more questions.

"This is the fun part." Amran's interlocutor doesn't seem suspicious at all. Mischievous, rather. Nor does he look like the criminal mastermind or hard-bitten anti-Information fanatic Amran expected. Of course, she tells herself, they would hardly send a mastermind to meet an untested recruit. Vincent—for so he introduced himself, and his public Information claims the same name—looks young, enthusiastic, and friendly. "How did you find this place?"

The meeting location they gave her was a test. Amran had been told to go to "the bar where the librarian's daughter was offered an unusual prize for her artistry near the school of engineering."

"I asked around," Amran says, the lie she believes they want to hear. She did ask people about the mysterious clue on her way there, but only for show. Mishima had arranged for different people—Information grunts, Amran supposes, although they could have been people off the street, for all she knows—to look up different parts of the prompt, so that there was no one search history to jump out at anyone keeping tabs. Mishima had wanted to know where Amran would be. There are no feeds in this bar (she wonders if she could have found it just by searching "bar with no feeds in Nairobi"), but Amran is sure the surrounding feeds are well-monitored right now.

"The point," Vincent says, "is that there are things Information doesn't know." Amran nods seriously. "The more local you get, the more specialized the knowledge is." For emphasis, Vincent throws up a map and dives down to the sidewalk level. "Every neighborhood has *layers* of microculture. Secrets, argot, history, dynasties, shortcuts, inside jokes. Incredible stuff that someone from the outside would never know about."

"Isn't that exactly what Information is for?"

"Sure. But Information isn't accomplishing it." Vincent is leaning forward now, small starbursts of numbers projecting as he raises his fingers. "One, they depend too much on algorithms and automated feed searches, and not enough on people. Two, the people they do employ move around too much. They don't have time to take root in the local culture, and when they use locals, they don't promote them." Amran has to bite the inside of her cheek not to respond to that. "But the most important reason, three, people hate them."

Skeptical, Amran tells herself. *It's okay to be skeptical, but not defensive.* "So, people hate them," she shrugs. "They still have all the feeds, all the staff to sort through them, all the data transmitters, all the . . . I don't know, the stuff that lets them do what they do!"

Vincent is nodding. "Exactly! They have all of that and they still can't pull in the hyperlocal content I'm talking about. Why? Because people hate them. Fairly or unfairly, nobody wants to tell Information anything anymore."

This isn't far from the truth. "So, what do you do?"

He grins. "We use people. We recruit the best"—with a small nod at her. "We keep them local. The goal is that someone—you, say—could walk into a neighborhood, a subdivision, a tenement, a prison, an office park, a shopping center, a high street, a village, anywhere in the world and know it as if you, and your parents, and your *grandparents* had grown up there."

"When you say *know it,*" Amran asks, skeptical, "you mean *have access to the data about it.*"

"Yes, of course," Vincent concedes. "Although you can turn that into knowledge by learning the data before you go."

Amran shakes her head. "What's your real goal?"

Vincent seems pleased by that too, although he pushes back at first. "What do you mean? I told you, the goal is foreign familiarity."

"No," Amran says, and reminds herself that her cover identity works in the private sector. "That's the customer experience. How do you make money?"

"It's not about the money," Vincent says, seriously.

"It's always about the money. Otherwise, how are you going to pay me?"

"Investors," Vincent says. "But to your other question. Let me ask you: is Information fair?"

"Fair?" Amran wrinkles her nose. "Impossible. Information is transparent, which is as close as you can get."

Vincent looks startled at that, and Amran realizes she's just spouted Information boilerplate. Flustered, she doubles down. "Are you telling me you're going to be *more* fair?"

"Information *claims* transparency, based on the idea that they cover *everything*, that they *know* everything. And yet, as we've just seen, they don't."

Amran pretends to consider while privately not conceding the point. "You collect the data Information misses, distribute it, and . . ."

"And that shows the world how Information manipulates everyone!" Amran catches a brief glimpse of fanaticism before Vincent relaxes again. "Politics, trade, international relations—they are managing it all, and no one even notices."

"You're going to be invading people's privacy in exactly the same way. Won't people hate you, too?"

"We're not the same! We use people, not video and

algorithms." He must know that's a weak point, because he moves on quickly. "More importantly, we're not trying to run the world. We don't force people to understand politics in a certain way or make businesses conform to a certain conception of 'honesty.' We're just trying to tell stories—and yes, make a little money along the way."

Amran freezes up when he says *telling stories*, wondering if he's gotten a whiff of her narrative disorder. Then she remembers he thinks she's a content developer; "telling stories" is the pitch that's supposed to snag her.

"It does sound like fun," she allows.

"It *is* fun!" Vincent proclaims. "You get to snoop for neighborhood gossip in service of a great cause. And it's historic; you'll be a part of the first hyperatlas."

"What exactly do I need to do?"

"As much or as little as you like—although, of course, if you don't do much, we may end up hiring another person to help cover your beat. Just give us stuff you find, anything at all related to anywhere at all, as long as it's not already available on Information—or at least not easily found."

"But doesn't—" Amran pretends to squirm. "Doesn't Information get upset at what you're doing? Am I going to get in trouble?"

"There's no *law* against it. They don't *own* this data—in fact, they don't even know about it! But the best thing to do," Vincent adds, less reassuringly, "is not to get caught. Since we're looking for stuff that's not *on* Information in the first place, this isn't hard. Just keep your head down and do your research in person. We'll set up a drop point and meet periodically as well."

"But . . . feeds and all . . . they'll notice, won't they?"

"What's for them to notice? You talking to people? Us meeting occasionally? Nothing wrong with any of that."

He sounds defensive, and Amran doesn't want to push too hard. "How do you distribute this . . . hyperatlas?"

Vincent winks at her. "That's the trick, isn't it? I'm afraid it's proprietary intel for now, but once you have something in it, I'll make sure you see the final version."

Amran pretends to dither a little longer.

"Look," Vincent says, offering his pay toggle. "Here's an advance, or maybe I should say *an investment*. Use this to drink a lot of tea or coffee and listen to people talk. If you learn something, come back to us and tell a story to the world!"

"All right," she says, with the smile of a won-over skeptic. "I'm in."

Vincent grins, offers her his palm to slap.

"By the way," Amran adds, offhand, "what do you call yourselves?"

Vincent's grin stretches wider. "Opposition Research."

There's an extra buzz around the Secretariat debate after the attack on the null-states event. Mishima can tell they've ramped up security for the rich spectators who've paid a lot of money to attend the debate in person. Even the candidates are put through an in-person pat-down and mental-emotional scan, in addition to the usual long-distance body scan for weapons. Mishima used to be indifferent to these things, but that was before the whole world knew her for a badass with a penchant for concealed weapons and a severe narrative disorder; now she feels like even the most professional of security staffers are looking to confirm their expectations when they search her.

The Secretariat debates are a side show compared to the mainstage, all-out publicity fest of the government debates. It seems fair to Mishima: your choice of government is likely to affect your life far more than whom you pick to be on an abstract council no one knows much about yet. Unlike the major governments, which have been discussed and analyzed and measured for decades, no one knows the candidates for this position, either. Of the five candidates on stage, only she and Nougaz have any broad name recognition, and Mishima is the only real celebrity. Her public persona has some disadvantages, though. She doesn't need the pollsters to tell her not everyone wants a neurodivergent assassin as their representative.

She has always appreciated the audio-only rule on principle, but now she is truly grateful. Nejime offered to set her up with a projection appointment with a stylist, but Mishima couldn't convince herself that was acceptable behavior for a candidate. She chose a paneled dress that she considers muted but classy. Two podiums over, Nougaz is wearing something bright-colored and angular, Rothko-esque while still somehow looking professional. Watching the sight lines of the audience, Mishima is pretty sure Nougaz is getting most of the attention.

She is beginning to realize that of all the career bureaucrats, diplomats, and spies on this stage, Nougaz is the only one who has been training for politics her whole life.

The debate develops a cavalier flair once it gets started: it is the first time anyone has done this, and there's still some uncertainty about what exactly the job is. The central moderator, a well-known news compiler (they couldn't use someone from Information for this one) named Souad Mourad smiles as she stumbles over the explanation for one question. Gerardo Vasconcielos, the first respondent, laughs with the crowd on a casual joke in his answer. Mishima's life has not, she thinks, prepared her to be so relaxed with strangers whose approval she needs.

It is a debate in only the most recent, specialized sense of the word: rather than an exchange of opinions among the participants (which would, in fairness, be unwieldy with even the truncated list of top governments), it is more of a panel discussion. The moderator takes them through key topics, aiming to create balance among the participants and to draw them into disagreements that throw divergences into relief. *Hardly a neutral and transparent process,* Mishima notes, as Mourad shifts in her seat to look at her. Mishima can feel herself bracing for the question, even though she knows that is counterproductive.

"You are a security expert, with long experience in the field," Mourad comments, her pace suggesting that she's reading the prepared question from an eye-level projection.

Mishima feels her face go hot: *not neutral at all.* The lead-in will remind the audience of her highly public, widely publicized fight a few years ago.

"We have recently seen renewed threats against our way of life," Mourad continues. Mishima's anger flares again, because this will bring back her gaffe during the null-state debate. "How do you see Information's role in ensuring the security of the micro-democratic system?"

This question is predictable enough that Mishima has the skeleton of an answer memorized. Maybe, she thinks as she starts talking, Mourad's giving her an opportunity to recover from that error. Maybe Mourad thinks she's on Mishima's side—or maybe she thinks giving Mishima an opportunity for bonus points is in the interest of fairness. As she considers these possibilities, Mishima can hear her own voice, deliberate and calm, using all the correct honorifics and exalted grammar, skating through the answer, but when it's over she can't remember what she said. Her recollection is so blank that she considers playing back the audio, but she's afraid to miss something in real time. Besides, the audience shows no sign of shock or surprise, so whatever she got out must have been reasonable.

Mourad turns her attention to Nougaz. "What about you, Director? How do you see Information's role with regards to security?" There's a mild flicker of interest across the audience: everyone knows the key face-off here is Mishima versus Nougaz, and security is a prime arena.

Nougaz gives it a moment before she answers, letting the attention build and focus. "Micro-democracy is, as you say, under threat from many different sources," Nougaz says, her voice carrying easily. "On our borders, the null states are growing in strength. Within, destructive and senseless organizations like Anarchy take shots at our institutions whenever they can. The latest attack, which disrupted an event much like this one, shows the grave risk we are facing: our enemies want to destroy your connection to Information itself." She pauses to let that sink in. "Corrupting or disrupting Information for even a brief period would have a terrifying effect on the economy, on those who depend on Information for their livelihoods or their lives—as some of us remember all too well." A reference to the events of the last election. Nougaz's role in the response to that outage is well known; Mishima's much less so. "That is why," Nougaz continues, her tone shifting from portentous to energizing, "I propose to strengthen Information's infrastructure, security protocols, and mandate. Individual governments—including and perhaps especially the Supermajority—cannot be expected to safeguard your access to the independent data you need. It is imperative, therefore, that we do."

"Speaking of internal and external threats," Mourad says, realigning herself toward Mishima, "we've all been following the Williams trial, which raises questions about the power of Information staffers to affect election outcomes. How would you deal with such incidents?"

Mishima, who has faked out more mental-emotional scans than she can remember, hears her heart thudding as soon as Mourad says *Williams*.

"I can't speak about that investigation," she says, her voice overloud in her own ears. "I'm not privy to the details, and in any event it would be inappropriate to discuss a trial in progress."

"Of course," Mourad says in an eminently reasonable tone. "But in this *kind* of trial . . ."

Fuck presumed neutrality. The moderator is definitely, no question about it, against her. "A hypothetical?" Mishima asks, trying to regain ground, but knowing it will be played as an evasion. "Each case is different. I'm not going to rush to judgment on a hypothetical."

She's expecting more pushback, and thereby a chance to expand on the point, maybe think of something to say, but instead Mourad turns to Nougaz. "Director?"

"I have so much respect for the women and men who collect, collate, and distribute data for us. They make the world go around." Nougaz doesn't sound warm, exactly, but for her, it's not a bad approximation. "While we must be vigilant to avoid bias and influence, Nakia Williams's is a particularly difficult, nuanced case. As my colleague quite correctly noted, we shouldn't discuss the details of an ongoing case, but as Hub Director, I've done everything I could to support my staff. As Information representative to the Secretariat, I hope I would do the same."

Mishima had been planning to jump in again when Nougaz finished, regardless of whether the moderator turned to her, but she's so surprised, she misses the (miniscule) window, and Mourad takes her question to the other candidates. The worst of it, Mishima thinks, is that she really shouldn't have been shocked, because it's true: Nougaz goes to the mat for her people. She pushed hard for her deputy Abendou to get his own directorship and supported Garza during that incident with the Starlight liaison. When did she start thinking of Nougaz as a bad person?

CHAPTER 16

When Maryam gets back to La Habana, the apartment is empty. Núria is in a SavePlanet centenal in the Amazon for three days, something about resource protection. She left the apartment on their usual timed-and-primed away settings, so it is neither dark nor musty nor sweltering when Maryam arrives. It still feels quiet, but at least there are no camaradas to contend with or difficult questions to answer, and Maryam tries to savor the prospect of a quiet night. She goes to bed early but lies long awake, running over the events and conversations of the last few days.

Without Núria, there's little appeal in going out for breakfast, and Maryam slurps some coffee, eats three-day-old bread, and hurries in to work, the colorful striped cloth from Oaxaca covering her head. At the Hub, she grabs a colada and settles down to work.

She is looking at voter identification protocol updates when she finally gets a ping from Taskeen. It's a response to the message she left in the plaza, suggesting that they meet "in the regular channel." Maryam looks at the message for a while, trying to figure out any other way to read it, but it's clear what Taskeen wants her to do. Maryam has to admit to herself that the secret linkage will be a much easier way to talk than these vague and time-consuming public messages. It's not technically illegal, probably because no one thought to make it so (something Maryam could remedy, if she felt so inclined). And yet, she can't deny a deep unease as she programs the hidden path into her communications protocol as a temporary hard mandate.

She's nervous enough about it to leave the office and walk the eight blocks to El Chismoso. Fortunately it's not too busy, and she's able to get a booth for one without a wait. The connection goes through, and Taskeen peers at her. "My, but it's good to communicate in a more modern fashion! Can you see me all right?"

"You're a bit flat," Maryam says drily. Taskeen's image is two-dimensional, but getting even that from a fifty-year old desktop camera impresses her. "It'll do. And on your side?"

Taskeen head-waggles. "Good enough. I found conversion software from when three-dimensional projections were starting to catch on. Now, what did you want to talk about?"

"This attack on the null-state event." Maryam pauses, because Taskeen shows no recognition of what she's talking about. "You heard about it, right?"

"I'm not encouraged to follow politics. As I'm living in 2008."

"You are going to *vote*, though, right?" Maryam hears the shock in her voice and immediately feels naïve.

"It is possible to vote without following every twist and turn of the pre-election novela," Taskeen says mildly. "In any case. You were saying something about a null state?"

Suddenly cautious, Maryam briefly summarizes the public facts, without saying anything about Hassan's efforts to figure out how the data paths were corrupted.

"At least no one was hurt" is Taskeen's response. "Too bad we didn't implement that program in time to stop them, but . . ."

"Rajiv was working with them."

That does get a reaction. "That snake! I knew there was something funny about him and his questions. Did you catch him?"

"He escaped with the rest of them. Taskeen, I think they used a trick like this—like this hidden channel—to keep the data from finding alternate transmission routes."

"You think they hid the nodes?" Taskeen is silent for seventeen seconds. When she speaks again, her tone is casual. "You must have wondered how Exformation communicated with each other across Hubs. Before they left Information I mean, how they were able to coordinate while they were still working there."

"Of course we wondered!"

"I think I may have had something to do with that. Before I retired, I noticed difficulties in sharing of experiences and lessons across departments and locations, particularly with people worried about what the upper leadership would think." Taskeen's shrug comes across on the two-dimensional image. "So I did something about it, developing the technique we're using now. It started as just among friends," she adds hurriedly. "But I believe it spread from there, and continued to gain popularity after my involvement ended. I'm surprised you don't know about it, actually."

"Before you went into the sana—time capsule?"

"Naturally." Taskeen blinks at her. "I could hardly do it from here, could I? Nor was employee satisfaction of any particular interest to me after I retired."

"So, you're saying they knew about it even before they left?" Convenient, if Taskeen wants to avoid being accused of working with them. "You gave them the tools they needed

254 · MALKA OLDER

to communicate clandestinely." And the worst of it is there's no decryption-key equivalent; knowing the technique is of no use at all in finding the channels.

"Well, I could hardly know fifteen years ago that some of our staff would become corrupt, quit, and adapt my techniques to their purposes."

"You could have told us earlier!"

Taskeen raises an eyebrow. "Don't you think it's really Rajiv you're angry at?"

"Pop psychology went out in the twenties," Maryam snaps.

"Amateur narrative analysis is no better!" Taskeen retorts. "You are looking for a villain who is suspicious but not too suspicious, unmasked through a key revelation about their history. You should be figuring out what you want the result of this conflict to be and how you're going to get there. Or at worst what *they* want the result to be and how to stop them! Come on, Maryam! Something is going to change. We need to make sure that things move in the right direction!"

"Right now," Maryam says, "all I know is that they're using your tool to undermine Information. And now you have me using it, too! You built this; you figure out how we can stop them from using it against us!" Maryam cuts the connection.

Roz and Hassan decided on the Istanbul end of the tunnel because Djukic is still based in Berlin: whether she's trustworthy or not, Roz doesn't want her involved in secretly tapping into the legal part of a mantle tunnel project. As they walk around the site, Roz realizes that she'd hoped the Istanbul site would be less orderly and well guarded than

the terminus in Berlin: a stupid assumption based on antiquated stereotypes. The tunnel construction site, in a corner
of Saraçhane Park, is thoroughly fenced and patrolled.

"How deep would the cable be, say, here?" Roz asks,
stomping the pavement when they've walked out of sight of
the guards along the trajectory of the tunnel.

"Too deep to yank it up without everyone noticing," Hassan says, rolling his eyes. "Why can't we just tell them we
need to inspect the cable for some other reason?"

"We can try," Roz says, "but it will make them suspicious.
If they realize we're trying to get to it, we'll be worse off than
if we say nothing and just . . ."

"Just what, exactly?"

"Just sneak in and check it out. We can get in to the construction site easily enough in the daytime," Roz points out.
"I have every right to be there, as do you. I'll come up with
some other reason to inspect the site and distract the people
in charge long enough for you to check the cable where it
emerges. It's not like they're going to have separate guards
for the cable area within the compound."

"And if they catch me?"

"You were acting on my orders," Roz says firmly. "Inspecting the scanning cable was . . . further down on the
agenda for the meeting, and you saw an opportunity to get
it done quickly. Any ideas for the rationale for inspecting it?"

Hassan shrugs. "Almost anything. Let's say: uploading a
patch with greater seismic sensitivity. That should distract
them."

They could have stayed in a hotel, but Roz, increasingly
nervous about the possibility of going into early labor while
traveling, preferred to stay in the crow, and Hassan had no
objection. They moor it in the park and go to bed early. The

next morning they walk down Şehzadebaşı, looking for some breakfast. The first few shops they pass are still shuttered. Roz, distracted by her efforts to plan for the coming infiltration, doesn't look up until Hassan says, "What's going on with *that*?"

Roz glances in the direction he's looking, at the storefronts and restaurants lining the street, and shivers. All of the windows and glass doors have blank indigo projections up behind them. "It means there's about to be a demonstration," she says. "I've seen it before. The shopkeepers and business owners blank the windows so that looters will think twice before breaking them. Blanked windows might hide fewer goods or more guards than they expect." She starts walking more quickly, looking down the street until she finds a window projection that hosts a gaily fonted slogan her translator interprets as *No to the Tunnel! Vote down 888 before they dig up your house!*

"They support the demonstrators?"

Roz shrugs. "Or believe supporting them will do more to protect their assets." She peers up the street nervously. "Look, I support their right to demonstrate"—meaning, as Hassan knows, *I support their anti-mantle tunnel stance*—"but I don't want to get caught in the crowd." Her hand flutters around her belly.

They end up eating energy chews from the crow's supply cabinet, which Roz feels guilty about too, because she's been trying to eat real food for the baby, but at least she gets nutrients into herself that way.

The meeting is easier than she hoped. The 888 officials and contractor reps are so used to updating Information on project minutiae that they don't even notice the conversation is pointless. It's possible that they are distracted by the demonstration; Roz catches more than the usual update flashes against their eyes, and one of the contractors keeps getting up and going to the window, which is useless since the fence blocks any view of the road. Hassan excuses himself early on, and nobody seems to notice when he doesn't come back. As soon as Roz gets the ping from him, she winds up the meeting and, after a round of handshakes, extricates herself from the pop-up shelter.

Hassan is not immediately apparent outside the shelter, which is probably a good thing. Roz finds him near the entrance to the site, sitting on a low stone wall with his legs swinging. He's expressionless, which she guesses means that he found something.

Outside they find ordered chaos, too loud and crowded to talk about anything. The demonstration has swollen to fill the street. Protestors are wearing sunglasses or hats with attachments designed to blur their faces on feeds, and the air above jostles with projected slogans:

STOP THE TUNNEL, SAVE OUR CITY!
PLANET OVER PROFIT!
INFORMATION WON'T SAVE US
WE HAVE TO SAVE OURSELVES!

Roz leads them off the road into the park. There are protesters scattered around the grass there too, resting and rehydrating, but they find an empty swath of ground with no feeds close enough to read lips.

"So?" Roz asks.

Hassan nods. "A braid of six."

Roz whistles. "Did you have enough readers?"

"Just. I thought I was being excessive, bringing that many.

We'll see how long the readers last. There's no particular reason for anyone to look at the cable, so it might be fine, but anyone who does will see them right away."

Roz looks back toward the colorful, bobbing mass of protesters. Someone brought a professional-grade projector and is putting up a massive slide show: images and vidloops from the Tokyo earthquake five years ago, interspersed with statistics and infographics on Istanbul's seismic risk factors. These people believe stopping the tunnel is life or death for them, and they may be right. Roz could stop it today if she wanted to, end their worry and stress just by throwing documentation of the illegal comms cable up on Information.

Hassan reads her thoughts. "We have to keep quiet for now. We need the data."

"It could take months! Have you decrypted any of the lines from the Heritage tunnel yet?"

"We'll get there," he insists. "Besides, the construction is still frozen. They're not going to dig tomorrow, or next week, or before the election. You can stop it anytime you want to."

"These people don't know that." Roz nods at the avenue.

"And odds are there are other people who are getting screwed over in ways we haven't even thought of, and we won't know until we listen in on those cables. Because whatever they're talking about, for sure it's nothing good."

CHAPTER 17

I t was *awful*," Mishima says. She managed to snag a privacy booth in the Lagos airport lounge while waiting for her flight out. Perquisites of her candidate status; the charge goes directly to Information. She's going to miss that, but not much else. "Anyway, I'm toast, so I guess I don't have to worry about the election anymore."

"Hardly!" Ken's attempt at a reassuring tone sounds overly earnest. "It's true, it didn't go well . . ."

"Understatement," coughs Mishima. "Outright lie. If you were a politician, they would annotate you."

"Plenty could still happen before the vote. It's not over. Nobody expected Policy1st to win the last election."

"If it's going to take two recounts due to sabotage and lies, I don't want the position," Mishima says, rolling her eyes, and then realizes she is shading one of Ken's proudest moments. Contrite, she turns the conversation away from herself. "What about you? Did you decide anything?" She's pleased at herself for framing it so tactfully, as if it were entirely his decision, rather than asking whether Geoff Forth has fired him outright. While he's answering, she flips open the polls—not her own, just the government side—and checks: Policy1st is still significantly behind, 888 still ahead, with PhilipMorris between them.

Ken fidgets. "Geoff hasn't said anything, but that doesn't mean he hasn't decided to fire me."

"Not the best communicator."

"The thing is, this idea of Policy1st's, the new way of working with other governments—I mean, it's fascinating, right?" Ken's face is alight with excitement. "It could be a whole new evolution of democracy—it could be what comes next." The phrase is a part of their ongoing conversation about the increasingly precarious future of micro-democracy.

Mishima considers. "There are two weeks left in the election. Would you want to work for Policy1st after the campaign ends?"

Ken tries to imagine it, but Policy1st is so different from Free2B, and has grown so much since he worked for them, that he's not sure what it would be like. Are they a giant, tedious bureaucracy now, like so much of Information? Have they managed to cling to their ideals through the morass and temptations of the Supermajority? "I don't know," he says. "Maybe I'll talk to Xavier about it. But . . ." He ponders. "I think I'm ready for a change." Maybe it's wounded pride, but since his last conversation with Geoff, Free2B has come to seem intolerably provincial to him.

"Then do it," Mishima says immediately. "You should talk to Geoff, though. Just because that bridge is a little singed doesn't mean you have to burn it down."

"I could say the same to you."

"Fuck this bridge," Mishima says.

In between checking election prep and fishing around Information for hints about disintegrating tourist guides with non-Information hints, Maryam goes back and rereads all the background intel she compiled on Taskeen before meeting with her the first time.

Most of it she knew even before Nejime suggested Taskeen Khan was the person to talk to about Information infrastructure. Born and brought up in Dhaka, higher education in Chennai, Bangalore, and la Ciudad de México— of course, the Spanish. Then positions, sequentially, with Google, Facebook, and the United Nations. Most of the founding Information staff worked for at least one of those, but Taskeen hit the triumvirate, and was a part of that core early group at the UN who not only came up with the idea but did most of the work to get it up and running.

Maryam falls into a daydream about what it must have been like for those early adopters: while the geopolitical system fell apart around them, they chose to run with a radical revision of the world order that was technically and politically unimaginable at the time. She has read books about the establishment of Information, of course, played through the interactives, seen some crappy films, but none of them were convincing about how it happened: how they decided, *Yes, this time, we're really going to burn it all down*; how they managed to create enough momentum to reach critical mass. Did they imagine the behemoth they were creating? Did they suspect, in those turbulent, nuclear days, that the Pax Democratica would hold for a quarter of a century?

Reluctantly, Maryam turns back to her suspicions. She runs a quick program to look for any connections between Taskeen and any of the Information staff who disappeared, but it's inconclusive. There were overlaps when Taskeen visited Hubs where those staff worked, but none since Taskeen retired five years ago, and nothing to suggest she met with those specific people out of the several hundred who would work in a medium-sized Hub. Maryam tries to check the sanatorium's visitor log, but of course that's not available on Information. She thinks of writing to Saleha to ask her, but that seems unnecessarily invasive. Maryam can easily imagine Saleha casually mentioning it to Taskeen over a cup of tea and some laddoo. Grumbling—it's late, and it's been a long day, and Maryam doesn't like spying on her heroes, even when they might be traitors—she sets up a face-matching scan to run on the feeds nearest the door of the sanatorium over the past five years.

If she's lucky she might get a result back before the election.

At least Núria is back.

Mishima exits the privacy booth and heads for the bar, an icy structure with built-in condensation as part of the new "design cool" aesthetic. She orders a bourbon, planning to spend her flight in drunken oblivion.

She is on her third tumbler and not too drunk to notice when a woman slides into the seat beside her. Mishima glances over, groans, and orders another drink.

"It's been a while," the woman says. She's older than Mishima and dresses like it, in a stuffy wool twist dress and itchy-looking legwear.

Thank goodness for cool design, Mishima thinks, and then realizes she said it out loud.

"I'm flying to Baotou from here," the woman says mildly. "I enjoyed your performance at the debate."

Touché. This time, Mishima manages to keep her thoughts to herself. "Glad somebody did." She drinks. "I suspect you enjoy how it benefits you more than out of aesthetic or intellectual appreciation."

"It does not in the least diminish you in our estimation,"

the woman says. Mishima has actively avoided learning this woman's name, calculating that knowing more about her and her position of power within China's null-state regime will not make any essential change in her decision not to listen to her recruitment attempts. "Filling a seat in Information's latest example of political showmanship would be a poor use of your abilities. With us, you could be using your talents to the utmost, not hiding them."

Mishima drinks. Sometimes, it's easier to ignore than to respond.

"You know your world order is falling apart," the woman says softly. "You must have seen this coming. The sooner you distance yourself, the less likely it is you will be hurt in the collapse."

Mishima drinks. "There's a lot of distance that doesn't include you," she says, and immediately regrets allowing that much of the premise. Lounge access isn't worth dealing with this. She taps in her payment, gets off the barstool, and wanders toward her gate.

CHAPTER 18

By the time Mishima gets home, Ken has a new job: Deputy Liaison for Semi-Autonomous Sub-Governments for Policy1st.

Mishima sees, her anger dulled because she expected it, that they've played him exactly right: yes, he's disappointed that the job isn't high in the campaign hierarchy, but it has an important-sounding title and is in the area he's excited about. By this point, he's talked himself into believing he was aiming too high and that he doesn't care about status anyway, it's about the work, and he's barely on the near side of ebullient. Mishima is happy to see him happy, but there's a bitter aftertaste to watching him settle, and she gets herself a beer and loses focus several times while he's telling her about it. Why can't she convince him he deserves more?

"Besides, they haven't hired the Chief Liaison yet." He doesn't say it, but there's clearly some hope, probably dangled by Vera or whoever he talked to, that he can slide up into that job. But if there was any chance he would get that position, why wouldn't they just hire him for it? "I have to go to Copenhagen next week for orientation," he says with a bit of a scoff: what can they teach him about working for Policy1st?

"It will be an exciting time to be there." Or depressing, if the semi-autonomous gambit doesn't pay off. But whatever, elections are exciting, even when you lose.

Except the ones you don't want to win.

Before she can mope too much she gets a ping.

"I have to go to the Hub tomorrow," she says, scanning the message. "Nejime's in town." Mishima says it casually, but for Nejime to travel out here almost certainly means something big.

"Tomorrow, though?" Ken asks, with a suggestive smile. He reaches out for her almost-empty beer bottle and puts it on the counter as he leans in. "You're still free tonight?"

"Tomorrow," Mishima confirms, just before his lips meet hers. She flicks on the audio for Sayaka's room: nothing but quiet breathing. She turns it off again. "Tomorrow."

Maryam and Núria are lying in bed, watching a projection of the rock-climbing at the Olympics. "Listen to them," Maryam says. "One athlete from Resilient Tuvalu wins and the announcers can't stop yammering on about how that proves it's not all about money, how the games aren't unfairly tilted toward the big governments. Just because one supremely talented person is able to break through. So hypocritical."

"Oh, yeah," yawns Núria. "You know all about tiny governments."

Maryam opens her mouth, then closes it again. Núria snuggles closer and kisses her, as though to soften what she said, but doesn't add anything. Annoyed, Maryam decides to make something out of it. "Tell me, then. What's it like?"

Núria pulls back a little and tilts up on her elbow to answer. "You know, it wouldn't be so bad if all the people in the small governments didn't have such a chip on their shoulder about it."

Maryam has to laugh. "Case in point?" she asks, eyebrows up.

Núria laughs too. "I suppose. Sorry, amor." She kisses Maryam again. "Sometimes, it feels like we're model victims. Everybody wants to say a word for us, even when they don't know anything about it. But I was thinking about my parents."

"I'd love to visit your centenal sometime," Maryam says. What she really means is *meet your parents*. They've had dinner with Maryam's father several times, twice when Maryam was still living in Doha and Núria's visits coincided with her father's, and once when he came to see them in La Habana, but Maryam has never met, or even been projection-introduced to, Núria's parents.

"There's nothing to see in my home centenal," Núria says, yawning again as if to emphasize how boring it is there. "Just a bunch of small hamlets where everyone has the same three or four apellidos. The food is unremarkable, there are no beaches. Half the population is convinced that we should join EsteladaBlava"—the largest Català nationalist government—"and the other half are rabid about maintaining our independence as a single-centenal government that gives no fucks about anything and that nobody gives a fuck about. Politics gives them something to talk about after long days of gold-farming or content-production or making cava."

"I like cava," Maryam offers.

"Who doesn't like cava?" Núria answers. "Other than the champagne producers and one-Spain fetishists, of course." She sighs, and flips the channel to randomizer; the Olympic compiler had fallen into a long run on the tragi-triumphant backstories of the two leading climbers, and if there's one thing Maryam and Núria agree on, it's that they hate that stuff.

"How about Barcelona?" Maryam suggests after a few minutes watching a cooking show, a chase scene, a snippet of intense dialog, and a pride of lazing lions in successive three-second bursts. Núria's reluctance to introduce her to her family, or even show her her home centenal, is starting to make her queasy.

"Oh, Barcelona's much better," Núria says. "It's so cosmopolitan. Even the nationalist centenals there are completely different! But you know that—you must have been there, right?"

"Once or twice when I was a teenager. But I meant maybe we should go there for a holiday."

Núria groans. "I mean, if you insist. But we both travel so much. Don't you think you'd rather stay here? Or go somewhere nearby? There's so much to explore around this region."

Maryam feels a ping on her work frequency. She's about to take it in bed—it's fine for Núria to hear her half of the vast majority of work calls—when the protocol requests her code key. She takes a deep breath. "I'll be right back," she says. "Sorry, work stuff." Before Núria can respond, she's out and closing the bedroom door softly behind her.

She vacillates about where to take the call but ends up in the kitchen with a mug of water. "What's going on?"

It's Nejime on the other end. "Maryam. We need someone to go talk to Halliday."

"Halliday?" Maryam was expecting a coding job, more attacks on distribution centers, maybe something about the tourist guides. "Halliday?" It's a name she knows well, but

it's so out of context and it's been so long since it was important that it takes her a few seconds to place it. "*Cynthia* Halliday? Isn't she in . . ." She stops.

"Guantánamo," Nejime says. "Yes. Rather convenient
from your current location."

Maryam moves from the counter to lean on the window-
sill. She can see the sharp line where the city lights end at
the edge of the Caribbean. She would like to open the window to get some breeze and listen for the surf, but she can't
risk someone in a neighboring apartment overhearing. "What
does she have to do with anything?"

Nejime grimaces, unusual for her; she must hate talking
about this stuff via projection. "We received intel during the
secession threat two and a half years ago that Heritage had
an off-Information comms channel that Halliday was in
charge of, but we were never able to identify it."

There's a pause, and Maryam stands up and faces into
the dim kitchen again. "This is about that tunnel Roz
found?"

"We haven't been able to decrypt any of the comms yet.
We're hoping that we can leverage our knowledge of the tunnel to get her to talk."

"This is not what I do," Maryam says. "I have no idea
how to . . . get someone to talk about something that they
don't want to talk about."

"We're hoping she'll *want* to talk after all this time,"
Nejime tells her. "And you know the latest thinking in terms
of comms vulnerabilities and opportunities better than
most." Better than anyone, actually. Except Taskeen Khan.
"You'll be able ask the right questions. And you're believably
not empowered to offer her anything; that's important too."

Maryam sighs with relief: at least she won't have to deal with negotiations.

"There's something else I'm not sure whether you're aware of," Nejime goes on. "At the time when this was going on—immediately before she became a fugitive, in fact—Halliday tried to kill Valérie Nougaz."

Maryam can't say anything.

"I've never been sure why Nougaz was such a compelling target for her." Dully, Maryam registers that Nejime has switched to the singular. "It's possible she was utterly nuts by that point, but I'm wondering if there's an angle there."

Maryam tries to clear her throat silently, which goes about as well as she expected it to. "Well," she says. "I'll keep it in mind."

Amran knows the spying should be the cool part, but she is distracted by how excited she is about her content-design job.

Technically, that's part of the spying, since it's her cover identity and not everyone knows that she's not really who she says she is. But at the office, she doesn't have to look for intel or try to gauge what's available on Information and what is secret. She just has to read scripts and think about stories, and that's what her brain has been trying to do her entire life. The thought of the office—the jewel-toned workstations, the small staff of fascinating, complex content experts, and the endless, unfolding storyboards—fills her with energy when she wakes up in the morning.

Before and after office hours, she does what she thinks of as gateway spying: she doesn't learn anything of interest, but it buys her the chance to learn more about Opposition Research. At first, she doubts whether what she collects will be of value to them, because initially she learns nothing at all. She walks the streets of Ngara and the Central Business District and murmurs to herself, scribbling down in offline message drafts all the quirky neighborhood incidents and secret slang words she can remember. She's not sure how this intel is useful to anyone, but most of it isn't on Information, which was still getting started when she was growing up here, so it hits the minimum benchmark.

Within a few hours, Amran starts to feel uncomfortable about what she's doing. She is literally selling her neighbors' secrets to spies. She tells herself they aren't particularly secret secrets: way back when, this was all open gossip, and today, it's extremely old news.

It feels a little better when she thinks about it as a memorial to a community that no longer exists. In her childhood, Ngara was at least 50 percent Somali, part of a LittleMogadishu government cluster of five centenals extending into Eastleigh and Huruma. Demographics have shifted and the areas she strolls through are more mixed: a small Meru enclave, a larger but scattered population of Luo, and a persistent contingent of Somalis, along with an uncharacterizable mix of other tribes. Governance is divided among Liberty, 888, and Policy1st, with one remaining LittleMogadishu centenal, its streets besieged by pop-up ads from larger governments. Amran has never been a fan of LittleMogadishu—in principle, she's a pluralist and a policy rationalist—but she still finds herself heartened when she checks the polls and learns that they hold a thin lead over Liberty in that centenal. They're not even bothering to contest the others.

Amran knows that it's all but inevitable for neighborhood

demographics to change over time, and while her childhood was not unhappy, she doesn't cherish her memories of the area enough to want to enshrine it forever. But thinking about all the bits of local trivia—the family that ran the shop on that corner, long gone; the holy man who used to mumble in the park; the restaurant everyone used to go to after mosque—Amran wonders if it would be such a bad thing to chronicle what the neighborhood was like, once upon a time. It occurs to her that such a guide—what did Vincent call it? A hyperatlas?—could speed the turnover process by making it easier for newcomers without clan ties to acclimatize to the neighborhood. That could affect economics—rent and housing costs, for example—as well as elections.

Of course, this has happened before. The detailed data Amran is recording now isn't on Information, but back when Information was established, it suddenly offered vastly more intel on local neighborhoods than had previously existed. The next day at work, Amran goes on the office Information connection, which is purposely anonymized to encourage staff not to shirk potentially embarrassing searches on questions relevant to their narratives, and does some painful analysis. There's a correlation/causation question mark in her results, but the pace of demographic change increases on average by six percent in the four years after Information comes online in any given area.

So (Amran tells herself, musing over her faux content designer workspace), this is normal, nothing to feel guilty about. It's all happened before; it's a natural progression of technology.

Clinging to that perspective, Amran has given Vincent three small articles, all of them historical. He's accepted them without much comment, but also without much enthusiasm, and without any hints that Amran will soon be initiated into the secrets of his organization. She has to do more; she has to find something current that's not on Information.

So, she makes up some wink-wink-nudge-nudge excuse to be out of the office in the middle of the day and walks around Ngara. She has removed all of her usual filters and sees the world overlaid with more data than she can parse. She's concentrating so hard on trying to figure out what is missing from the partially transparent words and numbers in her vision that when she sees a face she half-recognizes, she stares at it. Where did she see this person before? Still thinking about gaps in the data record, she stares so long that the familiar woman looks at her. Amran's mouth widens into a slight smile, because surely the woman knows her too, and she doesn't want to ignore her.

The moment their eyes meet, Amran knows who it is. Of course that face looks familiar: she has practically memorized her file. She knows her age, her hometown. She knows that she was recruited to the Information office in Jaipur as an entry-level data cruncher, then moved to Goa, Bharatpur, Chennai, and Dhaka while climbing the ranks to data analyst before disappearing, presumably to a null state, two and a half years ago. The person she's looking at is Gowri Misra. And Amran has just attracted her attention.

She drops her gaze, but that current of recognition has already passed between them. She can feel Misra looking at her, wondering why she stared. Amran keeps walking, looking at her feet and then, because that seems too obvious, at the shop windows on her left. She feels Misra approach and resists the temptation to look up, blinking up a feed of their location instead. Misra looks at her curiously as they pass, but doesn't make any move to address her, and Amran breathes a tiny sigh of relief that turns into frustration. That was her chance, an unexpected opportunity to crack the case, accomplish the mission, surprise everyone, and she pretty much made herself to the target. She brushes away the layers of data cluttering her vision and concentrates on the feed, and then the next one after that. Camera by camera, she follows Misra as she walks away. When she thinks there's enough distance between them, Amran ambles into a U-turn that she hopes looks casual and follows on foot while she tracks her on Information feeds.

There are no commercial domestic airplane flights on the island, so Maryam travels to Guantánamo by crow. She boarded dreading what she assumed would be a pointless milk run of local deviations as the algorithm determined the most efficient route to get everyone to their chosen destinations. That is exactly what happens, but Maryam finds the meandering route surprisingly pleasant. Varadero, the first stop, is a mess of extravagant high-rises and pop-ups for beauty products and beach amenities with the occasional election ad thrown in, and Maryam has to close her eyes against the impending headache, but after that they are in the quieter interior. They stop in a quick series of small towns with names—Cascajal, Mordazo, Hatillo—whose automated welcome processes include proud paragraphs of history scrolling through everyone's vision. Vendors tuned to the crow itineraries hover during their standard three-minute pickup/drop-off time, offering resealed coconuts of ropa vieja or (in a Liberty centenal) mentiritas, long chains of beads, fresh coffee beans. In Santa Clara they hear a professional pregonera calling out election ads; a few minutes after she finishes, Maryam realizes that it reminded her of Roz's wall project, another strangely compelling antiquated comms technology. She scrabbles to find a clip to send her. There are more small villages after that—unpaved roads, viej@s calling out to each other in greeting, even once a man on horseback—and longer stretches of undeveloped land, the light green, tangly jungle of late twenty-first-century tropics. Skimming over the treetops is a reminder of the wildness that once was, and forms a soothing background to Maryam's troubled thoughts.

Those thoughts are mostly about the attempted assassination of her ex. It is an odd atemporal feeling: the attack was years ago, but she didn't know about it then. If she had, she might have felt differently; that was not long after they broke up, the first time Nougaz was out in public with her new girlfriend. Maryam didn't *seriously* want to kill Nougaz, but she often felt like she did. Now, with a new lover, and the schadenfreude of seeing Nougaz get dumped on the world stage, it is horrifying but distant. Yet there is still a tenderness in her heart around Valérie, a protectiveness for that spiky, competent bureaucrat.

There's also something about the assassination attempt that triggers admiration and annoyance in Maryam. She spent much of the previous night after Núria went to sleep huddled in the sala, watching and rewatching the vids of the event, seeing Valérie's face, utterly cool and unaffected. Thinking about her icy response makes Maryam mutter "typical" out loud and then glance quickly at her fellow passengers to make sure nobody noticed. Then she imagines that impermeable exterior breaking down in private, and Vera comforting her. Maryam finds that scenario more tormenting than she would have hoped.

Maryam has never put a lot of computation time into understanding internal politics or personal manipulation, and it is not until after they pass Holguín that she wonders why Nejime shared that particular piece of intel with her. Was it really necessary for the interrogation? Or was it an attempt to make her angry at the target? Or maybe the better question is: was she really chosen for this assignment because of her proximity to Guantánamo, or was it because of her proximity to Nougaz?

Misra disappears.

More accurately, the feed does. There's supposed to be a camera covering her; it was available to Amran a second ago, and now it's gone.

Amran slows down to think. If the feed went down on purpose, if it's related to Misra, it might mean they know someone's watching her, tracking her feed to feed. They might have already traced Amran. She slows more and remembers to glance at the shop windows to cover it. She didn't think that was possible, blanking the feed from that specific camera on cue. Assuming it was intentional and not random, it must be so she would lose track of her quarry.

Or it could be because Misra's going to do something that they don't want anyone to see.

Or it could be to set up an ambush.

Amran can see the missing section of sidewalk ahead of her in real life, even if she can't distinguish it without checking for reference points on the surrounding feeds. It's just as sunny and real as the rest of the street. It's still two blocks away. Amran can't make out details; she can't pick Misra out from the other pedestrians, doesn't know if she's ducked into a doorway or a vehicle or started to run. She feels like she's heading into a cave, dim and shadowy compared to the multi-perspective street around it.

But that's not even the worst of it. She hasn't sent any messages to Information since she took on her undercover identity, but she knows the desk officers will be checking on her periodically, sometimes live, sometimes on recorded feeds. But if she's attacked in that blind area, her backup at Information won't know. If she's bundled into a car or a building, they won't be able to trace her, not until her face hits another feed—and even then, it could take days or weeks of facial recognition scanning if they don't know where to look.

A block away now, Amran's fingers twitch with the urge to send a message to Information, or ping anyone she knows. But that would only put her in more danger.

The only way out is through, she tells herself as she nears the edge of the missing feed. It's not true; it's not remotely true. She could turn around and walk the other direction. But she's already turned around once, when she circled back to start tailing Misra; if they're looking for confirmation, a U-turn now will do it.

Amran's walking through the middle of her hometown, in broad daylight. She's surrounded by people. She is not going to run away, even if this feels like running into a haunted house without a flashlight.

Amran steps over the edge, watches herself disappear from the last feed. The sidewalk is unchanged beneath her feet. She doesn't see Misra ahead, but she might just have moved out of sight.

Or she could be peering through the window of the hotel on her left. Or waiting in the shadows of that overhang.

Amran wonders if they are watching her now, to see what she does. She glances around, affecting unconcern, while the blank space that should show her as she walks hovers in the corner of her eye. She tries not to go too fast or too slow.

And then she's out of it. She can see herself on the next feed. Amran exhales slowly.

Misra is nowhere to be seen.

Mishima doesn't go in to the Saigon Hub any more than she has to. It's not that she doesn't like it. It's a perfectly nice building, but her apartment is nicer. Well, really, it has nothing to do with the building; she just doesn't like people, especially when she's working.

That thought reminds her she meant to call Roz, one of the people she does like. She compromises by sending a message as she rides to the top floor, enjoying the increasingly spectacular views of the river (Hey! How are you? Remind me when you're due? Everything okay? Ugh, so artificial. She hates messages almost as much as calls). Then she turns her attention to whatever's coming.

It is long past time for Mishima to admit it explicitly to herself: she doesn't want to be Information's representative to the Secretariat. The only thing she likes less than that idea, in fact, is campaigning to be Information's representative to the Secretariat.

She has known for a long time that she would rather be a spy than a candidate, but after China blew her cover, she didn't have the choice. She got this far by reminding herself that she can't slip into anonymity the way she used to. Occasionally she found herself thinking about facial reconstruction, but for the most part she was resigned to being absurdly famous.

Now, though, she wants out. Even if she can't be a spy, she definitely doesn't want to be in politics. She just has to figure out how to tell Nejime.

Fortunately, Nejime provides her with an excellent reason to quit. "Have you seen it?" she asks as soon as Mishima walks into her office.

"Seen what?"

Nejime grimaces, throws her a file, a short vid. "This hit an exponential pattern of replication in the plazas about an hour ago. No news compiler has picked it up yet, but they will soon."

Mishima opens the clip. It's taken from a feed overlooking a street in—she checks the stamp—Brussels a few days ago. She watches a long-haired teenage girl stalk into the frame, followed a few steps behind by a man Mishima immediately recognizes as Gerardo Vasconcielos, former Information liaison to Policy1st and current candidate for representative to the Secretariat.

"What . . ." Her question trails off as, in the projection, the teenager spins around and shouts at the man. "Just leave me *alone!*"

"Calm down," urges Gerardo through tight teeth.

"You *always* say that, you don't care at *all* what I think, you just want me to shut up so you can get on with your stupid, *stupid* work."

"I don't—I'll listen to you, fine; just express yourself in a more contained manner, *please.*"

"Contained! That's all you ever want me to be, contained, and reserved, and quiet, and pretty, to fit the perfect political family you wish you had!"

"That's not—I don't—I never told you to be pretty!"

Mishima winces. She was a teenager once and is anticipating raising one of her own in twelve years or so, and she knows a tactical error when she sees one.

"Of course you did!" the girl screams, with the self-righteous triumph of someone who is never believed, and she throws up a small projection between them. It is at an angle to the camera, making it foreshortened, but it's clear enough to make out that it's a clip from another feed. The teenager has ramped up the volume to the loudest supported in public places. The nested clip clearly took place some time ago, because the girl is appreciably smaller. She and Gerardo—with less gray in his hair—are sitting on a bench in a park, and he has his arms around her. "Just be yourself," he is telling the girl. "Smart, pretty, wonderful as you are."

The nested projection winks out, and Gerardo's figure judders in the projection Mishima is watching, as if he is mastering the impulse to slam his head against one of the nearby stone pillars. "That's not what I meant," he manages to get out, in a sort of strangled yell. "Obviously! I didn't say you *had* to be. I just—you know, when I was a kid, we didn't have a perfect record of everything our parents had ever said to throw in their faces whenever we felt like it!"

The teenager throws up her hands with a grunt of incoherent frustration and pounds away. Gerardo staggers after her, the beginning of an exclamation—his daughter's name?—audible just as the clip ends.

It takes Mishima some time to recover speech. All she can think about is that girl, how she must feel now, with her ugly, normal, blameless teenage emotions made public and weaponized against her father. Mishima imagines Sayaka in that position, closes her eyes. "I quit."

Silence. Mishima keeps her eyes closed while Nejime plans her attack.

"There are larger issues . . ." Nejime begins, and Mishima opens her eyes and glares at her.

Nejime pauses delicately. "The involvement of individual candidates in the election process may have been premature." It's not the first time a politician or a politician's family has been caught in an unguarded moment on a public feed. However, despite the public's stubborn focus on representatives—spokespeople, heads of state, centenal governors—such scandals are usually blunted by the fact that micro-democratic voters choose governments and their policies, not individuals and their personalities.

"Premature?" Mishima's rage is still burning. "You think humans will someday be enlightened enough to manage a competition for power without being completely vile about it?"

"There's no indication that this was a directed attack. As perfect as the staging is, it was probably just luck. Which is why it has been so successful in the viral sense; something scripted might not have had the same . . ."

"Train-wreck quality?" Mishima suggests.

"I was going to say je ne sais quoi, but yes. We don't think it was propagated out of any motive other than rubbernecking."

"What are the impacts so far?" Mishima asks with a sort of resignation.

"Not too much, honestly. His numbers have fallen a point or two, but he wasn't doing that well to begin with. Perhaps that will dissuade others from trying the same tactics."

"Or maybe now they'll go after the frontrunners instead," Mishima points out. "Which should mean I'm safe." She waits for Nejime to deny it, but data is data. The attack comes from a different angle.

"If you're not going to win anyway, you might as well ride out the race," Nejime says.

"How is Gerardo's daughter?" Mishima asks.

"She hasn't left the house, so I don't know. I was just going to call Gerardo and check in with him, if you'd like to join the call?"

"I don't think it would be appropriate," Mishima says, after consideration. "But please express my sympathy and dismay." It occurs to her that, as a candidate, that's something she can express publicly, too. She wonders if quitting the race because of the incident would be a stronger statement than staying in and using the platform to denounce this. Then it occurs to her that the latter could focus attention on her family. "I'm quitting," she says again. "As you say, I'm going to lose anyway."

"Quit, then," Nejime snaps. "But pretend not to."

"What?"

"I want you undercover as yourself, a public candidate rather than a spy. Quitting would only draw attention to you, and that's the last thing we need."

Mishima scoffs, but she can feel herself vibrating with the idea of being undercover, even as herself. "How could I get more attention than I already get?"

"Doubts, then. As a candidate, you appear to be a known quantity, with specific motivations and interests."

"What is it you want me to do?" Mishima tries to sound noncommittal.

"You are aware that former centenal 0924682 is holding a referendum on returning to micro-democracy?"

"I've heard something about it," Mishima says. Nejime

waits while Mishima blinks up the basic data at eye level: an island in the Baltic Sea with dispensation for an under-100k centenal despite its proximity to the mainland, Saaremaa voted itself out of micro-democracy in the last election. Officially independent, they are largely seen as a client state or even de facto satellite territory of the Russian null state, whose borders are only a short crow flight away, separated by six centenals via ground transportation from the nearest coast. Saaremaa's loss was downplayed after the last election—it is, after all, a tiny place, not even a full centenal's worth of population—but Mishima remembers a lot of angsting within Information over whether it and the handful of other jurisdictions that chose to leave would turn out to be bellwethers.

Mishima hasn't followed that hand-wringing closely, but from what she's seeing now the past five years have not been kind to Saaremaa. Withdrawing from micro-democracy crashed its economy, which was largely dependent on tourism. While there has been an uptick in Russian visitors, that was hampered for all but the richest by the need to cross micro-democratic territory or airspace, and tourism overall is way down. Assistance from the null state was apparently not as generous as the secessionists had believed. The economy seems to have stabilized lately, but it's still not where it was under micro-democracy, and so she's not surprised that the polls predict the referendum will succeed.

"We think Russia will let them rejoin?"

"They wouldn't let them hold the referendum otherwise," Nejime points out. She's more fidgety than usual today, the usual being not at all: her hand taps the frame of a workstation as she answers. "Saaremaa was never more than a symbolic victory for Russia; they aren't geographically contiguous, which still seems to matter to null states in general and Russia in particular, and they don't bring in much value in terms of people or resources."

Mishima refrains from pointing out that symbolism *is* value and waits for the point.

"We recently received some intel." Nejime has steepled her fingers now. She's nervous about something. And the phrasing is odd. Information doesn't "receive intel"; they collect it or analyze it or (on occasion) fabricate it. ". . . suggesting that Saaremaa has become home to a significant concentration of our former staff."

"I would have assumed they'd be buried deep in null-state territory."

"The liminal territory has certain advantages for them."

Focused on the image of a remote, frigid, rural island, Mishima takes longer than she should to get it. "Information left hardware behind."

Nejime nods. "Physical infrastructure for them to practice on."

Mishima imagines a squad of former staff running drills in a dark, echoing, defunct data transfer station. "They must be clearing out now, with the referendum about to send the island back under our jurisdiction."

"We haven't seen any sign of it," Nejime says. "We can't be sure, but there's a chance they'll wait until the vote itself."

"In case the referendum fails?" Mishima frowns: polling on this sort of issue is usually pretty accurate.

"Or because whatever they're planning will make the election irrelevant."

"We knew they were in Russia," Mishima says. "The theory was that they were working from several different sites, possibly fragmented, possibly in concert. Does the new intel identify the group in Saaremaa as the brain trust?"

"The new intel suggests that Rajiv Lama is there."

Mishima is plunged back into the red fury she felt when she found out about Rajiv's treachery. *How dare he?* She had pushed it out of her mind, but knowing that he is alive and well and out of reach brings it slamming back. When she can manage, she says thickly, "I suppose he would be where the power is."

"His sacrifice would earn him status," Nejime agrees. "The election is in two days. They are planning an attack; I am sure of it. I want you to go there and find out what it is. Stop it there if you can, or bring us the intel we need to stop it elsewhere."

Another silence, marred by the sound of Mishima's blood pumping.

"I can't go. Everyone knows who I am. They'll know I'm a threat."

"We'll have to turn that into an advantage. It is so unbelievable that you would go back to spying that they may take you at face value." The language sets off alarm bells in Mishima's already clanging brain. "We'll dress it up as a drastic last-ditch campaign strategy highlighting reintegration as a potential Secretariat issue, coupled with an offer of technical assistance as they move toward the transition. I'll arrange for the governor to send you an invitation. We can suggest you are laying the groundwork for a post-campaign career. It's not ideal, but it's probably good enough."

Probably good enough? "But why me? There are plenty of other people who could go." She grasps for a possible explanation. "Rajiv turning traitor doesn't mean no one else in the unit is trustworthy."

Nejime lets that hang for a moment before she responds. "Your participation was specifically requested by those who passed on the intel." She waits, her fingers working at the smooth wood of her bracelet, but Mishima is not, not, definitely not going to offer any possibilities herself. "The Chinese."

Mishima has no difficulty keeping her face still and her mouth shut, but she can feel the silence shift and change, like a liquid freezing slowly. The incident in the Lagos airport was the fifth time the Chinese have contacted her over the past three years with quiet recruitment efforts. It gives her gooseflesh to think of them working together with her employer to dictate her assignments.

"And you think giving them what they want is a good idea?" She asks at last.

"I'm not worried about your loyalty," Nejime says, with unusual gentleness.

That's not the point! Mishima wants to scream at her, but she lets her silence freeze deeper.

"Isn't this what you wanted?" Nejime asks, still gentle. "A return to the field? Undercover?"

Yes! Yes, but. "What does China get out of it?"

"They're concerned about Russia too," Nejime says. "The Baltic is obviously a little out of their sphere—"

Mishima can't let that go by without an expression of disbelief. China has long been working to bring the entire world into their sphere.

Nejime ignores her. "But they, too, are concerned about our ex-staffers. A group of them was in China for a while, the Yunnan area, I think. China permitted them for a time, hoping to gain some advantage, perhaps some inner knowledge of our workings. Then they expelled them, hunting down any who refused to leave."

"And now they've told you why?"

"They were building new intel networks, setting up competition for China's intranet."

"Competition for us."

"Presumably that was the intent, but they tested it on the locals first. The Chinese government was not amused."

"Saaremaa, on the other hand, would be fertile ground for something to replace Information." Mishima's brain is sliding easily into its old mode of professional analysis, when learning about a job meant accepting it. She yanks it back to the less-perfect present. "But why me? You must admit my identity adds risk."

"The Chinese believe you're the best."

"The Chinese are the ones who compromised me!"

"If your concern is based on bitterness, I don't want to hear it. This is a rare opportunity for us to collaborate toward common objectives, precisely what the Secretariat is meant to facilitate. And if you personally don't want to deal with China, then don't! Ignore their involvement. They have already provided us with the critical intel. What matters now is shutting down the threat. Do it for us, not them."

"They are manipulating the entire situation! It's not about me 'being the best,'" Mishima snarls. "It's about finding ways to coerce me onto their team."

"Surely they wouldn't go to such trouble if you weren't the best?"

"This is not a joke! They are manipulating you, too!"

"I've seen the intel. The campaign ads, the new intel channels, the Nakia Williams problem, probably the tunnel from Heritage, although we haven't been able to confirm that, it all points to Saaremaa. We can't—"

"Wait. The Nakia Williams problem?"

Nejime studies her. "You haven't looked at the data?"

"I went through it after the debate. I didn't think it was a good idea to look before that."

"It wasn't. What did you see?"

Mishima shakes her head. "I've only skimmed it." Her narrative impression was of a subtle but disturbing imbalance in the coverage that she doesn't want to admit to and is already preparing to defend.

"The complaint has validity," Nejime says, "but we believe some of the evidence was planted. Our new intel suggests it came from the Saaremaa group."

Mishima is caught between relief and anger. "You put her through all this and you *knew she was framed*?"

"We don't *know* anything. We suspect. And it's not clear whether the evidence was planted to discredit her or if she was working with them to defeat AmericaTheGreat."

Mishima's mind slides along the different possible interpretations, fractalling out into suspicion after suspicion. "You think she was working *with* Exformation?"

"It's one possible explanation," Nejime says. "After Rajiv, we have to assume they left other sleepers in place within our organization."

"And so the trial is to neutralize her while you investigate."

"Information had to look into the complaint; you know that. When the investigators found intel from non-Information data streams, it scared them. They had no idea what to do with it or what it meant about her. And those who did understand the implications were even more terrified. This poses an existential threat for our organization."

"If the point was to protect Information, they are going about it the wrong way." The fury is bleeding through into Mishima's voice. "The trial is only turning people against us! Look at what happened in my debate!" She wishes she hadn't said that, because she doesn't want this to sound personal.

"Then go to Saaremaa and help us deal with this properly!" Nejime holds her gaze. "Mishima. We need you on this."

Justice for a friend. Justice for a traitor. "I'll leave in the morning," Mishima says. "That cover story better be ready." She turns back long enough to receive the briefing file Nejime line-of-sights her. "If you're lucky, I'll report back in when I'm done."

CHAPTER 19

They want you to *what?*" Ken thought this was over.

"Look, I know you had that trip planned, but Marguerite can take care of Sayaka—or you could take her with you—it's doable—"

"I'm not worried about the trip! You are one of the most recognizable people in the world. How can you be a spy?" He is imagining some elaborate disguise and prepares to shoot it down with a thousand references to bad movies and undone plots.

"That's the thing," Mishima says, unusually subdued. "No one would expect it."

This makes no sense. "But they'll know who you are!"

"Yes, and that why it works," Mishima explains, getting slightly more animated. "They'll never expect—"

"Of course they will!"

It's so rare for Ken to explode that Mishima the steely and unstoppable leans back. Ken feels justified: she must be faltering because she knows he's right. "The people you're spying on are going to be on the alert as soon as they see you. No matter what you say or do, they're going to suspect you're spying for Information. Nobody trusts Information, and nobody trusts you!"

Mishima is still regrouping. "You never felt this way before," she tries.

"Of *course* I did! I worried every time you went on a

mission! But I never said anything, because I stupidly trusted you. I thought you wouldn't do anything foolhardy and amateurish, anything so stupid." Mishima goes hot, remembering numerous missions that could, objectively, be described that way. In her defense, they've also worked out fine, and she opens her mouth to say so, but Ken is still talking, which is fortunate because she realizes almost immediately that defense would not have gone over well. ". . . don't know if it's misplaced loyalty to your insidious, Machiavellian excuse for a world government or just your desperate compulsion to be a hero! But for once, you need to think about people other than yourself."

"Like you, you mean?" Mishima intends to say it evenly, but her words are wiry with anger.

"Like Sayaka!" Ken yells. His hands are shaking. "You're not just risking yourself anymore. It's not just *your* sacrifice, *your* heroism." He pauses, quiets, moves closer to her. "You and I both know what it's like growing up without our parents. Why would you do anything, *anything*, to risk that happening to our daughter?"

Mishima leaves. She opens the door, walks down the stairs and into the street. And she keeps walking.

The municipality of Guantánamo includes two urban centenals and one that stretches into the surrounding rural areas. Maryam gets a hotel in the ElOriente centenal, because the idea of staying in GuantánamoLibre, where the criminals live, gives her the creeps. It's silly, really: they're a minuscule fraction of the population, only twenty-two out of the 99,993 inhabitants. Maybe it's the skeezy implications of *Libre* in the centenal name—*Hide from the law here, and you'll be "free" (within centenal borders)!* Maryam knows the arrangement is tacitly sanctioned by Information as an easy and cheap way to keep political criminals contained and marginalized, but it still makes her queasy. Especially once she's walked along the pleasant bayside neighborhood with its walkways, cafés, carefully engineered marshland, and breeze-channeling. She knows that tourist money, driven by the weird desire to spot famous criminals, pays for these amenities for the 99,971 unconvicted citizens, but she can't help being angry the criminals get to enjoy it too. Attempted assassination should not be rewarded, and megalomaniac criminals shouldn't get to keep being famous.

Since she has to be here, she might as well enjoy it herself. She lingers over café con leche y tostadas on a pontoon chiringuito rocking in the surf before taking the new, beautifully designed tram—more tourist money—to Halliday's street. She lives in a row of old-fashioned Cuban houses, single-story, pastel-colored, and built to stay cool with awnings reaching out over the windows, upgraded to adjust themselves automatically based on sun exposure. Maryam walks up to number 38, knocks, and waits. She knocks again. And, without much hope, a last time. Not home. Why couldn't Halliday be under house arrest?

Maryam wanders back to the main street, debating whether to wait for Halliday to return. She could find her contact details and set up an appointment, but she doesn't want to let Halliday know she's coming. She is loitering at the corner, flipping through Information data on Halliday to try to guess at her routines and feeling very stalkery about it, when a tour crow meanders by, 360-degree feed cameras on every surface so the tourists can have a complete record of the experience, including their own reactions. Maryam is about to dismiss it with a sense of disdainful superiority when she notices the banner projection above the crow: GUARANTEED SIGHTINGS OF AT LEAST 18 CELEBRITY PRISONERS OR YOUR MONEY BACK!!

She immediately hails the crow. Those are good odds.

It's not that Mishima doesn't feel fear, but she can time-delay it. She bottles up what she feels in the moment—easier if that moment involves fighting or fleeing—and does what she needs to do. That doesn't mean the fear evaporates. Two and a half years later, she still wakes up shivering sometimes remembering her interrogation by a Chinese official, enclosed by imaginary walls showing images of violent death. It seems that the bottling process ferments the fear: in exchange for forty minutes of cool negotiation, Mishima has suffered through at least five hours of retroactive terror. It's worth it: if she had shown fear in the moment, she might never have gotten out.

Not that it's a choice.

She can't choose to feel fear now as she walks and walks along the streets of Saigon. No butterflies, no anxiety, no hesitation about hunting down her enemies alone in unfriendly, unsurveilled territory. She half-notices that she is abstractedly avoiding any landmark that her five years of living with Ken would make painful (taking a cross street before she passes their favorite breakfast café; the housewares store that furnished the majority of the apartment). Her mind refuses to process the argument with Ken, skipping instead to the logistical details of her mission. She doesn't even seriously think about not going. Which means everything he said about her is true. She can't process that now;

she has to pack and get into character—a character that will (as Ken said) be herself, but also not. She'll be playing someone dejected about her imminent election loss, when in reality she is completely elated to be back to her real job.

Not that she's really back, of course; she shouldn't kid herself into thinking that this type of tailor-made opportunity will come along often.

All the more reason to grab this one.

She needs to remember to read up on Saaremaa. She knows next to nothing about it, and there's nothing recent on Information; once she gets there, she won't have access to Information anyway, so she'll have to download everything she can from before they left micro-democracy: geography, recent history, demographics, although those are likely to have changed a lot in the past five years . . .

Mishima stops. Inhales. Exhales.

She finds herself in front of Tân Định, where their evening walks often ended before Sayaka shortened their range. She starts walking again more slowly but realizes her feet, or subconscious, or narrative fucking disorder, are taking her toward the park and her usual route home, and veers away. She's not ready. She hasn't decided how she feels or what stance to take, if she's apologetic or conciliatory or really, really angry.

She has to go back before she leaves. Packing aside (and Mishima has always considered packing overrated), she has to say goodbye to Sayaka; she can't leave her without a word. Her anger surges again as she remembers that's what Ken accused her of doing. She'll say goodbye and explain to her about her trip, as she always does, even if Sayaka interrupts with unrelated questions and forgets it all immediately. Then Mishima realizes: usually when she's away, she projects in at least once or twice during the day to say hi to Sayaka, say good night, read her a story. She won't be able to do that this time, stuck in what is still technically a null state for another two days. Maybe she'll find some place to send messages, but projection is almost certainly impossible.

Maybe she's wrong to go.

It hardly matters. Thinking narratively as she always does, she can't turn away from the mission; parts of her character have long since hardened into place. And if it's dangerous, she's been in danger before. She can take care of herself. She always has.

Ken might not believe that, but that's because he's emotionally compromised, predisposed to want to protect her. Traumatized, too, by his childhood loss.

He doesn't have to believe her, as long as she can justify it to herself.

She's definitely not ready to go home yet.

Mishima keeps remembering a moment, years ago, when she and Ken first met, when she stabbed him in the leg. It was due to a reasonable misunderstanding—she thought he was an enemy asset who had seduced her into a private vacation to get her out of the way while his colleagues overthrew the world order—and when she realized that she was wrong, she immediately gave him medical assistance. It's been a long time since she noticed the almost-imperceptible scar on his thigh with anything but the slightest vestigial memory of guilt.

Now Mishima keeps replaying that moment, except she is the one staring at a weapon protruding from her body, shocked by the rapid change in a relationship she thought she understood. It's a shitty analogy, she castigates herself; it's her narrative disorder insisting on a false symmetry. In the present (and she has to rub tiredness out of her eyes), Ken is entirely justified. He didn't attack her out of nowhere; he was responding to something that she did, that she's been doing for years. That might be what stings the most: all the time while she thought they were happy, while she imagined she had finally found someone who could forgive her for who she is, he's been feeling this way and smothering it.

Mishima's hands are fists. She keeps walking.

The tourist crow is set to an agonizing crawl, ostensibly to let the passengers see everything but in fact, Maryam suspects, to allow the driver to scan Information for location data on their target celebrities. It takes a stultifying hour and fourteen minutes before the guide's ongoing monologue, broadcast directly into her earpiece, squeals the name *Cynthia Halliday* with unnerving excitement. Maryam cranes her neck with the rest of them to see the "harridan of Heritage, William Pressman's final undoing, the head of state who almost splintered micro-democracy" sipping from an imported Nestlé water bottle at an outdoor café along the waterfront, white tablecloth fluttering in the wind. Figures. Maryam talks her way off the bus and, relieved to be back in the cool offshore breeze, saunters over to Halliday's table.

Halliday is sitting with a man Maryam doesn't know. His public Information shows nothing beyond his (instantly forgettable) name, but he's extremely, blandly attractive and has his hand on Halliday's thigh, so she assumes he's the replacement for her husband, left behind in the land of the unindicted.

As Maryam walks up, Halliday says, "No autographs, no

vids," and forks a neat triangle of frittata between her shimmering pink lips.

"Actually, I was hoping we could speak briefly," Maryam says, pulling out a chair.

Halliday's first glance is to the centenal cop standing on the corner. His eyes are on her, but before giving him the nod, she looks at Maryam, taking in her clothes and style and settling on the space next to her face where "Information" is listed under "employment" on her public Information. "Have a seat, then," she says, ignoring the fact that Maryam already has. She dabs at her mouth with a cloth napkin, briefly disrupting the projected shimmer effect on her lipstick. "Well? What do you people want now?"

Maryam wonders how often Information gets in touch with fugitive criminals. "We had some questions about your communications channel." She has no idea how to approach an interrogation; might as well dive right in.

"Hmm," Halliday murmurs, sipping at her coffee, which is served in a large china teacup instead of Cuban-style.

"We found the tunnel," Maryam tries.

Halliday bursts out laughing. "Finally!" She laughs so hard that her companion starts chuckling along sympathetically. "That was Pressman's deal. He had to find a way to stay in control, even if it meant digging into the mantle of the Earth, the entitled sonofabitch."

Maryam hopes her face doesn't show what she thinks of that display of hypocrisy. "So you're saying you never used that tunnel?"

"Of course I used it; why wouldn't I? It was already there." She takes a sip of her coffee, followed by a sip from her water. "It wasn't that useful."

Maryam frowns.

"Well, think about it!" Halliday snaps. "You can communicate secretly with a single location. Yes, it's clandestine, but at some point it loses its appeal."

"If that one location is in a null state," Maryam points out, "secret communications can easily branch out from there."

"Still." Halliday waves her hand dismissively. "Null states are so *limited.* As you can see, they haven't been very helpful to me in my hour of need."

Did she expect Russia to offer her asylum? Bust her out of Guantánamo? "Who's in charge of the tunnel now?" Halliday's eyes flicker up at her; Maryam can't tell if it's amusement or a challenge. Next to her, Male Companion is leaning back in his chair, watching the pedestrians along the waterfront.

"What makes you think it's even in use?" Halliday asks.

"We've seen the transmissions," Maryam says, trying to sound bored rather than excited that this is going better than she hoped.

"Then you know more about it than I do." Halliday leans back in her chair and takes another sip of her coffee, letting her eyes drift to the dark shine of the Caribbean against the horizon. Attentive now that she's stopped talking above his pay grade, Male Companion puts his arm around her shoulders and squeezes; she ignores him.

"What were you working on with the null states before you left?" Maryam tries. She has trouble imagining that Halliday has given up all her ambitions for a life of tropical leisure.

Suddenly, Halliday turns her hard gaze back to Maryam, eyes narrowing. "You're that techie she was with, aren't you?"

Maryam is startled; unlike the subsequent relationship

with Vera Kubugli, her own entanglement with Nougaz didn't make the tabloids. It wasn't secret, by any means, but she hadn't thought it was widely known beyond the Information circles in Paris and Doha. Then again, Halliday is exactly the kind of ambitious social-capital climber who would track that sort of thing. And maybe it wasn't the horizon she was looking at after all but search results. "Yes," Maryam says without thinking. "And I'd like to know why you tried to kill her."

Halliday smirks. "I would have thought you'd appreciate it."

Maryam, too furious to speak, lets her stare bore through Halliday's obnoxious expression.

"You should be thanking me," the former head of state snaps. "That double-crossing bitch."

Maryam has an unexpected impulse to slap the woman. "What did she do to you?" she asks instead.

Halliday leans back in her seat, back under control and smarmy as usual. "Let's just say that if you want to know about that tunnel, you should ask her."

CHAPTER 20

The farewell is almost unnoticeable, a meager bridge that signals an ellipsis in the fight without advancing it in either direction. Mishima is dry-eyed but raw, exhausted to the point of apathy. Ken comes off slightly better: he is calm without seeming hollow. Sayaka, fortunately, is too sleepy to say much; what she notices and folds away into her ever-expanding brain is another question.

Mishima walks from the apartment to the Saigon Hub. It would have been more efficient to pick up the crow first, but it feels better to walk away than climb aboard an extravagant personal crow. She didn't tell Ken much about the mission before he exploded, and doesn't want to inspire any questions or speculation at this point.

The personal crow is an unusual luxury for her these days. She's gotten used to flying commercial, and she spends the first part of the flight prowling around the crow: standing up from the controls to walk around the space; tapping the edges of the bunkbeds; stepping into the bathroom, seeing her face in the mirror, and stepping out again. She is passing Sardegna before she realizes what she's doing.

Years ago, Mishima had her own crow, on loan to her from Information. She arranged it for her own comfort and ease; it was her living space as well as her means of travel. This crow, a standard Information vehicle, is nothing like that. The bed in the cabin is a single with a thin mattress and basic climate control. The main room, behind the control space, is obstructed by a set of bunkbeds meant for missions where multiple people need to sleep on the road. There's a small climate-controlled locker with energy chews, desalination kits, and other basic supplies, but no facilities for food prep.

Layout, comfort level, personal touches—it's all different. And yet, she finds herself looking for her old crow, expecting it every time she glances up from her content. Mishima throws herself on one of the bunkbeds, which is less jarring, somehow, than the uncomfortable single bed situated where she once kept a duvet-covered double futon.

It wasn't just the romance of living on the road; she spent long enough based out of her crow to know that it suited her. At home yet detached; sheltered yet in motion. She hasn't thought of it much over the busy past five years. She loves her apartment in Saigon, and the fact that she knows the woman at the bánh mì takeaway and the outdoor dance instructors and even some of her neighbors. Sayaka has friends there, although at that age, friends are little more than other toddlers that she comes in contact with repeatedly. But Mishima is feeling the itch to move. Is it possible some semblance of rootlessness would be enough for her, even without the espionage and the danger? Mishima starts imagining what a family layout might look like in a crow, and goes so far as to look at prices, which sobers her. Maybe they could afford a small one. But would Ken agree? Would she have to guarantee him a safe, crisis-free life in exchange?

That thread of thought quickly becomes untenable, and Mishima diverts to a related one, also inspired by memories of her previous crow: what Information owes her, and what she owes them. From there she gets to the question of what

Information owes the world, or at least its staff. She fumes again over what Nejime said about Nakia, with an anger that's only partially displaced. The way she evaded the issue during the debate still rankles her, and it only makes it worse that Nougaz provided such a complete contrast. Mishima was not only wrong but timid, a characteristic she's not used to associating with herself. That reminds her of the disastrous interview after the null-states debate attack. Why doesn't her fear-delay mechanism function for speech as well as action?

She will play to her strengths, then, and take action. Feeling doubly the spy, Mishima redirects the crow toward New York City.

Maryam has no desire to write her report. She isn't sure she's able to repeat Halliday's accusation against Nougaz. *It might,* she tells herself, *be slander.* Halliday is the sort of underhanded politician who would make something up to get what she wants. She tried to poison Nougaz; it's not a stretch to imagine she would falsely accuse her of treason.

Maryam takes another lap around her small hotel room. It's a single-story hotel, a group of rooms opening directly on a small courtyard. Moths and other bugs are fluttering up to the porch light outside her door, crashing against the windows.

Telling Nejime about the accusations feels like admitting her own wrongdoing. If it's true, then Maryam misjudged Nougaz when they first went out, then fell for her wiles again when they got back together.

She can't stop rehearing Halliday say "double-crossing bitch." She sounded angry, unfakeably angry. Nejime said

302 · MALKA OLDER

they never figured out why Halliday wanted to kill Nougaz. The anger could come from betrayal if Nougaz threatened to give Halliday away, and now Halliday is trying to
smear her.

But if Nougaz was in a position to give Halliday away, why
didn't she?

Maryam keeps hearing it over and over. The memory
makes her squirm. Could what Valérie did to her be considered double-crossing, or was it just normal relationship fall-
out? You want someone, they leave you because you're their
superior, you get back together, but it's long-distance and you
fall for someone else. This happens, it's understandable, it's
not treason.

Treason. She sighs and sits down in the ancient wooden
chair provided for her use. Is that the nerve this is hitting?
Does she think Valérie is a traitor?

Yes, Valérie is calculating. She can be deceptive. She gives
the impression of being cold, and although Maryam knows
that's a front, it's a front that over time has become deep and
mostly real. But for all her faults, Maryam can't believe that
Nougaz would betray Information—she loves it far too much.
Probably more than she loved Maryam, or maybe that's the
self-pity talking.

Still, it's not worth telling Nejime until she's sure. If Valérie does know something about these communications, she
may have a good reason for keeping it to herself. Maryam
gives up on the report and drops into the cool, climate-
controlled bed instead. She falls asleep to the relentless rhythm
of Halliday's angry epithet running through her head.

CHAPTER 21

Nakia moved out of her apartment before the trial, out of the whole centenal, based on what Mishima heard, and she has understandably kept her new address closely guarded. Mishima doesn't want to try to initiate comms and leave a data trail. Instead, she flies directly to the Hub, which will bolster her shoddy cover story of needing some intel from the team there before she proceeds to her primary mission. Fortunately, when she comes out of the stairway from the crow mooring area into the lobby, she finds Velazquez on the twenty-four-hour desk. He knows her and Nakia well enough that he's willing to give her his colleague's new address, in an Académe centenal in uptown Manhattan.

The apartment is up a narrow flight of steps, the fluoron banister glowing faintly in the dimness. At the top, Mishima knocks on the only door without a number. She never visited Nakia's old apartment, but she can feel the comparison like a ghost: where she would have been if she hadn't been driven away.

Mishima knocks again, and then remembers: if Nakia had ever been the type to answer an unexpected guest in the night, she's certainly not now. Swallowing away her fear of giving herself away to the wrong person, Mishima leans her head in close to the ancient door and calls out, pitched as low as she can: "Nakia! It's me, Mishima. Are you there?"

The door opens so quickly, Mishima leaps back, nearly

propelling herself down the stairs. Nakia is inside, wearing an oversized T-shirt and a haunted expression and looking as if she's just climbed out of bed but couldn't sleep anyway. "Mishima!" she hisses. "What are you doing here?" She glances quickly around the hallway and drags Mishima in. "Of all the people who would get in trouble for seeing me, you have got to be the one it would hurt the worst!"

"Oh, I don't know," Mishima says. The door opened onto a midsized living room, worn varnish on the wood floors and peeling plaster on the ceiling. "I'm pretty sure I'm going to lose the election regardless." There's a thick mattress folded up on one side of the room, and Mishima wonders if she's supposed to sit on that.

"Well, in that case," Nakia says. "What can I do for you? Coffee?"

"I'm fine," Mishima says automatically.

"Obviously not, or you wouldn't be here."

Hard to argue with that. "I'm . . ." Mishima cuts herself off before she can explain that she's made a clandestine stop on the way to a clandestine mission. "If I'm losing anyway, I thought I might as well check up on you."

"And lose in style?" Nakia responds with a smile. "If you say so."

"So, how are you, then?" Mishima asks. She thinks again about sitting on the folded mattress, but Nakia is still standing.

"Ahh, it could be worse, I suppose," Nakia says. "Come on, sit down; I'm not mad at you." She settles herself on the folded mattress and pats the space next to her. "Sorry about the—" She waves at the room. "I put my good stuff in storage because, I don't know, I guess I'm still expecting a Molotov cocktail through the window."

"This," says Mishima, "does not sound like it could be worse."

"It's gotten a little better since the election drowned out the trial. Although I'm thinking of moving out of the city."

"Have you talked to Information about a transfer?" Once she's reinstated. Assuming she will be.

"I haven't decided." Nakia looks down at her hands. "I love New York City. Parts of it, anyway. But I don't know. Maybe it's time for a change." She looks up again. "So. How are you? I have to say, your campaign didn't exactly make me want to run for office."

Nakia softens it with a grin, but it's not necessary: Mishima thinks that's one of the nicest things anyone has said to her about the whole debacle. "You shouldn't!" she answers. "It was awful. The only comfort is that winning might have been worse."

Nakia laughs. "Before I got distracted by my own life, I was trying to figure out why you would do it, give up espionage for life on a committee, but I guess once you're famous, you might as well." Her smile cuts off: she's famous now too, but not in a way that gives her the option of running for office.

"You saw the debate?" Mishima doesn't want to ask, but she can't help it. "I feel terrible . . ."

"Why?" Nakia asks, surprised. "What, the question about me?" She shudders. "You didn't say anything wrong. It was a terrible question and you were right not to try to answer it."

"I should have defended you, like Nougaz did, on my way to not answering the question." Mishima says it with the soberness she feels, but she's aware that below that, as so often happens, her subconscious is angling for something.

She wants to know if Nakia has had any indication as to whether Nougaz's support was legitimate or faked.

Nakia shrugs and repeats, "It was a bad question. And I suppose you hadn't read up on the case."

"I hadn't," Mishima agrees, "but I have now. Do you know why they did this to you?"

Nakia throws her hands up. "There was *always* the potential for this to happen. We *knew* that. We trusted the organization—at least, I did. And I knew I shouldn't; we all know Information is never going to value our well-being over their reputation for neutrality, but what option did I have? There's a degree of paranoia you can't maintain if you want to live in society. So, I trusted them, and I got screwed."

"But why you? Why now?" Mishima asks.

"I've been thinking about that," Nakia says. "Either it's personal—I can't think of anyone in the hierarchy that I've pissed off that much, but I could be wrong—or—or they're freaked out about this bug in the system, their incapability of dealing with exclusionary supremacist ideologies. My downfall was a by-product of that shame and difficulty."

"There's something else." Mishima waits for Nakia to focus on her. "Some of the postings that showed bias may have been planted."

"Planted? I didn't think AmericaTheGreat was that sophisticated."

"Not by them. By Exformation."

Nakia frowns. Maybe that slang hasn't made it to North America.

"The former Information staffers," Mishima clarifies. "The ones who disappeared two years ago."

"Why would they . . ." Nakia trails off, trying to make sense of this.

"Did you know any of them?"

Nakia shakes her head. "Only by name. Why would they do this to me?"

Mishima shrugs. "Maybe they were using you to make a point about the segregation problem. Or maybe it's a small part of their grand plan to take over the world by chipping away at our legitimacy."

"That explains a lot. I couldn't understand why Information would give so much credence to a group like America-TheGreat." Unexpectedly, Nakia starts to laugh. She stands up and starts to pace, still chuckling. "It makes so much more sense now!" she says, to Mishima's worried look. "Information upper management has been freaking out about when the other penny's going to drop ever since those guys disappeared. Still, though," she adds, more quietly, "why me?"

"You haven't had any contact with them? Received any messages?" Mishima had been hoping Nakia would be able to explain.

Nakia shakes her head, then plops back down on the folded mattress, puts her head in her hands. "Why wouldn't they . . . No, of course they wouldn't tell me." She looks up again. "They thought I might be working with them?"

"They considered the possibility. Still are, I think."

"I had no idea—I hadn't even thought about those people in ages. I was so focused on AmericaTheGreat and how Information was letting them destroy my career." Nakia lifts her head and stares up at the wall in a way that makes Mishima think she's trying not to cry. "The worst of it is—I was trying so hard to be fair! I didn't make anything up or push any-thing. I was doing my job. Although—after the algorithmic tribunal, I did start to think I might have unconsciously . . ."

"It was the forged posts."

"You don't know that. They might have pushed it over the edge, but that doesn't mean I wasn't already failing at my job."

"You weren't! You shouldn't have been put in that posi-tion!"

Nakia doesn't seem to have the energy to argue any more. "I loved my job, you know. I believed in Information, with all their problems."

"And you don't anymore?"

"I don't know." Nakia stands again, moves around the bare apartment. "I wouldn't have chosen to give up my home to make this point about segregation, but it is a point that needs to be made. I wish Information would get its shit to-gether. But I don't know what the alternative is. Living like a null state?"

"The null states aren't as bad as we tend to imagine," Mishima says automatically. It's been one her hobbyhorses since her deployment to China. "So what are you going to do?"

"I don't know. I guess I should say *move on with my life,* but even though I'm not sure that I want to work for Infor-mation anymore, it's hard to let go of this. I guess I need—*closure* seems too weak a word. Vengeance?" Nakia laughs.

Mishima doesn't.

"Maybe I'll write a book. Or that dishy novella we were always saying someone should do on what it's really like to work for Information."

Mishima thinks longingly of her personal crow and the

ten-hour flight to Saaremaa during which she could be completely alone. "Nakia. Can you leave the city?"

"What? Oh, you mean because of the trial? Nobody's told me I have to stay. I probably shouldn't leave micro-democratic territory, but . . ."

"What if you left micro-democratic territory but only for a short time?"

"What are you talking about?"

"Vengeance."

M aryam holds out for one interminable day of scrying the results on tourist guides and, the next morning, goes to see Batún before he's had his café.

"I need to go to Paris to follow up on a lead." Maryam has never felt comfortable lying, but she convinces herself this is close enough to the truth.

"This is for what you're working on for Nejime?" Batún asks. They are in the corridor now, headed straight for the caffeine.

"Yes"—*sort of.*

Batún cocks his head at Maryam to see if she wants coffee and, when she demurs, punches in his order with long-practiced skill. "I guess we'll see you when you get back."

It's not like she's gotten away with anything, Maryam thinks once the long-haul crow is over the Atlantic. She didn't even really have to ask Batún; hierarchies within Information are typically loose and shifting as needed, and working remotely is a part of life. But Nejime is going to notice. There's no way she won't notice the timing, if nothing else. Given the fact that Nejime told Maryam about the assassination attempt, the whole thing is probably a trap to see what she'll do. She is expecting a call at any moment, asking her exactly what she's up to and where her report is, and every moment that passes without a ring or a jolt makes her more nervous, until at last she immerses herself in a re-boot of *Entre tu y yo*.

The flight to Paris is almost direct but for a few stops scheduled in Breizh. Maryam takes Information's advice and gets off at Brest to switch to high-speed rail. It's partly for the novelty of it: long-haul ground transportation has proven challenging to negotiate across the variety of governments that it almost always has to cross. That is part of the appeal of mantle tunnels: if Information courts continue to rule in favor of a borderless subterrane, it will bypass all the multi-lateral negotiations and complex investor agreements re-quired for train lines. The routes that are starting to revive around Europe, on the other hand, are being hailed by most commentators as a sign of micro-democracy maturing and beginning to overcome some of the early hurdles of a strange new system.

Maryam experiences an odd bidirectional nostalgia as she boards the maglev: it echoes a world she's never experi-enced except through fiction, but most of the ache comes from the worry that if micro-democracy collapses, these artifacts will fall into disuse and disappear again.

Practically speaking, the train is somewhat less comfort-able than a long-haul crow, although the unfamiliarity makes up for some of that, and she arrives a solid thirty minutes earlier than the crow was scheduled to. From the Gare Mont-parnasse, newly restored as a transport hub after years as a commercial center, Maryam walks across the broad plaza, empty but for the slender spire that replaced the old high-rise, and hails a public transport crow. Convinced as she is that Nejime (or anyone else trying to track her) will already have figured out her destination, she nonetheless hesitates before tapping in Information Hub, and instead registers her destination as Jardin du Luxembourg.

Once there, she doesn't immediately walk to the Hub but strolls the green space of the park. It's a chilly day, with that wet cold that Maryam hated when she lived in Paris, and there are few park-goers other than a group of basketball players at the courts and a few hurried pedestrians using it as a shortcut. The jardin is a no person's land between the surrounding centenals, and the governing charter prohibits pop-ups, so she doesn't have to swim through the frenzy of late-stage campaign ads that color the streets around her. Because of concerns about possibility of crime, it does have feed cameras. Maryam watches herself in a small square of the vision of her right eye as she wanders aimlessly along the broad solar paths and stops to get a chocolate to warm herself at the kiosk.

This is not about throwing anyone off her trail. (She almost laughs, thinking of what Rajiv's assessment might be, and then remembers he's in league with the masks.) No, she is wandering in this cold park because she is nervous about seeing Nougaz. As soon as she admits that, Maryam throws the rest of her over-sweetened chocolate into the reclamation bin and turns toward the Information Hub.

CHAPTER 22

It's an awkward flight. They try to make small talk in the main cabin. Mishima, hoping to distract Nakia from the trial, asks about her latest girlfriend. Nakia answers shortly that they broke up and asks how Ken is. Mishima answers even more shortly that he's fine. Finally, Mishima goes to bed. Closing the door of the cabin, she sees Nakia perched on one of the bunk beds, flipping through projections of her last six months of work decisions. Mishima doesn't sleep much, instead lying in bed and reviewing the files of the Exformation staffers while distracted by thoughts of Ken and Sayaka.

When she emerges into the main cabin twenty minutes before arrival, Nakia is curled up asleep on the bunkbed, still in her clothes. Mishima gnaws on an energy chew and watches their progress on maps projected over the darkness beyond the window. As they approach the island, Information winks out, and Mishima switches to downloaded maps. Most of the island is almost as dark as the Baltic Sea—it is very rural and does not have the energy resources to spend on things like streetlights—but there are enough lights in Kuressaare for Mishima to navigate to the mooring spot on the hotel-spa she had picked out.

Turning away from the controls, she sees Nakia rubbing her eyes.

"Where are we?"

"A once and future centenal," Mishima answers. "Come on, let's go find breakfast."

"Dinner?" Nakia suggests, peering out at the darkness.

"Food," Mishima says firmly.

"What's the plan?" Nakia asks over muddy black coffee and sprat herb omelets in the hotel restaurant.

"Find traitors," Mishima says, shoveling more food into her mouth. "Learn plan. Save the world. Or if not the whole world, maybe just Information; I don't know."

"How are you going to find them?" Nakia stifles a yawn.

"To be honest, I'm a little surprised they haven't found us." Mishima calls the waitress over. "Where do the foreigners stay?"

The waitress walks away without a word.

"Uh-oh," Mishima says. "Might have to do some legwork."

But the waitress is back a moment later. She slaps a coin-sized disk on the table. "It's a guide. I'll add it to the bill."

Mishima eyes the disk suspiciously; the technology has gone out of style over the last few years and is now widely seen as a vector for viruses. But the fact that it came from the hotel, and even more that they seem to be using it to make money, reassures her. She scans it with everything she's got and uploads the data, projecting it on the table in front of her so Nakia can see.

"What is it?" Despite the coffee, Nakia still seems half-asleep.

"The local version of Information, I guess." Mishima pages through. It's divided into sections—pages and pages of data on this sparsely populated island. Curious, Mishima picks a background chapter at random—native flora—and checks it against what she downloaded from Information before she arrived. Almost certainly an automated rewrite.

After that, the first section she goes to is connectivity, which is probably less a rational choice than a symptom of her addiction to Information but is still useful. After voting to leave Information, Saaremaa set up a rudimentary network, initially using abandoned Information infrastructure and eventually building a completely new if minimal system. Mishima wonders if that was out of concern over possible surveillance traps left in the Information broadcasters. On the other hand, the hyperatlas is surprisingly blunt in explaining that Russia provided technical assistance in setting up the new network, and that no assumptions can be made about them not listening in.

"I think I'm going to start with these guys," Mishima says, jabbing at the projected guide with her fork. She flips through until she finds a signature page: XXII Century, with an address in Kuressaare. "If they aren't who we're looking for, they'll know where to find them."

"Do you need me to come with you?" Nakia asks.

"No. In fact, I'd rather you don't. Stay in the crow." After paying the exorbitant bill, Mishima goes back to the crow with Nakia and rummages in its kit until she finds an old-fashioned walkie-talkie and slides it on her finger. "I should be able to raise you on the radio with this. Stay alert; we may need to leave quickly." Mishima climbs back down and heads out onto the dark street.

Maryam's nerves only get worse as she walks down the block toward the Hub where she worked for years. As an Information employee, Maryam still has clearance for the small side door used by most of the Paris staff, and can avoid the security at the front entrance, which is a good thing because her hands are clammy and her stomach rebelling and she can't deal with any delays. She doesn't want to give Valérie a chance to prepare for her, but more importantly, she doesn't want to change her mind.

She takes the spiraling west staircase to the fifth floor without seeing anyone. As soon as she steps out into the carpeted corridor, she sees Liam Iyengar, but she nods and keeps walking, quickly, and although Liam turns toward her, he doesn't call out or follow, so Maryam ignores him and continues until she is in front of Valérie's office door. She might not even be in, and Maryam lets herself hesitate long enough to check, but Information tells her Valérie is definitely in the building. Allowing that pause was a mistake, so without waiting longer, she knocks and opens the door.

There are three people standing around the workspace: a meeting, but not a long or formal one, just some quick discussion. Benyamin is there, and Valérie's new deputy, Massi, but Maryam's eyes go straight to Valérie's face. She is gratified to see surprise there, but something more complicated surfaces as Valérie closes the meeting and asks the others to step out. Maryam isn't sure, but she thinks she sees something brief and unsure that looks like hope.

When Valérie and Vera Kubugli broke up, Maryam was already with Núria. The relationship was long-distance at that point but heady and thrilling, the bubbly first gulp of champagne, and Maryam didn't have to think too much about how she felt about Valérie's breakup. She may have felt a tiny bit vindicated, or even triumphant: the rumors claimed that it was Vera who dumped Valérie, the best possible vengeance. Maryam was careful never to consider whether Valérie would have wanted her back, or whether that would be acceptable. She did not obsess over what Valérie was thinking or feeling, instead immersing herself in her own romance. She has not laid the groundwork for a psychological analysis, and now she is entirely unsure how Valérie might react to seeing her.

By the time Valérie has closed the door and turned off transmission on her workstation (the way it was when they started their first, semi-illicit relationship, in this office, so many years ago), whatever emotion flickered through her face is gone, and her expression is the usual mask: a single eyebrow raised under her pale bangs. Expectations, but not high ones.

"To what," she asks, and there is a care in the pacing of her speech that makes Maryam think she is still shaken, "do I owe the pleasure?"

Maryam doesn't feel like she can control her tone at all. She has to take a breath. Why *is* she here? Then she remembers Halliday and is able to grab some of that anger. "I spoke with Cynthia Halliday recently," she says, and is pleased at the steel in her voice.

Valérie's brows snap together. If there's any disappointment, it doesn't show. "Oh? Is she considered an accurate source now?"

Maryam can feel her hands trembling. It's been years since she's seen Valérie except in news-compiler vids or tabloid stories or, occasionally, across a busy room, projected into a large high-level Information meeting. "She told me to ask you about the clandestine comms Heritage used to plan their secession. So here I am."

She tacked on that last sentence as an unconsidered afterthought to fill the silence, and she watches Valérie take it in, wondering if she understands it means Maryam didn't tell Nejime.

"I take it this is relevant to something you're working on?" Valérie asks finally, turning to take a seat among the cluster of chairs in the corner of her office, and gesturing Maryam to do the same. Maryam follows warily: she would prefer to remain standing, but maybe this signals a long story. Or maybe Valérie is trying to unsettle her further by reminding her of everything that happened in these chairs. Maryam sees she's redone the upholstery.

"Maybe," Maryam says. "I take it it's relevant for you." Attack is her only strategy.

Valérie considers silently, then nods. "You're right. It's time. During the secession crisis, I discovered that Halliday was using an underground tunnel to conduct clandestine negotiations with Russia. I was never able to find out to what degree this was sanctioned by Heritage, or whether Halliday was trying to set up her own contingency plans. In any case, I was able to blackmail her into turning over control of the tunnel to me."

Maryam realizes her mouth is open. She can't believe this is real.

"At first," Valérie continues, "I pretended to be Halliday, using the tunnel to draw Russia out. I had the idea that they might be attempting to negotiate independently with microdemocratic governments, and that I could use what I learned from the tunnel to protect us."

"But you didn't tell anyone about it." Maryam doesn't understand why Valérie is volunteering all of this, but it makes her nervous. She doesn't want to let her wiggle out of any of the culpability.

"I didn't," Valérie agrees. "I thought it was too risky, and the opportunity for intel outweighed our transparency mandate, at least temporarily. I was only planning to use it for a few days, see what I could find out about Halliday and Heritage and, of course, Russia before I shut it down. It's possible"—she looks down at her hands, but maybe she's only signaling sincerity—"that all of that was just an excuse. I had a secret channel to an almost-unknown null state, and I wanted to know. I wanted the leverage that knowledge would give me. I wanted to understand what was going on. If I had made the channel public, it would have been closed. Also, it is likely that many Heritage supporters would have taken it as a threat, pushed harder for secession. As I said, these are excuses. But in any case, it is done."

"No wonder she wanted to kill you." Maryam is starting to recover. This is not so bad: questionable, yes, a possible firing offense, but not treasonous.

Valérie barks out a laugh. "Sore loser. The problem, of course, was that once she disappeared so publicly, I could no longer claim to be her."

"And you started talking to them as a representative of Information," Maryam says, sinking.

"Very, very cautiously. At first, it was perhaps one communication per month, or every six weeks. Keeping the channel open, that's all it was. I had set up an alert to let me know when a message arrived at this end of the cable, then I would fly to Zurich and ping them back. Sometimes I initiated. No intel was exchanged, just a back-and-forth of greetings. You can read them, if you like; I saved them all."

Maryam shakes her head silently. That offer proves Valérie feels guilty, and she has trouble imagining Valérie feeling unnecessary guilt.

"A little over a year ago, that changed," Valérie goes on. "A message came through, requesting data. Nothing specific," she tells Maryam, smiling slightly into her shocked face. "They wanted a selection of innocuous content, commonly available news, and so forth."

"You gave it to them." Maryam is underwater with shock.

"I did. I judged that engagement of this type would, in the long term, support the eventual inclusion of additional territory into micro-democracy."

"But you didn't tell anyone! You didn't even bring it up with the other directors. Did you?"

"That is perfectly within my prerogative," Valérie says sharply. "I have complete control over decisions within my area of responsibility."

"That doesn't—" Maryam was about to say *that doesn't include foreign policy*, but she's not sure that's true. The Information charter and the rules that have been formalized since its establishment have little to say about foreign policy.

Valérie waits for a moment, then goes on. "In exchange, I received intel from Russia."

Maryam finally explodes. "You had intel on a null state that you didn't share?"

"All of it unconfirmed and unverifiable," Valérie says. "None of it particularly useful for anything more than satisfying idle curiosity."

"As far as you know," Maryam grinds out. "There could have been someone else hiding similar intel that would have confirmed yours. There could have been someone running espionage who needed to know some of those details to carry out their missions!"

"I've seen to it that I'm well informed about all the null states surveillance programs," Valérie says.

"So why do it?" Maryam asks, frustrated. "If you were found out, no one would understand. You'd lose your job, at the very least. Why take the risk?"

"Rapprochement," Valérie replies, as if that explains everything. Maryam scoffs. "You have to understand." Valérie's voice gentles, bringing back all sorts of memories that are worse than useless to Maryam. "Information as we know it is over. Oh"—waving dismissively at Maryam's shocked face—"I said *as we know it*. It will continue in some form, most likely. But if we're going to manage this change, we have to face it."

Maryam sucks in her breath. It's one thing to hear this at a party from a tipsy radical she never liked, and quite another to hear it from Valérie in her Information Hub corner office. "So, what?" she asks. "You're just giving up on it?"

"Whether I give up on it or not will not change the outcome."

"Why run for the position on the Secretariat, then?"

"It's the aspect of Information I think is most likely to maintain any influence."

"Really?" Maryam has trouble seeing the usefulness of the Secretariat now, let alone in this uncertain future.

"Anyone can collect data. Governing how it is used is going to be important."

"And you don't trust Mishima to do that."

"Mishima is formidable, certainly. But she is young." *Like you* hangs in the air between them, and Maryam wonders how Valérie managed to switch the dynamic in their relationship to make *her* age the problem. "She is still idealistic. She would try to be fair, which is all well and good, but the system is inherently unfair. The large governments—the corporates, 1China, even Policy1st now—they all have excessive power, and they are all trying to grab more. For a fair result, we need to balance out their unfairness. Meanwhile, the null states will become more aggressive. She would want a solution that keeps everyone happy and productive. In short, I don't think she's up to it."

"So, Information is over." Maryam tries to sound as blasé about it as Valérie did. "What happens now?"

"That," Valérie says, "is what I am working on, and what you should be working on, too!"

Maryam's spine tenses as though frozen into a sudden column of ice. She does not want to work with Valérie.

Valérie is silent for a few seconds, as though gauging her reaction, then goes on with the story Maryam had assumed was over. "A few months ago, I received a different sort of message from my Russian counterpart: a warning. According to the message, the ex-Information staffers living in Russia are planning a coup during the election."

"A coup?"

"Some kind of takeover. The source—assuming they were speaking in good faith, which I don't—wasn't specific on the details."

"Surely, this kind of threat should be shared with others in Information," Maryam argues.

"And I shared it," Valérie snaps back. "With the appropriate cautions and without revealing my source. Of course they haven't been able to decide what, if anything, to do about it. It's amazing Information has lasted this long. With all the warning they had, InfoSec couldn't even manage to prevent the attack on the null-states debate." She leans forward in her cushioned seat. "I'm glad you came to me now. We are at a crisis point in history. The next few days could be very dangerous, especially for people with your skills."

Maryam is still recovering from that when Valérie goes on. "I wanted to warn you, but . . . your new paramour, she is a soldier?"

"You've forfeited your right to comment on my love life." It's a line Maryam has honed and practiced late into the night, a defense against the moments when Valérie's voice took over her own worries. She had imagined delivering it at some formal, social, stilted occasion, with Núria on her arm in a gorgeous gown or full dress uniform. This will have to do.

"I'm not talking about your love life!" Valérie's tone is so sharp that Maryam can't tell what's behind it: jealousy or manipulation or actual concern. "Has it occurred to you she may be a spy?"

Maryam laughs spontaneously, but it sounds wrong even to her. "That's ridiculous," she says, and then has to think hard for a reason, a good, logical reason, in response to Valérie's raised eyebrow. "I'm not important enough for anyone to spy on."

She thinks back to the night she met Núria: the smoky autumnal air of Shida Kartli, the disruption of that time of assassinations and war and mystery. She remembers the first sight of her, when Roz introduced them: dark hair bound up tight soldier-style, that tailored uniform. Even in that microcosm, Roz had been the important one, the one in charge, the one finding the answers. Maryam just helped her along. But as she remembers it, she doubts. She flew in to help in a moment of crisis; could it have been unclear who was in charge? And Roz had just begun her whirlwind romance; maybe Maryam was the opening, the only option, the fallback plan. And Maryam is the techie. Anyone would know that.

They've been targeting Information's infrastructure.

"Don't worry. You taught me to expect my lovers to use me." Awkward and acrimonious, but the best Maryam can manage at that moment. Then she remembers something.

"It might be," Valérie says, breaking into Maryam's thoughts, "that I'm just not suited for a long-term relationship." Her voice is strained taut in a way Maryam has only heard twice before. "I'm not sure why that is—maybe you could tell me—but the point is, I am not trying to keep you from having one without me."

Maryam is so far from being able to deal with that statement that she ignores it. "You used the tunnel to communicate with an unidentified Russian interlocutor. What about the other cables?"

Valérie looks blindsided, and in the space before she answers, Maryam has time to replay her last comment and realize that it was emotionally significant. "Other cables?" Valérie repeats.

Maryam finds she cares more about world peace than Valérie Nougaz's vulnerability. That seems healthy. "How did you access the tunnel comms?" She presses. "Through a terminal?"

"In Pressman's house."

"There were dozens of cables in that tunnel, some of them still transmitting. All of them encrypted, all with different codes." Maryam is trembling, but she stills herself long enough to deliver the thrust. "Halliday played you."

Then, because she can't handle sitting in that office any longer, she stands up and walks out.

After losing Misra, Amran feels desperate to get something of value to her investigation. She sits in a tea shop in the Liberty centenal and listens to gossip until she hears two young civil servants talking about the governor's brother's plan to skim data off their next satellite, writes it down, and sets up a meeting with Vincent for the next day.

When she walks in, Misra is sitting next to Vincent.

"Oh! You!" Amran says. It's not a slip. It's the only way she can think of to cover her previous slip.

The other woman gives her a questioning look.

"I saw you on the street the other day, and I thought I recognized you."

"Did you?" Misra asks.

"You looked familiar," Amran says. "I thought I must know you. But then I remembered that we had passed in the street a few weeks ago. In Guelph." It's a lie, and a verifiable lie, but not easily verifiable. A casual search will uncover that she and Amran were in Guelph at the same time. Hopefully Misra won't look any further.

"Ah," Misra says, without introducing herself.

"You had something for us?" Vincent asks.

Amran line-of-sights him the file, cringing at how slight an excuse it is. But Misra starts talking to her without reading it.

"You're a content designer?"

"Yes."

"What have you worked on?"

Pulse escalating, Amran names the novellas with uncredited writers' room–style staffs they added to her backstory.

"You're on the narrative-disorder scale?"

Amran nods. "I've been diagnosed at two," she says, which is what her backstory claims, two degrees lower than her actual test results.

"We need someone to communicate our story. Are you trustworthy?"

Reluctance is less suspicious than eagerness. "Look," Amran says, letting her eyes dart between Misra and Vincent. "I was told this was a part-time job. I'm not going to tell anyone, but I don't want to get involved in something . . ." Amran can't finish the sentence. She doesn't have to fake being terrified.

"Don't worry." Vincent still has that goofy, ecstatic smile. Amran wonders if he's on drugs, or if that's just the way he is. She shudders again. "We're not going to hurt you. We just thought you could help us."

"We have a proto-storyboard," Misra says, ignoring Vincent. "All the material is there: vid clips and stills of our history, even some location shots for the events that are going to take place over the next few days. But we don't have anyone with the experience or aptitude to put it together in a professional way, and we need the initial product to roll out immediately. After that, we can hire other people to build off of it and expand through the media spectrum—at that point, resources shouldn't be a constraint."

"When you say 'immediately,'" Amran responds, "how much time would I have to do this?"

"Thirty-six to forty-eight hours," Misra says. "Depending on how events play out."

Election Day.

"It's going to be hard to get that done in that amount of time." Amran quavers a little as she comes to the end of the sentence.

"We'll make sure you don't have any distractions."

That knocks the wind out of her.

"Don't worry," Vincent says again, just as cheerfully. "We'll send a message to your studio."

"We'll pay you for your time, too," Misra says. She leans in. "If you're really good, we'll even offer you a job."

CHAPTER 23

Mishima passes four people on the street before she realizes why that feels strange: nobody seems to recognize her. Even the waitress at the hotel looked at her with perfect boredom.

Maybe that's the answer: spying in null states.

As if Ken would countenance such a thing.

If she's honest with herself, it doesn't appeal much to her either. She remembers her time undercover in China: the lack of connection, the oppressive sense of distance. And she wouldn't be able to discount the likelihood that someone in government leadership with a clandestine Information connection would recognize her.

Still, she files it away as a possible option if Ken leaves her.

Mishima pulls her woolen hat down against the chill. Her heated jacket is keeping her core warm, but the cold is seeping in against her trousers and boots. She wishes she had thought to bring more warm clothes, but it's been a while since she's been this far from the equator.

"Mishima!"

She turns, taking a few large steps back to set her back against the stone wall of the house on the edge of the garden she was passing, finds her stiletto. A tall figure is coming toward her out of the dimness, and she hears a low laugh.

"It's been so long." Movement in the darkness delineates a smile.

Another step and Mishima distinguishes the features. "Domaine." Of course. Domaine. "What are you doing here? Isn't your party about to lose this jurisdiction?"

He laughs again. "The rumors of the resurgence of Information may yet prove to be exaggerated," he answers. "And you? I'm sorry to tell you, but you aren't going to find the votes you need in Saaremaa."

Mishima is annoyed to feel herself flush. Why did she ever agree to run for office? "I'll be better off without them."

Domaine looks bigger than she remembers, although Mishima guesses at least part of it is his leather trench: it must have been scaled up to hide the bulkiness of climate control and maintain those stylishly clean lines. It's not often Mishima feels dowdy, but cold weather does that to her, especially, she finds, after nearly five years in Saigon.

"I've been looking for you everywhere," Domaine says. He is still smiling, and it's making Mishima dissociate, as though just the fact of their meeting again after many years has fundamentally changed their antagonistic relationship.

"How did you know I was here?"

He pulls out a handheld and a detachable extended antenna. "We're not that far from Information territory, you know. You're all over the news compilers."

"Oh, right." Mishima sighs.

"No interest in how your desperate campaign gambit is playing?"

Mishima ignores him. "Who are you working for?"

He tut-tuts softly. "Working for myself, Mishima. Working for a better world."

"XXII Century?" she tries.

"You're too late, you know," Domaine says, and he turns

as if to draw her into walking beside him in the direction she had been headed, but she doesn't move, and he turns back to face her again. "That's where you were going, right? Come on, I'll show you around." He gestures again for them to continue.

"Why don't you just tell me about them instead?" He seems eager to get her there, and she's not interested in following whatever script he's got.

He blows out a blustery sigh: frustrated with her already, Mishima notes with satisfaction. "Obviously, a local network was necessary once Information pulled out . . ."

"Was voted out," Mishima corrects. "Micro-democracy, if you recall, is voluntary."

Domaine glowers. "Oppression by the majority," he snaps out, and goes back to the story. "XXII Century is the third attempt at providing the service, and the most successful."

"So successful that they've expanded into other markets?" Mishima guesses.

Domaine shrugs his broad shoulders. "There are a lot of places that are interested in a lighter, less surveillance-intense version of connectivity."

"Third attempt?"

"This time they didn't try to do it all themselves."

"Is that what you're doing here? Helping them?"

"On occasion," Domaine says. "If by *helping* you mean *providing services for payment*, and only in fairly unimportant ways. Most of the heavy lifting gets done by people who used to work with you."

"What are they after?" she asks, making an effort not to stomp her feet in place to try to revive her toes.

Domaine looks her up and down, but rather than suspicion, his eyes glitter with combined approval and desire. Mishima has to stifle a laugh. Not because she finds his regard ridiculous but because it has been so long and now they have fallen into the same strange relationship of antagonism and attraction. Also because the cold and four cups of coffee are pressing on her bladder.

"The usual," Domaine drawls. He's leaning in now, one hand on the wall she's leaning against, although far enough from her head to keep it from being obnoxious. "World domination. Revenge. Dinero."

"And you?"

"Something much simpler." His eyes flick up and down again.

This time, Mishima does laugh. "Ahh, fuck this," she says. "Want to go get a drink?"

It took some time before Roz could check the PhilipMorris cable to see if that, too, was compromised. She was busy and Hassan was busier, stretched between preparing for Election Day and decrypting the null state data, which Roz suspected he did in his spare time. She thought he might be stalling the trip because he didn't want to relitigate their discussion about whether or not to report the illegal comms, but in any case he and his team were close to peak volume of work.

Eventually, when irritation at not knowing began to outweigh the urgency of other demands on her time, Roz solved the problem by asking Djukic to accompany her instead. There was no conflict this time, since Djukic wasn't working on the project (and had never, a bit of due diligence showed, worked on any PhilipMorris infrastructure). Besides, she wants to test Djukic's reaction to the idea.

"Possible," Djukic declares, when they are alone in the crow and Roz has explained where they're going and why. She thinks about it. "In our tunnel, my team prepared the sensor cable, but there was input from some of the other engineering teams. The threading was handled by the primary contractors, and it was somewhat ceremonial—politicians with their hands on the wheel, you know, nobody else getting too close. A few comms cables added in wouldn't have—" She stops. "You don't suppose—" Djukic cuts herself off again, eyes narrowing. "You do suppose."

"I do more than suppose," Roz answers, convinced that Djukic isn't playacting. "I know."

"Those bastards! Those slimy, smarmy, double-crossing, lying, obfuscating scum! Of course they found a way to use the environmental assessment for their own benefit; *of course* they did! Why am I even surprised? And you!" For a moment, Djukic seems ready to start in on Roz. She grapples with her annoyance and then, perhaps remembering whose crow she's in, lets it go. "You saw it on our cable?"

"Hassan did. I was the distraction."

"You didn't confront them? They still don't know you know? It's not public?"

"Hassan wanted time to listen in on the comms, try to break the code."

"You could have stopped the construction right there!" Djukic is resentful but no more so than Roz herself.

"He has a point," Roz says, justifying it to herself as much as to the other woman. "We don't know who is talking along the cables or about what. As soon as we make it public, they'll shut up—maybe even try to withdraw or destroy the comms capacity—and we'll never know whom to prosecute or where to look for their next attempt."

"Enigma," Djukic says thoughtfully. "Still . . ."

"I know," Roz sighs. "If either of them get past the injunctions and actually start digging, I'll zap them with this before they can clear a meter of dirt."

"Good," says Djukic, but she's shaking her head. "The more contact I have with Information, the less I feel like I know."

It takes Roz a beat to work through that, but when she does, she's struck: she's gotten so used to Information hiding things that she almost doesn't notice anymore.

F irst, we need to set the scene. Make it clear to the audience just how boring and taxing and thankless it is, analyzing their data." Misra projects out story panels with vid clips of Information drudgery. Vincent has gone to get food and coffee.

In her guise as Idil, the content designer and hostage, Amran nods. Inside, she is cringing, because being an Information grunt *is* awful, and she is one of the lucky few to escape it. Her time as field lead for the DarFur government was hard and at times could have easily been described as "boring and taxing and thankless," but she never would have traded it for life as a data analyst. She still feels unwarranted guilt about getting a field job so quickly. *Is that what this is about? Workplace dissatisfaction?*

"Dangerous, too."

Amran almost laughs at that: occasional assassination attempts excepted, Darfur wasn't dangerous, but it was more dangerous than working in some climate-controlled Hub.

"Like Nakia Williams, all data analysts are at risk of being attacked for doing their jobs! Not to mention the isolation and the stress. Information assigns humans tasks better done by machines, like sorting and compiling, and treats us as if we are robots!"

Amran, still obediently tracing the preliminary outlines of a storyboard, mentally notes that the use of humans for data management is partly a mass-employment program. People forget the history of Information.

"Meanwhile, the jobs that should be done by humans—data collection and field observation—are left to machines! That's why so much data is missing from Information right now. Feeds can't capture everything! And stringers, who should be the most important people in the organization, are paid a pittance and expected to work without contracts, and even so, they don't hire nearly enough of them."

With this, Amran wholeheartedly concurs. It makes her antsy because she would really prefer to hate everything about these people. "So you organized?" She knows she should keep her mouth shut and let Misra talk all she wants, but she can feel the precariousness of her situation pressing against her mind, and she's not sure how long she can stave off the panic.

Misra, apparently also of the opinion that Amran should keep her mouth shut, gives her a long look. "At first, such organization was localized," she says at last. "It's not as easy as you might think to create bonds across far-flung hubs."

Amran hides her scorn, while as Idil she reflexively starts cultivating an idea for a novela featuring star-crossed lovers based in different hubs.

"There was disagreement about what direction to take. Some people wanted to agitate for better working conditions, others for a full restructuring. Others wanted to overthrow Information entirely. Even among the last group, there were differences in approach. And there were mistakes."

"I'm going to need some more detail in this section," Amran ventures. She's interested in mistakes.

Misra waves her hand. "We'll get to that later. I prefer to sketch the broad outline first and then flesh it out. Suffice to say that as part of one of the divergent strategies, an unsavory group was contracted and called attention to our subtler initiatives through a series of violent acts poorly disguised as accidents."

At this point, Amran should leap up on the table, reveal her true identity with a roar, and dive forward to cut Misra's throat with the tiny billaawe hidden under her clothes, crying vengeance. But Amran is not much of a hand-to-hand fighter and she doesn't think the tips Mishima gave her will substantially change that. Moreover, while the assassination of the DarFur head of state known as Al-Jabali—for surely that's what Misra is referring to—seriously complicated Amran's life, Al-Jabali wasn't *her* head of state, nor even her friend. Besides, cutting down Misra is no guarantee of an escape. She has no idea how many other people are in this compound. She'll do more good by listening than by getting killed. "And then?"

"Our cover was blown. Eluding Information is difficult anywhere, but as Information staff it is worse. We activated our emergency protocols and fled to the null states."

•   •   •

Domaine leads the way to a spot several blocks away (nothing is much more than several blocks away in Kuressaare). Most of the room is taken up by long common tables in the same light wood as the ceiling and fixtures, but Domaine finds them a tiny table in a nook by the window. Mishima uses the bathroom, tucked under a flight of stairs in the back, before she sits down, and is relieved to see Domaine hasn't ordered for her.

"Vodka?" Mishima asks, settling on the backless wooden box of a chair.

Domaine blinks. He probably didn't expect her to want to drink with him. "Sure. Or they have reasonably good shōchū if you—"

"Done!" Mishima says, and taps in the order. The room is warm, and although it's still early, there are enough drinkers scattered along the common tables to create a convivial buzz of background conversation. Mishima had been on the point of characterizing these other bar patrons as locals, but she catches the assumption and wonders how many of them might be ex-Information staff or Russian operatives instead. Without public Information, it's hard to guess.

"Hmm?" she says, realizing Domaine was talking at her.

"I said, your career has been easy to follow recently."

"Mmm," Mishima says, not wanting to show him just how much she hates being famous. "You better tell me about yourself then."

She's not surprised when that fails as a conversational gambit. The drinks come and Mishima sips cautiously, then with more confidence. "You mentioned you were consulting, or contracting? So was I, coincidentally."

Domaine downs half his glass in one. He knew this bar, so he's probably been practicing. "Yes, since the election, I've been working for a number of different—"

"Did the fact that micro-democracy survived the election debacle depress you so much, you moved to the null states?" Mishima's not sure exactly how she got into this cut-the-shit mood, but she sees no reason to rein it in.

"As you may recall," he answers, leaning on his dignity a bit, "I made a few non-Information enemies." *Oh, yeah.* That stupid vid he made. And then the other stupid vid, the one featuring Mishima saying something taken out of context. "Combined with the number of people at Information who hated me, that left few options."

"What about your old group? Are they still flailing around?"

Domaine growls under his breath. "Mostly disbanded after the election." A pause. "It *was* demoralizing, you know." He sucks down the remains of his shōchū, looks at her inquiringly, and taps in the order for another round. "After a series of critical election errors like that, we really believed that people would see the problems with Information, with micro-democracy. But most groups are so invested that there is a desperate need to believe . . ."

"I suppose," Mishima says, not caring. It's the system they have, it works reasonably well, they are always working to improve it. She still hasn't heard any better suggestions from him. "So, about these former Information staff . . ."

"Oh, yes," Domaine says. As he gets drunker, his gestures are getting more extravagant, his emphasis more marked. "Saving the world, overturning authority, blablabla. Suffering for the cause, you know."

Mishima's laugh spurts out unplanned. "Are you telling

me," she asks when she can speak again, "all this time, they've been thinking of themselves as heroic rebels?"

Domaine draws himself up. "I was a heroic rebel before these people realized they were working for the enemy!"

"And how is the rebellion treating them?"

He flops down toward the table. "You have no idea. The motherfucking intrigue! The *dra*ma!"

Mishima, who has spent the past years living novelas and interactives by night and Information internal politics by day, is not impressed. "What's their story, then? The nano-version, please."

"Oh, they're righteously angry about Information"—funny to hear such scorn, when *righteously angry about Information* is Domaine's middle name—"not so much because of what it does but because they think they could do it better. And they aim to prove it."

Mishima scoffs, only partly to keep him talking. "Take-over? For how long do they think they can take over Information? That's like saying you're going to conquer Russia: fine, conquer it, but what are you going to do with it then? It takes us an army just to keep the lights on."

"As I said"—Domaine takes another swig—"they are *so* sure they can do it better. But they aren't aiming to hold on to Information forever, per se. The idea is to break your monopoly long enough to allow free competition to flourish. Although I suspect they believe they will be able to win that competition and thereby rule the world, so maybe it comes to the same thing."

There's a silence during which Mishima thinks about but does not enumerate the ways in which Information is not a monopoly, and also drinks. "Why are you telling me this?" she asks finally. "You must be rooting for them."

Domaine shrugs. "I'm a free agent." Mishima checks her translator to make sure he didn't say *rōnin* and quells her eyeroll. "Do I want your monopolistic, holier-than-thou, hidebound organization to face competition? Yes. But I don't want you to go to war when it happens."

"We wouldn't—" Mishima stops. She's not going to predict what Information will or won't do.

"Always the idealist." The words are fond, but Domaine is looking at her hungrily and Mishima feels the sparks of the old attraction rising on the thermal current of his desire. She doesn't move, doesn't say anything, but something in her face must encourage him, because he leans forward, his fingers touching hers on the smoothed wood of the tabletop. "You don't know what it's been like, seeing you everywhere," he murmurs. "No matter how I tried to forget you, I couldn't avoid you. In vids, in interactives, in tabloids, all over the news compilers . . ."

That knocks her out of it. Mishima leans back, angry. "That wasn't me. Those mediated images have nothing to do with me." She realizes that Domaine has never been close enough to have any idea what she's like beyond her image, and draws more strength from that. "You're not the only one who sees them, who wants some stupid idea of me because I'm everywhere, so don't pretend it's some kind of link between us."

Domaine backs off, hands up. "Look," he says, cool again. "I always liked you. You know that. Seeing you everywhere just made it more difficult to ignore."

"Try harder." Mishima stands up, wavering only slightly, and heads for the bathroom again. It's a cramped space, and the wood-plank walls dampen but do not entirely block out the voices from the bar. When she gets back to the table, Domaine stands, face all contrite.

"I'm sorry," he says. "I'll shut up."

"A little late for that," Mishima mutters, slinging herself into her seat. "Keep talking, but talk about something useful."

"Do you remember how five years ago I warned you about problems in your own house?"

Mishima does remember. "You said, 'Be careful of your friends.'" In the heated atmosphere of the election, it had made her suspicious of Ken. She had known Domaine far longer than Ken at that time. And he had been right, but he wasn't talking about Ken. It had been her own unwillingness to trust herself that had turned her on her paramour.

"Your friends have, I think, borne me out in the meantime," Domaine says, not inaccurately. "And these former colleagues of yours hate Information with an intensity that makes me look like a dilettante."

Mishima snorts, only half-listening. She knows Ken much better now. Or she thought she did. It was the shock of his accusations that has so upset her, as much as the substance: he had never before tried to control her or complained about her job or—

"Right now you need to watch out for the governments."

Mishima snaps out of her reverie. "The governments?" She laughs, hoping for more details. "What, all two thousand of them? Or are you talking about null states?"

Domaine shakes his head. "I'm saying, your ex-staff hate you, but even with the reluctant backing of a couple of null states, they don't have the resources. It's when they connect with one of your big governments that you need to worry."

"Which one?" The large governments have their own military forces; they have legitimacy and devoted citizens.

"I don't know. I stay as far away from the violent element as I can."

Mishima's nerves dance on the word *violent*. "And the part you're involved in?"

"Can't talk about that," Domaine replies immediately. "Clients. Plus, they're right."

Doubtful. "Where's Rajiv?"

Domaine blinks at her, probably disoriented by the idea of talking about someone other than himself. "Who?"

"Rajiv Lama? The most recent Information defector?"

Domaine slurps his drink. "Sorry, I can't keep track of them. But they all hang out at XXII Century."

"Tell me something, Domaine," Mishima says. "That American cleric you annoyed so much with your vid five years ago—"

"I didn't *annoy* him," Domaine says, offended. "I exposed him! And, along the way, the hypocrisy of Information . . ."

"Right, right," Mishima says. "Wasn't he recruited a few years ago to head up AmericaTheGreat?"

"Exactly my point!" Domaine hits the table with his fist. "Unbelievable hypocrisy! I don't know which is worse: the priest for joining micro-democracy after years of railing against it; those idiots for hiring him; or Information for letting it all happen!"

"So, you took steps to reduce his influence."

Domaine grins. "That is, indeed, one of the jobs I've been working on here."

Mishima taps her finger on the table, pulsing the walkie-talkie with the signal she and Nakia agreed on while she was in the bathroom.

"Somebody had to do it," Domaine goes on. "How can you defend the existence of that government?"

"And letting an Information staffer take the fall for your actions?"

"That wasn't the intention," Domaine answers. "But as it turned out, that case brought far more attention to the problem of—"

Mishima stands up. "I have to go," she says, tossing some rubles on the table. "But you can explain it to Nakia."

Domaine twists in his seat to follow her gaze to the door, where Nakia has just stepped in.

Must have been hard, living in the null states." Amran is pretty sure that's what Misra wants to hear, but she's having difficulty ginning up the requisite sympathy, and when Misra doesn't immediately answer she tries for curiosity instead. "What was it like?" That comes out a little better. Amran has wondered often how people live in the null states; her time in DarFur gave her some insight into low-data environments, but that was different from no data or an actively anti-data government. Besides, it's not just the lack of Information: null states are cut off from trade and technology, stuck in the past.

"It was a change for all of us," Misra says. "We were scattered to different places. Some of us were lucky in our landing, others less so." A certain grimness of tone suggests she was not one of the lucky ones. "This is a great place to tap into the exile-slash-training montage trope, by the way. I hated those stories while I was going through it, but in retrospect I can see how it seems romantic."

Amran murmurs something noncommittal and Misra, keying into the ambivalence, leans forward.

"We've been portrayed as evil, or, worse, as nonentities,

for far too long! We have to make people see our heroism. And it's there, believe me! All it requires is the proper framing and contouring." She calms a little and continues. "For a while it looked as though we wouldn't be able to reorganize ourselves, and we would live out our lives in exile. But enough of us persevered. Some of the null states, with their own reasons to dislike Information, helped us, while others at least left us alone. Some threatened and harassed us."

That's what you get for not appreciating micro-democracy. Amran schools her face before it can give her away.

"The group splintered over the acceptable use of violence. Some people felt we had gone too far."

Amran doubts that Misra is among that faction.

"What with the complications of dispersal and clandestine communications, it took time to develop a new strategy. There's a broad scope at this point for exploration of the various dynamics at play, clandestine love affairs, secret messages, jostling for power, and so on. Eventually, we were able to regroup, but during the interim"—Misra leans forward—"a schism! Members of our core leadership had been corrupted by outside influence."

That sounds promising.

"They took another direction. Friendships were destroyed, relationships damaged—keep in mind, this is all still going on in various null states."

"We might have to consolidate the action," Amran suggests. "Are there one or two important settings?"

Misra frowns. "The bulk of us were in Russia, but that group was broadly scattered. Travel within Russia isn't as easy as it is in the micro-democratic world, particularly when the government is trying to keep an eye on you. Still, you could manage a lot of local color in there—freezing sleet storms, piroshki, internal combustion engines, televisions, borscht, you know."

"So . . . corrupted by outside influence?"

"Right. They started working on smaller projects, incremental change, approaches that either won't work or won't be noticeable if they do."

That would be the nonviolent clique, presumably, Amran thinks. Which makes it definite that Misra is not among them.

"The core group, however, managed to persevere and even grow, recruiting new members in the null states or among other exiles and malcontents." *How many of those are there, really?* Amran wonders. Misra looks crafty: "We even forged partnerships with some of the top governments."

"With governments?" Amran asks, surprised. "What kind of partnerships?"

"It's the governments that suffer most under Information," Misra says, as if this is obvious. "*Especially* the competent governments, the large ones." *The rich ones.* "They provided us resources, financial and military."

"And now you're planning on taking over the world?" Amran didn't mean to say it, but she's shaken by the reference to military power. Misra gives her a long look. Amran tries a smile: "Narrative disorder."

"We're planning on freeing the world," Misra says finally. "From the tyranny of Information!"

Laughter spurts out of Amran, squeezed between terror and hysteria. Misra stares her down until she gasps out, "Tyranny? Information facilitates democracy."

"How would you know?" Misra asks. "You get all your data, every smidgen of what you know about the world, from Information! Of course you think they're the good guys!"

"That's not true. I've been places; I've seen how things work . . ."

Misra regards her with interest. "A true believer? That might not work for us. I wouldn't want you to skew the narrative. Then again, if we can bring you around, it might be even better." She leans forward, speaking slowly and clearly as if Amran were a brainwashed Info-zombie. "Wherever you were, whatever you thought you saw, it was what Information wanted you to see."

This is too unhinged for Amran to even try to argue with it. "And you're going to change all that?" She scoffs. "By writing tourist guides?"

"Tourist guides are fundamental in framing how people experience new areas," Misra says, without a smile. "But no. Those efforts began as one of many fragmented initiatives but at this point are mainly for practice and recruitment."

"Practice?"

"Data collection and presentation. We need to raise an army of staff to take over from Information, and we need to do it quickly so that there can be a smooth transition once the other operations are completed."

"And what are those?" Amran asks, heart pounding, stomach queasy.

"Don't worry," Misra says, showing her teeth. "We will be democratic. Eventually."

The XXII Century headquarters is topped with huge neon letters spelling out *XXII* with *Century* in Russian on one side and English on the other. Casino-grade tacky, but easy to find. There's a head-high wall around the compound, but the gate is unlocked.

Mishima circles the building, checking on windows and doors, then settles into the shadows of the wall just inside the gate and waits in the cold, watching the people going in and out and looking for faces in the lit windows. She counts three ex-Information staffers among the many she doesn't recognize. The place is full of activity, even in the middle of the night. All the rooms she can see from the road are busy, and when she's been watching for twenty-eight minutes, a van pulls up and unloads trays of food and drink at the door. Mishima watches, breathing into her heated scarf, learning what she can about the layout, trying to figure out the best way in. Then, five minutes after the caterers leave, a figure she recognizes slips out the front door and starts toward the gate.

Mishima steps in behind him and slides one arm under his armpit, spinning him around while she secures an armlock on his right arm and finds his throat with the flat of her stiletto. "Rajiv," she breathes into his ear. "What *are* you doing here?"

He twitches as though to struggle, and she presses the cold blade of the stiletto against his skin.

"Well?" Mishima whispers. "That wasn't a rhetorical question. What is going on?"

The gate rattles.

Mishima drags him around the corner of the building to the unlocked bulkhead doors she found earlier and pushes him down the six steps in front of her. "Ready to talk yet?" She keeps the armlock and uses her knife hand to snag the doors closed. The cellar is completely dark.

"Fine!" Rajiv hisses. "Hit the lights, though."

"So your people can see and come running?"

"No windows down here! Light switch on your left."

Wondering why he's so familiar with the layout of the cellar, Mishima kicks the back of Rajiv's knee, controlling his fall so she doesn't rip his arm out of his socket, and reaches for the light while he's off-balance. The fluoron flicks to life. One door, open onto a stairway, but a quick glance upward shows her it is closed off with another door at the top. The room is bare except for a small broadcaster connected to a cable coming out of the dirt floor.

Mishima checks Rajiv for weapons. Finding none, she lets go and shoves him away from her. He stumbles, turns, rubbing at his neck. "Mishima. You came."

"Attacking a data transfer center, Rajiv?" Mishima had been furious, but now she feels something more like disappointment. She can distinctly remember laughing with Rajiv, a few months after the initial disappearance, about the feckless renegade staff. "What are you doing with these yahoos?" It was at that conference in Kandahar, one of the last events Mishima attended as a member of the security intelligence team, and she remembers feeling pathetically grateful that they had something to laugh about besides her sudden fame.

Rajiv, always at ease, leans back against the stone foundation wall. "You remember in the last election how we were all running around, trying to make sure that sabotage didn't derail the voting and, heaven forfend, make the wrong government win?"

Mishima nods, cautious. She still has her stiletto out, hovering in his direction.

"We managed it. We were all exhausted and traumatized and yet elated, because finally there was a Supermajority transition. But I noticed something in the months after that." He spreads his hands. "Nothing changed."

"Come on!"

"No, really. Think about it. Policy1st stumbled through the transition, but everything kept running. And it ran in the same way as when Heritage was in charge."

"There were big changes in the centenals that turned over." Mishima didn't come to this damn island to discuss the finer points of micro-democratic theory. "The Supermajority was never supposed to rule the world!"

"Exactly," Rajiv says. "And they don't. Information does. Unelected, unquestioned—"

"I get the point, and it's not a new one." Mishima growls. "That's a reason for you to start blowing things up?"

Rajiv grins. "Sorry, Mishima, if you're looking for mass destruction, that subgroup is in Sebastopol. Here we work on rebuilding."

"What?"

"You're in the wrong place. And I'm afraid the Sebastopol team has already moved out, so you're a little late to stop them."

Mishima rushes him, forearm up under his chin, stiletto pressed to his ribs. "What are they planning?"

She hears his head knock against the stone wall, but he is still smiling. "I have no idea," he wheezes.

Mishima pushes the knife harder against him. "Who does?"

"No one here. Unlike Information, we manage our OpSec."

Mishima pushes away from him with an extra shove of her forearm into his windpipe that leaves him gasping. "You must have some way of keeping in touch." Switching her stiletto back to her left hand, she pulls out her hunting knife, drops to one knee, and starts hacking at the cable coming out of the floor.

"Hey!" Rajiv yells. The cable is parting into a dense braid of fibers. "Stop!" He rushes her, and Mishima pops up into a side kick, the heel of her boot crunching sweetly into his ribs. Rajiv lets out an *oof* and falls back against the wall. Mishima gives the cable one final blow, slicing through the last strands, and goes over to him.

"What should I be worried about, Rajiv?" she asks him. "What's going on here?"

His face is a mask of anger now. "There's nothing here for you. You want to know who's going to bring you down? Khan's the one you should be worried about!"

Footsteps pound the boards above them.

"Khan?" Mishima knows three Khans who work in different hubs, and one more—no, that's a character from a novela. "Which Khan?"

"Taskeen Khan," Rajiv says, practically spitting. "She'll take you out before we do."

The door at the top of the steps is thrown open. Mishima leaps away from Rajiv and folds her knives away in apparent innocence. Two men rush down the stairs.

"What's going on here? Is something wrong with the—" The taller of the men stops talking as he sees the cable, then notices Rajiv. "Are you all right?"

"That man attacked me!" Mishima says. "He's a traitor wanted by Information."

The tall man looks at her. "The latter is hardly our concern. And the former—" He stops, studying Mishima, then smiles. "I know who you are."

"Congratulations," Mishima answers, edging toward the stairs to the bulkhead door.

"Wait," he says. He turns to his companion. "Call the doctor. Get security down here and someone to fix this cable." Then he looks back at her. "Mishima—am I saying that right? My name is Anton Verne. I don't know what you're doing here, but it seems serendipitous. I would love to give you a tour of our facility."

Mishima *hates* being famous. "I'm good, thanks." She leaps for the stairs, but the bulkhead doors are opened from the outside before she reaches them, and two heavy men peer down at her.

"Fine," Mishima says. "A tour."

Maryam wanders out of Nougaz's office, unsure where to go. She wanders into the staff lounge. It's empty except for a man Maryam doesn't know sitting at one of the tables, manipulating a tiny projection of a datacube. She nods at him and goes automatically to get an espresso from the machine, then takes it to a corner table.

She covers her face with her hands, trying to find some anchor. She can't decide whether Nougaz was trying to distract her by slandering Núria or telling an improbable truth. At least in here, she doesn't have to worry about figuring out where feeds are; she is so tired of thinking about that. It's only since Dhaka; she never worried about it before. Is Núria one of those people who automatically thinks about them all the time? In the midst of her confused thoughts Maryam hopes Nougaz was lying about the tunnel, because she doesn't want her to have been telling the truth about Núria.

Maryam raises her head at the sound of rushing footsteps in the corridors, and someone shouting. She stands up, feeling shellshocked already, and her gaze meets the stranger's in the other corner. She has the feeling her face is mirroring his: startled, wary, ready for the next crisis to hit. Then the projection from his workstation flickers and extinguishes.

X XII Century is, Anton tells Mishima, less a producer than a facilitator. "Very much like Information," he says, with a marketing timbre to his voice. Each suite in the building houses a different organization, all of them working on data provision.

"Not compilers," Mishima says.

"No," Anton confirms. "Most of them hunt their own raw data, although we do have one group that specializes in packaging."

The data peddlers have names like Opposition Research and Omnivision, and seem to employ happy young people, all of them slightly manic.

"It's almost showtime for them, you see," Anton says as they walk into his office on the second floor, followed by the two security guards. "Market share is everything, and even a few hours' delay in jumping into the breach could be fatal for these young companies."

Mishima blinks. "And what is it you do, exactly?"

"Finances. I have been managing the investment flow."

Verne is slender with dark shiny hair and prominent dark eyes. Mishima doesn't recognize him. "Where did you work when you were at Information?"

He shakes his head, laughing. "I'm afraid I've never worked for your organization. In fact, I have spent most of my life in Russia. But I'm one of your biggest fans. And in a way, we're your greatest ally out here."

"What do you mean?" Mishima leans back and laces her

fingers behind her head, squeezing them to activate the beacon in her walkie-talkie ring.

"We are extending your reach into the null states. We receive data from your world and propagate it here. Of course, our technical means are far clumsier than what you have, but we are slowly building our own networks here as well."

"And you push Russian intel back out to micro-democratic governments, secretly." She is terribly out of practice at Morse code.

He shrugs. "We have to pay for what they give us. But I'll be honest: they get far less than they give. Part of the data-arbitrage conditions."

She studies him. "Why hasn't Russia shut you down?"

"They've tried a couple of times, but only halfheartedly. I think they see this as a relatively controlled outlet for inevitable data contraband. They also don't believe we'll be able to spread far beyond Saaremaa, because of the lack of infrastructure. And where we invest in new infrastructure, I am always expecting them to snatch it away from us." He stands and goes to the coffee machine.

"Then why do you bother?"

"After tomorrow," Anton says, coming back with the coffees, "our focus will shift entirely from the null states to the micro-democratic territories. There will be immense potential for growth and gain. Once that has settled, we can return to the question of Russia."

Mishima studies him. "You all seem very sure that Information will fall."

Anton smiles and offers her the sugar bowl. "I was hoping Information would send someone this way. Communication has been . . . difficult, for obvious reasons, but in fact, cooperation is in both our interests at this stage."

"Why should we cooperate with you?"

"Assuming that I am right, and Information collapses within the next thirty-six hours, a smooth transition is greatly preferable from the perspective of our investments." Anton's smile widens. "I was particularly pleased to see you out of all the possible Information agents, because I hope we can do business together in the future."

Mishima stands up. "I doubt it. And if you're wrong and Information doesn't fall, you'll all be arrested for the selling of unvalidated data."

"Well, that's the other reason I was glad it was you who came." Anton is still genial. "I'm sure the safety of the most famous Information staffer will buy my safe conduct to Russia. But I doubt that will be necessary. We'll be in business by this time tomorrow, and your presence will go a long way toward legitimizing our clients."

Mishima turns to the door. The security guards loom on either side of it, watching her.

"You should sit down," Anton says behind her. "We will be here for a while yet." She hears him slurp on his still-hot coffee.

The door bursts open. The coffee splutters from Anton's mouth as Nakia strides in, holding a large flamethrower, which she swings on the guard to her right. Mishima pulls her hunting knife and covers the other guard. "Nice," she says to Nakia.

"Hey." Anton stops patting at his coffee-spattered shirt to stare at Nakia. "I know you, too. You're that woman from New York!"

"You're a genius," Nakia says as they back out the door.

"No, really," Anton says, pushing past the guards to follow them, although he stays beyond flame range. "You two, together? That would be—" The gushing noise of the flamethrower covers his word choice; Mishima suspects *dynamite*. "Listen," Anton yells from the singed corridor as they turn to run, "if you decide to get into the business, call me!"

"Who are these people?" Nakia mutters to Mishima.

"I'll tell you later. Where are you parked?"

"Roof." She pulls open a door to an external staircase. "Over here."

The crow is waiting on the rooftop. Mishima launches as soon as they are both within the vehicle, jostling Nakia against the wall as she accelerates. As they pull into the dark sky, an elongated shape launches itself upward from beside the building.

"What is *that*?" Nakia asks, scrambling into one of the pilot's chairs in the nose and strapping herself in.

"Too long and skinny for a tsubame," Mishima says, dropping altitude and swinging around south toward the closest point of micro-democratic airspace. "But it's got to be something similar."

"It's fast!" Nakia says as the smaller vehicle swoops after them. "And it's shooting at us!" A dark blob flies toward them, and Mishima banks hard, then accelerates.

"It's a simple grenade," Mishima says as it falls harmlessly past them. "Do you think they'll follow us into Information territory?" They are almost past Saaremaa territory already; if it were light out, they would be able to see the edge of the island below them.

"Maybe not," Nakia says doubtfully. "I thought that guy was your biggest fan."

"I'm guessing he's not the final word on security," Mishima answers, thinking of Rajiv clutching his ribcage.

She suddenly swings the crow around to face its assailant and lets off a gout of flame from the crow's weapon. Their pursuer dodges away, and Mishima continues her sweeping turn and accelerates again.

Like a light switching on, Information is suddenly there. "Lastochka," Nakia reads from her vision. "A Russian tsubame knock-off."

"Anything useful?" Mishima asks, corkscrewing again as a grenade plummets past them.

"Just what you've already discovered," Nakia answers, skimming. "Faster than a crow but not as nimble."

Mishima sets off an SOS signal, then sends the crow into a loop with a sickening plunge at its height.

"There!" Nakia says, pointing at the coastline rushing toward them.

There is a *thunk* and both of them freeze, but the grenade bounces off and explodes between them and the waves.

"Still coming?" Mishima asks as they tear over the shore.

"It's slowing down," Nakia says. Mishima decelerates and takes her eyes off the forward view, and they both watch as the Lastochka veers back toward Saaremaa.

"Phew!" Nakia slumps back in her chair. "You were right, Mishima; this does put my troubles into perspective."

Mishima grunts an acknowledgement. "What did you do to Domaine?" she asks, keeping an eye in the rearview vid.

"Oh, he got me the flamethrower, but he didn't think you'd appreciate it if he came along."

"Astute." Mishima snorts. "How did it go with him?"

Nakia gets up to get two glasses of water. "He talked himself into knots, trying to explain to me why taking down Information is more important than respecting my life, and then when he couldn't defend it anymore even to himself, he broke down and groveled."

"I thought you were going for vengeance," Mishima notes mildly. She's trying to decide whether to aim for Doha or Saigon or New York.

"I did too. But I'd prefer to get it from AmericaTheGreat or our esteemed employer."

"Looks like you're not the only one." Mishima projects the navigation screen between them so Nakia can see it blink on and off. "Locators are down, the Information intranet is inaccessible, and voting starts in seven hours. Information is under attack."

PhilipMorris chose a construction site for the Rome terminus of the Rome-Cairo mantle tunnel on the outskirts of the city in hopes of avoiding any troublesome historical artifacts during the excavation. Roz is annoyed when they disembark to see another visiting delegation. She recognizes a staffer from Veena Rasmussen's organization, presumably looking for dirt for the next lawsuit, or maybe on court-ordered mediation.

"Maybe Veena's people will keep them busy enough that I won't have to sit through a fake meeting. Come on."

Roz knows exactly where the cable is anchored; she remembers standing there for hours during the ceremony when they turned on the scanners. They navigate around the various free-standing pop-up offices.

"Okay, here." A gilded spike sticks up from the ground, running a constant projection of crowded numbers in a cube above its rounded head.

Djukic takes a look at the projection and snorts; clearly,

the data isn't as interesting or sophisticated as it pretends to be. "Now what?" she asks Roz.

Roz had figured that Djukic could take it from here. "Uh, can't you just . . . dig or something?"

Djukic sighs and drops into a crouch by the spike. "We could have brought a spade," she grumbles, but she's already scrabbling in the dirt. Roz drops down to join her, but Djukic shakes her head. "Keep a lookout. Good thing it's cold and I was wearing gloves anyway."

The surface is hard with cold but not frozen, and the dirt isn't packed. It only takes a minute or two for Djukic to clear half a foot of space on the southeast side of the spike, where the cable feeds into it. "Hang on," she says, and lies down, getting her head close to the cable.

Veena's group arrived at the compound forty-three minutes ago, so there's a good chance the meeting is still going on. The engineering group seems to be in their offices, which makes her a little nervous, since they could come out of them at any moment and three of their shelter doorways look out directly on the spike, but hopefully they're all deep in calculations.

"Yep," Djukic says. "They bundled comms in here. I see at least . . . seven different strands."

"Can you attach these readers?" Roz asks, squatting to pass them to her. She's annoyed with herself: she only brought six. She stands again and goes back to looking around. Her annotations stutter and disappear. Roz blinks, and blinks again.

Djukic, climbing to her feet, notices too. "Are you guys doing maintenance today or something? I suppose it must be easier on Preelection Day with fewer pop-ups."

Roz starts toward the crow. Annotations flicker back on.

"Ah," Djukic says. "Just a glitch, I guess." They go off again. "Happens to all of us."

No, it doesn't, not to Information, not in fricking Philip-Morris Rome. The digital environment has changed. Pop-ups are blossoming around them in the relative quiet of Pre-election Day. One is asking them to connect to AltraRoma. What is that, a virtual reality site? Another is streaming headlines like ticker tape. Another, under the rubric Opposition Research, is promising *The Best Information Not on Information*. Roz starts to feel dizzy. "Come on," she says. "We need to get back." She remembers that moment during the null-states debate. If everything's really falling apart this time, she wants to be home with her husband and her obstetrician.

On the way to the lot where the crow is moored, Roz spots Veena Rasmussen and two of her staffers clustered outside the management office.

Veena sees her too. "Roz!" she calls. "Did something happen?" She doesn't sound scared but slightly shrill, braced for catastrophe. Roz wonders what dire event she's reliving. The blackout during the last election? The Anarchy attack? One of the multiple failed attempts on the Policy1st headquarters during the four years she worked there?

"I don't know." Roz bends her trajectory so she can lurch close enough to Veena to preclude anyone else from hearing. "Check the scanner cable, the one they put in to test the proposed route. There's more on it than there should be. I've only just found out myself," she adds over her shoulder as she makes for the crow.

CHAPTER 24

Where are we going?" Mishima asks. "Should I drop you back in New York?"

"I'm in no hurry," Nakia says. "This is the best vacation I've had in years."

"So . . . Doha?" Mishima wants to be in the middle of whatever this is, and in the current constellation of Information power, Doha is the center of gravity.

"Sure, Doha," Nakia says without enthusiasm. "What's going on with you and Ken?"

Normally, Mishima doesn't talk to anyone about her love life. She's never enjoyed it, and becoming famous enough to have her relationship dissected in public by so-called experts without her consent or participation has made it less appealing. But even though she and Nakia have never been especially close, she finds herself narrating the fight, point by point.

"And where is he now?" Nakia asks. They are sprawled on the lower bunkbed, munching on energy chews.

"Saigon, I guess," Mishima says. "Locators are off. No, wait! He's in Copenhagen for his Policy1st job orientation. Probably."

"Then why are we going to Doha?"

"I have to report in to Nejime," Mishima mumbles.

"Really. What do you have to tell her?"

"That Exformation and their Russian backers are prepared to take over the second Information goes down."

"And how are they going to take it down?"

"I don't know, but"—waving her hand at the wavering navigational projection in front of them—"it looks like they already started."

"Are you still mad?"

"Yes. Oh, you mean at Ken. No, not really. Annoyed, maybe. But I miss him." Mishima rolls over to hide her head in her arm. "I don't want to lose him," she reports from that darkness.

"Then you should go talk to him. Besides"—with a sudden inspiration—"you said Domaine warned you about governments? Maybe visiting Policy1st will shed some light on the plot."

"Policy1st doesn't have a military," Mishima argues, but she's already setting the course for Copenhagen with her eyes closed.

Ken's first meeting as Deputy Liaison for Semi-Autonomous Sub-Governments is going well. His future boss, the Senior Liaison for etc., hasn't been confirmed yet, so he's meeting directly with Vera Kubugli and six other senior directors. There's a large projection in one corner of the room counting down to the start of voting, and a smaller but more distracting area below it that cycles through feeds from Policy1st centenals around the world. It helps to keep the upper echelon in their ultra-modern offices connected with the real people, he imagines.

The discussion is thoughtful and evidence-based, as he would expect from Policy1st, and Ken is able to make a point about the identity function that everyone nods about, so he's feeling pleased with himself.

Then Vera jolts up from her chair. "Sorry," she says. "Emergency call." She steps toward the window and everyone else in the room politely looks away, but a moment later she's coming back and opening the projection. "You all can hear this," she says.

It's Veena Rasmussen on the other end, looking windblown and harried in some bare-earth area. "The mantle-tunnel construction," she begins, and Ken immediately grows skeptical: this has been her bugbear for years, and while he's not in favor of mantle tunnels, he's long found her repetitive if not obsessed. "It's being used as a cover for illicit intra-governmental communications."

That's a new angle.

Veena seems breathless with the excitement of it. "I saw it. I have vid." She tosses through a file that opens up into a separate projection, a bundle of wires and amazed experts' faces. "This is what we needed! We can stop the construction of this environmental travesty right now."

"That's marvelous," Vera says, and Ken is almost sure she's even more fed up with Veena's single issue than he is, "but it's too late to affect the election. It's Preelection Day; there's no way you'll be able to get intel about other governments past the no-campaigning rule."

Veena starts to laugh. She sounds unhinged, and Ken sees uncomfortable glances being exchanged among the senior directors. "I guess you haven't been outside," Veena says. "But I think we can find a way to get the data out into the world."

.   .   .

Maryam stumbles out of the Paris Hub while the staff are still yelling in the corridors, and does her own diagnostic on a park bench. Information is back up, but not all of it. Locators are down, pop-ups are behaving strangely, and annotations keep blinking off and on. Something happened during those moments while it was down, some shift. The rules have changed. What was it Taskeen said? That next time, she would program in regular upheavals? Maryam shudders.

All she wants right now is to be home with Núria. It's a familiar feeling, deep-rooted even as she dismisses it as irrational. She felt the same hollow in her chest when she was eight and fighting broke out between two rival militias while she was in school. She could talk to her parents and know that they were safe, she wasn't in any danger where she was, and it was obvious even to an eight-year-old that traveling the streets would be worse. And yet, the urge to be physically in their presence was so strong that a teacher had to hold her back from running home. Now all she wants is to be home and to be with Núria. But Núria's a soldier—if the world's going crazy, she probably isn't home either. And Maryam has no idea where she is, because locators are down.

She can't face going back into the Paris Hub, where sooner or later she would have to talk to Nougaz. She's not going to sit this one out on a park bench, either. Maryam hails the next public transportation crow she sees. It is crowded and algorithmically confused, and it takes her four hours to get to the airport, but once she does she finds that most flights are in service, and she's able to get a ticket for Doha.

· · ·

When Mishima and Nakia get to Copenhagen, locators are still down, and Mishima points the crow to the roof of the Policy1st headquarters. It reminds her of the aftermath of the Kanto earthquake, just after she and Ken met. With Information down, Ken sought her out on the roof of the Tokyo Hub.

The Policy1st headquarters is much swankier than the squat, practical Tokyo Hub. The angled roof sports a small turbine and is plastered with enough solar panels to make the offices energy-positive, and the interior is expansive and airy, constructed from naturally fallen wood and accented with sea glass. Mishima is listed as Ken's partner, which gets her past the receptionist, but he refuses to contact Ken until his meeting is over. Fortunately, Mishima knows exactly where he will go next.

And so, when Ken emerges from his meeting, he finds her sitting by the crèche, watching Sayaka play among the dozens of Policy1st toddlers. He watches her back for a few seconds; then, though he hasn't moved and is still several meters away, she turns and sees him. The great spy in action.

"Hey," he says cautiously as he approaches.

"Hi," Mishima answers, and then, to say something: "It's a great crèche. Look how much fun she's having with the other kids! Maybe we should move here instead of you working remotely."

"I quit." Ken hopes he sounds as confident and matter-of-fact in his decision as Mishima would.

She whirls on him, everything else forgotten. "Why? What happened?"

Ken immediately loses his equanimity. He's been desperate to talk this through with her since it happened. "They hired Suzuki as Chief Liaison for Semi-Autonomous Sub-Governments."

Mishima concentrates for a moment on not showing any expression. Suzuki is, in her non-expert opinion, a sociopath: charming, successful, likable, and ruthless. But Ken has a long, close history with him, laced with gratitude and betrayal, and she's never wanted to tell him something he's not ready to hear. "You would have been working under him again," she says as neutrally as she can.

"Suzuki helped me out when I had nothing, but he's always going to see me that way, as the kid he helped out, and never on my own merits. And he's never going to let go of his position, so there would have been no way for me to advance."

"I'm sure Vera would move you to a different department if you talked to her."

"Yeah, but then it would look like I was rejecting Suzuki, and I can't do that after all he's done for me. Besides, the election is over." Ken gives a half-shrug. "Working for Policy1st in"—he almost said *peacetime*—"normal times has never been as exciting."

"Sounds like the right decision." The silence grows again. Mishima is tugged by the temptation to let the tacit reconciliation stand. "I'm sorry," she says at last. "I . . ." She has to struggle again to be more specific. "I should have talked to you about it."

"I just don't understand." Ken looks away. "I know you love to take risks, but surely there's a limit?" He shakes himself. "Maybe I got used to the idea that you couldn't go undercover anymore."

"I need something else," Mishima says. "The politicking wasn't it, but I'm sure I can find something."

"There's going to be plenty of opportunity. Remember how we talked about Information ending?" Ken asks. "It's happening now."

Maryam expects to find the Doha Hub a disturbed anthill, like after the null-state debate attack, but it's eerily quiet instead. As she climbs the stairs that zigzag up the edge of the atrium, she starts to see why: everyone is fully immersed in their workstations. The disturbance was subtle and threatening, and no one understands it enough to talk about it yet.

She goes to Hassan's office first. "What do you know?"

He blinks at her. "Hi! I didn't realize you were here. Is La Habana . . ."

Maryam remembers suddenly that she hasn't been where she was supposed to be. Of course there's no reason Hassan would have checked. Nejime might have, though. She wonders if the locators are retroactively blanked. Seems unlikely; way harder to delete than to block.

Hassan is still waiting for an answer to his undefined query about La Habana. "Uh, same," Maryam says, hoping it's true. "Do you have anything yet?"

"Not much. Software attack, we think, although we're having difficulty verifying hardware status. We're not sure whether they achieved what they were aiming for. Locators are out, and coverage is still spotty in some areas, but most services are up and running fine—it's not like five years ago."

"Al hamdu'illah," Maryam murmurs automatically, and then wonders if they were better off when the damage was obvious. She's not confident that this attack failed.

"We're working to check if there are specific segments that have been blocked off or if there was a spate of comms hidden by the brief brownout, but so far, we haven't found anything definitive."

"And voting?" Maryam asks. She glances up at the count-down clock projected on his wall: 122 minutes to voting.

Hassan flips his hands palms up, helplessly. "As far as we can tell, everything is fine! I can't find any change to the vote casting, collecting, and counting mechanisms. But that is all dependent on the assumption that we are getting good data from our network."

"Are you pinging—" Before she can finish the question, Hassan has projected a window showing a long string of ping responses, and Maryam laughs. "You're way ahead of me."

"Not at all," Hassan says modestly. "Oh, by the way, there is one bit of good news—we were able to crack one of the encoded comms."

"Really?"

"Get this: you know how people used to type?"

"Mmm." Maryam makes a wiggling motion with her fingertips, imitating the click-clacky typing she's seen in old films and series.

"The code was based on transposing the letters on an old keyboard. Easy to break once you see it, but almost impossible for someone today to notice."

"Wow. How did you find it?" And as soon as she says it, Maryam can guess the answer.

"You know Taskeen Khan? Nejime suggested I send samples to her, and she cracked it almost immediately."

Maryam is too confused to speak at first. *It's not sinister,* she tells herself. Nejime proposed Taskeen as a resource for her; there's no reason she wouldn't suggest her to Hassan. Maryam tells herself not to be jealous that someone else has access to her special contact. "What—what did the messages say?"

"A lot of talk about timing and guarded references to events or operations that the people involved must have already agreed upon. We haven't been able to figure out who's talking. Here." He throws a file to her. "Take a look, if you have time."

"Thanks. Do you know if Roz is in?" Maryam needs to talk to someone about what happened with Valérie.

"I think she's pretty much working from home at this point." Hassan's hands describe a large half-sphere in front of his belly.

Roz's apartment isn't far, and the more she thinks about it, the less Maryam wants to see Nejime, so she leaves and walks there along shaded streets. When she knocks, the door is answered by a portly middle-aged woman. Maryam gapes at her, and she smiles back.

"Are you one of Roz's friends?"

"Uh, yes . . ."

"Maryam!" Roz scrambles up from the daybed and edges past the older woman to throw her arms around her friend. "What are you doing here? This is my mother, Elizabeth. Come in! Did you just arrive? Do you need to eat?"

"Sorry," Maryam mumbles. "I should have called first."

"Not at all," Roz's mother says, patting her arm. "You're very welcome."

Roz ushers Maryam into the room, introduces her to her father, who is occupying what Maryam is pretty sure is Suleyman's favorite chair, and keeps her moving until they're out on the balcony. "Is everything okay?" she asks once the door is closed behind them. "I've been trying to listen in on the intranet when I can, but . . ."

"I don't know," Maryam says. "I just got in, kind of on the spur-of-the-moment."

"Tell me," Roz says, and Maryam does.

"Wow." Roz is leaning against the balustrade ("I spend way too much time sitting these days"), and Maryam has collapsed into one of the lounges. Every once in a while, she catches a peripheral glimpse of Roz's mother drifting by the door to check on her daughter, but they have the awning up and a breezeway in the airscaping, and it's not too hot.

"I don't know Nougaz as well as you do—" Roz blushes. "I mean, of course. But I barely know her at all. I have no idea. But claiming your new girlfriend is spying on you is out of line."

Maryam nods, miserably.

"Unless she has hard evidence," Roz adds. "Did she say anything substantive?"

"No," Maryam answers. "Just that she's worried about me, and that she wasn't trying to ruin my relationship."

Roz makes a rude noise, but Maryam doesn't smile.

"Do you think she might be?" She asks.

Roz sighs and puts her arm around her friend's shoulders. "I can't tell you for sure that Núria isn't a spy. But even if she is, I don't think she's spying on you."

"Really?"

"Look, let's say, even though it's terribly improbable, that she hooked up with you initially because of some confusion over your level of influence and access. Do you really think she'd have stuck with you this long? She'd have to know by now that she's not getting anything out of you."

Maryam's traitor heart lifts. "Maybe . . ."

"Maryam, I was there when you met," Roz says. "Nothing that happened looked calculated."

It didn't feel calculated. It felt stunning.

"And I met her first, remember? I didn't think she was acting strange in any way. Listen, I think Nougaz was . . . Even if she had your best interests at heart, her analysis may have been swayed by her personal feelings for you."

Maryam manages a laugh. "Maybe."

"And—sorry to get back to work, but are you sure Nougaz didn't know about the additional cables in the tunnel?"

"She definitely wasn't faking that," Maryam says, and then looks a little sheepish. "I guess I shouldn't have mentioned it, since it's not public knowledge yet."

"That's nothing," Roz says. "This morning I told Veena Rasmussen that there are seven comms cables in the PhilipMorris tunnel."

"Wait, what?" Maryam sits up. "There are comms cables in the—what PhilipMorris tunnel?"

"The scanner cable," Roz explains. "The one they put through to run tests on the proposed route? The one that is supposed to address all the ecological concerns?"

"Wallahi," says Maryam. "And nobody knows?"

"We chose not to go public until we could analyze the comms." Roz's voice is threaded with resentment.

"And you told Veena."

"Yeah." Roz laughs. "Not likely to keep it quiet, is she?"

"Well, people need to know," Maryam answers. Part of her indignation is in support for her friend, but most of it is genuine. A few months ago, she wouldn't have thought twice about this kind of international, espionage-related intel quarantine, but now it seems grotesque.

"I've been thinking," she says, and at the same time, Roz starts, "You know—"

They both stop. Roz makes a small motion with her head,

and then her fingers bobble. A moment later, she sends Maryam a quick-typed message by line-of-sight: Would it be such a bad thing?

Maryam almost smiles, but she's nervous. People believe line-of-sight is less likely to be hacked than comms that go through Information, which is true as far as it goes, but these messages still leave footprints on both the sending and receiving systems. At least Roz's phrasing is oblique. She writes back I'll be almost disappointed if in the next few days and then, when she sees Roz reading, adds out loud, "Nothing changes."

Roz laughs and nods. "True," she agrees. "I think. The question is, what should we do about it?"

Maryam can't believe they're having this conversation, however obliquely. She tries to remember Rajiv's lessons, but that was all about moving around cities, avoiding casual surveillance, hiding her critical messages in a mess of mundanity. None of it applies to sitting a few feet away from her best friend on a dark balcony, plotting sedition. "I don't know," she says seriously. "I'm not sure there's anything we can do."

Roz hesitates, her hands absently drawing patterns along her belly. "That can't be right, Maryam. Look at us, where we are, what we do. We—" She stops, but Maryam gets the picture. She thinks suddenly of the camaradas. Their talk of revolution always seemed so fictional and far away.

"Maybe you're right," Maryam says. "But I still don't know." She types: what to do.

"It might not mean . . ." Roz stops, thinks, then gestures with her hands: a total upheaval.

"Let's hope not?" Maryam says, but it turns into a question as it comes out. She pauses, then types: I think there might be someone I can talk to.

Roz thinks. "Mishima?"

"With her new job?" Running for Information rep in the Secretariat certainly seems like a commitment to the status quo. She types: someone you don't know. I'll let you know if it works out.

"Mm," Roz agrees. "Let me know?" She sends another message: How can we talk?

"I don't know," Maryam says again.

"But we're on the same page?" Roz asks, and their eyes meet.

"I think so."

They're quiet for a few minutes, but Roz's parents are waiting on the other side of the glass and Maryam keeps thinking about the file of decrypted messages and possibly compromised voting and everything else she should be getting into at the office.

"I'm sorry I can't offer you a place to stay." Roz breaks the silence at last. "My parents were planning on coming out for the birth anyway, and when this happened they got nervous about whether I'd be able to get in touch with them and took the first flight out."

"That's all right," Maryam says, blinking to make a hotel reservation. The mechanism glitches once, but then she's able to get through. "I should get back to the office."

"Let me know if anything happens?"

"You too," Maryam says, nodding significantly at Roz's belly. Roz glances at the wafer on her wrist and sighs.

"Nothing yet."

CHAPTER 25

As she leaves Roz's apartment, Maryam sends Taskeen a message. There's no immediate response, and Maryam calls the sanatorium to ask to be connected, but the receptionist tells her that policy is not to connect to residents' phones this late at night except for family emergencies. Maryam considers arguing that it is a family emergency, on the reasoning that Information is Taskeen's baby, but hangs up instead and walks into the Hub.

Zaid waves her on into Nejime's office without a wait. Nejime is standing at her workstation, frowning at some global projection, which she closes without hurry when Maryam enters. "I didn't realize you were here," she says.

Maryam is faced with the sudden temptation not to tell her about her detour to Paris, about Nougaz. *She'll find out; they always do,* she thinks, and is surprised by the spurt of anger.

"I came from Paris." She throws it out like a challenge. "Nougaz knew about the Heritage tunnel."

She expects Nejime to be disoriented by the shift in crises, but she processes it quickly. "How long?" Then: "*That's* why Halliday tried to kill her?"

Maryam nods. "She blackmailed her into letting her take control over the comms."

"Oh, Valérie," Nejime murmurs to herself.

Maryam's eyes snap up. She's never heard Nejime use

that name before, or talk about anyone in so gentle a tone. Could Nejime and Nougaz have been a couple once?

"There are other types of affection." Nejime has come back from her memories and sounds amused, but Maryam blushes to realize her thoughts were so legible. "What has she done with these comms?" Nejime's fingers flutter on her workstation: setting up a recording, or maybe opening a file to take notes or prepare a message.

As Maryam opens her mouth, Nejime jerks suddenly, and her eyes refocus in front of her face: a message or a projection. Her mouth moves slightly, and then her fingers twitch: calling up some other file. Twitch. Twitch. Then she staggers.

"It's over," she whispers. "We're done."

S o you basically stole this crow?" Ken asks. They have ceded the bedroom with its single bed to Nakia and are lying side by side on the top bunk bed in the main cabin after persuading Sayaka to fall asleep on the lower one.

"Borrowed?" Mishima tries. "I'd really prefer not to give it back."

Ken laughs. "Maybe with all the problems they're having they won't notice."

"So, these alternative datastreams are already online?"

"That's what Veena said," Ken answers. Mishima has thrown her leg across his stomach, and he lets his fingers play along her shin. "She claimed they were all over the place in Rome. I haven't seen them myself, but I haven't been outside in public space since early this morning. And you saw where they are making them?"

Mishima considers that. "I think so. At least, they were

doing some of the work there, although it seemed too small to account for this level of disruption. There may be other incubators as well. Anton sounded like he was expecting competition."

"They are using the data transfer stations they attacked before to get these streams out on Information infrastructure?"

"I don't know," Mishima said. "If so, maybe we can still shut it down."

Ken doesn't answer immediately, and Mishima turns her head to look at him. "Or not," she says.

Ken turns to look back at her and grins. "Who do we want to win?"

"I'm not sure yet," Mishima admits. "Speaking of which." Mishima checks the time. "It is now officially Election Day."

"Oh, good," Ken says. "We should vote, then."

He doesn't sound enthusiastic. "Do you know how you're going to vote?" Mishima remembers suddenly how they went into separate rooms to vote five years ago, when she and Ken had only just met. Now she thinks nothing of asking him outright, which is fortunate because at this moment, how Ken wants to vote might be her main criterion for deciding her own.

"I think I'm going to go with Policy1st after all. I know you think they use me"—Mishima drops her eyes: once again, Ken has been reading her far better than she gave him credit for—"but . . . yeah, I don't know. Even after all this, I guess I can't shake the feeling that they're the good guys." Mishima can make out faint squint lines beside Ken's eyes: she's been telling him for months to get his vision recalibrated.

"Fair enough," Mishima says, and opens the voting

mechanism. She had been planning to vote for Free2B because she can't think of any way Policy1st would make her centenal better and there are a few ways it could make it worse. The idea of voting for a small government with no chance in the Supermajority race is strangely appealing, as if it were incredibly transgressive to think only about the best outcome for herself and several hundred thousand of her co-citizens instead of the whole fucking world.

But Geoff Forth's bullshit has been more annoying than usual lately, and she feels an irrational need to demonstrate loyalty to Ken in any way she can, so Policy1st it is. In her own race, she throws Gerardo Vasconcielos a vote that is only partly sympathy: he's got the right skills and he believes in the system, for whatever that's worth. She expects the usual smug congratulatory message after she punches that one in, but instead she gets another voting screen.

> *Who should control your data?*
> 1. Information
> 2. Whomever you choose

Mishima rereads it twice before slamming her hand against the wall.

Ken jumps.

"Did you finish voting yet?" Mishima asks him through clenched teeth.

Ken blinks back into his ballot, and a moment later, she gets to watch his face open in shock—eyes, mouth, even the tiny corkscrewed spikes of his hair seem to be leaping apart. "What?"

And *of course* the Information intranet is down. She was

one of the first to vote; only a couple of million people have seen this yet. "They're making it official."

"What now?"

"I'm not sitting this out," Mishima decides. "We'll be in Doha in three hours."

Maryam is at Nejime's elbow. "What is it? What happened?" She is expecting a terrorist attack, mass casualties, the armed revolution she has feared from childhood.

"The election," Nejime says, and throws the projection up in front of them.

Maryam studies the question about who should control data in growing shock. "That was on the official ballot?"

Nejime doesn't seem to hear her. "How did I not see this? All those distractions, the different points of attack . . . and now this." She sits back into a chair Maryam has rarely seen her use. With a quick movement of her hand, she changes the projection to up-to-the-second voter data, the numbers spinning upward as they watch. "Millions already. There's no running this back." Her eyes come back to Maryam. "You don't remember what it was like before Information." Nejime's voice trembles, and Maryam wonders if this is going to be the melt-down-and-admit-all scene, but Nejime has far more self-control than a film villain and she continues in her usual dispassionate tone. "Competing data sources tore down any idea of truth; people voted based on falsehoods. We didn't invent surveillance: there were plenty of feeds and search trackers, but they were fragmented and firewalled by governments and private companies. The surveillance was *used* to propagate falsehoods."

Exasperation creeps in, and she stands and walks to the

window, staring at the monochrome desert sky before swinging back to face Maryam. "I hate feeling like a parent raging
at an ungrateful child who doesn't understand my sacrifices.
We *knew* our system wasn't perfect; we *knew* it wouldn't last
forever. But." She strides back to stand in front of Maryam,
gestures as though about to take her hand. "Don't ignore
what we were trying to do, the lessons that we were taking
from our early lives. Don't swing the pendulum back too far,
if you can avoid it."

"I'm not . . . I'm not the person in control of this." Maryam
still feels as though she's here by accident. She should be reading about this, or watching from against the wall while the
important people around the table make the decisions.

"You're here," Nejime says, grim. "Right now, you're
what I've got." She shakes her head. "It's my fault for connecting you with Taskeen in the first place."

Maryam panics. "I only called her to—" She remembers
that she was calling her for exactly the reasons Nejime is suggesting, stumbles, and picks it up again. "Ask for her help
figuring out what was going on with the outages."

"And what did she say?" Nejime's voice is cold, and
Maryam realizes that Nejime hadn't seen the call after all.

"She didn't answer." Nejime says nothing; she has already shifted her attention to something Maryam can't see.
"Maybe . . . maybe this is fixable. We can shut it down, explain it as a joke, an attack . . ."

Nejime sighs. "The problem with democracy," she says,
"is that sometimes the wrong people win. But go ahead; work
your techie wizardry and let me know what you come up with.
Remember," she adds, as Maryam turns toward the door,
"no announcements or action without approval. We must be
careful here. People have a tendency to cling to their votes."

CHAPTER 26

Maryam walks out of Nejime's office shaking her head. An hour ago, she and Roz were agreeing that a change would be a good thing, then Nejime tears up and she's fighting to save Information. She hates herself for being so fickle.

Realizing Zaid is looking at her funny, she goes out into the corridor. The news about the voting mechanism hack has spread. The quiet intensity has been obliterated by an urgent buzz of reaction, gossip, and brainstorming. Maryam hesitates by the railing of the atrium. She could find Hassan and figure out how to help him or . . . Or what? Leave? Work on her own, try to figure out what's going on, and then decide how to act? She is wondering whether there's any chance she can find a quiet place to work (probably not) when Taskeen pings her on the secret channel.

"Did you do this?" Maryam whispers.

"Do what?" Taskeen asks in a normal voice.

Maryam almost stamps with frustration. "Stop playing with me! What is going on?"

"You called me," Taskeen points out.

"If you have nothing to say to me," Maryam hisses, "then this isn't exactly the best time—" She stops. Five floors below her, coming into the main lobby of the Hub, she sees the glint of garnet from a dark head.

Maryam ducks behind the fronds of one of the palms

ornamenting the lobby and peers down, only partly aware of Taskeen gabbing something in her ear. "Hang *on!*" she whispers. The figure below her turns toward the reception desk, and the angle reveals enough of her face for Maryam to confirm what she already knew. "I have to go," she murmurs.

"Wait!" Taskeen commands, but Maryam has already cut the call. She takes the stairs at a run, and gets to the lobby, breathless, while Núria is still negotiating with the receptionist.

"Hey," she gasps.

Núria turns, cries out in relief and recognition, and throws her arms around Maryam, who can see Saeed roll his eyes toward the ceiling and go back to whatever he's projecting at eye level.

"Come over here," Maryam says, and draws Núria over to one of the sets of chairs airscaped to provide some measure of privacy in the panopticon of the Hub lobby. "What are you doing here?"

"It was the only place I could think of to look for you." Her eyes fill. "I knew it was stupid, that you'd probably come home and we'd cross paths in midair, but . . ."

"But I didn't," Maryam says, stunned. A long time ago, she developed a theory that one of the key indicators for relationship success is compatibility in translating love into action and action into love. Some people say *I love you* a lot, some don't. It doesn't mean the latter love less. But knowing that is going to be small comfort if hearing *I love you* is one of your primary routes to the feeling of being loved, especially since studies have shown that these habits, in both directions, are particularly hard to change. Núria has just maxed Maryam's feeling-of-being-loved meter. Maryam, faced with the same predicament, felt the same impulse but didn't act on it.

"It's fine," Núria is saying, smiling through the tears. "I wasn't home, anyway. It's fine, really."

Maryam realizes that her face isn't expressing the complexity of her feelings, that she probably doesn't look as happy and moved as she is by Núria's presence, so she throws her arms around her. As their lips meet, Maryam's brain, determined to ruin the moment, wonders whether Núria might have just played her perfectly.

They go to Maryam's hotel, sneaking around the feeds in the lobby like teenagers because Maryam's room is designated single. She's already turned off all her notifications; Taskeen and her games can wait, and she doesn't want to have to answer a call from Nejime asking how the work is going.

As soon as the door closes behind them, Núria grabs Maryam in another hug, murmurs, "I was so worried about you," into her ear, but Maryam can't help feeling like it's forced this time.

She disengages. "Why didn't you send a message?"

Núria drops her arms. "Why didn't you?" When Maryam doesn't reply, she goes on. "I wasn't sure you'd answer, and I didn't want to sit around waiting, not knowing if you weren't answering because something had happened to you, or because you were too busy for me, or because you didn't want to talk to me—"

"Why wouldn't I want to talk to you?" Maryam asks.

"I don't know!" Núria shrugs exaggeratedly. "With all

this going on, I figured you'd be working on something you couldn't talk to me about! Which I understand, it's fine, but I just wanted to see you, you know? I know it was silly . . ."

"Of course it's not silly," Maryam says, but automatically: she is thinking about the *all this,* wondering how much Núria knows. "Have you voted yet?"

Núria gives her a quizzical glance. "No, but there are, what, twenty hours left? I think we have other things to talk about first."

"Just—try to vote. You'll see why."

As Maryam watches Núria's skeptical face clicking through the options, it occurs to her that she hasn't voted yet either, but right now, she can't face that decision—any of the decisions, really, because she's still not sure whether she can vote for Valérie, or whether she can vote against her.

"¡Coño!" Núria's eyes rise from the unseen voting mechanism to meet Maryam's. "How did this happen?"

Maryam shakes her head, holding Núria's gaze. "I don't know. But I have to ask you: given that choice"—she hesitates, takes in a breath—"Which side are you on?"

Núria answers without hesitation. "Yours."

Maryam swallows. "What does that mean?"

"What does it mean? It means I don't care about any of this stuff! If you ask me, really—" She stops for a moment to think. "I guess I'd vote for whomever I choose, because, bé, maybe there's something better?" She shrugs. "But if you tell me to vote for Information, I'll do it, not"—one finger up—"because you are corrupting my principles or any such comemierdería, but because I don't care that much and you do and I trust you to lead me well."

She stops as though she's run out of words, and Maryam

lets air out that she didn't know she was holding. "You—you don't know what this is about or where it comes from?"

"How would I?" Núria asks, incredulous. "I'm a soldier, not—I've never dealt with anything like this."

"You had nothing to do with this?"

Núria laughs. "Of course not!" Seeing that Maryam is still skeptical she casts around for an explanation. "I wouldn't even know where to begin, whom to talk to . . . I'm not connected to anything like this, not really! Why would I be dreaming revolution with my friends if I were already a part of one?"

"I hate your camaradas," Maryam blurts.

"What?"

"I'm jealous of them. All the time you spend with them, your shared cause . . ." *Their beauty, their style, their effortless wit . . .*

"And you think I'm not jealous of Valérie?" Núria tightens her fingers around Maryam's.

That possibility had, in fact, never occurred to Maryam.

"Mira, amor meu," Núria starts. The Catalá possessive pronoun makes it sound so much more intimate and real than Núria's usual flippant use of the endearment. "Yes, there are some things in my job I can't talk about—just as there are in yours. But believe me"—another little laugh—"I have never been such an important person in YourArmy as to work on things like these. And I never wanted to be."

"I never was, either," Maryam murmurs. "Until now."

Núria pulls her into her embrace again. "I don't care!" she whispers fiercely. "I don't care if you have to keep secrets all the time. As long as they're not secrets about you cheating on me. But keep your work secrets. I don't want them. I just want what we have together."

Maryam sighs, trust rising in her like slow floodwaters. "I do too."

Maryam wakes up a few hours later, Núria's arm over her belly, Núria's face in her shoulder, Núria's hair against her cheek. The futon feels luxuriously clean and *flat*; Maryam remembers she hadn't slept since the flight from Paris, and before that in Cuba. She should still be asleep. But there is daylight glowing faintly through the window filter and her mind is wide awake, clicking away.

Núria stirs when Maryam clambers off the futon but doesn't wake up until Maryam is dressed and kneeling beside her. Núria smiles. "You're going in?"

"Yes," Maryam says, running her hand through her lover's hair. "Is that—"

"It's fine," Núria murmurs. "As long as you come back."

"I will," Maryam promises. And then, just in case: "If I don't, come looking for me."

"Flamethrowers blazing," Núria agrees. "Oh," she calls as Maryam walks out. "Don't forget to vote. The last polls showed Liberty ahead in our centenal."

Maryam stops. "Ahead by how much?"

"By enough." Núria shakes her head, furious. "I don't understand how anyone can vote for them, knowing what they did."

Núria works for YourArmy; she and her friends worked to clean up Liberty's mess. "Maybe they don't know," Maryam offers.

"In that case," Núria says, "I'm sorry, amor, but Information failed."

Maryam has no answer.

As she leaves the hotel, Maryam pulls open the voting mechanism. There are still fourteen hours left in Election Day, but this is probably the latest she's ever waited to vote. *888. Valérie.* And then, after a brief hesitation, *whomever I choose.* Having the choice means she can still choose Information, she tells herself.

The choice made, she opens her comms again and calls Taskeen.

CHAPTER 27

Maryam expected Taskeen to be furious or at least frustrated, but although she answers immediately, her voice is distracted. "Yes?"

"You wanted to talk to me yesterday?" Maryam tries to sound equally blasé.

"You called me first," Taskeen says, sounding more guarded now.

Maryam cannot deal with coyness any more. "I wanted to know if you were responsible for the Information flicker. Now I need to know if you are responsible for the new voting category." When she thinks about it, over the last week she's talked truth with a former head of state, two of the most powerful women in Information, and—no less intimidating— her own girlfriend. No need to doubt herself now.

"Oh, that. Yes, of course."

Maryam finds herself doubting. "¿Perdona? Yes, of course *what?*"

"I arranged for both those things to happen. Collaboratively, you understand; I'm not trying to take all the credit."

Maryam stops walking. She's on a small side street, it's early in Doha, next to her a shopkeeper is pushing a display case out of his store, down the street a woman is programming the daily menu projection for a restaurant. "Credit?"

"Look," Taskeen says, reasonably. "We're a little busy here taking over the world; what exactly do you want to know?" Before Maryam can manage an answer, she amends, "Well, not taking over the world, exactly. We don't want to end up running it. But definitely kicking Information's ass."

"Why?" Maryam gets out at last, thinking as she does it's a stupid question, a comic book question for an evil mega-villain. "Information's not that bad."

"And there you have your answer," Taskeen says cheerfully. "'Not that bad' was worth something at the beginning of this experiment, but it doesn't cut it anymore."

"So, you're upending the status quo and just hoping it works out."

"That's the only way to do it, dear. Nobody ever knows whether something this big is going to work out. Political systems, macroeconomic policies, coding languages, algorithms: there will always be unintended consequences."

"Except," Maryam says, remembering Nejime's warning, "we do have an idea how this will turn out. Multiple sources of data means people will believe what they want."

"Unless we do better at teaching them how to choose. No reason Information can't fill that role."

Maryam tries to imagine Information as an underfunded public media literacy service. "That's going to be a tough transition for a lot of people."

"Exactly!" Taskeen pounces. "That is exactly the key issue right now. The important thing is for the transition to be as smooth as possible. Thankfully, we are finally at the stage where we can truly have a bloodless revolution."

"Bloodless because most people won't notice!" Maryam shoots back. "You did this with no discussion, no debate—"

"We didn't hide anything! If people aren't paying attention, that's on them!" Taskeen snaps. "Are you going to tell me you of all people pine for the false heroics and desperate actions of trying to get everyone to agree with you?" Taskeen throws up a projection of Maryam's public history and draws lines in the air from places she's lived—Beirut, La Habana, Lima—to images of violent revolution. This is not a prepared projection; she is finding and throwing up the images in real time, and adeptly.

"You've been practicing." Maryam swallows. "You haven't been locked away from Information technology in that sanatorium."

Taskeen ignores her. "Tell me that you haven't bought into the narrative of the heroic resistance paying in blood for some abstract notion of freedom! Do you really think it's better if people wring some small concessions from power by dying?"

"And what are you giving the people? Not more power."

"A deconcentration of power. The removal of the giant undemocratic blockage in the system."

"That you set up!"

"In part, yes," Taskeen says. "The system was supposed to evolve."

"It has! The Secretariat, the new environmental regulations . . ."

"The environmental regulations are a sop, and the Secretariat barely worth mentioning. Maryam! You know that Information holds the power in this system, and it is completely unelected. Are you really arguing for that?"

"I'm arguing that we need a source of data as close to impartial as we can get! We need a way to give people the data they need to make the decisions democracy depends on."

"Information has spent the last twenty-five years trying to force people to pay attention to issues they don't care about. And despite all your meddling, people still care more about their friends, and clothes, and sports, and what to eat for dinner, and whether they can find a better job or where to go on vacation than about any question of governance. And how has that worked out?"

"So, your solution is to let people not care." Maryam is walking again, angrily, toward the Hub.

"No, my solution is to decentralize and democratize the process. It won't be perfect. But it will be a step, an improvement. We have to keep finding ways to improve! We have to keep trying, we have to be willing to break in order to build! Now, Maryam, you have to decide: are you going to help?"

Maryam sucks in breath. She is almost to the Hub.

"We've already won," Taskeen says. "Getting the question into the voting mechanism, that was everything."

"I thought the infrastructure was everything. I thought you needed our infrastructure!"

"A bit of misdirection," Taskeen admits. "I didn't want you looking too closely at what I was trying to do, but I certainly didn't need to cut off your power supply to hack your election ballot, and for distribution we've worked out a transmission method using a network of small, cheap antennae. The technology has been improving rapidly, and all of my partners are outfitted and operational. But I needed your help to block those other idiots, the Exformation crew. *They* can't manage without infrastructure. Clumsy fools! Trying to control something they don't understand. That's the risk right now, that they do something stupid to try to hijack your network. The sooner we can settle this, the safer everyone will be. Look around you! The advids from our competitors are starting to go up. The Election Day adblocker is broken. The information market is open. So, when I ask for your help"—her eyes coming back to meet Maryam's—"it is only in making the transition as painless as possible."

Maryam dawdles under the overhang outside the main entrance of the Hub. When she looks up, Roz is getting out of an autocab and walking toward her. "Maybe," Maryam says. "Let's see what's happening inside." She turns down the volume but leaves the connection on as she and Roz walk into the building together.

W hat are you doing here?" Maryam asks Roz.

"Mmph," Roz says. "Suleyman's not happy about it. And my parents are worse. But with all this happening, I couldn't not come. Supposedly I have another week anyway. Besides, this is hardly farther from the hospital than my apartment."

"So, you're planning to go into labor in the middle of the showdown?"

"Careful, they'll say you have a narrative disorder." They start toward the elevators. "Is that what this is going to be? A showdown?"

"What else could it be?" Maryam asks, conscious of Taskeen listening in.

Roz looks at her sidelong. "You heard Nougaz is here?"

"What?"

"I assumed that's why you called it a showdown," Roz says sheepishly. "She came in last night."

Maryam is flipping through the messages she missed during her Núria interlude. Nothing from Valérie. Several messages of varying degrees of panic from Batún, asking what he should tell the tech team to do about voting. "Do you know where she is?" Maryam hears herself asking.

Roz shrugs and tilts her head toward the reception desk. "Where will you be?" Maryam asks, already moving.

"I'm going to say hi to the Wall team before the meeting," Roz says. "I'll see you there, unless I go into labor first."

"Wait, Roz?" Maryam flushes, hurrying back to get close enough to whisper. "There's a meeting?"

"You weren't invited? Oh, right, I keep forgetting you're not supposed to be here." She flicks the message about it over to Maryam. "I'm sure they won't mind if you sit in."

"I hope not," Maryam says. "Um. Remember I mentioned a person we could talk to?" She waits until she sees understanding click in Roz's face. "I'm connected with them." She taps her ear.

Roz's face shows shock now. "What—now?" she whispers, as if that would make a difference.

"I think—I hope this is the right decision. What we talked about." Taskeen sends an old-school emoji, a face with a waving hand, to dance in front of Maryam's vision. Maryam stifles a laugh. "Sorry. Didn't get much sleep. Anyway, this meeting. If I can't get in . . ."

Roz studies her face. "I'll call you," she promises, pressing Maryam's hand. "But I'm sure Nougaz will get you in, if nothing else. See you soon—it starts in twenty minutes."

Nougaz has taken over the office of Lily Cohen, deployed to Kashmir to monitor the election. When Maryam walks in, she is observing a projection and making notes, so enthralled it is half a minute before she can drag her eyes away from whatever she's looking at. She doesn't seem surprised when she does. "What do you know?"

Oh, Valérie. Maryam hears herself say it in her head in

the same tone Nejime used. "I told Nejime about your involvement with the tunnel," she says, before she can lose her nerve.

"She is looking well," Taskeen says in Maryam's ear.

Nougaz shrugs, eyes dipping back to the projection. "It would have come out anyway. Moot now; we have bigger problems."

Maryam moves farther into the room, closing the door behind her. "Whose side are you on?"

"Hmm?"

"Whose side are you on?" She enunciates it loudly, and Valérie finally turns her attention on her.

"What are you doing here?" Nougaz asks. "Don't you work somewhere else now?"

"I'm supporting the transition." Maryam hears a pleased sigh from Taskeen.

Nougaz offers her classic eyebrow-raise. "*Transition,* is it?"

"You said yourself Information is over."

"I didn't think you believed me." Nougaz examines her. "*Transition* sounds . . . promising."

Taskeen snorts. "Commitment problems?"

Maryam flinches. "I'll assume you're still on your own side. Assuming there is a transition, where do you want to end up?"

"What's on offer?" Nougaz asks, cautious. "Where does this transition idea come from? Nejime?"

"You're giving away too much and she's not telling you anything," Taskeen grumbles.

"Taskeen Khan," Maryam says, piqued, and is gratified by Taskeen's annoyed grunt.

"Taskeen Khan?" Nougaz's features startle from their

resting position of authority into a rare expression of surprise. "You're working with her? She used to be my senior, back when we were starting."

"Used to be!" Taskeen explodes in Maryam's ear. "I am *still* very much her senior! People think that age and experience are only good up to a point and then it's a fast downhill slide, but believe me . . ." Maryam lowers the volume on her earpiece to background Taskeen's rant as Nougaz goes on.

"Taskeen Khan, back in the game. And how is she communicating? No, never mind, don't tell me, I'm sure I won't understand your explanation, anyway. Everyone seems to be trying to squirrel away their own secret comms these days: Khan, those other lines in the Heritage tunnel . . ."

"What Heritage tunnel?" Taskeen asks sharply.

"Where is Taskeen these days?" Nougaz asks.

"Dhaka." Maryam is relieved to have a question she can answer quickly, even if she's omitting the fact that Taskeen is listening in on their conversation. "Shall we go to the meeting?"

Valérie raises her eyebrows. "We still have a few minutes. Are you well?"

"Fine," Maryam says. She can feel Taskeen hovering silently on the connection. *Don't pick this moment to get sentimental for the first time in your life, Valérie, not right now.*

"Your—" Valérie stops, and Maryam wonders what she had been about to say: Your job? Your girlfriend? Instead, she shifts her position to make room at the workspace. "Have you seen these?" she asks.

Maryam steps in next to her. She can smell the dry, clean scent of the older woman, see the energy contained in the angle of her neck. Nougaz enlarges the projection. A shimmery flash gives way to an image of a beautiful, middle-aged white woman—the ad is picking up Nougaz's identity cues—reading something off of a projection and nodding with a satisfied smile. *For data you can trust* reads the italicized text, as a quick array of stylish infographics shuffles, *Opposition Research is on your side!*

Nougaz sniffs. "Not very sophisticated, are they?"

Maryam is stunned. "'On your side'—data is not supposed to be on anyone's side!"

"Data is on everyone's side," Nougaz corrects. "But yes, I think they're trying to suggest—"

"That they'll tell you just what you want to hear." Maryam covers her eyes with her hands. *Nejime was right!* She should have helped her. And now here she is, letting the architect of all this listen in on their conversations.

"It won't be that easy," Taskeen predicts in her ear. "Information will still be around, not to mention their other competitors."

"But no one will believe Information anymore!" Maryam feels like she's about to be sick.

Nougaz has stepped back, the better to eye her suspiciously. "Not that many people believe us now," she says. "But if you're so worried about it, tell Taskeen to stop these."

"I can't," Taskeen says. "That's the whole point. I don't run Opposition Research. I am not in charge. No one is."

This does not make Maryam feel any less nauseous. "She can't stop them," she repeats, for Nougaz's benefit. "She's not controlling them."

"Well, then," Nougaz says briskly. "Let's go see what the best minds of our generations can come up with." Having managed to annoy both Maryam and Taskeen, she leads the way out.

• • •

Vincent brings Amran a bowl of ugali, a spiceless vegetable stew, and a scoop of fried termites for protein. He hangs around and tries to make conversation while she eats, but she's not into Stockholm syndrome. She does accept his offer to take her to a toilet, and takes advantage of the moment of solitude to fit the handle of her billaawe in her hand, comforting herself that it is real. When she puts it back under her robes, she is careful to arrange it for ease of access. Amran knows she's not proficient enough to manage anything complicated, and she doesn't trust her resolve for a committed stab through cartilage, bone, and squirty bits, so she has decided her best chance is to the throat. She imagines the motions repeatedly as they walk back along the hallway: spring forward, slash, run. Spring forward, slash, run.

When they get back to the room, Misra is finishing a call. "There have been some unexpected developments," she says. "I think we're going to have to skip ahead to the climactic scenes." She projects some new backgrounds, and Amran is startled to recognize the silhouette of a building.

"That's—those are Information hubs!"

"Correct," Misra says. "A targeted strike on critical infrastructure and personnel."

"Personnel?" Amran waits for her brain to catch up with her sense of shock. Misra is smiling, obviously pleased with herself. "But," Amran says, speaking carefully, "how will attacking Information hubs win you any kind of lasting control?"

"With that physical access, we'll be able to speak as Information while having some of their most powerful and influential officials under our control. We will be able to enact our reforms. And then we'll be the most prepared to step in and take over. The same service everyone is accustomed to, but we will do it better. Just look at the data collection and distribution we've been able to do already, and then imagine it with all the logistical and political power of Information on our side."

"So, you're taking over but not making any real changes to this system you hate?"

"There will be lots of changes," Misra says. "We have all sorts of plans, but that can come later. What we need to have ready is the storyline of our glorious takeover. This is crucial because Information will be spreading their own perspective if they have any chance to do it. So: a spirited attack using the military might of our allies." She flashes vid clips of fighter planes. "Heroic hand-to-hand battles, I'd imagine. And finally, triumph and freedom of Information!"

"What hubs?" Amran asks.

"Excuse me?" Misra comes back from her daydream.

"What hubs are you attacking?"

"We were going to hit Doha, Paris, and Mexico City, but we have been tracking the Paris Director and she is conveniently in Doha at the moment, so we can economize. Again, local color is great. Now, it would be good if we can have the bare-bones version of this prepared to run later tonight, although I hope it won't be necessary until tomorrow or the day after."

"Sure," Amran says, and leaps across the space between them, unsheathing her billaawe.

The meeting is in the scrupulously designed Jaber conference room usually reserved for visiting dignitaries with large entourages or high-level internal meetings. The last time Maryam was here was five years ago, after the last election was sabotaged. She hangs back at the door, not wanting her entrance with Nougaz to be misinterpreted, but there are enough people milling around that she doesn't think it will be remarked on.

She searches for Roz and finally finds her on the other side of the room, but as she starts toward her, Maryam realizes the person she is talking to is Mishima. When did she get here? Maryam doesn't know Mishima that well, and a mega-famous assassin-spy-politician seems like the worst person to involve in touchy secret machinations. Unless she's most definitely *your* mega-famous assassin-spy-politician. But then Mishima touches Roz's belly, and Maryam notices a small child clinging to Mishima's leg. They're talking pregnancy and motherhood, not global political cataclysm. Or maybe both?

Letting her gaze drift, Maryam catches a glimpse of Batún projecting in from La Habana, and sits down hastily in the first seat she can find, not wanting to have to explain what she's doing here or why she hasn't answered his messages. In any case, the meeting seems to be wending toward a beginning; the hum of conversation has risen in anticipation of being cut off, and more people are sitting. Not far from her, Maryam hears Nougaz talking with Nejime and al-Mofti.

"If this had happened two days later, it would be the Secretariat debating this."

"Two thwarted elections in a row. Perhaps we *are* finished."

"You think so?"

Maryam cranes around to catch Nejime's expression, but she is already calling the meeting to order.

A mran goes in, slashing for the throat. She misses the neck but catches Misra across the cheek. It's clear Misra isn't a fighter either: she flails at Amran, shrieking. Amran dodges her and runs for the door. She throws it open to find Vincent running toward her. She aims for his belly but he yells and ducks away.

"What the fuck!" he screams.

"You kidnapped me!" Amran yells back at him. "You! Kidnapped! Meeeeeeeeee!" she screams in his face as loudly as she can. Then she runs.

K en slides into the room just after the meeting starts. Nakia decided she couldn't face a Hub full of strangers while still under suspicion, so they had dropped her off at Roz's apartment. Then they moored on top of the Information Hub, and while Mishima went straight to the meeting, Ken went down to the sweet cart he remembered in the lobby to get a few Lebanese pastries for Sayaka (and himself). He can't get close to where Mishima is sitting at that point, but as a non-Information employee he prefers to sit in the back anyway.

Ken was in this room, even more distinctly out of place, for a similar debate during the *last* election. He automatically glances down at Sayaka. Mishima set her up with a projection under the conference table, and she's lost to the world. She's a personification of all the time that has passed since the last time he was in this room, not only since her birth but also the years before that while he and Mishima were getting to the place where they could decide to have a child.

There are other differences, too. For one, he knows almost everyone's name here and more or less who they are. When he slipped in, Hassan was giving the tech perspective on what's going on; now Hub Directors from across the globe are putting in their comments on special local considerations and sharing the different ads that have been going up in their regions for new data services, which seems to be making everyone nervous.

"Maybe no one will see them," says one of the older directors, from northern Europe, Ken thinks.

"Are we going to have to start advertising now?" asks Lin, laughing at the preposterousness of the idea.

"Surely people won't fall for this crap!"

"Why not? They fall for everything else."

"And even if people see them, if they don't have any original content . . ."

Ken clears his throat, darting a gaze at Mishima. She nods, and he speaks. "They do." Faces turn to him. "They have original content. And some pretty exciting original content, too. Policy1st is using one of the new . . ." He doesn't even know what the word should be. "They're using one the new independent datastreams to inform the world about secret communication cables in the PhilipMorris mantle tunnel."

General chaos ensues. Nobody is looking at Ken anymore, because half of them are looking for friends or rivals to discuss with or shout at, and the other half are trying to find out about it on Information. Someone with a particularly loud voice is shouting, "How dare they! How dare they!"

and Ken wonders whether they're talking about Philip-Morris or Policy1st.

"You won't find it on Information," he tells the room. "It will be blocked because it's Election Day."

Horrified silence. Nejime breaks it. "Once the Secretariat is in place, we can manage these governments with their secret communications . . ."

"You knew about this?" someone asks.

Nejime bats the question away. "We were dealing with it. That is a minor threat compared with this problem of upstart data purveyors!"

"The question is how we can possibly maintain our authority under a deluge of competing sources," al-Derbi agrees.

"You are already accepting their premise," Nejime says, cutting through. "Back up. We can't let this election stand. The voting depends on a damaged elective process . . ."

"And what do you intend to do?" interrupts Nougaz. "When would you hold a new election?" She waits just a moment, for the quickest to get there on their own, and then spells it out. "To invalidate the election on those grounds, you would need to ensure that the re-vote was absolutely clear of those concerns, and we are not in a position to do that, not for the foreseeable future."

"You are suggesting we let it stand?" asks Lin.

"I'm suggesting we don't have a choice." Nougaz pauses, and when she speaks again, her tone is more conciliatory. "We need to consider the order of the election questions." Around the table, attention that had been focused elsewhere locks on to her. "If the question about intel provision had been first, the election would have been over then—the entire system, probably. How many people would have even gone on to the second question? But they put it into the final position, after the other voting choices had been made."

"If you're trying to say that means the election result isn't contaminated—"

"Of course it's contaminated! What I'm saying is that they could have blown up the entire voting mechanism, and they chose not to. They want the process to continue."

"You're saying this isn't a threat to micro-democracy?" Al-Derbi is skeptical.

"No, it's certainly a threat. I'm saying micro-democracy isn't the target of the attack. We are."

"Maybe we'd be better off considering where the attack is coming from," Mikolajczak says. "Who did this?"

"I suspect it's connected to the people who left the organization two years ago," Nejime says. "We've seen an uptick in activity from their suspected sites of exile."

Ken sees Mishima open her mouth, but before she can say anything, Nougaz has jumped in again. "I believe Taskeen Khan is involved."

There is a minor sensation at that. Ken, who has never heard the name, does a quick look-up, then realizes he's seen her portrait every time he's walked through the lobby of the building.

"What is she trying to do?" someone asks out of the hubbub of voices.

Ken can see Nougaz looking significantly at someone; following her gaze, he recognizes Maryam, who used to be the head techie in Doha and then moved to somewhere, in Latin America, he thinks.

"What does it look like?" Nejime responds. "Break the so-called Information monopoly."

"Would it be effective to, erm, compromise her ability to

lead this effort?" Ken didn't see who asked the question, but Mishima's voice is unmistakable as she answers.

"Are you suggesting that we assassinate a retired eighty-nine-year-old?"

There's a murmur in response, probably not so much to her words as to her presence. A lot of people seem not to have noticed she was here until now. Ken allows himself a moment of smug self-congratulation about how awesome she is.

"I appreciate the consideration," says another voice. Ken follows it to the doorway. The woman standing there doesn't look like she's eighty-nine, but she does look startlingly similar to the portrait in the lobby.

Amran calls Mishima and can't get through. She calls the Doha Hub and can't get through. She calls the Mexico City Hub, and when she can't get through there, she gives up on communications and runs along the sun-simmering pavements toward the Nairobi Hub.

Maryam closes her eyes and, while they're closed, revises her understanding of the last dozen hours, removing the premise that Taskeen was talking to her from her antiquated apartment in Dhaka and imagining her instead en route to or stashed away in the Hub, waiting for exactly the right moment to make her entrance.

Taskeen waits until the commotion has quieted before she goes on. "I thought it might be helpful for me to be here in person to explain exactly what has happened, and what is likely to happen next."

Nejime breaks in with an unexpected display of sentiment.

"How could you do this, Taskeen? How could you betray all that we've worked for?"

"Do you remember the principles we founded this system on?" Taskeen's eyes sweep the room; it is only to be expected that they touch on Maryam's before continuing. "Democracy. Choice of government. Political self-determination. It is time to expand our principles of choice to information management as well."

"Democracy doesn't work without an informed public," Nougaz puts in. Maryam is surprised: she had thought Nougaz would hold back before committing. She really has a talent for making people think the worst of her, even those who know her best.

"And a single source informing the public is more dangerous than none," Taskeen says. "Even if all of you are convinced that you are irreproachable, you must imagine the consequences if someone less principled were to take over this behemoth that we've built."

"A single source is less dangerous than many competing unregulated sources," Nejime cuts in, and she throws up a projection. It's a quick kaleidoscope of vid clips from old news programs and more recent documentaries: diagrams of media bubbles; glamorous news anchors getting caught in lies; analyses of voting influence. Maryam wonders if Nejime's been working on it since they talked yesterday. "It will be chaos."

Taskeen is ready for it. "I hope we aren't prioritizing order over democracy," she says, and throws a montage of official government news and propaganda efforts. The flashes of the competing projections put Maryam in mind of a battle of wizards.

"That's not us," someone says indignantly, and Taskeen bows as if she's proved her point.

"We made this system," says Taskeen, with the lightest emphasis on the *we* to remind them that, in terms of the architecture at least, she personally made most of it. "We can modify it."

"Tear it down, you mean," snarls Nougaz.

"I mean improve it. And for better or for worse, it's done now, so you best use this time to figure out how to address it rather than arguing the theory."

"She's right," Nejime says. "Even if we were to invalidate the election—and as you pointed out"—with a nod at Nougaz—"that is probably inadvisable—the idea is already out in the world, and it has been all but proven that people prefer it."

"That doesn't mean we have to accept it!" Lin is almost yelling, and for a minute, the room devolves into a babel of competing voices.

When it subsides, Hassan slips a question in.

"So, what do you need from us? Are you looking for some level of control over our infrastructure?"

"No, not at all!" Taskeen says, with pride. "In fact, I think it best if you keep your infrastructure proprietary as long as possible. No, we have found that with small antennae, we are able to maintain a network that is, though certainly less efficient and robust, entirely workable for a start-up."

The senior Information leaders in the room take a moment to digest the degree to which their long-term investment in global, world-class infrastructure has become obsolete.

"If that's the case," Hassan ventures, "why did you attack the data distribution centers?"

"That wasn't us," Taskeen says, and almost exactly as she finishes speaking, there's a dull but distinct *thud* and the lights go out.

The electricity flickers back on a second later; the Hub has robust backup systems. But the projections that have been looping silently in the air above the room are gone, and so, Maryam notices, is everyone who had been projecting in. Other than that, no one has moved except for Mishima, who is now standing and holding her daughter in her arms. The girl bursts into tears, and for a moment, her anguished sobs are the only sound.

Maryam sees Mishima's eyes meet Ken's across the room. There's a breath of intense communication in their gaze, and then Mishima is on the conference table, striding across it, leaping lightly down on the other side. She passes the girl to Ken and is out of the room without a word.

CHAPTER 28

The Doha Hub security center is on the ground floor, or at least it used to be; on her way down the stairs, Mishima tries to blink up a blueprint to make sure it hasn't moved, but Information is completely out. Annoyed, she focuses on getting to ground level as quickly as possible.

Simone, whom Mishima knows well, is no longer the head of security at Doha, and Mishima has never met her replacement, Jens. She's hoping that he won't give her any trouble about joining the team, but when she bursts into the flurrying crisis room, his eyes widen immediately with recognition and surprise. *Still a legend,* Mishima tells herself. She hovers by his side, listening to the quick updates and half-spoken questions and confirmations, and by the time he turns to her a few minutes later, she has most of the picture.

"Before Information crashed, we received SOS signals from the data transfer stations in Al Khobar and Jam," he tells her as soon as he has a breath between demands. "I suspect Al Hamra is out too."

"You think they're isolating us?"

"I'm sure of it."

"And the explosion?"

"Our grid connections," he says. "A targeted precision bomb that knocked out our power source."

"Bomb?"

"From an aircraft, most probably," Jens says. "Someone seems to be waging war on us."

Mishima sees Sayaka's sobbing face again, shakes her head to dislodge the image. "So the Information outage is probably localized. It should be working in the rest of the world?"

"Almost certainly. And they may not even have realized we're offline yet."

"Do you have any other comms available?" Five years ago, during a global outage, Mishima received critical intel through this hub's telegraph. From the look on Jens's face, he knows the story.

"Roman ran for the telegraph first thing. He's sending out a generalized SOS, but the closest connected hub is Baghdad, and they'll only come for us if they're following the protocol for keeping it on and linked to alerts."

"On Election Day, I would hope they are," Mishima says. "Still a minimum . . . three hours?"

"Very optimistically, I would say." Jens is starting to relax into the shop talk.

"And further attacks?" They are both watching a radar screen bolted uncomfortably high up on the wall: no one expected it to be the main source of data.

"We're expecting them, but we haven't seen anything yet." He gestures at the large projection display in front of him. The spaces allocated to feeds from the cameras at the hub entrances are blank, knocked out in the hack. "We have people stationed at the entrances, but of course we won't know anything until we hear from them."

"No walkie-talkies?"

"No, but we've set up a line-of-sight chain—not complete,

we don't have the staff for that, but at a few points to shorten the time."

"How sophisticated was the tech attack?" Mishima wonders. "Blanket EMP-style, or . . ."

"They're working on that." Jens nods at four people clustered around a horribly convoluted circuit diagram projected up in a corner. "All they've said so far is 'more a scalpel than a sledgehammer,' so I think there's some hope there."

"Okay." Mishima shakes off her professional curiosity. "Where do you want me?"

"You came in a crow, right? Post up on the roof. I want you in the crow and ready to take off."

"You're concerned about aerial bombardment?"

"If that's what happened to the grid connection." He points to a map projected against the entire side wall. "The transformer station, here. Close enough for us to hear the explosion but a little far for us to easily confirm."

Mishima gives an unwilling shudder at the thought of that amount of firepower, at the thought of Sayaka in the room above her. "From where?" she asks.

For the first time, Jens hems and hedges. "Look, I'm not super-proficient with this radar. It's not like we've had a lot of practice with it. And the map on it is just coastlines; it doesn't show any centenal borders."

"Well?" Thinking about the levels above her—floor, space, floor, space, floor, Sayaka, floor, space, roof, space, bomber jets—is making Mishima itchy.

"To me it looked like they were coming from the Heritage centenal just across the Gulf."

The thought of being attacked by a government is

shocking, particularly this government: Heritage has one of the best militaries in the world.

"I understand," says Mishima, reverting to Japanese syntax. She turns to go, then pauses. "Have you thoroughly Lumpered?" she asks, knowing the question is so basic as to be insulting, but he nods without any signs of offense.

"We do it regularly, and initiated a site-wide Lumpering as soon as the electricity was cut."

"Can I take some hardware?"

Jens nods her to a door in the side of the room and turns to a woman who's offering him an updated report on the grid connection. Mishima goes into the armory. She grabs a torch, the standard flamethrower the security teams carry, and, after a little searching, a pack of shuriken and a large dagger to add to the hunting knife and stiletto she's already carrying. Then she runs for the stairs.

It takes the collection of experienced, elite Information leaders in the meeting room twelve and a half minutes to come to the same conclusion that Mishima reached in two seconds. Maryam watches them argue back and forth about what should be done, but keeps an eye on Taskeen. The older woman jumped at the explosion and looks pale, shaky, and undecided. All of which, Maryam hopes, means she's not behind this attack.

The room might have kept discussing, but a runner from security stopped in to inform them that they suspected a bombing attack on the electrical transformer station, or possibly the power plant, and that an evacuation is recommended.

Even then they can't make up their fucking minds.

"Evacuate to where?"

"They might be expecting us to leave, pick us off once we're outside the building."

"They might *want* the building; they're probably just waiting for us to leave to take over."

"AlThani won't stand for this infringement on their sovereignty."

"They have no way to find out about it. Information is totally off."

"They might notice the flyovers."

"Maybe. Do they have radar or any other non-Information-based air surveillance?"

Nobody knows.

"Maybe we can do something about communications," Taskeen says, standing. "Maryam, can you find us a place to work?"

Maryam is on her feet. "Hassan?"

A moment later, the three of them are in the corridor. It's a distinct relief to be out of that room full of talk and confusion.

"Hassan took over my job when I left," Maryam tells Taskeen as they charge down the corridor toward his office. "He's the most up-to-date on everything we have related to comms and codes."

"Perfect," Taskeen says, with a quick nod. She seems to have recovered her sangfroid and is striding along with every appearance of aplomb.

"Taskeen," Maryam says. "What is happening?"

The older woman tilts her head slightly. "I don't know exactly."

"But you suspect."

Taskeen nods.

"Why don't you tell us what you know?" Maryam says, frustrated. "Who are you working with?"

"Some of your former colleagues."

Hassan joins in. "Did you start working with them before or after they left?"

"That's complicated. Before, but we weren't planning on any of this at the time. It started as a consultative relationship, and the contact was broken for a while after they deserted."

And during the assassinations? Maryam wonders.

"As you know, there were quite a number of people who exiled themselves two years ago. It is not a monolithic group. A large segment of them have been working with me toward the goal of what some call 'free' and what I prefer to call 'competitive' data services. However, I am aware that there are others who are more interested in toppling Information than in what might replace it."

"And these others . . ." Hassan starts.

"Are violent, yes."

"Are they working with Heritage?"

Taskeen and Maryam both turn to look at him. They have just walked into the techie department—largely empty, evacuation is underway—and Hassan is leading them to a workroom. "I think so. Why?"

"There was a spike in traffic on the comms in the Heritage tunnel shortly before the power went out," Hassan says.

Heritage again. Maryam shakes her head in annoyance. "Why can't these people stand to lose power? Don't they understand this is a democracy?"

"So what are we doing here?" Hassan asks.

"Maryam and I believe," Taskeen says, "that they attacked the null-states debate by hacking into the algorithms that find alternative data transmission routes when one is blocked or overloaded. If they did the same thing here, maybe we can counter it by either reloading the algorithms"— Hassan and Maryam make identical faces: this is unlikely to be feasible—"or manually entering new pathways."

"And we're aiming to connect to AlThani security forces," Maryam says.

"That's the best place to get military reinforcements quickly?" Taskeen asks.

"Definitely," Hassan says. Maryam thinks of Núria in the hotel room. Is there a YourArmy contingent anywhere near here? Could Núria convince them to deploy?

"After we alert them," Taskeen says, "or maybe simultaneously, I'd like to suggest connecting with some of the local data services groups." She throws up a file and flips through it, looking at a series of node maps.

"Why?" Hassan asks. "You think this will be a good publicity stunt for your new project?"

Taskeen ignores his hostility. "The attackers are hoping to control this narrative. They'll tell people they were being heroic and fighting tyranny. Attacking the Information Hub in public view is a very different proposition. Particularly for a major government."

Chilled, Maryam meets Hassan's eyes. "Let's get to it, then," she says, as steadily as she can, and they start pinging.

It's harder to be fearless when you're worried about other people besides yourself. Mishima tries to shut down the images her narrative disorder is playing ceaselessly, of Ken but mostly of Sayaka. Her face, red and wet with startled tears as Mishima pulled her away from her vanished projection;

her clinging arms as she handed her over to Ken. Fear and fury are twin wires running between her heart and her guts, one cold and one burning. Every time she feels the icy pinch of fear, she tries to send more anger pulsing through her veins, but it's hard to stave off the cold, standing alone on the roof, waiting for something to appear out of the cloudless, desert-burnished sky.

She is keeping an eye out for other modes of attack on the roof—grappling hooks, or crows or tsubames carrying assault teams—but fighter jets would be faster and more devastating. The AlThani military might have some limited anti-air capacity to defend against them, but InfoSec certainly doesn't.

Mishima gets a ping to her handheld: a line-of sight message from the InfoSec Jens has stationed near the roof access. *Suspected take-off from same site. Eight bogies.*

Mishima cranks the crow into the air, heading straight up a couple of dozen meters. Crows don't get a lot of altitude; there's not going to be any way for her to engage directly with fighter jets. The best she can hope for is to deflect the bombs or whatever they're planning on raining down. She makes herself not think about anything, not feel the cold bringing goosebumps out on her skin despite the perfect climate control, but it's not easy during the wait. She misses her old crow.

There! Faint discolorations in the sky still, up and to the northeast. Mishima stares until her eyes water despite the protective coating on the viewer. Faster than seems possible, the blur separates into shapes that grow and sharpen. Mishima gets as high as she can, taking a quick glance downward in case this is a distraction for a ground assault. When she can hear the roar, she pulls back slightly from the roof, tilts the crow upward as far as the air pressurizers allow. She has no idea if it's possible to divert a bomb as it's falling. Don't most of these things have directional controls? But there's nothing else to do. She relaxes her hands, ready to control the crow with instinct instead of brain, and focuses everything on the air above her as the jets shatter the sky.

One breath. Two breaths. Would she see a bomb by now? The jets scatter dark blots in their wake, but as Mishima watches, they bloom and slow: paratroopers.

Mishima lets out the third breath with a whoosh, forces herself to breathe slowly until her hands stop shaking. This enemy wants control, not destruction. And now she has time to figure out what she's going to do.

This is taking too long," Maryam says. Hassan is still working doggedly, stringing together node after node, but it's slow going.

"Remind me to hardwire in emergency paths after this is over," he grunts.

Taskeen says nothing, and hasn't for a while; Maryam suspects she is working on connecting to her local contacts instead of AlThani. Which, who knows, might work even better.

"I'm going for help," Maryam says. Taskeen doesn't look up, but Hassan does.

"What are you going to do? Run all the way to the Al-Thani hall?" Their seat of government is on the other side of the city—no one thought it was a good idea to have two such powerful institutions close together—nearly ten kilometers away.

"No, I'm going to see if we can contact YourArmy."

Hassan, who knows about her relationship with Núria, looks at her through narrowed eyes. "Don't do something stupid."

Maryam doesn't care. She wants to be with Núria now. The last time she felt this way and ignored it, she ended up feeling like a jerk. She stands up.

Taskeen finally looks at her. "I've left messages for some people. I told them to wear white armbands. They'll help you if they can."

Maryam tries a smile. "No neutral press, huh?"

"No such thing," Taskeen answers.

While waiting for the paratroopers, Mishima checks the crow's weaponry. Nothing but a flamethrower on the nose. She wishes she had thought to grab a grenade launcher from the armory. She has time to think about how hard she wants to work to avoid killing people—aside from anything else, she would like to know exactly what the fuck is going through their heads when they decide to attack Information— and then they drift into range.

Mishima lets the crow sink slowly with them, staying slightly above the bulk of the chutes so the paratroopers can't see her. The tricky thing is going to be taking them all out while they're high enough to be injured but low enough not to be killed by the fall, but her fear is gone now, leaving anger alone beating through her body, so she doesn't spend a lot of time worrying about it. Mishima's impatient for a real fight. At five meters above the roof, she starts torching parachutes.

. . .

Maryam hurries down to the ground floor. She should probably go to the security office and get some intel on what's going on, but she's afraid they'll talk her out of leaving. She goes through the lobby, past the ground floor restroom and the small logistics office, and back through the janitorial offices to the service door where food is brought in for the canteen. Feeling silly and scared, Maryam lies down on her belly and pushes at the door. It's heavy and hard to push open in that position, and she has to get up on her knees and elbows to edge it open. She pauses and waits. The hot air is steaming in from outside and her arm aches holding the door open. She can feel the sweat gathering on her forehead.

Maryam crawls forward and pushes the door open more, leans her head up to the doorjamb and peers out. The Information hub is set away from its neighbors, with an access road that circles half the building to a small auxiliary parking lot by the door and a driveway up to the loading dock next to it. Maryam's eyeing a small stand of climate-modified bamboo a few meters from the door when she is startled by a growling roar that gets louder and louder until it rips the sky and crowds everything but fear out of her brain: *They're coming for us!* She squeezes out through the door and wriggles her way behind the bamboo, cowering there until the noise has faded.

The building hasn't exploded, and she can think again.

Carefully, Maryam pulls herself into a crouch and looks around. It's a dozen meters or so across bare ground to the next building, an anonymous glass-and-concrete parallelogram that houses a content factory, a logistics company, and a firm specializing in custom workspaces. Maryam sprints across the ground to the side of the building and works her way around it. When she leans around the corner, she sees a hundred or so people in business wear standing in front of the building, chatting. She stands up and walks into the crowd, listening.

"They're probably just doing drills."

"Or an airshow? Have you seen anything about that?"

"They could have waited until closer to lunchtime."

"Hey, have you voted yet?"

"No, and I can't seem to get on Information. I sure hope this isn't a repeat of last election."

Maryam winces. She's worked her way to the middle of the group and feels like she can breathe again. She blinks to call public transportation, but of course nothing comes up. Well, she walked here from the hotel this morning; she can walk back as long as no one stops her.

A few of the paratroopers miss the roof, but the rest scatter over it, crashing through trellises and destroying the bulk of the solar cells. Mishima lands on the roof of the access stairwell and leaps down from the crow in front of the door. She's just in time. Several figures wrapped in reflective flight suits are struggling upright and scrambling from the pile of comrades who cushioned their falls. Mishima raises her flamethrower and moves forward to roast the first one, but they are quicker than she expects after their fall and leap aside to avoid most of the blast. Those suits look fire-retardant, but what got to them must have hurt.

"Reinforcements!" Mishima yells into the access doorway, hoping the runner is there. She steps back toward the door and arcs flame across the faces of two more of the glimmering blue-white figures as they converge on her, drawing their own weapons. She hears screaming and then is knocked backward when something hits her in the shoulder.

Mishima hits the ground awkwardly but manages to roll back up to her feet and get herself into the lee of the access doorway. Her shoulder is throbbing. She's pretty sure she's bleeding but doesn't dare look down at it. The two she just torched are rolling on the ground screaming, but she hears something ricochet off the doorjamb in front of her and finally understands: they are armed with plastic guns.

"Chikushou," Mishima swears. She fumbles for her stiletto and peels a healing pad off the hilt. She hears a ping but she's too busy with the pad to read the message; hopefully it's confirmation of reinforcements on the way.

Mishima can't see the hole in her shoulder well, so she has to position the pad by touch, patting around the halo of soreness and then gasping when she touches raw flesh. When she has it aligned as well as she can manage, she presses her palm against it, biting her lip against the pain. She inhales as deeply as she can, exhales, and forces more air into her lungs the second time, working past the pain. Then Mishima holds her flamethrower above her head and ducks around the doorway, spouting flame.

The first few bullets are aimed at the shoulder-level flamethrower and give Mishima time to find her assailant lying flat on their stomach behind one of their companions' bodies. Mishima levels a steady plume at them and runs in under its cover. She sees the gun melted against her assailant's hand before she plunges her hunting knife into their back. She lets the momentum carry her into a crouch and stays low to strip guns from all the bodies within reach and then scurry back to the door. Mishima slides inside to find two InfoSecs pounding up the stairs.

"Most of them are immobile, but I can't guarantee how many are still alive, and they have plastic guns," she pants, hoping her relief isn't audible.

"Did you get the message?" asks one of the InfoSecs as the other launches a grenade through the access door.

Mishima shakes her head, heart sinking.

"Six more jets on the way," he says, and then both Info-Secs charge out the door in the wake of the explosion. Mishima climbs back up toward the crow, leaving them to handle the situation on the roof. She can already hear the roar of the jets.

CHAPTER 29

Maryam is limping down Khalifa Street as quickly as she can in her sandals when the second set of jets passes overhead. She hovers in place until she is sure that they didn't blow up the Hub this time either, then jogs on. It is not until she passes Al-Jamiaa Street that Information comes back up. She almost collapses with relief, stops in the middle of the sidewalk to blink up everything at once. She doesn't see anything about the Hub attack at first, until a new window pops up in her vision, bold headline streaming across it: **Heritage attacks Information Hub on Election Day!** She opens it up. The data is scant, and she suspects it wouldn't pass publication muster for Information, but it's there.

Maryam keeps reading as she walks, and almost bumps into Núria.

"What are you doing here?" Núria asks, throwing her arms around her.

"I—" Maryam looks around. She's still a couple of kilometers from the hotel. "I was coming to you. What are *you* doing here?"

"I saw about the attack, and I came to find you." Núria holds up the lighter-sized mini-flamethrower she carries with her, smiling. "Flamethrowers blazing, remember? You're all right?"

"Fine," Maryam says. "Where did you find out about the attack?"

"Something called . . ." Núria blinks it open. "Proto-data. Is that a new compiler?"

"I don't think so," Maryam says. She checks the meta-data on the site she was reading: Omnivision. "No, it's not a compiler. It's something new."

Mishima pulls the crow up in the air and circles once to make sure the two InfoSecs on the roof didn't run into any trouble. When she sees their thumbs up, she rises higher, preparing for another round of parachute hunting. How long can they keep this up? The jets zoom overhead, dropping their payloads of troops, but the roar of the engines doesn't fade away. Mishima peels her eyes off the chutes and scans the horizons. Two more jets are approaching, but from the west. They roar over the paratroopers and follow the others. Mishima cranes her neck, but there's no way she can see the insignia on the tail. Still, they have to be Al-Thani planes, right? With that in mind and the two Info-Secs below her waiting with confiscated plastic guns, she decides to let the paratroopers get close before she incinerates their chutes.

It doesn't take long to neutralize the second set of paratroopers. Two of them get shots off, and one of the InfoSecs will have a bad bruise on the chest tomorrow, but the armor prevented any serious injury. Mishima and the two Info-Secs are still checking the prisoners for hidden weapons when a runner comes up to confirm: the AlThani fighter jets have pursued the attackers to the coastline of the Heritage centenal across the Gulf, and are now patrolling the border. Al-Thani ground security forces are in the process of securing the building.

Mishima leaves the InfoSecs and clatters down the stairs, loose-jointed with relief. No one is left in the Jaber room, which feels slightly eerie, but she finds Ken and Sayaka in the lobby, coming out of the bunker adjoining the crisis management center. She picks up Sayaka and hugs her until the girl squirms. Then she puts her arms around Ken and lets him hold her for a long time.

Ken wants to sleep in the crow that night, and Mishima wholeheartedly agrees. After she gets him and Sayaka settled there with plans to order some tsubame-delivered kebabs, she searches out Nejime to let her know.

Not entirely surprisingly, Nejime is back in her office. "Another night in the crow?" she repeats distractedly when Mishima asks her. "Not a problem. Is your daughter all right?"

"She doesn't seem to have registered anything after the initial shock of the lights going out."

"Good job with that," Nejime says, but she sighs. "One might say the same about the rest of the population. There's been no outrage, barely any condemnation of Heritage."

"Did you expect them to hail us as heroes?" asks Mishima.

"They're too busy exploring all their new data options." She changes the subject. "By the way, how did you end up getting word to AlThani?"

Unexpectedly, Nejime laughs. "We didn't! No one told you?" Mishima shakes her head. "It was your protégé, Amran. She learned about their planning in Nairobi and alerted the Nairobi hub. They alerted AlThani and sent a couple of crows up here themselves. Amran came with them; she's being debriefed by the lawyers downstairs."

"I'll go see her," Mishima says.

"Yes, you should. She'll make a good operative . . . or she would have, I suppose."

Reluctantly, Mishima slows her retreat. "You don't think you'll be continuing the program?"

"I don't know if we'll be continuing at all. We were so close." Nejime has turned her gaze to the window; Mishima suspects it's to hide her emotion. "Four elections, two peaceful transfers of power—that is significant in the annals of new forms of government. If we could have just gotten the Secretariat up and running, if we had just thought of it in time for the last elections . . ."

"You really think the Secretariat could have prevented this?" Maybe it is sour grapes, but Mishima can't think of the Secretariat as anything but another sad layer of self-important bureaucracy.

"You always undervalued these things," Nejime says without ire. "Processes, pomp, consensus, taking that extra step for democratic inclusion. And especially legitimacy. Look: we started with nothing." She turns her soft elderly hands palms up. "You start by making something out of that nothing, creating. But it's still almost nothing! You have to roll it, build on it, feed it, recruit others. At some point you gain traction, and it gets easier, but you still have to push, and push, and push. Finally, you get some momentum, it has taken on a life of its own, but you still have to guide and push some more. And then you hope, someday, it will go on without you. But it is all imaginary and invisible. As you well know, government only works because people believe in it."

"Maybe what comes next will be better." Mishima can't help being cold: she is just so sick of this shit.

"Maybe it will," Nejime says, in a tone that does nothing to admit the premise. "But you have just knocked all that legitimacy we built up down to zero."

"I didn't do it," Mishima says. "And I wouldn't have chosen it. But holding on too long can strangle legitimacy just as easily." Nejime doesn't answer. "Speaking of which, what will happen to Heritage?"

"I would like to decommission them, the way we did SecureNation," Nejime says, her usual fierceness returning. "But I'm not sure we have enough legitimacy capital to manage it. For the moment, Agambire is under arrest, but do you know he's blaming it on his wife? He says she masterminded it all from exile. Meanwhile, she was interviewed by one of these new data peddlers"—Mishima wonders how long it will take for that term to seem unforgivably derogatory—"and she claims it was all William Pressman managing it from prison."

"Maybe now that it's not running the world, Information can do more work on accountability," Mishima suggests, and turns to leave.

"Oh, Mishima?"

Mishima pauses, almost at the door.

"Keep the crow."

Mishima turns back, startled. "What?"

"I think you've earned it."

When Mishima finds Amran, she's been in debriefing for three hours. They might not be done with her, but she is clearly done with them. Mishima pulls rank to get her out of the room and takes her to get some food.

"I'm not sure I'm up for this spy stuff," Amran says for the third time. Her plate is still mostly full, and she's pushing the rice around.

"You don't have to be. But you were amazing," Mishima says.

"I was terrified! I messed up the escape!" She hides her face in her hands.

"You acted under pressure. And you saved us."

Amran mumbles something and draws more designs in her rice with the spoon.

"No need to go back to it if you don't want to," Mishima repeats. "There's plenty of other work to do." Assuming they all still have jobs tomorrow. "Hey, Maryam and Núria are coming up to the crow later for tea; do you want to join?"

Amran nods, brightening. "Sure. I think I'll go to the hotel first to freshen up." She is still in the clothes she was wearing during her imprisonment.

"Come up to the Hub roof and whack on the mooring line when you're there," Mishima says. Information is still glitchy in the Hub and its immediate vicinity. "I'll get an alert and we'll come down to get you."

Mishima stays at the restaurant after Amran leaves to finish her tea, and then orders some bourbon, which is discreetly delivered in the same teapot.

She's on her fourth cup of alcohol when a middle-aged woman slides into the seat across from her.

"Congratulations," the Chinese agent says. "You survived."

Mishima has learned from experience that it's better to say as little as possible on these occasions.

"If you happen to be looking for a job . . ."

"I'm not a fucking hired gun," Mishima says.

There is no noticeable hesitation, and yet Mishima senses a minute recalibration of approach from her interlocutor. "Of course not," the Chinese woman responds. "You work for what you believe in. But to be happy, you need to do the work to which you are most suited. You need to use your talents." Had she been slightly more drunk, Mishima would have put her head down in her arms at this point. "Information cannot give you that anymore. They never really could, as they did not respect your unique abilities. But we can. As a superpower—"

"The world doesn't have superpowers anymore," Mishima says, trying to feel certain of something.

"Of course it does. One superpower is falling, which means another will rise."

"Not necessarily. There could be a, a"—Mishima wishes her alcohol-impaired brain could come up with examples, wishes she hadn't accepted the premise—"a warring-states period." Ugh, that was worse than no example.

"Maybe briefly, but I doubt it. The world wants a leader."

"It won't be you."

"Oh, we think it will. We've been watching how you do it."

Now Mishima wants to bang her head against the bar. "People will want something different."

"We know." The woman tilts her head. "Why are you so prejudiced against us? Has it occurred to you that most of what you know about us might be propaganda?"

"Did you know that Heritage was involved? Did you know where they were planning the raid?" She stands up, still leaning on the table. "Did you send me to Saaremaa to distract us from the real danger?"

The woman doesn't answer. Instead, she reaches her hand out to Mishima's unbandaged shoulder, which sways under her touch. "Are you all right?"

"I'm fine," Mishima blurts. "I'm going to bed. I can tell that if you ever want to talk to me again, you'll know how to find me."

"Indeed," the Chinese woman murmurs.

On the way back from the bar, Mishima's attention is caught by a pop-up from one of the new data providers. **NEW SUPERMAJORITY MIRED IN SCANDAL! 888 cache of secret communications found in mantle tunnel.** Mishima stares at the pop-up while it scrolls gently, urging her to read on. Then, as she watches, the familiar annotation appears, disputing *mired* and *scandal* although not the substance of the sub-headline. It unrolls slowly, letter by letter, and Mishima can picture the exhausted, confused Information grunt, unable to leave their post, doggedly correcting each new headline. In that moment, the thankless work of that grunt, the lowest on the Information hierarchy, seems far more important and worthwhile than any mission she's ever been assigned.

Nougaz and Taskeen have joined Nejime in her office. Nougaz is sipping at a tumbler of whiskey; Nejime has indulged herself in a cheekful of qat, which she got a taste for while running the Sanaa Hub decades ago. Taskeen is drinking tea.

"So, that's that, I suppose." Nejime has been saying some version of this since she saw the modification to the voting mechanism, but she can't get over it. They were so close. Or maybe not; maybe Mishima was right and the Secretariat would only have made things worse.

"You should be grateful, you should be *singing* with joy"—Taskeen sniffs—"that of all the plans to overthrow Information, mine was the one that succeeded."

Nougaz offers only an icy smile, but Nejime shuffles her shoulders in something like acquiescence. "I suppose one can hope that this chaos will eventually work its way into something better."

"'Hope!'" Taskeen scoffed. "'Work its way into!' You'll be the ones working on it, I should think. You must have at least ten years left before retirement, no? And look at what I've managed to accomplish from the sanatorium. There's still plenty for Information to do. You'll be far better off moderating and watchdogging independent sources of data than you were producing it all."

"I'm not sure the world will see it that way."

"Even if you're right, the end of Information isn't the end for you. You two are eminently employable. I'm sure you'll find lots of interesting ways to shape world history." Taskeen is enjoying this a little too much.

"Shouldn't you have shriveled up by now, running around in the present like this?" Nougaz's tone is more amiable than her words.

"Modernity isn't kryptonite," Taskeen answers, her voice just as mild. "I have cultivated physiological changes in my body through the mental practice of time capsule therapy. They'll last me for as long as I need to visit this time and place."

"So, you're going back?" Nejime asks.

"My work here is done," Taskeen says judiciously.

"You're going to leave us to deal with this mess while you retire to your safe little nostalgia-haven," Nougaz offers.

"By *mess* I presume you mean *democracy*?"

"We know what will happen," Nejime says. "This is not some bold experiment. People will hear what they want to hear, believe what they want to believe. That's not democracy, or at least not any useful form of democracy. That's anarchy."

"That's already happening even with Information," Taskeen points out. "Might as well have it without the enormous unelected powerbroker in the room."

"Are you talking about Information or yourself?" Nougaz asks.

Taskeen chuckles. "Whatever happens next, it will be fun to watch."

They gather in the crow. Even Roz comes, glancing at her wrist monitor every five minutes.

"Do you think the election results are going to stand?" she asks. 888 won the Supermajority, but the news of the illegal data tunnels is breaking now, and there is talk of a challenge. On the other hand, no one knows if the hidden comms are still illegal.

"Probably," Mishima answers. "There's only so much upheaval we can take at a time. Besides, I think the voting was . . . as legitimate as voting ever is." With the help of some concentrated hydration pills, she partially sobered up, and now she's working on getting drunk again. She and Ken and Roz and Núria are drinking plum wine; she made tea for Maryam, Amran, and Suleyman.

Núria turns to Maryam. "Our centenal went for Liberty."

"What?" Maryam blinks open the results. "When I saw 888 won the Supermajority, I assumed they had kept power there. I didn't even look!"

"I won't live in a Liberty centenal," Núria says.

"Me neither," Maryam agrees. "Where do you want to go?" She projects a small map of La Habana between them, spins it to check the post-election government affiliations.

"Actually," Núria says hesitantly. "I was thinking. I don't know how happy you'd be working remotely, but . . . I've been thinking I'd like to get away from all of this. Just remove a little from the whole Information tussle. What do you think about the Independentista territory?"

"It's amazing how many of these new intel services already exist," Roz is telling Ken. She shows him the infographic she's set up; the numbers jump even as they watch.

"So, what do you think?" Ken asks. He respects Roz's opinion second only to Mishima's, and Mishima's been unwilling to talk about it. "Anarchy and misinformation, or competition and accountability?"

"I really don't know what to think yet," Roz says, hand on her belly, "but I'm in a mood to hope for the best."

"With this many services, there must be a wide range of professionalism."

"Hopefully some of them are quality."

"Information should reinvent itself to keep an eye on them," Nakia comments.

"Hopefully one of them will fill the SVAT niche for personalized services." Roz shakes her head. "It's so important. Maybe if we'd done more of that . . ."

"I wonder who's coming up with all these different services."

"We met one of the investors, in Kuressaare," Mishima says. "People are jumping in to try it. They think they're going to make money off of data peddling."

"Half of them won't last a month, I bet," Ken says.

"Still, they could be incredibly useful."

"If they're any good," Mishima says. "Someone needs to weed out the ones that were tied to the Heritage plot."

"Like the one I worked for," Amran says, so quietly that no one answers.

"Maybe we could work on accountability," Ken suggests.

"For the data services?" Maryam asks, interested.

"Or we could build our own?" Amran says it, and so it has an uncertain inflection, but they latch on immediately.

"More open."

"More human."

"More humane!" Nakia says.

Mishima catches Ken's eye. They were both in that meeting, and she knows he is thinking what she is: *This is what they thought when they created Information.* But they have to do something, even if it's incremental, even if it's the tiniest increment, and so she adds her voice in agreement.

"Better."

"Ours."